TOXIC SIREN: AWAKENING

Lauren Gage

NEBULOSUS LITORE PRESS

Nebulosus Litore Press
13359 North Highway 183
Suite 406-509
Austin, TX 78750
www.nebulosuslitore.com

Library of Congress Catalog Number: 2019918333

ISBN: 978-1-7343878-0-3
ISBN: 978-1-7343878-3-4
ISBN: 978-1-7343878-4-1

This is a work of fiction. Names, characters, businesses, places, events, locales, and incidents are either the products of the author's imagination or used in a fictitious manner. Any resemblance to actual persons, living or dead, or actual events is purely coincidental.

To my husband, Jim, for his patience with me while I wrote. A thank you to my friends and family, who were incredibly supportive as I undertook this journey.

1

"Never fall in love with a sailor," Nan's words echoed in my mind as I sat in the sand, sinking my toes into smooth grit still warm from the dying sun. Sage advice. The women in my family had the worst luck with men in the military, those in the Marines and Navy were the worst. I joked with my mother that we were cursed with the blood of sirens, the mythical creatures whose beautiful voices lured sailors to their deaths at sea. She didn't find it the least bit funny.

Just this morning, my cousin Claire became another victim of the family curse. Her husband announced that he was leaving her for a younger, cuter blonde. Claire called in tears moments before I left for school. I'd handed the receiver over to mom, who was better equipped to deal with the heartbreak of a broken 7-year marriage. Me? I was only 17 and hadn't had a boyfriend in ages. My last one died, along with my best friend in a freak accident. All I'd figured out in my brief conversation with Claire this morning was that giving up personal dreams and bearing progeny did not break the family curse. Her husband was in the Navy. Maybe she was lucky. Most of the so-called sailors didn't make it beyond the engagement period and died before they could marry the women in my family. Maybe the family curse was losing its power.

I sighed, returning my senses to the present. I let my head fall back to soak in the remains of the sun's warmth before it dropped beneath the horizon. Orange and purple hues overtook the sky as the sun sank behind the tree line. Dark, distant clouds lit with intermittent firefly glow. I sank back onto my elbows and clawed my fingers through the sand as the scent of rain drifted through the trees and across the lake. A sense of electric anticipation rode the night air. The raised hairs along my body told me that it would be an incredible night.

My name is Shell, actually Michelle, but I hadn't gone by that name since the accident. I told people it was Shell, as in seashell. I loved water. There was something about water that felt like magic to me. It was the same with rain and fog. Around water, I felt energized and alive, a feeling I didn't experience much since the accident. Those who knew me before that day said I was a different person. I agreed. I barely remembered Michelle.

Not many people remained on the small beach. A small group of people I loosely called friends stood around a bonfire that roared and danced in the growing breeze further down the beach. A familiar voice called my name and I looked toward the fire to see my friend Julie, Jules, staggering in my direction. Her short blonde hair whipped in the wind. I watched as the waifish pixie flopped bonelessly into the sand next to me. Cute as she was, coordinated she wasn't, especially when she'd been drinking.

"Jay's asking about you. Says he hasn't seen you all night." Julie belched hoppy brew in my face and I waved a hand to get the noxious gas away from me.

"Why's he care? I'm enjoying myself right here." I looked toward the bonfire where an unfamiliar, but gorgeous blond guy stared in our direction. His strong jawline and cheekbones stood out in deep contrast by firelight. My breath caught and heart sank into my stomach. I forced myself to suck air into tight lungs as my heart pounded. While I struggled to breathe, the tingle of ozone and warm scent of smoke mingled in the atmosphere, bringing images of past campfires, smoldering skin, and fading green eyes. I blinked away the stinging behind my eyes.

"Who's that?" I asked, with a shift of the eyes, trying not to point. I let my long black hair fall into my face.

"Who's who?" Jules slurred, sounding more like "whose shoe?"

"That blond guy next to Jay," I whisper-hissed.

"That's why he's looking for you. He wants to introduce you to his friend," she said in sing-song.

"Jules, I don't need friends. I'm good right here." I settled further into the sand and leaned back on my elbows, enjoying the pre-storm smell of petrichor from the opposite shore. The boy looked like trouble, hot trouble, the kind I didn't need.

"He's been staring at you all night like a piece of rare steak," she whispered in my ear. She giggled loudly and nudged my shoulder.

"Uh, gross," I said, pushing her back. From the corner of my eye, I caught movement near the bonfire. Jay reached into the cooler for another beer and started toward us. "Crap. Your boyfriend's coming this way." The urge to spring up and run away tugged at my chest and I struggled to rein myself in. I'd had a mini crush on my friend's football player boyfriend for some time. Nothing huge, just enough to make me super awkward around him.

Marcus, a classmate and coworker raised his drink to us and smiled. I wasn't sure if he was greeting both of us, or just Jules. I nodded in response, just in case. He'd offered to tutor me in Precalculus last week when he saw my quiz score. I cringed at the thought of so much red on white paper. Michelle had been a math whiz and straight A student. She would have cried to see my grades now. Although grateful for the offer, I didn't see when we'd have time to study together. Between work, school, and band rehearsals, I didn't have much down time. That was the problem. I could catch up on my own if I just found the time to review my notes, read the chapter, and actually do the homework.

Jay wove his way across the empty beach, stumbling over his feet as he neared. How much did he have to drink? They hadn't been here that long, maybe 30 minutes. I got to the beach a good hour before they arrived. Guess he'd been pregaming. I wondered who drove.

"Shell! Just who I was looking for!" He said. Yuck. It seemed he could sense my discomfort. Oh, wait, he could. Jay loved to torment me.

"Huh? What?" I feigned disinterest as he smirked. I remained on the sand, making him look down at me. After brief eye contact, I returned my gaze to the water. The wind whipped hair across my face.

"Come to the fire. Join us," he said, chugging his beer and crumpling the can single handedly. Wow, what a Neanderthal. How could I find that remotely attractive? I wasn't sure, but I kind of did.

"You know I'm not much of a joiner. I'm a loner." I wondered why I'd come. A normal Friday night involved sitting in front of the television or reading a scary book while I kept an eye on my little brother, Andy.

"Shell, the rain won't hold off forever," he said. "Come on, join us." In my mind popped a movie scene, twin girls in blue dresses asking a young boy to join them, forever and ever. I bit my lips together and breathed deeply to stop myself from laughing.

"Afraid of a little rain?" I asked as I sat up and stretched. I took my time standing up, pulled my shirt over my head, revealing a low-cut black swimsuit, and shimmied out of my shorts. I'd slimmed down over the summer, and continued to shed pounds through the beginning of the school year. Although I saw these guys every day at work or school, the clothes I wore were ill-fitting, baggy. My stomach had never been this flat. I ran into the water. Screw Jay.

Thunder crashed and lightning brightened the sky as it hit the ground somewhere on the distant lakeshore. I grinned and waded further into the lake, enjoying the cold water against my legs. Someone waded in behind me. I turned around when I was hip deep. Blondie stood about three feet from me, bare chested in gray shorts. In the light of the distant bonfire and the occasional flash of lightning, he looked near perfect, symmetrical but for a few scars on the left side of his body. One in particular, ran in a long white line down his chest. Nothing to complain about. I had plenty of scars of my own. My back and left arm were covered with tree-like Lichtenberg scars from the lightning strike. I clenched my hand to stop myself from running fingers down his intriguing scar.

"Daredevil!" He said with a laugh. "You're living dangerously."

"What?" I cocked my head. Why was he talking to me? Gosh, he was gorgeous. Amazing bone structure. Strong jaw.

4

Blue eyes shone under a flash of lightning. Beautiful blue eyes, not like mine. His were more aqua. They'd glowed for a moment in the lightning.

"Hasn't anyone ever told you it's dangerous to be in the water when it's lightning outside?" His voice rumbled as his lip curled in amusement.

"Oh. Yeah, my mom would have a heart attack," I said, regaining my composure.

"I'm Dylan," he said, holding out a hand.

"Shell," I replied reaching out to shake his hand. It was warm and firm. With that touch, a tingle raced from my hand to my chest and I let go. My face flushed.

"Nice to meet you," he said as he waded forward to stand by my side. Warmth radiated from his bare arms and chest. Wow, he was literally hot, a furnace in the winter. He stared off into the distance. "What do you do for fun around here? Besides stand in the water during a lightning storm?" He asked. I laughed before I could stop myself.

"Yeah, not the safest thing to do," I admitted. I knew a thing or two about getting struck by lightning. "Hike, read. Not much to do out here, it's country, but with modern conveniences not far away. Weird place." Was I rambling?

"We should hang out sometime. You could show me around."

"You don't want to do that," I said, eyes falling to watch my fingers part the water as my arms moved aimlessly.

He turned toward me, brushing a strand of long black hair behind my ear. A flash of lightning illuminated his blue eyes, bringing that odd glow. "Why not?" He asked quietly. His voice woke something in me, a desire to touch him, and warmth spread through my body. I fisted my hands under the water to stop myself reaching out. He stood so close.

"I keep to myself. I'm a loser, a loner, not popular."

"I'm sure that's not true. Come on, give me your number," he prodded, moving closer. "We could form a loser's club."

I laughed and shook my head. Had he just dropped a hint that he read the same books I did? He'd never call anyway. Guys like him didn't call girls like me. Rain began to fall in slow, heavy drops. "You're a funny guy."

Shouts from the shore drew our attention. Jay waved his

arms wildly and yelled something unintelligible. He started to hop around. I wondered if he'd fall over in his drunken state and my lips turned up in a smile at the mental image.

"Gotta go, he's my ride and he might leave without me," Dylan said.

I nodded, though he couldn't see it, and followed him back to the shore. Sounded like something Jay would do. I hoped Dylan was driving, he hadn't been drinking. As we stepped onto the wet sand, he looked back over a shoulder.

"Later, Daredevil," he said with a smile and wink that I caught through the contrast of dying fire and night.

The security light blinded me as I parked next to mom's car. I climbed the deck stairs and fumbled with the key at the front door. I didn't like going into the house through the driveway-level basement at night, not anymore. It was just creepy. I hadn't minded when my bedroom had been in the basement, but since it was now unoccupied, the vibe held no welcome. Luckily, the security light stayed on long enough for me to make it up the deck stairs and through the front door where I let myself in. It was late and mom had gone to bed, but Andy was up watching TV.

"What'cha doing up Andy?" I asked as I leaned over the back of the love seat and showered him with rainwater from my hair.

"Yuck!" He squeaked, batting at my wet hair. "I just wanted to make sure you made it back. The fog was thick when we came home from dinner," he said. For a 12-year-old, Andy could be thoughtful. I hadn't really noticed the fog. I'd been preoccupied.

"You're so sweet," I said, ruffling his damp hair with my cold fingers. I hoped it was damp because he'd recently showered, but with him, I never knew. He was an active kid sometimes with his ADHD. I wiped my hands on my rain damp pants.

"Nah, I'm just not tired." He turned his attention back to the TV, dismissing me. I looked at the clock on the wall and saw that it was nearly 11:00 p.m., but I hadn't planned to be back before 2:00 a.m. I worked tomorrow, but not until ten in the morning.

"Night Andy."

"Goodnight." Andy mumbled into the arm of the love seat.

I headed back to my room, floor creaking with each step. I fumbled against the wall, flipped the light switch, and closed the door behind me. My eyes sought out my nightshirt, a purple tee with a cartoon sheep jumping over a fence. I found it tossed over my desk chair and started to change, then realized I still wore my damp swimsuit and needed a shower before I went to sleep. I sighed and stumbled to the bathroom, nightshirt in hand.

I barely stopped a frightened squeal from escaping when I captured my reflection in the mirror. A cave dwelling savage stared back at me, hair tangled from the wind and dampness combined with the raccoon eyes of running mascara and smudged eyeliner. Great, she looked like someone who would go well with Jay's Neanderthal traits. They'd probably have a great time together.

I stripped out of the swimsuit and tossed it into the hamper, then stepped into the pounding water. I stood under the cascading jets and rinsed off the fishy lake water and sand. I loved the lake, and the feel of the sand under my toes, but I didn't like the dirty result. I shampooed my hair and conditioned it twice, knowing it was knotted from the wind. I spun the dials and the water slowed to a light drip. It would stop after the shower head drained, but in the meantime, the drip-drop sound would drive me nuts. I stepped out of the shower and dried off in the misty room squeezing the water from my hair carefully with the towel before pulling on my nightshirt. Then, I began the ridiculous task of detangling my hair. A comb died in the process.

I wiped some haze from the mirror and found a cleaner version of myself staring back. Her eyes were still ringed with black liner, but at least she no longer wore a smudged raccoon's mask. I braided my hair to prevent it from being unmanageable in the morning, brushed my teeth, and returned to my room. A stab of pain in my shoulder made me wince as I closed the door behind me. It happened since the accident, especially when the storms blew through.

2

The alarm sounded and I sat up like a vampire in a casket from one of those old black and white movies. My arm stiffly reached for the clock, but knocked it off the table and onto the floor. Great. Muscle spasms and poor motor control. Today was going to be really fun. My friends and co-workers thought I was clumsy, but in reality, I had neural and muscular damage from a lightning strike a few years back. Me, my boyfriend, and best friend all got hit. I survived, they didn't. I have a large network of scars that run along my back, over my left shoulder and down my arm. Lichtenberg figures, they were called, tree-shaped scars that traced the path the lightning took through my body. The scars were cool, but most people didn't get the chance to see them. I didn't want the questions, so I kept myself covered with lots of long sleeve shirts and layers. Even when I wore less, most people didn't notice. At first, the marks were a deep red against my vampire white complexion. Now, the scars barely stood out from my pale skin, just a network of shiny pink branches, branded into me.

Crawling on the floor, I located the alarm clock under my bed, dragged it out, shut it off, and returned it to the bedside table. I stretched my shoulders and arms, trying to loosen the muscles. I wanted to avoid the alternating numbness and pain that followed the stiffness and muscle spasms. I put on my work uniform, a button up short sleeved blue shirt, black slacks, and anti-slip shoes. So sexy. I grabbed my matching apron and hat and headed out to the car after I said goodbye to my brother for the day. Mom had already left for work.

I rushed out the door to avoid questions and small talk, not that my little brother Andy was big on either. Ted, my best friend, had plans to meet up with me after work to tweak some songs we were working on. He was the bassist, other songwriter, and occasional singer in our band, Toxic Siren. Yes, I came up with the band name. I was the singer, the Siren.

As I walked down the stairs to the car, I wished the rocks would stop tumbling around in my stomach. There was no reason to be nervous. It was just work. My hair stood on end. I stopped and looked around, feeling watched, but saw no one.

I breathed in the foggy air and walked toward my car, gravel crunching under my feet. I startled at a loud huff. Frozen, I looked into the nearby trees where a 10-point stag stood motionless, staring at me. It eyed me as I slowly got into the car, still and creepy as a wraith. Our house was a rental in one of the Pocono area housing developments. There were lots of trees, but Andy called them 'fake trees' for their diminutive circumference compared with that of the older ones we'd grown up around. Deer weren't uncommon in the area, but didn't normally act like this one. I looked out the window, but the stag was gone. I started the car, and a catchy grunge number blasted through the speakers, bass shaking the frame. I drove to work, singing along to the new Transcendence album as the trees flew by.

It was 1992 and music had changed drastically as the grunge scene of Seattle began to take over. I loved the expression of depression and dark experiences and emotions combined with the new sound that seemed to draw from metal and punk. I'd been a fan of punk and hair metal along with the standard 1980s music that was falling out of favor with listeners. Our band combined a similar mixture of punk and metal, but did not quite have the sound of music coming out of Seattle. What can I say? We were Toxic Siren.

The parking lot held only three cars as I parked behind Norma's fast food restaurant. If it were the 1950s, Norma's would have been one of those drive-in burger joints where the waitresses brought orders to cars on skates. Now it was a locally owned burger joint with salad bar and woodsy hunter decor in the dining area.

I recognized Raif's car and relief spread over me that the younger, cooler, manager was on duty. Pat was the older, uptight, General Manager, and shifts under her were far less enjoyable. I smiled when I saw Jules' white Neon. It was nice to work with Jules because sometimes when it was slow, we got the chance to catch up. She also did her share of the work without complaining. I grabbed my hat and apron, headed to the back door and pressed the buzzer. Jules let me in.

"Girl, it's good to see you!" She greeted me with a hug.

"Huh? What do you mean?" I just saw her last night.

"We need to talk. Jay was miffed last night," she said in her conspiratorial voice as she pulled me inside by my bad arm.

"Why?" I asked with a wince. She dragged me into the walk-in refrigerator and closed the door.

"Didn't like your hard to get act," she said, hands on hips, voice sharp.

"What act?"

"Yeah, like, running into the lake? Remember that? With the storm so close?" Her brow crinkled, "what was with the striptease?"

"Just practicing." I teased. She glared at me. "What? Thinking about a change in career. How'd I do?"

"You can have him," she said abruptly. She turned around and reached for containers of peas and cauliflower.

"Huh? He's not interested in me. He's your boyfriend. Duh!"

I had noticed she was getting annoyed with Jay more often lately. Maybe she had noticed my crush. I followed her out of the walk-in and eyed the assignment board to find that I was working salad bar and that Jules was only helping me set up. She was working the cash register for her shift. I ran my time card through the clock, placed it back in the card holder, and peeked into the manager's office, "Hi, Raif!" I called, channeling my inner cheerleader smile.

"Hey, Shell. May need you to shift duties today. Just got a call that Marcus was in an accident. Ambulance took him to the hospital," Raif said, tapping a pen on one of the financial reports. My smile dissolved. I'd talked to Marcus last night. He'd walked me to my car after the rain started, not at all bothered by it.

"Not a problem. Just let me know what you need," I said as I turned to look at the assignment board and saw that Marcus was scheduled to work grill. I shrugged. Never worked it before, but how hard could it be? I joined Jules in the walk-in and began filling my arms with metal containers of vegetables. "Hear about Marcus?" I asked.

"Yeah, Jay called it in. He saw the accident while running errands before work. Road was blocked. They just reopened it so he's on the way in, running late."

I rinsed a head of broccoli in the industrial sink, then took it over to the metal prep island to cut it into bite-sized pieces. I washed my hands and slid them into plastic gloves. Jay came in as I chopped the broccoli, his face ashen. He walked straight into Raif's office and closed the door. I continued prepping vegetables and took them out to the salad bar. Julie had already prepped the bar with ice and fake kale leaves for decoration, but otherwise had disappeared. I began placing vegetables in their places on the bar, with refills in the refrigerator.

"Hey, Hot Lips!" I turned around to see Raif smirking as he set up behind the counter, a change from his earlier mood. Must be his version of the cheerleader smile.

"Huh?" My eyebrow raised.

"The guys voted you the girl with the sexiest lips."

"Um, ok." Heat flooded my cheeks and I turned away. Well, at least I had one good feature. My figure was not what most would consider ideal. I was heavier than I should be, although I'd lost a lot of weight over the past year. I'd finally reached a healthy weight. I had long wavy hair, dark auburn that I dyed black, and my skin refused to tan, leaving me with a pale vampirish complexion. My eyes changed from blue to gray. I rarely smiled. People often told me to smile and when they did, it was a struggle not to punch them. My disposition leaned strongly toward depression and morbid thoughts. This was probably why the managers liked to hide me behind the scenes rather than at the cash register.

"I've got it under control back here," Raif said. "Finish setting up and come back to the line when we open."

I gave him a thumbs up, eyes on him longer than polite. Raif was handsome. Not regular handsome, but model or movie star handsome and he knew it. His hair, a light brown still graced with sun-kissed highlights of summer, glinted under the recessed lighting. His eyes, greener than hazel, really drew a girl in.

"Girl, you need to get laid," came a gravelly smoker's voice. Cheeks red, I spun to face Vicki, who smiled innocently at me. Her square jaw and muddy hazel eyes did not fit with her new curly hairstyle. The extra volume of permed hair made her face extra square.

"What are you doing here?" I snorted. "I didn't see you on the board."

"Raif called me in. Something about Marcus and an accident," she croaked.

"Well, it's nice to see you."

"Raif said to help you out. What do you need?" The perm gave her mousy brown hair a brassy sheen. Between the hair color and low voice, she reminded me of a red headed character from an old comic strip that had been translated into occasional seasonal cartoon specials on TV. Made me want to go around calling her 'Sir.' She needed to lay off the cigarettes.

"Double check the salad bar and make sure I put things where they're supposed to be?" Not that it mattered if the peas were where the carrots were supposed to be.

Vicki nodded and strode off while I grabbed restroom supplies and went to refill toilet paper and paper towels. It was easier to take care of these things before the doors opened. I looked at my watch. Fifteen minutes until we unlocked the doors. Having completed my mental checklist, I returned to the salad bar prep area and found Vicki eating a blueberry muffin.

"Late breakfast?" I asked.

"Yeah, late night. Wasn't planning to be here this morning." She shrugged and continued nibbling at the muffin.

"What'd you do last night?"

"Stayed over at Brent's. His parents were away. Played house," she said as crumbled muffin tumbled from her mouth.

"Ah." My lips twitched. My mother would never allow me to stay over at a guy's house. Unless she didn't know what I was up to. I didn't like lying to her.

13

"Sorry I missed out last night. I heard it was a blast," she said after a swallow. She tossed the wrapper into a trash can.

"It was ok. Wasn't into the whole beer thing, so I kind of stayed away from the gang, but I loved being at the lake."

"You're so weird."

"I know." My mouth twisted into a half-smile. "So, how's Brent?"

"He's working hard, saving up," she talked around a large bite of muffin, pieces falling from her mouth and onto her navy apron.

"That's good. What are you guys going to do after graduation?" I asked. Vicki, like most of my crew mates were a year ahead of me and getting ready to graduate from high school. I should have been graduating with them, but got held back after the accident.

"I'm going to college, Kutztown. Brent plans to keep working. We'll see what happens after that."

"Hard to make plans right now, huh?" Spaghetti sauce splashed my arm as I placed its container into a slot above steaming water. I sighed then tried to feign interest in Vicki's plight, but just didn't get what she saw in Brent. His mustache turned me off big time and I didn't like the way he looked at me.

"Yeah. I like him a lot, and he says he loves me. But, with me moving away for college and him staying behind, it's hard to know what's going to happen." She grabbed a sanitizer rag and began tidying the bar around the hot items. Sauce painted the metal between the plastic bins. She checked the temperature knobs and nodded. "Looks good."

Raif unlocked the doors and the first customers streamed in and up to the counter to make their orders. I headed back to the grill and started some burgers. One of our unusual regulars, Larry, showed up and ordered his standard coffee and fries. He sat in his usual spot, dressed today in old fashioned military greens with a Hitleresque mustache. As he sipped his coffee, he began a guttural conversation with himself.

"Sad about Marcus." Jules said when the line died down. She'd reappeared with puffy red eyes as Raif unlocked the doors.

"Any more news?" I asked.

"Not yet. Jay saw it happen. Drove right up a bank and into a tree. Looked like he was racing another car," she said. "The jerk didn't stick around."

"Oh. That sucks." Jules nodded. My fingers started tingling and I shivered. I tried to shake it off. It was nearly eleven. "I saw him at the lake last night. He was by the fire, talking with the guys." We'd spoken briefly before Jules had arrived. Just normal everyday topics like when was the band playing again and how things were going in our classes. If I hadn't known better, I might have thought he was trying to flirt with me. But Marcus was just being nice. We had several of the advanced prep classes together since I'd moved to the Poconos. We weren't particularly close, but he was friendly. Last time that I'd seen him, he was getting in his car, barely visible under the dome light for a moment before he shut the door.

After work, I rushed into the shower and did my best to scrub off the greasy fast food hamburger smell that permeated my hair and skin. Despite my best efforts, I still smelled of the nasty grease. Giving up, I stepped out of the shower, pulled my hair back into a bun, and got dressed into some relaxed ripped jeans and a Calabrias tee-shirt. The Calabrias were a punk rock band that started as a garage band in the 1970s and grew in popularity over time. I just adored them. The tee graphic showed four brothers in torn jeans leaning against a Cadillac convertible. They weren't great looking, but they were awesome! It gave me hope.

The phone rang and my brother got to it before I'd even made it halfway down the hallway.

"Shell, it's your boyfriend," Andy called from the kitchen. I rolled my eyes and took the phone from his hand.

"Hi, Ted," I said, smiling. It was embarrassing to be teased when it came to Ted, because it was true that I'd been crushing on him for years. He was my best friend and the bass player in our band. He'd never shown any interest outside those roles.

"I'm your boyfriend now?" Ted asked with a chuckle.

"According to Andy. Still coming over, boyfriend?" I asked, emphasizing the word "boyfriend" for Andy's benefit.

"Um, yeah. Be there in about fifteen."

Ted was still laughing when he hung up. Andy snickered from the living room. I sighed. I went down to the basement and into the garage, our normal practice space. It was more private and spacious than upstairs. It also held the amps, guitars, a couple of mics, and a drum set. Moving equipment upstairs was a pain. There was a chill in the air, so I turned on the space heater before going back upstairs to grab a couple of drinks, my notebook, a couple of pens, and a red plaid flannel shirt to ward off the chill. I returned to the basement, unlocked the outside door and waited in the garage for Ted to arrive.

I flipped through the notebook until I ran across one of my newer songs. I picked up my acoustic Gibson guitar and began strumming some chords until I found a progression that I liked. Then, I began to put a melody to the lyrics. Ted came in while I was messing with the chorus. My eyes met his and my lips split in a wide grin. He carried his bass in and set it down on the guitar stand. I had a wicked urge to hug him, but Ted had issues with people touching him. I did too, but for different reasons. I did my best to respect his boundaries, as much as they frustrated me.

"What was that?" He asked.

"Girl I Used to Be," I said. I handed him the notebook and he started to look at my notations. He cocked his head and raised an eyebrow. "You do know I haven't always been this awesome, right?"

He laughed and handed the notebook back.

> Staring from the mirror she's a stranger
> That girl's not the one I used to know
> What's that dreadful gleam of danger
> Shining from her eyes as tears flow
> Bubbling up, anger like lava from below
> What happened to the girl I used to be?
> What happened to the girl I used to know?
>
> She used to be fine
> She used to be free
> A great future in a straight line
> Someone's special honey

16

Yeah, I was gonna be somebody
What happened to the girl I used to be?

"How different could it have been?" He asked. My eyebrows drew together.

"Trust me, a lot different."

"I don't believe you."

"You don't?" I asked. "Dude, I was a cheerleader." He broke out laughing. In the nearly three years we'd known each other, I'd never let that slip. Oops. Well, at least he thought I was joking. Sad thing was, I was totally serious. I had been a cheerleader, and a lot more. Getting struck by lightning had more than just physical repercussions. I suffered brain damage, which caused memory loss and personality change. The scarring, pain, and muscular issues were all a part of the physical issues I'd suffered. The memory loss was severe, years of memories gone. Some had returned, but not many. Photos and stories people told me sometimes triggered a return of memories, but not always. My confusion with the past was part of the reason I didn't bring it up much. I also didn't like the reminder that my boyfriend and best friend were dead, not to mention everything else that I'd lost.

I had recurring nightmares, not just about the accident, but other things as well. As happy as I looked in photos, I knew my life prior to the accident wasn't as cheerful and awesome as other people made it out to be. I'd seen some of it play out in my head, confused bits of arguments, physical conflicts, and random images. It wasn't just when I was asleep. When memories came back, or I experienced a flashback of the accident, it was a living nightmare. I'd lose myself to the experience and the present faded away.

Ted continued to laugh. He bent over gasping, all semblance of collaborating on our music forgotten. Well, maybe Ted needed a laugh. Poor guy had more issues than I did. It was probably why we got along so well together. I told him I'd be right back and headed upstairs to grab an old photo album from my bedroom closet. I'd hidden the albums the last time that Jules had come over. She had a bad habit of snooping through my things whether I was in the room or not. I didn't want to explain my blonde hair and cheerleading outfit. She could be mean spirited at times.

I pulled the rose covered album from the top shelf of my bedroom closet and scurried back to the garage. Ted was still chuckling between gasps when I returned. I put the album down on the work bench and turned on the fluorescent light. I motioned for him to join me at the bench, where I opened the album and pointed to a picture. Me, blonde hair in a pony tail, normal makeup, not the vampy stuff I wore now, wearing a cheerleading outfit complete with pom poms. Standing next to me with an arm around my shoulders was my redheaded boyfriend, Joe, the JV quarterback.

"See?" I said. He squinted.

"Who's that?" He pointed at the smiling blonde girl in the red and white cheerleader outfit.

"Me."

"No, really. Who is that?" He asked again, pointing at the picture in confusion.

"Me and my boyfriend, Joe. He was the quarterback."

"That's not you."

"Sure, it is. I frosted my hair blonde and didn't wear the dark makeup I wear now. I could get out my old yearbooks too. You'll see my name next to pictures that look like this one."

He moved closer to the picture and stared at it, inches from the album. I laughed. He did a double take between me and the photo.

"You did not date the quarterback," he said, wide-eyed in mock horror.

"Yeah, I did." I flipped the page and showed him a picture of me and my best friend Christy. I'd frosted my hair when she did. It looked better on her. Made me look like a ghost. "That was my best friend. She was basically my sister. We grew up down the street from each other. Our moms were best friends. Went on vacations together. It was great." Christy was a year older than me. Joe was Christy's age, but had been held back in third grade.

I let him flip through several more photos. He asked occasional questions as he ran across photos of my piano and dance recitals. Michelle wanted to be a professional ballerina. Didn't have the body for it. Too curvy. But she still dreamed of a career in dance. After the accident, the muscle and neurological damage killed that dream. He made it through to the end of the album, where I'd kept copies of the articles about the accident. His eyes shuttered.

"What's this?" He asked, finger pointed at a black and white photo of the three of us huddled together on the football field under the headline, "Teens Struck by Lightning - Two Dead."

"We were in a freak weather accident. The three of us got struck by lightning. There wasn't a cloud in the sky. They died, I didn't."

"Wait, you were…"

"Struck by lightning," I said slowly, nodding. "I've got scars and plenty of other issues from it."

"I've never seen any scars."

"Have you noticed what I wear?" I laughed. I guess he hadn't. He didn't really look at me like I was a girl. Couldn't blame him. "Yeah, we'll save that for another time." I wasn't in the mood to strip for him. It wasn't like he'd appreciate it. He might never talk to me again if I started stripping. I couldn't even hug the guy.

3

I walked into the high school Commons before first bell. Jules and Vicki sat on a bench in front of the school's main office. They appeared to be deep in conversation and I wasn't in the mood to listen to how serious their relationships were or how much I needed to get laid. I turned away and beelined toward Ted, sax case leaning against his leg. He was my bandmate in two ways. We were in Concert Band together, he on alto sax, me on flute. I sat next to him on the recently polished stairs.

"What's new?"

"Huh?" His eyes turned to me, startled as if woken from a daydream. "Oh, hi Shell."

"How was the rest of your weekend?" I forgot the rules, leaned into him and let my head rest on his shoulder. No reaction.

"Worked for dad, slept, mixed some tracks. You?" He asked, his breath brushing my forehead.

"Hung out at the lake Friday night, worked Saturday, and slept yesterday," I said. It felt so good leaning against him. I realized what I was doing and moved away, turning to face him.

"Exciting…" he said, voice dry.

"Totally. So, tell me about these tracks."

"You know those lyrics you gave me last week? The ones about the building storm?" I nodded. "I was thinking how it

21

should start off slow and build up into a loud, crashing, fast rhythm. Like a thunderstorm. Then, slow down again at the end, but quickly. I sampled some metal in the background."

"Can't wait to hear it. Just don't forget there're only four of us, and our skills aren't that well developed yet. I can barely play guitar while singing." Zane grabbed us both by the shoulder. I jumped.

"Hey guys!" His eyes glinted with mischief as he peered down at us. "Ted, you putting the moves on Shell again?" Ted's cheeks tinted cherry against his light caramel skin.

"Not at all, bro." He raised his hands in the air like a kid caught shoplifting.

"It's all me, Zane. Forgot the boundaries for a sec." I grimaced at our lead guitar's firm stance and mocking grin. Geez, he was like a mean little brother sometimes.

"I knew it. I knew there was something between you two."

Behind Zane followed Jay and Scotty Baylor, star athlete. Jay leered at me. I narrowed my eyes and leaned back against Ted, who again, did nothing. It was almost as if I wasn't touching him at all for the reaction I got.

"So, tell me about the kind of bass line you're thinking about for *Thundering Heart*." Zane stepped down to stand in front of us. Ted took out a cassette recorder and handed us some earbuds.

"Here, take a listen," Ted said, smile playing at the corners of his lips.

I popped the earbud in and a deep pounding riff assailed me. I bobbed my head with the rhythm as it built, getting faster. It stopped suddenly and I removed the bud, lips stretched into a wide grin.

"That's what I've got so far," Ted said, eyes intent on our reactions.

"Love it. Can't wait to see what everyone else comes up with. How are we doing on demo CDs?" I turned to Zane.

"Still have about 65 left," he said. "Need to order more soon."

"Can I get 10?" I reach into my pocket for some cash and handed it over.

"I'll bring them to practice tonight. I've got at least that many in my trunk."

"Awesome." The bell rang and we split up. The heaviness of eyes on me made my skin crawl as I walked toward the cafeteria for study hall. I hated being watched. I didn't turn around.

Vicki's brother Aaron, former Biology lab partner and recital accompanist, approached me during study hall.

"How's Monica?" I asked. Monica was Aaron's girlfriend, and a friend of mine who sat behind me in Civics the previous year. She was the cheerleading co-captain this year, but off the team due to injury. Cheerleading was more dangerous than people realized. Injuries weren't uncommon.

"She's good. Says she misses seeing you in Civics class."

"Man, Ms. Min was so boring, but that EMT kid - Sam, was it? Always shook things up. Our field trip to the landfill was nuts!"

"Monica mentioned that adventure. Something about the heat and the smell."

"Yeah, it was terrible. The recycling center smelled like sour milk and rotten vegetables. Gross. Surprised your class didn't go too."

"Mr. Dupont didn't feel that recycling was a good enough cause to subject us to the landfill. Are you taking AP Bio next year?" Aaron asked.

"That's the plan. I need lots of science if I want to go pre-med."

"Cool. Me too. We don't see each other much outside of recitals." We both took lessons from the same private music instructor, Mrs. Bates.

"No, we really don't. Send Monica my best."

"Will do." Aaron stood up and walked off as the bell rang. I wondered how he could be so cool and nice when Vicki was, well, Vicki.

Madame Bouvier paced the front of the classroom drilling us on conjugated irregular verbs in the irregular past tense. I was bored, having learned the verb tense previously. The school had combined French III and IV this year due to low enrollment, and I was doing independent study in preparation for next year's AP French V. Review of irregular past tense done, Madame Bouvier moved on to discussion about the weekend.

"Michelle, qu'as tu faire le weekend dernier?"

"Le samedi, j'ai travaillé et le vendredi, je suis allé au lac avec mes amis."

"Dans la pluie?"

"Oui, la pluie était magnifique sur le lac."

Madame nodded and moved on to the next student. I mostly tuned out the rest of the class, taking an occasional note to look like I was paying attention. Gwen, one of my co-workers tossed me a note to ask about Friday's party. She hadn't been able to go. She was grounded due to a school suspension she'd earned last week by talking back to one of her teachers. I wrote a quick note to tell her I'd met a new guy and that Jay had been a jerk as usual, then tossed it at her when Madame was facing the board again.

When the bell rang, Madame motioned me to the back of the classroom where she opened the closet and handed me a new novel, *Madame Bovary*, by Flaubert.

"Read this and we'll talk about it next week."

"Yes Madame. Thank you." I took the book and headed to Precalculus, my last class before band. Although it'd been a standard day, I'd found myself slow blinking in class, and now struggled with heavy limbs. I looked forward to going home after Concert Band.

I sensed Stephanie, or maybe heard that telltale shrill laugh first, before I took my seat as section leader. In my position, I faced the clarinet section and the bells, where Stephanie attempted to flip her fried blonde hair, which was sprayed into a high unmovable wave of bangs and a crispy frizz of shoulder length curls. Her hooked nose had a big pimple on it, which she'd tried unsuccessfully to cover up with concealer a couple shades too dark. Eye makeup heavy and melting, she hung off the arm of Chad, a 6-foot-tall, 200-pound football player and part-time band geek drummer. He shook her off like a gnat, rolled his eyes, and twirled his drum stick as he took his place at the bass drum. The guy had skills. Mr. Seagram tapped the conductor stand.

The phone rang from the band director's office, and Mr. Seagram barked at us to play a C-scale in whole notes while he took the call. He motioned Max, the drum major, to take over conducting. Max waved his arm slowly in the air as he instructed us to play a scale in fourths, followed by an F-scale, then ran us through arpeggios until Mr. Seagram returned with his hair mussed and face red. Max stepped down.

Mr. Seagram barked out a song title, counted down, and we began to play. After only four bars, he motioned us to stop. "No, no, no!" He pointed at the trumpets and told them to play the first four bars. Knowing that he would beat on the trumpets a while over those same four bars, I leaned back in my chair. I felt a tap on my shoulder. I turned to find Ted's face inches from mine, his breath warm on my cheek.

"We still on for practice after school? Your garage?" He asked.

"Yeah, as planned," I confirmed.

He squeezed my shoulder and a goofy smile spread on my lips. Seemed like yesterday that he wouldn't even touch me and shied away from any physical contact. He still didn't let anyone else within three feet, except for Zane. Ted leaned back and Zane punched his shoulder, giving me a nod and one of his "go girl" looks. My eyes rolled and I faced front as Mr. Seagram signaled for us to ready our instruments and tapped a four-count.

At measure 16, the bell rang and we packed up for the day. Didn't get much practice in thanks to that phone call. I wondered what got Mr. Seagram so pissed off. Then again, he was always mad. Zane and Ted waited for me with their alto saxes already cased as I slid my flute into my backpack. We walked to the parking lot together.

"Zane, you'll bring those demos to practice tonight?" I asked in reminder.

"Yeah."

"7:00, your garage, right?" Ted confirmed with a side hug. Whoa buddy, body contact. Crazy.

"Mmm-hmm. Either of you know if Barry's coming? Might sound a little weird with no drums." He'd missed Concert Band.

"Saw him in Geometry. He said he'd be there." Zane waved

as he dumped his books and alto in the trunk of his car.

"Need me to bring anything?" Ted leaned in for another side hug. My eyes widened.

"Only if you want a specific drink or snacks," I said, unable to stop a goofy smile from spreading across my face.

"See you soon." As he walked away, my skin creeped and the hair on the back of my neck rose. Again, that sense of being watched. I surveyed the parking lot, saw nothing, and got in the car.

4

When I got home, mom's car waited in the driveway. She'd taken the afternoon off to because Andy had a doctor's follow up to check on a healing broken ankle. He'd broken it during a summer soccer game. He'd half-fallen into a hole while kicking a goal. He'd made the goal, but his planted ankle hadn't. Andy spent the rest of the summer on crutches, healing from a fractured tibia. Resilient as he was, he was already back into school sports and I hadn't seen him limp in over a month.

I walked in to find Andy sitting at the table working on his spelling and vocabulary homework. Although he struggled with language arts in the past, he'd really caught up recently. He'd taken to his new teacher's way of having students learn vocabulary by writing a sentence using each word. Andy enjoyed using those words to connect each sentence into a coherent story. Last week, he tied the word 'hubris' into a tale about a boy and his sled dog. The boy's grandfather was racing in the Iditarod and his hubris led him to use a shortcut that brought him to an untimely demise. I'd snuck a look at it after he went to bed. It actually wasn't bad.

I snuck up behind him and peered over his shoulder. He tried to push me away with a whining noise, "Stop it!"

"What's the story about this week?" I asked.

"It's about my sister's new boyfriend." He spoke in a sing-song voice that trailed into a squeal of laughter at the end. I playfully slapped his shoulder as mom walked into the room.

"New boyfriend?" Mom asked.

"Nope, just Ted."

"I see." Her brow crinkled into deep lines. "You know the rules, no going out unless I'm home and know where you are."

"Yes, mother." I grabbed an orange and began peeling it. "Oh, don't forget, the guys are coming over to practice tonight."

"Fine, just don't play too loud or too late. I'm working late shift tonight. Covering for Sherry."

"Really? You've been working an awful lot lately. Don't you work the morning shift tomorrow?"

"Yes." That was it. Just "yes."

"That's a double shift!" Which meant she'd be tired and grumpy when she got home in the afternoon.

"I'll sleep when I get home," she said. She might as well have used the tired expression that she'd sleep when she was dead. Work was all she did these days.

"Did you sleep at all today?" I asked, arms crossed.

"Some."

"Did you eat?" I asked, feeling like the parent.

"Had a sandwich when I woke up."

"No lunch break at work again?"

"You know how it is. Things pick up in the hospital and I can't just stop to eat."

"Take some granola bars or something. You have to eat." I examined my mother, dark circles under her eyes, skin sallow. I knew she stressed about bills since the divorce, but she didn't need to work herself to death. I worried about her. "I'm going to get the garage ready. Have a good evening at work."

"Sure. Have fun with the band. Oh, I told Andy that Mike could visit for a bit tonight. Do you mind?"

"No, that's fine. They'll probably just play video games and I'll order pizza after practice."

I hurried downstairs through the basement and into the garage, flipping the light switch and checking the equipment. The drum kit was set up and the amps plugged in. My guitar and mic stand stood ready to go. The floor looked relatively clear with just a few dried leaves littering the concrete. I opened the garage door to release musty air as a gold sedan pulled into the driveway. Ted got out, pulling his bass guitar from the back seat. He came in and set the bass on a guitar stand, then gave me a full hug. I raised an eyebrow as he released me. So much physical contact in one day.

"Guys will be here soon," Ted said. He swiveled at the sound of crunching gravel. Mike zipped up the driveway on his bike. Mike leaned the bike against the house and peered into the garage.

"Wow, cool set up!"

"Thanks, Mike. Come on in. Andy's upstairs. Oh, and I'll be ordering pizza around 8:00 if you're still here." I asked Ted, "you want pizza later?"

"Sure. You know I love pizza."

"Let's go upstairs until Zane and Barry get here. It's a little chilly." I pulled the garage door closed and turned on the space heater. He followed me up the dark stairwell and into the light of the dining area. "Want some soda?"

"Sure, something with no caffeine?"

"Got it." I grabbed a green lemon lime 2-liter from the fridge. "Ice?" He shook his head. "Guys! Want something to drink?" I called to the living room.

"No!" In stereo.

"Earlier you said you'd been sampling something metal? Did you bring a copy?"

"Oh, yeah." He pulled a CD from his pocket. I put it in the boom box and pressed play. Something that sounded like a slowed *Marionette,* but not quite issued from the speakers.

"Interesting." Not quite what I'd had in mind, but certainly interesting.

"It gets better." The song transitioned to something like the intro to Metallartig's *Insane,* a total change in pace, although from the same band's repertoire. "Just wanted to get your attention." His eyes met mine as his lips twitched. I pushed down the laughter trying to escape in a series of coughs.

"Definitely better." Something different, and definitely not Metallartig, started up with the bass riff that he'd played for me and Zane that morning. "Hang on, let me get the lyrics." I started humming a melody to the music as I rushed back to the dining table. "I reach for you through the clouds of my dreams, you're never there... I call for you over the thunder of my heart... Answer me, I'm dying here."

"Not bad. Let's get back to the garage and record some of this. The guys should be here soon." Ted stood, extending an arm to guide me to the stairwell. I picked up a flannel shirt from my chair before I followed him downstairs. "I wanted to ask you something." Ted said as Barry's van pulled into the driveway. Zane and Barry unloaded some gear from the van and held up a hand.

"Sure, can it wait a sec? Looks like the guys are here." I opened the door and greeted the rest of Toxic Siren. "Hey, guys! Good to see you. Come on in. Ted and I were about to work on some ideas for the new song. He's got some cool bass riffs and I'm toying with some melody for the verses."

We set up in the basement, while I listened to the guys banter. I enjoyed listening to them talk. It was so much less dramatic than listening to Jules and Vicki. I didn't have to work so hard to keep the guys entertained. All I had to do was be there and they were happy. I liked hanging out with them. Couldn't say that Zane's girlfriend, Tara, was keen on him spending so much time with me and the guys, but I didn't spend time alone with him. She was a petite brunette sax player in band who used to play flute. She was nice enough, but I could tell that Zane's friendship with me bothered her. Typical girl jealousy. Couldn't say I was immune. I loved my guy friends. Hated having to share them with other girls, even though the guys were just friends of mine. Made no sense and I knew it.

Ted brought out the tape player and set it up to record. "Alright, here's what we've got so far. Join in when you've got something." Ted started playing his bass line and soon after I began the first verse. I didn't quite have a tune for the chorus yet, so we went back to the first verse again a few times to jam and let the guys join in. I lifted my red electric Luna guitar and tried a few chords. Bear drummed a nice steady beat. After a while, Ted stopped the recorder.

"That's a good start. Something to work with. I'll make copies and bring them to school tomorrow."

"Anyone interested in pizza? I need to put in an order." I looked at my watch.

"Nah, Barry and I have to go soon. I promised Tara I'd help her with Geometry tonight. Maybe next time," Zane said. I knew it wasn't all about the Geometry because Zane wasn't the brightest of bulbs. If anyone was benefitting in Geometry from their study sessions, it was him.

"You know Tara's welcome to join us if she wants to," I offered.

"I know. Just think it'd be distracting. Sometimes I need time away from her," Zane said.

"Ok. Let me call in the order. You have time to run through a couple more songs before you go?" The guys nodded. I pulled Ted to the side to ask about what kind of pizza he wanted then headed upstairs to get the boys' order. When I got back downstairs, the guys were talking quietly among themselves. There was an abrupt silence when I walked through the door.

"Pizza's ordered. What do you want to practice first?" I asked, ignoring the odd silence. Tension rode the air.

"Let's run through that cover of *Medicated*." Barry suggested. I nodded and grabbed the microphone as he cracked a quick 4-count with his drum sticks. It was one of my favorite Calabrias' songs.

I tried to loosen up and practice my performance technique due to some unfavorable feedback at our last show. I jumped a little, walked around, tripping on the cord a few times, and worked a little interaction with Barry and Ted. I had a really difficult time forcing myself to connect with the audience during shows. I got super nervous when I had to look at people, so I tried to make up for it by looking at my band mates. During practice, I pulled my hair back so that I couldn't hide my face behind it. Tonight, I'd pulled it into two side braids that fell forward over my shoulders. It may have made me look younger than my 17 years, but I didn't care. I liked it. Perhaps the audience would be more forgiving if I looked young and inexperienced. Darned performance anxiety. It had never been a problem for Michelle, not that I could remember.

"Still a bit tight, Shell. You gotta loosen up!" Zane laughed. "Wish we had a video camera. You move around, but it's like your arms don't move! Does it hurt being so stiff?"

"You're kidding, right? Guys, was it that bad?" I swiveled my head between Ted and Barry who had trouble meeting my eyes as they broke into hearty laughter. "Seriously?" Tears streamed down Ted's face and Barry toppled onto the concrete floor, holding his stomach.

"Fine, I'll keep working on it." Laughter escaped my lips as I watched the guys try to recompose themselves and fail.

"And on that note…" Barry grabbed his drum sticks and pointed at Zane who was packing up his Gibson with hitching breaths. "We'll be off." The guys left with a see you later wave.

I was still giggling when Ted and I made it upstairs. Andy and Mike looked at me like I was losing it. Ted shook his head. "You had to be there, dudes." I pulled some plates and napkins from the cupboard and set out cups and soda. I paid the delivery guy, placed the pizza next to the plates on the island and we grabbed some slices. We headed to the living room where the television was turned down low and a Bianchi Brothers game was paused. Darned tune was catchy. Ted sat next to me on the sofa.

"Having fun?" I look to Andy.

"Sounded like you guys were having a lot more fun in the garage," Andy said.

"You could have come down and watched," I reminded him. He and Mike were always welcome observers.

"Yeah, you really missed something." Ted nudged me. Heat rushed to my face.

"What happened?" Andy leaned in.

"You had to be there. It can't be expressed in words." Ted looked at me as I hid my eyes behind a hand. He lightly took my hand and pulled it down to my lap. "No, really, it was kind of cute."

"Guess you'll just have to watch our next practice, Andy." Warmth surrounded my hand. I looked down and found Ted's hand still on top of mine. "So, Mike, what's new with you?"

"Not much. Grandma says we're going to visit my Aunt Tunia this weekend. She lives in Philly, and that'll be neat."

"Sorry, her name's Tuna?" Andy asked. I gave him a look trying to convey how rude he was being, but Mike took it in stride and just laughed. Good kid.

"No, no. Tunia," he said more slowly.

"Do you see her often?" I asked. He'd never mentioned an aunt before. I would have remembered someone named Tunia.

"Haven't seen her in years," he said with a shrug. He looked at the floor and picked at the shag carpeting.

"Looking forward to it?"

"Not sure. She and mom didn't get along, so we don't talk to her. Grandma says it's time for me to start making up my own mind about people."

"That's a good idea," Ted agreed.

"So, when does Lily expect you home tonight?" I asked.

"She said 9:30." He looked at the clock. "I better go home now."

"Need a ride? It's dark out there." I asked

"No, I'm good. My bike has a headlight and reflectors and you know I'm just a block over. Thanks for the pizza!"

"Good to see you, Mike. Good night!" He rushed out the door. "Is your homework done, Andy?"

"Yeah, finished it before Mike got here." He picked up the game controller and returned to playing Bianchi Brothers.

"Awesome." I sank into the sofa and leaned into Ted with my head against his shoulder. It was just so comfortable to touch him. Ted was non-threatening. My best guy friend. No, definitely my best friend. I looked up into Ted's brown eyes and asked, "What's your curfew tonight?"

"No curfew, my parents are trying something new."

"Weird. They're usually more protective than my mom," I gazed into his eyes, that goofy grin back on my face.

"Yeah, they are. Sick of me yet, or want to hang out a little longer?" He asked, smiling at me as his deep brown eyes looked down into mine.

"Any chance you brought over homework? I've still got some I need to do and I'd feel bad working on it with you here."

"Yeah, actually my backpack's in the backseat. I'll go get it." He left to get it, leaving my hand cold when he stood. I looked at my hand, confused by the chill. Had he been holding it all this time?

"Your homework's not done?" Andy looked at me with comic disapproval.

"Nope. Go ahead, tell mom. It's not like I haven't done my homework at all. It'll get done before it's due tomorrow. Planned to do it after practice." I moved to the dining room and got my books laid out on the table. I arranged a notebook with pencils and checked out the instructions for my first assignment. I opened my French textbook and began conjugating verbs. I looked up when Ted returned, backpack in hand, and gestured to the table. He took the chair next to mine and set up. We worked on our assignments for a while, occasionally getting up for drink refills and bathroom breaks. Andy got tired and went to bed. It was after 11:00 when I finished my assignments.

"Wow, got late quick. Done with your homework?" I stretched my arms overhead and looked over to see Ted staring at me.

"Oh, um, yeah. Been done for a while," he said, leaning on a hand and smiling.

"Sorry about that. Got absorbed in what I was doing. Do you need to go now?"

"You tired?" He asked, avoiding the question.

"A little, but I could stay up a bit longer. You?"

"A bit, but I was hoping to talk to you without your brother hanging around," Ted tapped a pencil on the table, looked at it for a moment, then put it down.

"Sorry, I have to keep an eye on him when mom's out."

"I know. I kind of hoped he'd get tired earlier." Ted frowned, then smiled.

"Usually stays up later than me." I said and laughed.

"These chairs are uncomfortable," he said, touching the oak armrests.

"Hmmm… what do you expect? They're wood." I stood up and stretched from toes to fingertips, exposing my belly as my tee shirt rose. "Come on, follow me." I led Ted back to my room and closed the door. I started up a Calabrias cassette on low volume in the dim yellow light of a lamp. I sat at my desk chair and gestured for Ted to sit on the bed.

"Never been in here before." He took in his surroundings.

"My private sanctuary. I don't let just anyone in here." Mom also had rules about boys being in my room, as in they're not supposed to be there. I trusted Ted. It wasn't like he'd try anything.

"Very 1970's. The brown shag carpet and dark wood paneling," he noted as his eyes surveyed the room.

"Yes, retro chic." My left eyebrow arched and I half smiled.

"Your voice was lovely tonight as always."

"Thanks. I really enjoyed your bass playing and mixing skills. Thanks for bringing that CD, by the way."

"We've really got to work on loosening up your body though." He leaned forward, tapping his chin.

"Same might be said for you, mister." I pointed at him as he leaned back.

"What, me? I'm a cool cat, loose, chill, and besides, nobody checks out the bass player."

"I've checked out the bass player." I mused.

"What?" He looked up from the floor, eyes wide.

"Seriously, at concerts, there have definitely been some bass players that piqued my interest." Not to mention, Ted. He was one fine bass player with his shoulder length wavy black hair, deep brown eyes, and full lips. I wondered what those lips felt like.

"I wasn't sure anybody piqued your interest," he said, pulling me away from my musings about his lips.

"I do my best to keep people away. It's not like I don't have feelings or desires, but the logical part of my brain, the part that reminds me I'm broken, keeps me from connecting and going after what I want."

"Broken? You seem pretty put together to me, even confident at times."

"Oh, sure. But, there's something wrong with me. There's this terrible numbness and anger. I'm not happy. I'm getting there. I'm happier these days, spending time with you and the band. But something's not right. There are times I can't get out of bed and I want to sleep for days and cry. My thoughts get really dark."

"Come here." Arms held out, he moved back against the wall and motioned me over. I sat between his legs and he began to massage my neck and shoulders. "Wow, your muscles are seriously wound up. Tight. Let me know if it hurts."

"So far so good." I leaned back, enjoying the feeling of his fingers loosening my muscles. "Wow, this is great, but now I'm getting tired." I leaned forward and looked back at him. "You?"

"Actually, yes."

"Too tired to drive?" I asked. I didn't want anything to happen to my best friend.

"Yeah," he admitted.

"You can stay if you want."

"Really?"

"Yeah, just don't tell my mom. She's working a double shift. You can stay in here if you want, but you need to be on the sofa before my brother wakes up."

"Got it." He smiled. What's a sleepover between friends?

5

I woke to Andy's cracking voice, "what are you doing here?"

I sat up in bed, wiping my eyes and looking around. Realization dawned and I quickly hopped out of bed and rushed to the living room where Ted spoke with Andy.

"Morning, Andy. Took us longer to finish our homework than expected and Ted was too tired to drive home so he slept on the sofa," I blurted. My little brother looked skeptically up at me and back at Ted's bed head and rumpled shirt. He looked cute in a disheveled way. Extremely cute. I shrugged. "It was really, really late." I panicked and looked at Ted. "Maybe you should call your mom and let her know where you are?" His eyes widened and he rushed for the kitchen phone.

Andy tapped his foot on the floor impatiently. "What really happened?"

"We finished our homework late and decided to talk for a while. It was too late for him to drive home safely so he stayed over. On the sofa." I spoke slowly and struggled to maintain eye contact.

"Oh-kay." He drew out with a sigh. "Gotta get ready for school." He shook his head as he headed back to his room to get dressed. He was such an old man at heart. Sometimes I felt like he was the guardian.

I hurried back to my room and shimmied into the first jeans and tee shirt combo that I could find. I grabbed my work uniform and stuffed it into a duffle bag for my after-school shift. After locating a couple of my longer concert tees, I returned to the living room where Ted sat with a stunned look on his face.

"What's up?" I asked, handing him the tee shirts.

"She's fine with it. Didn't freak out at all. Said she'd see me after school."

"Totally weird."

"Yeah. Hey, did you know that you talk in your sleep?"

"Actually, yes. I knew that. I also sleepwalk. Multitalented individual here," I said, pointing at myself. I cocked my head. "Did I say anything interesting?"

"Couldn't make out most of it, but I thought I heard you mumble that you liked me." He grinned.

"That's not very interesting." I turned around and backed into the wall to avoid my brother, who was running down the hallway.

"I'm late, I'm late!" He ran out the door to catch the bus.

"For a very important date!" Ted and I screamed in unison followed by a stream of laughter.

"Either of those tees work for you?"

"What's wrong with this one?" He looked down at the one he was wearing.

"Nothing, if you don't mind people thinking you're doing a walk of shame. Do you have another shirt in your car?"

"No." He looked more closely at the tees I'd handed him.

"I know you're taller and skinnier, but one of these might work. I left a new toothbrush on the counter for you." I had a growing stash of dentist promo toothbrushes. I kept forgetting I had the free ones from my visits lying around and kept buying new toothbrushes instead. Occasionally, like today, the dentist promos came in handy.

"Thanks." Ted took his turn the bathroom to tidy up and I went for the dining room to shove my books back into my backpack. I tossed a couple toaster pastries into the toaster and sat down to lace up my black combat boots. I looked up as Ted turned the corner. I'd tied my hair high in a pony tail that fell over one shoulder. I tried to blow a stray hair out of my face as I looked up. My tee was a little loose on him, but it looked ok. He'd chosen the black Hammer and Nails shirt. Nice choice, more fitting than indie, I suppose. I motioned to the toaster and he took one of the pastries, nodding with a bite.

"We gotta get out of here or we'll miss first bell." I thought about the white rabbit from Wonderland shouting about being late in my brother's distressed cracking voice and giggled. Ted raised a brow. "I'm late! I'm late!" I imitated Andy. Ted laughed, picked up his books, and walked out the door with me.

The school day flew by. Luckily, I'd finished the Precalculus homework. Mr. Fritz collected our assignments in class, nodding as he skimmed over mine. I looked forward to work, if only to avoid going home. I worried that Andy would blab about the sleepover, not that anything had happened. When the final bell rang after band, I bolted out to my car to get a head start on traffic.

As I drove away from the school on Highway 611, I wondered how Marcus was doing. We shared Precalculus, Chemistry, and Pre-AP English classes. It was unsettling to not see him sitting near me with his head in a textbook. No one in school seemed to notice his absence. Classes went on without him, or even mention of him, and I wondered where his acquaintances thought he was. Probably figured he was sick. As I pulled into the Norma's parking lot, I saw Raif's car and next to it, Pat's Dodge Ram. The lot was packed with cars, so I hurried in and changed into my uniform before clocking in.

Assigned to the sandwich station, I washed my hands and relieved the day shift worker, Sal. I gloved up and prepared orders until we caught up. Customers served, I used the lull to ask for news about Marcus.

"He's in a coma. Not sure he'll live." Raif wiped down the counter. "Spoke with his mom this morning. She's a mess, but hopeful. He flatlined twice last night. Second time, it took them 15 minutes to revive him. He may have some brain damage if he recovers." Raif let out a deep sigh. "I'm not sure how she's keeping her hopes up. Interested in some extra shifts, Shell?"

"Sure, I guess so," I said, reflecting on what Raif had said. Marcus was in worse shape than I'd thought. He might not make it? Coded twice? I thought his vitals were improving.

"Talk to Pat before you leave and she'll set you up. Have to cover his shifts until he comes back." Raif's eyes dropped to the floor. "If he comes back."

My eyes burned and stomach sank as I considered the potential loss of a classmate and co-worker. A peer, someone my age. We're supposed to live long lives, go to college, get a good job, and have families of our own. I felt my darkness descending.

"Raif, I'm going to check with Pat while things are slow." I tossed the used gloves into a trash bin and walked back to the manager's office where I found Pat bent over receipts, pressing calculator keys with the eraser end of a pencil. I stood in the doorway and knocked. She looked up, hair in a frizzy pony tail and dark bags under her eyes.

"Yes, Shell?"

"Raif said to ask you about covering some of Marcus's shifts?"

"Ah, good." She handed me a copy of the schedule and I compared his schedule with mine. "I can take Thursday and Friday night, and Sunday's day shift. Sound good?"

"Great. Pencil your name in." I picked up a chewed pencil from the desk, leaned down and crossed off Marcus's name, replacing it with my own.

"Mind if I take off Friday and Saturday next week? We've got a show in Scranton."

"Not a problem." She handed me a yellow sticky note. "Write it down and stick it to the schedule."

"Thanks."

"Oh, Shell, I'm moving you out to the salad bar from 9:00 'til close, unless it's really dead. You can head over and help Julie shut down and prep for tomorrow."

"Not a problem."

"Thanks for being flexible. Oh, and can you do a quick cleanup of the dining area before heading back to the line?" I nodded, grabbing the small sanitizer bucket and a towel to wipe down the tables. I let Raif know my assignments before I headed to the condiment area.

After the final customer rush, I helped Jules close and prep the salad bar for the next day. She was unusually quiet as we worked. Although she said she just wanted to finish closing the salad bar and go home early, something was on her mind. I didn't press for more information. We closed the station in record time and she left by 9:30 as Pat locked the door. I looked outside as I cleaned the dining area and stacked chairs on top of the tables while Jay vacuumed the carpet.

Fog settled outside, creating an ambient glow beneath the street lights. I suppressed the urge to run out and enjoy the fog. I loved the fog. That mysterious and wonderful feeling of prickly water droplets called to me, the scent, the way things disappeared and emerged like magic. Soon enough, we were released from duty.

As I drove home on Sterling Road, my eyes caught a deer to my left standing next to a tree with a big light spot on the trunk. I realized that it must have been the tree that Marcus hit. I fought chills as I continued home, watching for more deer that might run in front of me. A hazard of driving in the area was running into the bountiful deer that lived in the forests, and if you saw one, there were usually more nearby. In a trick of the light, or a hallucination of my eyes, I saw a runner in a red jogging suit along the side of the road. I turned my head to look as I passed him by, but there wasn't anybody there. Happened to me a lot in rain and fog, seeing things that weren't there.

I pulled into the driveway to find that once again, mom's car was absent. I got out of the car and savored the damp smell of the fog. I twirled, watching the grounded clouds drift and swirl around me. I grabbed my backpack and duffle and entered the house through the basement, started the washing machine and dumped my uniform in with a pile of waiting clothes. I emptied the dryer, tossed the clothes into a basket and carried it upstairs in the dark, not bothering to flip the light switch.

When I opened the door, all I could see was the pulsing glow of a familiar knife informercial on TV. First, the knife sliced through a can, then cut through a tomato without losing its sharp edge. I didn't immediately see my brother. As I walked by the love seat, a head with messy brown hair resting on an arm caught my attention. On closer examination, my brother stared at the television, eyes wide, mouth slightly open with drool bubbling and gathering in the corner of his mouth. I laughed and he slowly looked up at me.

"What?" He mumbled, drool bubbling and dripping onto the loveseat.

"Kind of creepy, watching that commercial so intently."

"What? It's so cool!" He looked up at me and wiped the

drool from his mouth using a shirt sleeve.

"Where's mom?"

"Staying at the hospital tonight. Called and said something about a pileup and being on-call."

I shook my head and took the laundry basket over to a mismatched armchair where I started folding and sorting laundry.

"You eat yet?" I asked.

"Yeah, sandwich."

"Good. Homework done?"

"Yep." He said with a yawn as he scooted into a semi-seated position.

"I'll be up a while. Need to wash my uniform and I haven't started on my homework yet. Lots of Precalculus tonight." I frowned, setting aside an unmatched sock.

"No boyfriend to help you tonight?" He wagged an eyebrow and I refrained from tossing a pair of underwear that I was folding at him.

"I don't have a boyfriend," I mumbled.

"So you say, but he was here when I woke up."

I tossed a pair of wadded up briefs at him, hitting his face. What could I say? They slipped.

"You doing ok? Home alone so much?" I asked, rethinking those extra shifts. Andy turned 13 next month. While I'd been babysitting younger kids at that age, including Andy, mom didn't like me to leave him alone for long. I couldn't blame her. I felt protective of him too. He was my baby brother.

"Not a problem. Do what you gotta do," he said.

"Just worry about you sometimes."

"Got the good ol' TV and video games." He Vanna White-ed the small entertainment center.

I finished folding and sorting the laundry and dropped off piles in our respective bedrooms. I returned to the basement to toss my uniform in the dryer. The phone rang upstairs.

"What time is it?" I grumbled, irritated, but also worried it might be bad news. Bad news or an obscene caller. I rushed upstairs as Andy called for me. I nearly knocked him over.

"Who is it?"

"Your boyfriend." He cooed in a singsong voice.

"I don't have a boyfriend." I took the phone from him. He

turned off the TV and stumbled to his room. I looked at the wall clock and read 11:00.

"Good to know," the voice on the other end said.

"Huh? What?"

"That you don't have a boyfriend," he said, chuckling.

"Ted!"

"Cheerleader," he teased. I groaned. "How much trouble are you in?" I asked.

"No trouble at all."

"You're kidding." His parents were way strict, more than my mom. Mom was slipping, a risk of not being home. Couldn't enforce strict rules if you're there. He laughed quietly. "Does she know where you were last night?"

"Yes. I told you, they're trying something new. Remember, I turned 18 last month?"

"Uh," I drew out while I thought about it. We had celebrated his birthday a couple weeks ago. Like me, he was a year behind in school and could have also been graduating this year. I knew it had been his birthday. It hadn't registered how old he was. "Yeah, I guess you did."

"We renegotiated the rules. Living under their roof, I've still got to follow some basic rules, but they're doing this whole loosening the leash thing. I just have to let them know where I'm going to be, who I'm with."

"Wow. That's a lot of trust," I said. His mom was so strict that I'd never seen his room, not even from the doorway. I was allowed in the kitchen, living room, bathroom, and garage when I visited. That was it. Then again, boys weren't supposed to be in my room either. Not even Ted. Definitely not with the door closed. Nothing had happened, but I'd still broken a few rules last night. But, I mean, it was Ted. "So, the phone rules have changed too?" He wasn't supposed to be on the phone after 10:00.

"Freedom," he said quietly. "But I wouldn't suggest calling me this late. Phone rings after 10:00, mom'll probably flip." My own mother wouldn't be happy with the phone ringing this late either. Again, not home. "What are you doing?"

"Right now? Homework. Still have about 10 more Precalculus problems and some reading to do for French. What about you?" I asked as I leaned against the kitchen island and twirled the phone cord around my fingers.

"Feeling kind of wired, not very tired."

"Any idea why?" I fished for information, wondering what was keeping my buddy up so late.

"No. Is it a full moon?" He asked. He knew I had a loose interest in things like astrology, but I wasn't that into it.

"No idea. It's so foggy that I can't tell. Hey, what did you want to ask me about?"

"What?"

"Yesterday, you said you wanted to talk to me about something, right before Zane and Bear showed up," I prodded.

"Oh, that can wait."

"I've got time," I said. I really didn't want to get back to those Precalculus problems.

"I'd rather talk about it in person."

"Is it something bad?" I asked, heart speeding up as scenarios ran through my head. Had I done something to piss him off? Did he want to ask me for dating advice? Did he think my songs were crap? Wait, he wasn't allowed to date. He didn't like people touching him anyway. We both had that arm length bubble of personal space thing going on, usually.

"I hope not," he said with a chuckle. I breathed again, realizing I'd been holding my breath. "Can't wait to see you tomorrow. Can we hang out again after practice?"

"Oh, sure. I'd like that." I would. I loved hanging out with my best bud.

6

When I got to school, I found Ted leaning against the wall next to the Band Hall doors. If I didn't know Ted, I might have thought he was waiting for me. He grinned, adorable dimples on his cheeks and tiny crinkles at the sides of his deep brown eyes. His shoulder length hair, dark and shiny with the slightest wave, flowed as he moved in for a hug. My eyes widened and mouth fell open as I was suddenly in Ted's arms. I cautiously reached around him and hugged him back. He smelled amazing, leather and sage. He squeezed me before letting go and I stepped back.

"What was that for?" I asked, leaning my head back to find his eyes.

"Just happy to see you," he said.

"I'm happy to see you too," I said, lips curving into a half-smile. "You just don't hug me like that."

"You didn't like it?" He asked, eyes hooded.

"Oh, no. I liked it." I liked it too much. Darn it, Ted. His intent expression made me uncomfortable. I preferred, in general, for people to ignore me. Sure. I'd gone on a few dates over a couple months with Carlo last year. He'd called himself my boyfriend, but a few dates didn't scream boyfriend to me. He'd been a creep and three years older than me. I'd broken up with him. He disagreed with my decision to end it. I hadn't dated anyone since. It'd been a while since any guy had really paid attention to me in the guy-girl way.

We stood there staring at each other quietly in the dim basement hallway until students began to pour in through the door. Ted looked away first and I shook my head. He lightly took my hand and pulled me toward the stairs. How was he touching me? Had he suddenly overcome his aversion to touch? The no touching thing came from a history of childhood abuse. He'd spent a few years in foster care before the Levins adopted him. My understanding was that the abuse happened at such a young age and for so long that he couldn't stand to be touched, except by a few trusted individuals, and even then, not for long periods of time. Even his parents could barely hug him before he pulled away.

Having experienced abuse of my own, I had an inkling of what it was like to be hit, kicked, pushed, knocked down for really minor stuff, accidents really. Eventually, you start to believe the lie of worthlessness and the value of invisibility and silence. I'd lost my memories of the early abuse, due to the lightning strike, but the abuse post lightning strike had been bad enough. It ended with me in the hospital with a concussion and cracked ribs shortly after moving to the Poconos. My brother got a dislocated shoulder, broken arm, and cracked ribs. Of course, I could never fully understand what Ted had been through. His experiences were his, as mine were mine. We didn't really talk about it, but it occasionally popped up in our songs.

I hadn't known Ted's history when we'd first met, but we had a connection. When we realized that we had similar tastes in music and played instruments outside of school band, we started hanging out. Or, rather, Ted invited me to start hanging out with him and the guys. Up to that point, he'd done the singing and all they'd done were covers. The band had pretty much been garage band karaoke. Ted had been writing songs for a while when I showed up, but hadn't played any with the band until I came along. I smiled at the memory of the first year hanging out with the guys in Ted's garage. His mom scared the crap out of me. She still did. She was a social worker, and strict. With my experience with social workers, I steered as clear of her as possible. They'd intruded, but hadn't really intervened or helped. Their focus had been my parents, when the problem was Grandpa O'Carroll.

Ted led me to a bench in a dark corner of the recessed Commons area and we sat down. I barely registered that he still held my hand. I was deep in memories, triggered by thoughts of why Ted didn't like to be touched. Yelling, my brother on the ground clutching his arm as our grandfather stood over him, kicking. An arm reached around my shoulder and pulled me close. I turned to find Ted's eyes on me. I struggled for a smile.

"Sorry," I said. "Lost myself."

"I could tell. Bad, huh?"

"Happens sometimes. It's been worse." At least I hadn't woken myself up screaming lately. Good thing that it hadn't happened when Ted stayed over. Wait a minute. "Did I actually talk in my sleep?"

"Yeah. You said you liked me, then mumbled some other stuff that I couldn't make out," he grinned and looked more his age than I'd ever seen him, more 18 than 80.

"Of course, I like you. If I didn't, I wouldn't spend time with you."

"Yeah, but you should've heard the way you said it," he said, elbowing me in the side.

"Huh." Well, maybe no more sleepovers with my best bud, who continued to hold me close with his arm around me. Felt really nice. I leaned my head against his shoulder. Felt natural, normal in an abysmal world. "You're lucky that's all I did."

"How so?" He raised an eyebrow.

"I told you that I sleepwalk too, right?"

"Yeah, so?"

"Who knows what else I'm capable of when I'm asleep. Takes some skill to walk and talk while asleep." I knew for a fact that walking down stairs while asleep was not one of those skills. I'd woken myself falling down stairs many times over the years. I smiled at the thought. As far as I knew, I hadn't walked in my sleep for a while. But, when I had, it had been when I was under a lot of stress.

"Hey," Ted leaned in, "mind if I stay over tonight?"

"Something up at home?" I turned, nearly brushing his lips with mine. Our noses touched. I froze.

"Just want to spend time with you," he said softly. He

leaned back.

"Mom might be home tonight. I'm not sure. Her schedule is jacked up. Andy's home."

"Andy's alright."

"Yeah, but Andy's got loose lips. I'm surprised he hasn't let slip that you were on the couch yesterday morning," I said, eyes rolling. "Of course, mom's schedule has been crazy, so she's only been home while we're at school."

"So, maybe?"

"Did you have that much fun the other night?" I asked. We'd stayed up late, talking, and fell asleep in our clothes on my twin bed. He was tall, almost 6 feet. It couldn't have been comfortable. I had no idea what time he'd moved to the living room, but I knew from experience that the sofa wasn't comfortable at my height. Always left me with a stiff neck.

"Yeah, I did," he said, his lips turned up at the corners.

"We'll see. I mean, I know I'm just one of the guys and all, but mom doesn't see it that way," I pointed out.

Someone cleared their throat and I turned toward the rude interloper. Jay and Jules looked down at us. I raised my eyebrows to express my annoyance and asked, "what?"

"Are we interrupting something?" Jay asked.

"No man, just discussing our plans," Ted said.

"Plans?" Jules asked, giggling.

"Band practice, hanging out," I said, not that it was any of their business. "You know, plans."

"So, you don't want to come to Jay's party tonight?" Jules asked. I shook my head.

"Sorry, I'm busy. Why are you partying on a school night?" I asked.

"Parents are out of town and they took my sisters with them. Figured we'd party after work," Jay said, rolling his eyes.

"Sounds like you'll be up late."

"Uh, yeah. That's the point," he said, barking laughter.

"We can reschedule if you want, Shell," Ted said.

"Heck, Ted, you can come too," Jay said. I shook my head.

"Nah, I'm good. I've already got plans. Thanks though. I appreciate the thought," I said. I'd take an evening with Ted over one of Jay's parties any night.

"So, are you two, like, together?" Jules asked, hand on her

hip.

"Yeah, on this bench," I said. Ted laughed. He squeezed my shoulder and reminded me that we were still touching. Jay shook his head. They waved as they walked away, Jules glancing back over her shoulder, half of her lower lip pinched between her teeth.

"What are you doing?" Zane asked loudly. I tensed at the raised voice and looked up at him.

"Sitting?" I said. I let my head rest on Ted's shoulder, and Zane's face reddened. I wondered what his blood pressure was like. I assumed it had risen quite a bit over the last few seconds. Ted's chest shook in silent laughter. It made me smile. I wrapped my arms around him in a reflexive light hug and squeezed. Zane's face, an alarming beet red, contorted into an odd expression I'd never seen. I thought it might have been fury. Not just pissed off, but furious. Huh.

I released Ted, although he hadn't made any sign of being upset by my touch. I'd been terribly familiar, considering. He just continued to hold me against him. Fine with me. Couldn't see him doing this with one of the other guys, but whatever.

Barry rushed over, probably noticing Zane's stiff posture and odd skin tone. Zane's hands clenched at his sides, fingers whitening at the knuckles. What did he care? Barry looked surprised to see me and Ted sitting so close but what stole his attention was Zane's body language.

"Hey man, you ok?" He asked Zane quietly.

"Do you see that?" He asked in disgust, body rigid, arm pointed at us in a stiff and jerky movement.

"See what?" Barry followed Zane's finger, directed at me and Ted.

"They can't do that," Zane hissed through gritted teeth.

"Do what? They're not doing anything, man," Barry said.

"It's going to mess up the band," Zane hissed.

"What's going to mess up the band?" I asked, leaning back against the wall and crossing my arms and legs.

"You two getting together. It's going to ruin everything."

"We're not together like that." I said. I looked at Ted, my best friend for the past three years.

"You two were almost kissing," Zane accused.

"Say what?" My voice raised and my body tensed, ready to

lunge at him.

"I saw you. You almost kissed." I didn't know what was up with Zane. He'd always kidded us about Ted making moves on me. It'd been a running joke. A mean natured one, now that I thought about it.

"No, we didn't. We were just talking. Get over yourself, Zane. Chill out." If we ever did kiss, I hoped it would be somewhere other than in front of everyone at school. Yuck. I was surprised Ted was showing any kind of physical affection in public to begin with. He didn't touch me in private.

The first bell sounded. I stood up slowly, trying not to spook Zane. Who knew what he'd do in this crazy state of mind? He was freaking me out. I couldn't tell what Ted thought about it. They'd been best friends long before I moved to the area. Ted took my hand and walked me to study hall, nowhere near his class. Zane, frozen to the spot, stared after us.

Ted leaned down and told me he'd see me in Concert Band. I nodded, crickets jumping around in my stomach. He wanted to sleep over twice in one week, and suddenly he was ok with us touching? What was going on with my friend? What was up with the sleeping over? I'd been kind of joking when I'd offered the first time. Not that I hadn't been crushing hard on him for ages.

The day dragged on. I couldn't stop thinking about Ted wanting to do another sleepover. It was weird. In French, I discussed what I'd read with Madame Bouvier. She was pleased with my progress. I'd nearly finished the novel, *Madame Bovary*. I'd probably be ready for another novel next week. I loved to read and I loved the French language. I planned to take the AP French literature exam at the end of the year. That's why I was reading so many extra novels. Next year, I'd be taking the AP French grammar exam. My breath caught when Ted greeted me outside the door. His class was nowhere near mine. My eyebrows shot up.

"Did something happen?" I asked.

"What do you mean?" He asked with a grin.

"I didn't expect to see you until last period. Figured you needed to tell me something."

"Oh, no. Just thought I'd walk with you to your next class.

Precalculus, right?"

"Yeah," I drew out. His previous class, US History, was nowhere near my French class. He must have snuck out early. "Well, it's good to see you. Nice surprise."

He took my hand again, and I was stunned. I mean, it was kind of hokey junior high stuff, but it was big for him. I wasn't sure what his motivation was. Maybe he was testing himself. Using me as a comfortable test subject. I didn't figure he was messing with me to be mean, so I decided to go along with it. He stopped at the side of my classroom door and I stood with him, against the wall as students passed. I got a weird look from Juan, a clarinet player from band, as he went into the classroom.

Ted told me he'd see me in band and I nodded. He squeezed my hand and walked off. I took a moment to appreciate his tight butt. His shoulders had broadened this year too. My friend, always cute, had gotten hot this year. I sighed and turned to go into the classroom. Juan waved impatiently at me to hurry to my normal seat next to him. It wasn't like anyone was racing me to take the chair. Marcus's empty chair sat lonely behind him. I missed him and his occasional under the breath snarky comments. I wondered how he was recovering and if he could have visitors yet.

"What's going on with you and Ted?" Juan asked, leaning across my desk and invading my personal bubble. I shrugged and leaned away from his pungent breath.

"I don't know. Nothing new. He's my friend, you know."

"But you were holding his hand," Juan said under his breath.

"So?" Wasn't Juan's business, whatever was going on was between me and Ted. I really wanted Juan to get out of my personal space. My body tensed up like a tiger prepared to strike an invading predator.

Mr. Fritz saved me from cross examination by space invader when he returned our last pop quiz. I looked at my score and turned the paper face down on the desk. Great. I could've used some of Marcus' tutoring on this unit. Stupid imaginary numbers. If they were imaginary, why did I care? They didn't exist. I sighed. Juan glanced over. I rested my head on a hand and listened as Mr. Fritz went over the correct answers. I wrote them down, but didn't want other people seeing all the red ink on my quiz. Looked like he'd graded it angry.

We reviewed imaginary numbers and learned some new skill that he promised would be on our test next week. He collected our homework and I was glad that I'd worked through all the problems last night rather than ignoring it. Mr. Fritz didn't always collect the homework, but it was worth points I needed when he did. I'd even gone through the trouble of checking my answers to make sure I'd gotten most of them correct. There were at least 3 of the 40 questions that I couldn't figure out. Rather than spend another hour working on them, I'd given up and switched to French. I had a hazy memory of being pretty good at math before the lightning strike. Since then, not so much. I blamed the brain damage. Mom refused to let me switch to a lighter version of math, claiming that my dreams of med school would be over if I did. I didn't exactly believe her and planned to skip math next year and swap it out for AP Biology instead. There was no chance that I'd pass the AP Calculus test.

My mind wandered as Mr. Fritz droned on and drew graphs on the board. Ted had told me that I said something about liking him while I slept. I wondered exactly what I'd said. He'd been vague on the details, but found amusement in the situation. Well, I guess that was a good thing. I mean, I thought that he knew I liked him. We were friends. People generally like their friends. But the way he'd teased me, I bet I'd said more than just, "I like you, Ted." I smiled thinking about some of the things my parents had told me I'd said in my sleep over the years. I'd had full conversations, at times sitting up in bed, talking with them, laying back down and falling right back to sleep. Of course, in the morning I'd remember none of it. This had started long before the lightning strike.

The bell rang and I tossed the textbook and notebook into my backpack. Mr. Fritz called out to me when I stood. I walked over to him, hoping he didn't hassle me too much about the failed quiz.

"Shell, you doing ok?"

"I guess. I was just thinking that I wish I'd taken Marcus up on that tutoring he offered me earlier in the semester."

"Ah, yes. Sad about the accident," he said nodding.

"Yeah. It's weird not seeing him in classes or at work. Never realized how often I saw him until he wasn't there."

"Any idea when he might be back?" Mr. Fritz asked. How would I know? I shook my head. "Well, if you want extra help, I'm sure Juan would be willing. He's doing really well."

"I'll think about it. I think it'll be fine. Just need to do some extra practice and review the examples in the book." I didn't want Juan tutoring me. He already had behaviors I wanted to avoid making worse, like constantly invading my bubble of personal space. I didn't want to give him the wrong idea.

Mr. Fritz dismissed me and I joined the throng of students in the hall. I hurried downstairs and across the Commons area to the basement stairs. I had to take a zigzag path to get to the band hall from Precalculus. It was a pain in the butt and after the talk with Mr. Fritz, I barely made it through the band hall doors before the bell rang.

I heard loud muffled voices from Mr. Seagram's office, but scurried to my chair as quickly and quietly as I could. I pulled out my flute case, put my instrument together and opened my folder. Max, the drum major took the director's stand and led us through warm up scales. The band was small today, being a chorus day for the students who did both band and chorus. Mr. Seagram rushed out of the office and yelled at Max to stop. He told us to put our instruments away and make it a study period. And, for goodness sakes, keep the noise down. I cringed. I hated being yelled at.

I put my flute away and returned the music folder to the shelf. When I came back to my seat, Ted reached around and hugged me from behind. I looked back at him, surprised. I rubbed his arm.

"Hey, what's up?" I asked him quietly.

"Wanna get out of here?" He whispered in my ear.

"Um, sure." I followed him outside. It was last period and the class had in effect been cancelled. When we got outside, I asked, "What did you have in mind?"

"Go back to your place. Unless you want to grab some food first?"

"Are you hungry?" I asked.

"Not yet."

"Me either. I guess we can hang out at my place until the

guys get there."

We split, me going to my car, he to his. Driving home, I listened to a grunge band, Pinctada Falls, sing about a student suicide, with Ted's car in the rearview all the way home. So, now he was skipping school? I turned in at my empty driveway and sighed. Mom was already gone, if she'd even come home. Sometimes, she stayed at the hospital and napped between shifts in a staff room when she worked back to back shifts. It was happening more and more these days due to the nursing shortage. There was also a flu-like illness going around knocking the nurses out like bowling pins. Mom had been getting tons of overtime recently, money she claimed we needed. We probably did.

Ted parked next to me and followed me up the deck stairs with his backpack slung over his shoulder and his bass in hand. I unlocked the front door and waited for Ted to go in before following and locking the door behind us. I left my backpack at the dining room table and checked the kitchen island for a note. Mom hadn't left one, so I assumed she hadn't left the hospital. The answering machine flashed a digital 2, so I clicked play and grabbed a pen. My doctor's office called to remind me of an upcoming appointment in the morning. Oops. I'd forgotten, but needed refills so I had to go in. It was also my first ever women's health visit and I was super nervous. I wrote down the time. The second message was mom. She was working another overnight shift and decided to stay at the hospital. She hoped to be home tomorrow.

I knew the earliest she'd be home was after we left for school. Night shift ended at 7:30 AM. We left for school around 7:00 AM, but I needed to leave earlier than that to get to my doctor's appointment. I got drinks from the fridge and handed Ted a can of soda. He suggested we hang out in the living room until Andy got home. I followed him and sat next to him on the sofa. He angled himself to look at me, so I did the same.

"So," I started, "we're having a sleepover tonight?"

"Yeah, that's the plan," he said.

"You just want to hear me talk in my sleep again don't you. You do understand that sometimes I wake up screaming, right?"

"So you've told me," he said. "I used to do that too. Haven't had the nightmares in a while. Do you? Still have the nightmares?"

"Yeah. Not every night, but sometimes." The nightmares and screaming came complete with racing heartbeat, shortness of breath, and sweat soaked sheets and pajamas. No more sleeping in the bed any night that happened. I wasn't sure where Ted expected to sleep, but I hoped that if he stayed in my room it wasn't one of those nights. I giggled. He looked at me. The topic wasn't funny.

"What's so funny?"

"I just realized that you're the first guy I ever slept with." I deflected, laughing harder. "In the literal sense." That I remembered, anyway.

"Replace guy with girl and ditto for me," he said, cheeks reddening.

It was true. I hadn't ever done more than kiss Joe. We'd been pretty young, me 15 and him 16. He'd started pressuring me for more not long before the accident, but nothing came from it. I was really inexperienced with guys. I probably needed a junior high romance. I'd been stunted by trauma. Even Carlo, three years older than me, did nothing more than kiss me. It was fine with me. He'd been a terrible kisser. More of a slobberer really. I felt like I was making out with a drooling dog. He'd also found it amusing to transfer his gum to my mouth. I'd nearly barfed the first time he did it. So gross. Joe wasn't a great kisser, but he'd been my first kiss and all I'd known up to that point. Who knew? Maybe there was no such thing as a good kiss. Depressing thought.

Ted took my hands in his. I looked down at our hands. His skin warm with the glow of a light tan that was actually his natural skin color, mine a nearly translucent white, even though I'd gotten some sun over the summer. I didn't tan. I burned, peeled, and returned to ghost white.

"You don't like to be touched," I said.

"I like touching you. I like when you touch me."

"Since when?" I asked, narrowing my eyes. Until this week, it seemed like the only times we'd touched were accidental. Hard to imagine only accidentally touching for three years, but it seemed that way.

"Almost as long as I've known you."

My forehead furrowed and I raised a skeptical eyebrow.

"You know how my parents have all these rules, right? Like I'm not allowed to date," he said.

"Yeah."

"Well, we talked and the deal was that mom didn't want me dating until I was 18." Ted was a displaced senior, like me. He missed a lot in school while moving around in foster care and fell behind.

"Is that what you wanted to talk about?"

"Yes and no."

I gestured for him to continue.

"She's loosened some of the house rules, especially since we've got that out of town gig, and more coming up. I think she wants to make sure I won't go all rebel crazy," he said, chuckling.

"Like no curfew as long as you tell her where you are and who you're with."

"Right, like that."

"Why'd you bring up dating? You plan to start dating someone soon? Are you going to ask me for advice?" I asked. He raised an eyebrow and pressed his lips together. "Ted, I haven't had the best luck with relationships. I wouldn't be the best source."

He leaned forward and kissed me, full lips warm and gentle against mine. I forgot to breathe in my surprise. My eyes widened, then I breathed in, wrapped my arms around his neck and kissed him back. Our lips moved softly against each other, then with a slip of the tongue, our kiss deepened and I lost sense of time. Really lost sense of time and everything else, because the next thing I knew, Andy slammed the front door and screeched.

"Gross!" Andy dropped his backpack on the floor and stomped off to his room. What the heck was Andy doing home? We'd gotten home 45 minutes early and Andy usually got home 30 minutes after I did. We might have talked for 30 minutes. Surely, we couldn't have been making out that long. My eyes searched Ted's after I checked my watch. I hid an embarrassed smile behind a hand. Andy was actually 15 minutes late.

Ted and I broke into laughter at the same time. Andy

stomped back into the living room. Ted and I turned to an irritated Andy. He stood with hands on his hips, glaring.

"I didn't want to see that!" He yelled, voice cracking into an upper register.

"Uh, sorry," I said, not sorry.

"Sorry?" He squealed. "Sorry? I'm blind!" He threw his hands in the air dramatically.

I laughed harder. Drama King.

"Andy, mom's not coming home tonight," I said, clearing my throat and changing the subject. "What do you want for dinner? Band's coming over to practice."

"Let me guess, boyfriend's staying after?"

"Yes, Ted's hanging around after. You know his name, Andy. What do you want for dinner?"

"Pizza, I guess."

"I could cook something," I offered. We'd eaten a lot of pizza lately.

"No," he grumbled. Looked like I was bribing little brother tonight.

"Fine, pizza." I eyed Ted. "Hope you don't mind pizza."

"Pizza's great."

"The usual?" I asked. He nodded. Luckily, I had cash. "Andy, you going to watch us practice?"

"No. You'll probably be sucking face the whole time," he grumbled, arms crossed.

"Don't know how I'd sing if we did that," I said. Ted laughed. It was an odd image. It would also be awkward with our instruments. My lips curved into a smile, they felt warm, tingly. Weird. I'd never been kissed like that before. It had been amazing.

Gravel crunched in the driveway. Great, the guys must be here. Ted told me to freshen up and he'd get the guys set up. I cocked my head, and headed for the bathroom. I hadn't been wearing lipstick, so I couldn't have clown face. I turned on the bathroom light and shut the door.

I squeaked. That darned reflection, she was a scary creature, hair wild. I couldn't remember Ted messing with my hair, but apparently, he'd run his fingers partially through my braids. They needed to be redone. And the lips, what the heck? I leaned closer. Yikes. My lips were swollen and kind of purple.

Could lips bruise? What on earth? Geez reflection chick, pull yourself together! I took a deep belly breath, turned on the water, rinsed my face, undid my braids, brushed my hair and pulled it into a simple wavy ponytail. I grabbed some tinted lip gloss and ran it over my lips. I hoped the guys figured I'd just applied plumping lipstick or something.

I didn't look quite normal, but I left it as good enough and met the guys downstairs. I heard Zane whining loudly as I descended and shook my head. I knew he was Ted's best friend, but sometimes wished we could replace his whiny butt. Zane annoyed the heck out of me. Barry sat behind the drum kit, tapping the cymbals with a stick. Ted strummed his bass. Zane glared at me with hands on his hips. Oh boy.

"Problem?" I asked.

"Is there?" He asked. "A problem, Shell."

"No. No problems. Don't see why you look so pissed. We've got that concert this weekend. We need to practice, right?" I asked, slinging the Luna over my shoulder. "We all sharing a room?"

"Uh, no, there are two rooms. Me and Tara in one, you and the guys in the other," Zane said.

"Cool. Sleepover! You're going to miss out on the nail painting and pillow fights," I said with a wink, trying to get a rise. He ignored me, leaned over, picked up his guitar and pulled the strap over his head. He warmed up with a couple riffs.

Barry tapped a quick 4-count and we jumped into *Medicated*, the punk number. I felt pretty relaxed, and let myself move with the music. I expected laughing at the end of the song, but just got a thumbs up from Zane and we moved into the next song on the setlist. Zane gave me a wobbly hand on my moves for slower songs, but apparently, I was doing better with the faster numbers. I'd just pulled from some old cheerleading and dance moves. A few memories had stirred when I shared the album with Ted. With the memories, a few simple moves resurfaced. Ted grinned at me, but not in a mocking way.

When we finished, I asked the guys if they wanted to stay for pizza, but they declined. Zane had plans with Tara and he'd come with Barry. Barry shrugged in apology. We watched them load up the van, then returned to the garage to make sure the amps and other equipment were all shut down.

Ted moved close and lightly placed his hands on my hips. He bent down and touched his lips to mine. My knees went weak and I sank before regaining control of my legs. I giggled and looked into his deep brown eyes. I hated giggling. So girlish.

"We should probably place that order. Don't want to lose track of time," I said. I worried the pizza joint would close if we lost track of time again.

"You might be right," Ted said, kissing my forehead. I liked this version of Ted.

When the pizza arrived, the three of us ate in the living room around the coffee table. Ted started up an action cop movie and we settled in to watch. Even Andy couldn't complain. He liked the movie, he had pizza and soda, and I'd pulled out a white box filled with comic books from my closet before the pizza arrived. I'd told him he could read any of them he wanted. All of them for all I cared.

"What's with the comics?" Ted had asked.

"Used to love comic books. Not so much for collecting, but the artwork. Sometimes the stories, but generally the artwork," I said with a shrug.

He'd grinned, eyes wide in interest and surprise. I wondered what was going through his mind. I looked forward to spending more time alone with him later, while Andy perused old comic books. The topic of comics had never really come up in our three years of friendship. I'd forgotten a lot about the comics I'd read and collected over the years. There were several more boxes at dad's house. I didn't have time for the hobby these days. Comics were from a time before I had a job outside of babysitting.

Done with the pizza, I sat wrapped in Ted's arm as the movie continued. Luckily, Andy was interested in the movie and ignored us. Ted liked action movies. We watched them together with the other guys sometimes, but it had been a while since we'd all shared a movie night. He enjoyed comedies too. We'd watched a couple superhero movies together, but I hadn't known if that was because Ted liked them, or if it was Zane or Barry who had a thing for men in tights. I figured it was a guy thing. Andy liked them too.

Ted got up in the middle of the movie and called his mom to let her know he was staying over. We were watching a movie with Andy and it was getting late. I smiled to myself. I liked how he'd included my brother in the explanation. I got up and tossed the trash in the trashcan and put the leftover pizza slice in the fridge. For some reason, nobody had wanted it.

I grabbed fresh drinks and joined the guys back in the living room, cuddling up close with Ted and pulling a blanket over my lap. There was a chill in the air. I reminded myself to check the thermostat before we went to bed and offered Ted half of the blanket. He draped it over his legs. Andy snorted. I eyed him warily, but his eyes were on the screen. There wasn't anything funny happening in the movie. I raised an eyebrow at Ted. He winked back at me. My heart stuttered.

When the movie ended, I turned off the lights and left Andy in his room with the box of comics. He was muttering to himself when I closed the door to my room. Ted sat at my desk. He'd brought our backpacks. We hadn't touched any of our homework. I frowned. I didn't want to do any homework. I could fake it in study hall in the morning, make it look like I made an effort. Well, except for the reading assignments in French and English.

"What's wrong?" He asked.

"I don't want to do homework," I whined.

"We should do at least some homework," he reasoned.

"Well, I know. I just don't want to," I said, lips turning down in a pout as I leaned back on the bed.

"What do you want to do?" He asked.

I patted the bed and gestured for him to join me.

"I don't think we'll get any homework done if I join you," he said.

"I know." Well, crap. I had that early doctor's appointment. Nope, no study hall in the morning. I could always just not go in after the appointment. I was betting I'd feel all violated and gross after the appointment. Mom had scheduled me for my first women's exam. Yeah, that one. I guess she'd been getting the vibe that I was becoming a horny teenager and needed birth control. Apparently, she was onto something. She probably thought I was already sexually active. She was a nurse. She'd seen gnarly stuff at the hospital. Teen pregnancies too. I was surprised she hadn't made me get the exams at a younger age. It would be over soon enough. I bit my lower lip as thoughts raced through my mind.

"What's that look?" Ted asked.

"The horror?" I asked.

"Is that what it was? Are you horrified at the thought of kissing me again?"

"No, I can't wait to kiss you again," I said. "The horror is about my doctor's appointment in the morning."

"Are you sick?"

"No. Getting a physical, complete with the whole adult women's exam. I'm expecting that to be painful, gross, and violating. I'm definitely horrified at the idea," I admitted. "Gross, right?"

He laughed. "A little bit."

"I mean, I guess it's better to be prepared rather than wait to get on birth control after the fact, right?"

"Huh?"

"Well, I've got condoms, but I've heard horror stories about them breaking, or guys not wanting to wear them, or people getting carried away and just not using them. So, since mom scheduled the appointment, I was just going to get started with something more regular. You know, preemptive, so I'm not having to worry about it at the last minute. Like the pill." I'd given it a lot of thought and talked it over with mom. It hadn't been a comfortable conversation.

"Ok," he drew out.

"What? I've thought about sex. I'm human." Great, now I was rambling. I'd barely even kissed guys. Only two guys before tonight, that I could remember. My mind raced through missing pages of memory scanning for other similar experiences, but only found an infuriating fog. "I'm not ready for kids," I mumbled.

Ted stood up and joined me on the bed. "Shell, you're not alone. I get it. I'm not ready for kids either."

He leaned over and kissed me. I think he did it to shut me up. His hand ran the length of my braids. I reached back and released my hair. I felt his lips lift into a smile as his fingers slid through my loose hair. I guess he had a thing for long hair. The brush of fingers sliding through my hair brought tingles through my body and I shivered. Magic.

I couldn't remember how we got from sitting to lying on the bed, but there we were, groping each other and lip locked when there was a knock on the door. I jumped to sitting as the door opened. Ted shook in silent laughter on the bed. Andy peeked in and swore. We were still fully clothed, barely.

"What's up Andy?" I asked, breathless.

"Just wanted to let you know that I'm going to bed. I'm supposed to remind you to set your alarm early for your doctor's appointment."

"Thanks Andy," I said. "Good night."

Ted cleared his throat. "Good night, Andy."

"Does mom know he's staying here?"

"No," I said.

"Ok," Andy said. And, that was that. He pulled the door closed behind him. I set the alarm, got my clothes out for the morning and found some pajamas.

"Ready to see those scars?" I asked.

"Sure," Ted said.

I pulled my shirt off and turned my back to him. I heard the bed move as he stood. His fingers slowly traced branches of the tree-like Lichtenberg figures that marked my back, shoulder and arm. They were easy enough to see in the dim light of the bedside lamp, shadows under moonlight.

"They're beautiful," he said.

"I like to tell myself they're nature's tattoo. A gift of the lightning," I said. I did tell myself that. At least the scars were kind of pretty, even though there was damage beneath the skin.

I turned around. He stood up and hugged me, maintaining eye contact. "You're beautiful," he said.

I'd beg to differ on the beautiful remark, but that was his opinion. "Thank you," I said. It was the best I could do with a compliment. "I think you're handsome. Really, really handsome."

"Do you?"

"Uh huh," I said with a nod as I hugged him tighter. I loosened my grip, stepped back a bit and frowned. "Are you staring at my boobs?"

"Well, um, they're right there."

"They've always been there," I said with a frown as I looked down, then back up at him.

"I've just never seen them like this."

"In a bra?"

"Not covered by a shirt," he said, meeting my lips with his. So soft, those lips were so amazingly soft. His fingers traced paths up my back and struggled with the clasps of my bra. I stepped back.

"Um, Ted?" I asked breathlessly.

"Yeah, Shell?" I heard the humor in his voice.

"Maybe we should do some of that homework and go to bed?"

"That's what I said, but you insisted that I join you on the bed."

I turned around and pulled the tank of my pajamas on. It wasn't like it covered me much and it didn't provide any support for the girls, but at least it covered the boobs. I looked at Ted and frowned. My forehead furrowed as I shimmied out of my pants. He grinned as he observed my black underwear. I pulled on my pajama shorts. It wasn't the most modest pajama set I owned, but it wasn't the sluttiest either.

"What's the matter?" He asked.

"What's going on here, Ted?"

"I thought we were having a good time," he said.

"I was. Then I started thinking."

"It's not like I came here tonight to screw your brains out," he said.

"Why are you here?"

"I wanted to ask if you'd go out with me. You know, date."

"I suck at dating," I said. But Ted rocked at making my body feel alive. He was so sexy.

"Well?" He looked at me expectantly.

"Well, what?"

"I know you like me. I like you. What do you say? Will you go out with me?"

"Sure," I said. "Let's give it a shot." Zane would be so pissed. I was in so much trouble. I really wanted to do more than just make out with Ted. Mom must have been psychic. I was highly motivated to get to the doctor's appointment on time in the morning.

Rather than do homework, I voted for bed. Ted shrugged, stripped down to boxers, and climbed under the covers. I slid in next to him and turned off the light. I made sure the alarm was set before turning to face him.

"Ted?" I whispered. He hadn't moved.

"Hmm?"

"I do like you a lot."

"I know you do," he said. I sensed humor in his voice. I wanted to know exactly what I'd said last night that was so entertaining, but had a feeling Ted wouldn't tell me.

"I like you too," he said.

He wrapped an arm around me and my fingers ran along his back as we began to kiss.

7

When the alarm sounded, I opened my eyes and reached behind me. I was tangled in the heavy limbs of Ted's nearly naked body. I couldn't remember falling asleep, which meant I'd fallen asleep in the middle of some very pleasant activities. I felt bad. My fingers found the clock and pressed the snooze bar. Ted groaned. I rubbed his back. I felt movement from below as he leaned the lower half of his body into mine, half pinning me. I smiled, then moved in and began to kiss him, deepening the kiss with a gentle slide of tongue against his. His hand found its way beneath my top and I drew in a deep breath. Wow, what a lovely way to wake up.

"You working tonight?" He asked.

"Yeah. You?"

"For a bit," he said, lips meeting mine as his fingers explored the skin under my tank top.

"Is your dad ok with you being here so much?" I mumbled against his lips. He pulled back.

"Instead of working? It's fine. I wasn't on the schedule anyway. Want to drive to Scranton together?" He asked.

"That would be nice," I said with a sigh. It was preferable to going by myself, but it wasn't like it was a long drive. Our shows on Friday and Saturday were at Club Del Sol in Scranton. I'd never been, but knew the general location. "What time do you want to leave?"

"We need to be at the club by 7:00. We can check in to the hotel as early as 3:00. If you want to leave mid-day, we could do something fun before checking in."

"I don't know about fun, but I need a couple new stage outfits. The old ones don't fit anymore." I'd shrunk out of them by several sizes. I needed smaller ones. "It would be nice to go to a leather clothing store."

"I'm up for that," he said.

"Going to help me pick out a new outfit?"

"Absolutely," he growled. He kissed me harder and ground against me. I kissed him back and the alarm sounded again. I reached behind me and turned it off.

I laughed. I knew what that meant. "Sounds like we're skipping school on Friday?"

"Sounds like. It's a date?"

"It's a date."

"So, when's my girlfriend going to get to school today?" He asked.

"Your girlfriend? I didn't know you had a girlfriend."

"Yeah, I think you've met. Her name is Shell."

"Oh, Shell Dean. Yeah. I'm not sure she's going to school after that very intrusive doctor's exam. Crap. I need to get out of bed."

He chuckled as I half slid out of bed. I wasn't sure this little dating experiment of ours would end well, but I was enjoying it. Felt a bit backwards. We shouldn't be sleeping together this soon. Didn't matter that I'd had a crush on him since we'd met, that we'd known each other almost three years, or that we'd pretty much just been sleeping. I shook my head as I stepped into the dark bathroom and flipped the light switch.

I took a rushed shower, dressed and checked the time. I brushed my teeth, combed my hair, grabbed a scrunchy and headed out. No time for makeup or fancy hairdos. I didn't bother to bring my backpack. I drove to Mt. Pocono and pulled into the medical clinic parking lot. I reached the doorway as the office assistant was unlocking the door. Well, at least I wasn't late.

I followed her to the waiting room and waited at the check in window while she gathered a thick packet of intake paperwork. In the past, mom had filled out the forms for me, but she decided it was time for me to act like an adult. She'd already sent over consent forms and spoken with the doctor. Next month, after my birthday, I wouldn't have even needed consent forms. She and I had narrowed down the birth control options to save time. I groaned as I struggled through questions about family medical history. I had no idea about some of the questions. It wasn't like I was the family historian. My family didn't talk about deceased relatives. We barely talked about some of the living ones, especially on the O'Carroll side.

I spent a couple minutes trying to count back to the day of my last period. I was really bad with counting and hadn't brought a calendar with me. Mom had warned me that I needed to know the date, and I forgot to check and write it down before coming. The nurse called me back before I'd gotten a quarter of the way through the forms. She took my height and weight as usual, then she handed me a specimen cup. I looked from it to her. She pointed toward a restroom and told me to go pee into the cup. Huh?

"Why?"

"Pregnancy test."

"I'm not pregnant. What if I can't pee right now?"

"Just do it."

Great. She thought I was being difficult. I'd peed before I left the house and hadn't drunk anything since. I slunk back to the bathroom and did my best to pee into the cup. I hated doing that. I didn't get much into the cup. There hadn't been much to capture. I left the minuscule sample in the metal cabinet and washed my hands. The nurse waited for me. I shrugged. I'd done the best I could.

She took my vitals in the exam room and asked me questions about my last period. I tried to think back to the date I'd written down and asked if I could look at a calendar really quick. She pointed to a countertop yearly calendar and I double checked the date and confirmed. Based on that date, my period was due to start next week. Lovely. I was really bad about tracking those things. Oops. The thought slipped out and the nurse told me that I better get good at tracking those things if I didn't want to get pregnant. Slam.

What'd my mom do? Tell everyone here I was having sex

with all the guys at school? Still a virgin here. Though probably not much longer. My cheeks heated.

"Um, what?" She'd just asked me a question while my mind wandered to Ted's bare torso and surprisingly toned abs. The nurse shook her head and put the clipboard down.

"How good are you with taking pills every day at the same time?" She asked slowly and with more volume, as if I were hearing impaired.

"Uh, not as good about it as I should be. Why?"

"You wanted to take the birth control pill?"

"Yes."

"I think you might want to consider another option."

"I think it'll be fine. I talked about it with my mom," I said, feet swinging off the exam table while I looked at the floor.

"If you don't take it every day around the same time, it won't be effective. Also, some medications make it ineffective."

"What, like something else I'm already taking?"

She looked at my chart. "No, but antibiotics, so if you get sick, the pill will be out of commission all month. What will you do then? What if you forget?"

"Don't I still have to use condoms anyway?"

"It's advised," she said. I nodded slowly. I felt like I was missing something.

"You think something would be a better choice for me. What are you thinking?" I asked, suspicious.

"Implant or IUD."

"Yuck. I looked into those and don't like the side effects." Images of errant IUDs, perforated uteruses, and the lumps and scars from the implant shown to my Sex Ed class popped into my head. I squirmed.

"They last years and you don't have to think about them. We could hook you up with an IUD today and it would be effective when you walk out the door."

Well, that sounded awesome, but I really had read all of the side effects. One of the IUD models had no hormones and could last up to 10 years. That would get me through college if I could manage the side effects. No daily pill. Just bad cramps, heavy bleeding. Other potentially deadly, but less common, side effects. But they also worked well for lots of women. We talked about the options until Dr. Drake came in.

"Have you decided which birth control method you want to go on?" He asked.

"Yeah, I'd like to try the IUD," flew out of my mouth. Crap. Well, it could be removed at any time. He nodded and told me he'd be back shortly, leaving instructions with the nurse to have me get ready. Getting ready meant stripping completely naked, then covering up with a paper top that opened to the front and a paper drape that would cover nothing. I sat on the table waiting until he returned with a rolling cart with freaky looking instruments that screamed "torture devices" and a set of tools labeled IUD in red.

He instructed me to scoot forward and stick my feet in the stirrups, then general nastiness ensued. Dr. Drake explained everything that he was doing, which didn't help the discomfort of having a male look at and touch my private parts. There was discomfort of instrument insertion, pressure, and scraping during the Pap smear. Then dilation, insertion, pain of positioning the blasted device, string trimming of the IUD, and removal of that horrid spreading device. After the exam and typical bloodwork, I was headed home with care instructions. Basically, ibuprofen for any pain and keep an eye on the bleeding. The bleeding wasn't expected to last more than a couple of days. The cramps would subside in a day or so. But, yeah, birth control wise, it was effective immediately. Pain wise, I felt like my period was just getting started. A week early.

I found a folded note on my pillow at home. I crawled into bed and set the alarm for afternoon in case I fell hard asleep. I had to go to work later. I opened the note and smiled. Ted had left me a little note and some potential lyrics. Cute. I fell asleep quickly and woke when mom tapped my shoulder.

"What are you doing home?" She asked.

"Don't feel so great after that exam," I said.

"Why not?"

"First, virgin, mom. Second, IUD."

She grimaced. "IUD, Shell? Really?"

"Really. Nurse worried I might not do well with the pill, what with having to remember to not only take it every day, but also around the same time."

"Ah. You would've been fine," she said.

"Well, if this IUD works out, I'm good for 10 years."

"You do realize you still have to go in every year."

I groaned. "Yeah, and in two months to make sure it's still in place. And, I have to find the stupid string every month after my period to make sure it hasn't come out."

She laughed. "You know, you really don't look good."

"I know. I feel like crap. That's why I came home," I said with a groan as I pulled the comforter tight around my shoulders.

"Virgin, huh?"

"For the time being, yes," I said. As far as I knew. The exam had certainly felt uncomfortable enough. I'd bled from the exam, but not as much as I'd expected.

"Time being. Prospect on the horizon?" She asked. She reached out and laid a hand on my shoulder. I raised an eyebrow. Did she really want to know?

"Yeah."

"Just don't rush," she said quietly, with a pat on my shoulder.

"Trying not to."

"Does Ted know?"

"Yeah."

"Is he ok with the guy?"

"Um, yeah, I think he is," I said, smiling just a bit.

I spent the rest of the afternoon in bed. When the alarm blared, I dressed in my uniform, pulled my hair back, dabbed on some lip gloss, and gasped. I looked closer at my reflection and hissed. What the… Oh man. Ted! A hickey stood out purplish black against white on the left side of my neck. I hadn't noticed it until I'd pulled my hair back. Had mom noticed? She hadn't said anything. When had that happened?

I ran into mom in the hallway. She commented on my pallor, but said nothing about the hickey. I laughed. I thought I looked a bit gray in the bathroom mirror, but figured it was the yellow light of the bathroom fixture. She suggested I take more ibuprofen before I left, so I did. I figured she knew what she was talking about.

"Mom?"

"Yes?" She eyed me from her bedroom doorway.

"Don't forget we've got that show in Scranton this weekend. We're staying in the hotel near the club. The one near the old train station."

"I remember. It's fine. Your dad's picking up Andy after school on Friday. It's his weekend."

"Ok."

"What are the sleeping arrangements?" She asked. Of course, she'd ask.

"Two rooms. I'm sharing with Ted and Barry."

She raised an eyebrow.

"It's a double room mom. Zane and his girlfriend are in the other." I knew from her puckered mouth how she felt about that. Judge-y.

"I don't think it's a good idea. Why can't you share a room with Tara?"

I shrugged. I wasn't going to lie and tell her differently. "What's it matter? I'm pretty much one of the guys. I think it'll be fun."

"What about this new guy? What's he going to think about it?"

"He's not new," I evaded with a shrug.

Mom's eyes narrowed. I smiled and walked out the door. She'd find out it was Ted soon enough. Unless one or both of us freaked out and quit the budding relationship. I looked forward to the weekend. It was our biggest show, but I looked forward to testing new waters with Ted even more. I wondered if he wanted to tell the guys we were dating. Zane wouldn't take it well. My cheeks tightened and my lips pulled up at the corners thinking about Zane's red face.

I parked behind Norma's next to Jay's blue Escort. I wondered how hungover he'd been that morning and hoped he didn't give me crap for the way I looked. I grimaced when I stood and a cramp hit. Well, decisions and consequences, I reminded myself. I closed the car door and wandered in.

"Girl," Vicki rasped as I passed her at the register.

"Hmm?" I paused with my hand on the swinging door.

"You don't look good," she rattled, dry like sand on paper.

"Thanks," I said, attempting a wry grin as my lower gut seized.

"You ok? Didn't see you in school."

"I'm fine. Had an early doctor's appointment and went home after. I'm not contagious or anything." I kept going, walked through the swinging door and checked the assignment board before clocking in. Working grill with Jay on sandwich station? Right, Marcus' shift. Ooh, fun.

I washed my hands and joined Jay at the grill. I think I scared him with my serious ninja sneaking skills, as Andy called them. I moved really quietly sometimes, but not on purpose. He jumped when he saw me.

"What happened to you? Did you die?" He asked, horrified.

"Maybe. You don't look so great yourself. Did you rinse your eyes with sand this morning?" I jabbed him in the ribs with my pointy finger.

"Ooh, that's a good one," he said chuckling. "Seriously, are you sick? You shouldn't handle food if you're sick."

"No, I'm not sick. Had a doctor's appointment this morning. I'm going to feel off for a few days."

"Um, ok?" He gestured, waiting for more information.

"Yeah, TMI for a guy. Girl stuff. You don't want to know."

He crossed his pointer fingers in front of me, vampire hunter style. "Keep the girl cooties to yourself."

"That's what I thought," I said, checking supplies for the station. Either Jay, or the previous crew member had it set up and ready to go.

"Whoa, what's that on your neck?" He asked, pointing at my neck with a snide grin.

"Why? Are you checking me out?" I asked. "Am I, like, a science experiment?"

He laughed. "Hey, Vicki! I think Shell has a hickey."

Vicki came over to check it out. My cheeks burned.

"Yeah, so?" I said.

"I guess things went well last night," Jay said, chuckling.

"Yeah, not that it's any of your business," I sulked. I hadn't planned on having proof of my activities today. Good thing I'd skipped school. It was gym day. All the girls would've seen. Possibly some of the boys, Jay included.

"I knew you two were screwing around," he smirked, proud of himself. As if. He hadn't been the only one to think so.

"We're going to date, go out, whatever," I said dismissively.

Did it need a label? Andy would continue calling Ted my boyfriend. Of that, I had no doubt. I wondered if he'd tell mom about the sleepovers when he got home. Andy had a big mouth tattling problem. He was a great kid, but geez, he couldn't keep that mouth shut. I shrugged. Vicki clasped her hands and squealed, but it came out like a gravelly croak. I narrowed my eyes.

"What?" I asked. She hugged me, hard, arms trapping me. I looked at Jay wide-eyed. He shrugged. Guess he thought it was a normal girl thing. I hated girl things.

"I'm just so happy for you," she said. Sure, she was. I never got that whole "happy for you" girl thing. When I saw another person happy, that usually wasn't my first thought.

"Why?" I asked. It just slipped out of my mouth. In the old days, I would've been jumping up and down, squealing, and hugging her back without hesitation. It seemed fake to do that now. Sure, I was excited at the prospect of a non-platonic relationship. Maybe I'd been spending too much time around the guys. Maybe I'd just experienced enough crap to understand that all things come to an end in time. I'd come to the conclusion that girls sucked as friends. Too flighty and backstabbing. My bandmates, well, Barry and Ted, were far easier to deal with on a regular basis. I put up with Jules and Vicki because I worked with them and Vicki and I had Concert Band together. I wouldn't say we were especially close. We didn't hang out. Not since they'd gotten regular boyfriends anyway.

"Girl, you're too much," she said with a flick of the hand before returning to the register to take the order of a customer who had just walked through the door.

"Dylan will be upset," Jay muttered.

"Huh?" I looked over, having forgotten he stood next to me.

"Dylan. Had his heart set on winning you over," he said with a roll of the eyes.

"Who?" I asked.

Jay shook his head, continuing to look to the ceiling. An image of a young blond man with blue eyes and incredible body popped into my head. Ah, Dylan. I hadn't seen him since the beach party. I thought he was new to the area and figured I'd see him in school, but I hadn't. Maybe he didn't go to school? How old was he? Did I care? Not really. Win me like a carnival prize? I frowned.

I flipped the burger, listening to the order over the speaker. Done medium well. Not much longer on this patty. No cheese. Jay waited with the bun. I moved the burger to the bun, he applied the toppings, wrapped it and set it in a basket while I scooped fries into a cardboard sleeve. I wondered why we didn't just directly dump the fries into the basket, when most of the customers ended up doing that anyway. Vicki took the completed order out to the customer. I felt eyes on me and turned to Jay's hazel ones, which appeared to be focused neck level.

"What?" I asked. It seemed I'd turned monosyllabic.

"Just surprised is all," he said, lifting his hands in surrender. He wasn't the only one.

Pat walked around to check out operations. The dining room was dead, but for the one customer we'd just served. Vicki snapped gum at the cash register, a big faux pas. Pat was about to pass by, but stopped.

"Shell, you getting sick?" Pat asked.

"No, went to the doctor this morning for an annual. He said I'd feel off the next few days, but I'll be fine. Not contagious or anything. Just girl stuff."

Jay groaned.

"Well, if you need to go home, just let me know. Rob's coming in soon. He's just floating, and it really isn't busy."

It wasn't. Not unusual for a Thursday night, but it was dinner time, and we should have seen at least 10 customers since I'd arrived. I hadn't seen Rob in a couple weeks. I worked weekends and he worked weeknights. He was a college student at East Stroudsburg University. Sweet guy. Kind of like an older brother. He had that protective energy and I looked up to him as a mentor. He studied Biology and was interning at Simon Labs as a sanitation tech. Even though it was basically a glorified janitor, he still had to gear up in a biohazard clean room suit.

I excused myself to go check on the salad bar. Gwen, former neighbor, from when I'd first moved to the Poconos and lived in a condo down the street, was assigned there. Jay nodded. It wasn't like anything was happening at our stations. He just kept making fun of me and I wasn't in the mood for it.

I picked up a small metal container filled with warm sanitizer solution, a fresh cleaning rag, and headed to the salad bar. I wiped down the tray rail and greeted Gwen while I eyed the veggie bins. I stepped through the knee-high swinging gate and set the sanitizing solution down. I sighed.

"Girl, should you be back here? You look sick," the ebony skinned princess in blue collared shirt said with a melodic voice. Her accent always sounded musical to me. Her family moved to the area from Sudan not long after I had. She was an actual African. I grinned.

"I'm not sick. Saw the doctor this morning. Just cramping and stuff." I shrugged.

"You should go home. It's dead around here."

"For cramps?"

"Looks like you got more than cramps, girl."

"Yeah, it's not just cramps. The doc said I'll feel better in a couple days."

"What do you mean not just cramps?" Gwen narrowed her eyes. I walked closer and spoke in a low voice.

"Birth control, IUD."

"Hard core." She scrunched up her face, her version of horrified. I laughed, then shrugged.

"I'm hoping it's a good solution."

"Solution to what? A period that doesn't cramp and bleed hard enough?" We'd shared the same sex ed class last year. She'd seen x-rays of the perforated uterus and heard tales of unbearable heavy periods too.

"The nurse told me it would be better than the pill," I said from the side of my mouth.

"Better for who?" She asked, hands on hips.

"Me and my bad memory."

She laughed. "I think you been had."

"I'm going to check the tables and head back to the grill," I said with a shake of my head that made me woozy. I shouldn't feel this awful. It's not like I was losing pints of blood.

"Why do you need birth control?" She asked. "You don't date."

"I haven't in a while. Doesn't mean I don't." I winked before walking off.

"Wait, what's that on your neck? Girl, you better come back here!"

"Later, Gwen!" I called over my shoulder as I began to survey the tables searching for dirty ones. I found one that may or may not have been dirty and wiped it down. I returned to the back room as Rob clocked in.

He grinned and rushed over to give me one of his trademark bear hugs, lifting me high into the air. I laughed and hugged him back. It was impossible not to smile around Rob, he was so goofy. Sure, he was at least 4 years older, but he acted like someone more Andy's age.

"Good to see you!" I said. I meant it.

"Good to see you too. It's been ages," He said as he looked me over, gray eyes darkening. "You doing ok?"

"Yeah, I'm fine."

"Hey," he reached out and rubbed my neck with his thumb. "You got something there."

My cheeks heated up. "Um, yeah, I don't think that's just going to rub off."

"Well, well, well. What have you been up to?" He pondered.

"Rob!" I lightly slapped his chest. "I don't want to talk about that."

He wasn't smiling anymore. I turned to the sink and washed my hands. I needed to get back to the grill. I dried my hands with a paper towel, waved and returned to the grill, where Jay stared off into the empty dining room. Well, darn it. Now there was a dirty table. The one customer had left while I was talking to Rob. Technically, Gwen was covering both salad bar and dining room. I'd only gone out there for the heck of it.

"Shell!" Pat called from the back. Rob passed me, gloving up. I went back to the manager's office where Pat sat at the desk, stack of applications on the desk in front of her. "Go on and head home."

"Yes ma'am," I said. I didn't need the money that badly. I had plenty in savings and it wasn't like I had regular bills to pay. I clocked out, waved to Vicki and the guys, and left. I checked the time. Ted would be home from work by the time I got home. His dad's hardware store closed at 9, but Ted had mentioned he was only working until 7 tonight. Covering dinner break for a couple employees.

I drove home, wondering what homework I needed to do, then remembered I was skipping school tomorrow to head to Scranton early with Ted. It was already the night before Friday. I would be so behind next week. I knew I had a Precalculus test on Monday. I could finish *Madame Bovary*. I was just a few chapters away from the end. I was nearing the end of *To Kill a Mockingbird* for English. I was prepared for next week's Chemistry experiments, I'd read ahead. Maybe the only thing I'd really be behind on was Precalculus homework. I'd missed out on getting the study guide. If Marcus had been around, I could've made a copy from his, but he was still in the hospital. Nobody had mentioned him in a couple of days and I wondered if there was any new news.

Even though mom worked as a nurse and was currently assigned to the ICU floor, where Marcus was, she couldn't and wouldn't tell me anything. I'd learned that in the past. Very professional of her. My guess was that there hadn't been any change.

8

When I pulled into the driveway, I was surprised to find Ted's Toyota parked next to mom's Escort. He knew I was working, so I wasn't sure why he'd be here so early when we hadn't made any plans. Had Andy told mom? Is that why Ted was here? I trudged up the stairs, feet heavy, gut in a vise, limbs weak. I unlocked the door and peered into the dim light. Ted sat on the sofa, standing up to greet me. I looked for mom, but didn't see her.

"How did it go?" He asked.

"Not too bad. I slept all day. I'm still cramping. Bleeding a little." I wasn't sure he wanted that many details.

"Your mom called and told me you weren't doing too well. Thought you might like some company when you got home."

I raised my eyebrow. Mom had called to ask him over? Where was she? I hugged him and rested my head against his chest. He held me.

"Mom?" I called out, mumbling a little with my head still pressed against Ted's chest.

"Shell?" She called back, voice nearing.

"Yeah," I said. Who else would it be? She walked out, finding me in Ted's arms. Her eyes widened. What the heck mom? "Thanks for calling Ted."

"Sure," she said. She coughed, then cleared her throat. "Um, Ted, are you ok?"

His head turned to look at her. "Yeah, I'm great. Why?"

She gestured at us. "Shell, should you be in Ted's space like that? Did you ask?"

Ted laughed and rubbed my back. I hugged him tighter. I guess Andy hadn't said anything. "It's fine, Mrs. Dean," Ted said. "My girlfriend is allowed to touch me."

"Girlfriend?" Mom looked really confused.

"We're together, mom," I said.

"Is that a good idea?"

"I'd think you weren't happy for us," I said, frowning.

"That's not it, I'm just wondering if you've thought what will happen to the band if things don't work out?"

"I think it'll be ok," I said. Ted's arms still held me against his warm body. He touched his cheek to the side of my head. "Did you already pack for the weekend?" I asked Ted.

"Yep, all packed up," he said.

"I haven't packed yet, but I need to. Mom, I know it's a lot to ask, but could Ted stay over tonight? I don't feel well and would really like the company." I must've been giving some serious puppy dog eyes, because she agreed that he could stay as long as the door stayed open. I hadn't even asked if he could stay in my room, she'd just assumed. Huh?

"Shell, how are you really feeling? You still don't look like you feel well," mom said.

"Should I?" I asked. From what the doctor had told me, I probably wouldn't feel great tomorrow either. Mom shook her head.

"Everyone's different," she admitted.

"No, I don't feel great. I'm cramping and bleeding. The cramping is about like a period and I'm still kind of spotting. Sorry, Ted. Nothing worse than what the doctor told me would happen."

"Good," she said. She looked at us and shook her head. "I'm assuming you two will behave yourselves tonight?"

"That's the plan," I said. I didn't feel sexy in the least. Although it probably wasn't, my belly felt painfully swollen. I couldn't wait to get out of my work pants and into some sweats.

"I don't know if I'll ever get used to this," mom said. I assumed she meant me and Ted touching, because we were still clinging to each other. Luckily, she hadn't caught us in more compromising positions like Andy had.

"You going to call your parents?" I asked Ted.

"Sure," he let me go and walked to the kitchen, where I heard the click and spin of the rotary dial of the wall phone.

"Are his parents going to be ok with this?" Mom asked. "I thought he wasn't allowed to date."

"They renegotiated the rules. He turned 18 last month."

Mom seemed to consider this. "You'll be 18 next month." She nodded. "Andy will be 13 soon."

"Right," I drew out. "I've still got another year of high school. You know, because, well, the accident and all." I reminded her. I should've been graduating this year. Missed too many days from hospitalization and recovery after the strike. Ted should've been graduating too, but moving around from foster home to foster home meant he changed schools a lot. Didn't help his early learning. I felt for him.

"Maybe we need to talk about the rules again too."

I groaned. I didn't want stricter rules. It was her house, her rules. I knew the drill. If I'd wanted a more laid-back life, I would've stayed with dad after the divorce. But, with all the bad memories, missing ones, and the pitying looks, I couldn't stand to stay there. Not being a year behind my classmates, different.

"No, no, don't worry," she said. "I'm thinking more freedom. You're going to be going out of town for more shows, right?"

I nodded.

"You'll be making your own decisions soon," her voice trailed off as her focus shifted to some distant point.

"True," I drew out. I looked at her hopefully. "Can I have the basement room back?"

"I'll think about it," she said, eyes narrowing as Ted returned. Great. Just what I needed, for her to dislike Ted, whatever he was to me now. I didn't want to call him my boyfriend, sounded so immature. "Go ahead, pack. Did you want to eat something?"

"I probably should. Have you guys eaten yet?" It was 8:30. Everyone should've eaten dinner by then.

"Not yet. Is there anything you want?" Mom asked.

"Chinese? Lasagna? Sandwiches? I don't care. I'm not dying of hunger, but I could eat," I said.

"Ted, preferences?" Mom asked.

"Whatever you've got," he said. He wasn't picky.

"I'll put lasagna in the oven. It'll take just over an hour," mom said.

With that, Ted followed me back to my room. I heard him sigh loudly behind me as I opened the closet door to pull out my duffle. I wasn't packing show clothes. We'd be shopping for those tomorrow. Just needed a couple changes of clothes, pajamas, underwear, and socks.

"What's up?" I asked as I tossed the empty bag on the bed.

"I thought your mom was going to kick me out."

"Why?"

"Did you see her face when I called you my girlfriend?"

"She didn't know who you were talking about," I laughed.

"Oh, uh uh, she sure did. She was pissed," he said, voice low as he looked back at the door.

"No, she was confused. She was upset I was touching you, knowing you don't like to be touched." I kissed his cheek. "Do you want me to pack anything special?"

"What do you mean?"

"I know you haven't seen my pajama collection or anything, but if you want to look, go for it."

His eyes perked up as he smiled. "You're giving me permission to go through your underwear drawer?"

"My pajamas aren't in my underwear drawer, but if you really want to choose my underwear, knock yourself out." It wasn't like there was anything especially exciting in there.

He opened the top drawer and started going through my underwear. He picked out the laciest black underwear he found. Fine. I had a couple of pretty things. I raised an eyebrow.

"Don't forget we're sharing a room with Barry."

"I can call ahead and see if there's an extra room available," he offered.

"I don't mind sharing the room," I said.

"Besides," he said, "He probably won't be seeing you in your underwear, right?"

"Probably not, pajamas yeah."

"True," he found the matching black lace bra. Although the set was cute, it was scratchy as heck. I'd wear it, but I'd be really happy when I got to take it off again. I watched as he found a similar set in red. He tossed them at me and I packed them. He opened the next drawer, finding pajamas. He pulled out a set of powder pink thermals and grimaced.

"You want me to wear that?" I asked with a smirk.

"Please don't." He continued to look through the drawer's contents, finding a couple of satin pieces, one a button top with shorts set, another a thigh length spaghetti strap babydoll. He turned around and wagged his eyebrow at me. I mouthed "Barry" at him. He held it out toward me and I tossed it into the bag. It wasn't that revealing. He tossed over a tank and shorts set in cotton knit and I packed it away. He started searching through my shirts. Apparently, he was looking for the tightest ones. I guessed that I could buy more form fitting clothes. I needed some clothes that fit in general. I had two pairs of jeans that sort of fit, and they slid down even with a belt.

"We may need to stop by the mall," I said.

"You think?" He held out a size medium Transcendence tee. I took it. I still wore my uniform and wanted badly to change.

"Hey, I want to get out of this thing and take a shower. I trust your judgment," I said pointing to the dresser.

"Mmm. You smell like burgers," he said.

"Yeah," I laughed. "That's why I need a shower."

"It's not a bad thing."

"I'm glad you don't mind, but I do. I'll be right back." I reached around him for a knit set of Capri pajama bottoms, matching tank, and fresh underwear then headed to the bathroom. I turned on the water, let it steam up the room and adjusted the temperature before stepping under the stream. I washed my hair, then scrubbed down with cucumber bath wash on a body pouf. I left it at good enough, stepped out feeling better, and dried off. I dressed in the pajamas, remembering to add a pad before heading back to the bedroom. I didn't want to scare Ted off with unexpected bleeding overnight. Although there hadn't been much blood during the day, I didn't know if it would be worse overnight. I didn't expect it to, I just didn't want to risk it.

The scent of lasagna greeted me as I returned to my room. The dim light of the bedside lamp lit up the space. Ted sat at my desk, writing. I walked up behind him and peeked over his shoulder.

"Hey," I said.

He turned around to face me and touched my face. I bent forward to kiss him. The position was uncomfortable. He guided me onto his lap, which was more comfortable and I draped my arms over his shoulders. His lips were warm, soft, and smooth against mine

"Shell?" Mom cleared her throat and we pulled apart. "Dinner's ready." She stood in the doorway, arms crossed over her chest. She obviously didn't approve. Andy's door opened and I heard him snickering as he tried to sneak past mom. "Andy, wash your hands." He groaned. She gestured for us to get up, so I stood and Ted followed me to the kitchen. We washed our hands there.

We got fresh drinks from the refrigerator and sat at the table, where the tray of lasagna and garlic bread waited. Smelled amazing. We helped ourselves and ate. Sure, it was a frozen lasagna, but I hadn't eaten all day, so it tasted great to me. Mom handed me the bottle of ibuprofen and told me I should probably take more. The cramps weren't bad, but I took it anyway.

I cleared the table when we'd finished and helped mom wash the dishes while Ted followed Andy back to his room to check out the comics. They'd started to geek out about comics over dinner. I'd smiled listening to them talk about the ones that Andy had liked so far. So, that's why I hadn't seen the kid all night. I'd started to think he'd gone over to Mike's house. But, nope, he was just holed up reading comics in his room.

"It was nice of you to hand over all those comic books," mom said as I scrubbed plates and handed them over.

"It was nothing. They've just been sitting in the closet going to waste. I'd forgotten about them. He and Ted were talking about superheroes the other day and I remembered them. I should probably bring some more boxes over from dad's and let him have those too."

"Seriously?" Mom stopped mid-dry and put the plate she'd been holding down.

"Yeah, why?" I asked, eyebrows rising as I shrugged.

"You loved comic books. You took such good care of them."

"I don't remember that. I kind of like reading them and love the art and stories."

"Didn't you notice all the plastic sleeves?"

"Come on, I bought a bunch of them at yard sales and flea markets. It's not like I was buying them new or anything."

She shook her head. Even if I had placed value on them at one time, they didn't really matter to me anymore. Lightning strikes and personality changes did that in the rewiring and frying of the brain. Broken circuits, that's all it was. When things reconnected, they were different. I'd never be the Michelle I'd been before the strike. She'd died that day. I was a shadow of her shining glory.

I joined Ted in the bedroom. He had a small pile of sleeved comic books piled on the bedside table. Looked like he was checking out some Art Gray. It was pretty cool stuff. Trippy stories and creepy art. I used to love it. I was still fond of Gray's work. I climbed in next to him and got under the blankets. I checked out the page he was on and smiled. *Sandman*. I remembered this one.

"You really read all those comics?" He asked.

"Mmm-hmmm. I've got at least 10 more boxes that size at dad's house."

His eyes widened. "I think I love you," he said.

"You're funny." I reached my arm over his stomach and squeezed. "What time do you want to leave tomorrow?"

"What do you think about 10:00? Is that too early? We're going to check out the leather store, and you want to go to the mall, and we should eat," he listed.

"10:00 is fine. There are other things we can do if there's a lot of time left before check-in. Do the guys know we're meeting them there? I didn't tell them."

"Uh, I didn't tell them either."

"Are we telling them about us?" I asked.

"I think we have to," he said. "Otherwise, we'll be sending Zane to an early grave every time he catches us touching. He'd have a heart attack if he walked in and saw us kissing."

I laughed, but Ted might be right. Zane had flipped out

seeing us sitting together on a bench and barely touching. Sure, Ted's arm had been around my shoulders, but it wasn't anything scandalous. Zane hadn't seen the hickey. Oh, the hickey.

"Uh, Ted?"

"Hmm?"

"You left something behind this morning."

"What?"

I pointed to my neck. He laughed. I carefully took the comic book from his hands and placed it on the table before drawing his face to mine. My eyes swam in the depths of his, almost black in the dim light of the lamp. I turned off the light and kissed him. The bed squeaked under us as we adjusted to a more comfortable position and I cringed on the inside. The door was wide open. Mom watched tv in the living room. Andy read comic books across the hall. I was making out with my boyfriend on my bed, with the light on. My uterus squeezed into a tight fist, then relaxed. Maybe it clenched, trying to dispel the foreign object. Things had obviously torn during the IUD positioning process. I'd felt the sharp pain as the arms were adjusted into place, and then there was bleeding.

Mom peeked in, finding us tangled together in an obscene, but clothed position. She closed the door, breaking her own rules. Eventually, we fell asleep, but I had no idea when or how. I was pretty sure I'd been kissing him when I lost consciousness. I was so embarrassed. We'd been slowing down, so I was pretty sure he was about to pass out too. He felt so good against my body that I tried to cling to consciousness to savor the feelings, but lost the fight.

9

I woke with the alarm, Ted's body wrapped around mine. I reached behind me and hit snooze. The alarm meant that it was 9:00 in the morning. I snuggled closer and got a better look at Ted, so cute in the morning. His eyes blinked as I stared, in what was undoubtedly a disturbing manner. I wanted to take in all the details. He rubbed his eyes.

"Hey," his lips turned into a smile before he reached his arms above his head and stretched. Wow, those were some defined arms. Not huge muscles, but there was some nice definition. Very masculine. Very sexy. I felt tingly and tight low in my body, in a really nice way.

"You're so hot," I blurted out. I moved in for a kiss before he could process what I'd just said. I pulled him close and he made a surprised noise that delighted me. We rolled slightly and he ended up on top of me, supporting himself on his elbows as we kissed.

"How are you feeling?" He asked.

"Mmm, good," I said as I reached a hand up to run my fingers through his hair.

"I mean, how are the cramps?" He asked.

"Oh," I said, taking a moment to think about it. "Uh, not that bad at the moment."

"Good."

He dropped his head to kiss me again and I ran my fingers along his jaw, slightly scratchy with stubble. He pulled back and crawled over me, getting out of bed and adjusting himself. I frowned.

"We should get ready and leave soon. Plenty of time to pick up where we left off," he said, grinning. "Unless you want to perform in street clothes."

"I've done it before," I said with a pout.

"Shell, this is a big deal, come on," he said, rubbing my thigh. I groaned and sat up. I wasn't a morning person. I preferred to stay up late and sleep all day. That's what I did if I didn't have any plans.

"You're helping me pick out clothes?" I asked. I hated shopping. Clothes never looked good on me. Nothing ever fit right. Waistband too tight, hips too loose. Although I had curves in terms of boobs, I was not gifted with the curvy hips and butt to match. Instead, my stomach tended to bulge. My stomach was the flattest it had ever been, but I couldn't shake the image of that bulging belly when I looked in the mirror. I guess I'd been eating less. I ran occasional mornings to burn off emotional crap. Activity was supposed to help depression, so my doctors used to tell me. But, otherwise, I wasn't doing anything to lose weight on purpose.

"Yes," he said. "I'm helping you pick out clothes."

I did need new clothes. I had very few pieces that weren't falling off at this point. The only thing that might stop me from running from the dressing room screaming was that Ted would be there. It'd be embarrassing if I ran out screaming in my underwear. Besides, he'd probably be a better indicator of whether the clothes looked ok than the salesperson. None of those false compliments, that everything looked great.

I let my legs fall to the floor as I watched Ted walk around the room. He bent down to grab clothes from his duffle. I couldn't tear my eyes from his body. I moved toward him and hugged him from behind as he stood holding his clothes. He laughed as if I'd tickled him. Maybe I had.

"Shell, aren't you excited to get started on our first date?"

"Huh?"

"It's like our first official date. We'll be shopping and going out for a meal in public," he said.

"Yeah, out of town. Nobody will know. We've done those things before," I said.

"This is different," he said.

"I know."

"It's important to me," he said. "I know you've been on dates before, but I haven't."

"We'll go on more dates, Ted. I guarantee you'll get your kiss."

"You think it's funny," he said.

"Not really," I said. I thought about it. "Although it might be a slightly awkward kiss with Barry in the room. Hey, are we sleeping in the same bed if Barry's in the room?"

"Oh, um, I don't know."

"Yeah, maybe it's creepy. I mean, I want to sleep in the same bed, but if Barry's in the room with us, it's a little weird."

"I'll sleep in your bed. Barry will just have to deal with it. He'll deal with it better than Zane."

"Good point." I pointed to his clothes. "You want to shower first?"

"Sure."

I watched him go then started to search through my drawers for clothes that almost fit. I found some black jeans that were only about one size too big and a 3/4 sleeve black baseball tee with red sleeves. I grabbed another lacy set of undergarments for Ted's enjoyment and wandered out to the kitchen. Mom had left a note on the counter for me to wish us luck. At least she hadn't barged in this morning. We'd only been sleeping, but it was nice to get uninterrupted sleep.

I realized that we hadn't called Zane or Barry last night to talk about driving to Scranton early to run errands and do other stuff. I waited for Ted to get out of the shower and let him make the calls. They'd left for school hours ago. He left the basic message that he and I were driving to Scranton early to run some errands and would meet them at the hotel sometime after 3 PM.

I took my turn in the shower, finding that the bleeding had pretty much stopped overnight. I applied light makeup, clear gloss, foundation and powder. I packed up stage makeup and basic travel toiletries and tossed them into my duffle. I braided my hair into 2 side French braids and met Ted in the kitchen, carrying my duffle and leather jacket.

"Want to eat before we go?" I asked. "I can cook

something."

"Or, we could head into town and drive thru, or wait until we get there and stop somewhere," Ted said.

"Either way. I think it would be a good idea to eat before we get far. I could eat drive thru. Royal B?" I asked, referring to a local fast food place with breakfast sandwiches and a drive thru.

"Sure," he said with a smile. We went out through the basement so I could grab my guitar from the garage. We packed up my car because it was bigger and had a large trunk that fit my guitar, his bass, and the duffle bags. For a girl, I managed to pack minimally. Maybe, because Ted had basically done it for me. Also, because we were going shopping and I hadn't packed my normal stage wear. I offered my keys to Ted and he shook his head with a laugh.

"Oh, no, it's your tank, honey."

"Honey?" I asked, laughing. "Ok." His car was newer and smaller, a gold 2-door Toyota. Definitely more compact than my 4-door gray Oldsmobile, aka "the tank" or "the boat." We got into the car and I handed Ted the CD organizer. I knew he had his own collection, but he'd decided to leave it behind. We had similar tastes in music. He paged through the discs as I backed out of the driveway and onto the road.

I made a left on Sterling and drove toward Mount Pocono. My eyes darted to the scarred tree, bare wood surrounded by shredded bark, as we passed. My thoughts drifted to Marcus, and I wondered again how he was doing in the hospital. He must be getting better. Was he still in a coma? Why hadn't anyone said anything?

"You're quiet," Ted commented.

"Just thinking about Marcus," I said. "Haven't heard how he's doing in a while."

"I haven't heard anything either," he said.

"It's just weird not to see him every day in school or at work. Lately, I've been wishing I'd taken him up on his offer to tutor me in Precalculus. I'm not doing so great in class."

"Sorry, didn't know you were that close to him," Ted said.

"We weren't close. He was nice, quiet. It's mostly that he was around every day, you know. I just notice that he's not there. He sat next to me or near me in most classes. Then I'd see him at work a lot too."

"He and I were in a few classes over the years," Ted said.

"Really?"

"Yeah. You're right about the quiet part. He's always been that way. Quiet, but smart. Have you asked Julie?"

"Julie?"

"Yeah, aren't their moms best friends?"

"Yeah? She hasn't said anything."

"In elementary school, third grade I think, Marcus' whole homeroom class got invited to his birthday party. Mom made me go. Thought it was good for me to socialize," he said with a bitter chuckle. "Julie was there with her mom. You know, if I remember right, Julie and Marcus were pretty good friends."

"Even though they're not in the same grade," I muttered. A little like me and Christy. Sure, Christy lived a few houses down the road, but really, the reason we spent so much time together was because our moms were best friends. If our moms hadn't been such great friends, would we have spent so much time together? I wasn't sure. She was fun, kind of bossy, a year older than me. There weren't a lot of kids my age in town. It was a tiny place.

I pulled into the Royal B lot and Ted suggested we just go in. I parked.

"You do know we're skipping school," I said. He grinned.

"Come on, live a little, Shell," he said. "You want to be seen together in public, don't you?"

Ah, that's what this was about. Of course, our classmates were in school, but I'd humor him. We got out of the car and walked in. We ordered, got our drinks and sat down to wait for our number to be called. There weren't many people inside. I reminded myself that with Ted, sometimes what seemed like little steps were big leaps. As for what had happened recently, well that was plain miraculous.

He picked up the food at the counter when our number was called and my eyes followed him. It didn't seem real, that I could touch him. I worried that I'd wake up and things would be back to the way they had been. Not that his friendship wasn't amazing. I was honored that he'd taken me on as a friend. His eyes met mine as he sat down, warm brown, like hot chocolate. They crinkled at the edges as he smiled. I loved that crinkle.

"What were you thinking?" He asked.

"When?"

"Just now. You almost looked sad."

"I was thinking how lucky I was to be your friend. I was also thinking that I'd wake up and things would be the way they were. Not that it was bad."

"I wasn't sure you were interested in being more than friends, Shell."

"Half my songs are about you, you know," I said. The ones that weren't about the old me and my dead friends.

"Are they?" His eyes drifted up as he seemed to think about it. His eyebrows drew together as he looked back at me.

"Yeah," I said. "I'll tell you which ones someday."

"Tell me that *Haywire and On Fire* was about me," he said with a grin. My cheeks reddened as I felt the heat creep up my neck and into my face. Yep. I nodded. It had been a song about frustration and unmet desire. Wow, what had happened to shy Ted?

Back on the road, driving on 380 toward Scranton, some of our favorite metal by Bosley played and we sang along. I knew I shouldn't sing along with anything. We had a show tonight. He'd be singing too. Maybe we were both nervous and trying to burn off some of that energy. I looked forward to spending the evening with Ted and Barry, especially with Zane occupied elsewhere. Felt like I hadn't been spending much time with Barry these days. Probably because Zane was always riding with him and had to take off so he could be with Tara. Of course, that had given me more time with Ted. If Zane had known what that would lead to, he might've rethought all those study dates.

"So, really, do you think Zane's going to get over us being together?" I asked. I knew he and Zane were close. They'd been friends since elementary school. I didn't want him to lose a friend over me.

"It's not for him to get over," Ted said. I caught the movement of a shrug from the corner of my eye.

"He might be right, to worry. Like mom said, think about the band. What'll happen if you and I don't work out?"

"Don't be so pessimistic," he said. "You're thinking about the end before we've even started."

"I know. I'm a downer, but I know he's not going to be ok with it. I get it. He never liked me, just kind of puts up with me. You two have been friends forever. I'm sure he doesn't want you to get hurt."

"Whoa, whoa, whoa. You're going a mile a minute, slow those thoughts down."

"I'm just nervous. They're going to know something's up."

"Of course, they will. I'm going to tell them," he said. I sighed. I hoped he waited until after the show. I didn't want a fight before. I decided to change the topic.

"Do you have the address for the leather shop?"

He shuffled through papers and read out an address. I knew the street and had a general idea how to get there. I'd spent a fair amount of time in Scranton over the years due to private music lessons and doctors' appointments. No options for either in Jackson, where I'd grown up. Sure, I'd taken piano lessons from Mrs. O'Brien, Joe's mom, but there weren't any good flute teachers there. The store should've been near an old used bookstore I loved to go to after visits to the neurologist.

Ted brought up the topic of comics and we geeked out for a while. I wished Andy were in the car so they could geek out together. Sure, I knew the comics he was talking about, but I hadn't kept up with any of them. I only knew the older story arcs, and what I knew was sketchy. I'd pretty much lost interest after the accident. I wasn't sure why I hadn't just sold off the boxes I had at dad's house. Maybe I'd figured Andy might grow into them. He had. I just hadn't turned them over. It was time.

When Ted brought up Art Gray and the *Sleeper* comics, I got more interested. Those, I could still get into, although again, I hadn't kept up with them. I thought Morpheo was a mixture of sexy and creepy at the same time. Ted laughed. I'd had a bit of a crush on the character when I was younger. I merged onto highway 81 and continued north.

"So, I know you like superhero movies and action movies," I said. "Are there other movies you like?"

"Don't forget comedy. I like those too."

"Ah, yes. I forgot the comedies."

"Did you realize that 90% of your movie collection is horror?" He asked.

"I'd say it's more like 99%. Horror is my favorite."

"Why is that?"

"I think I like the adrenaline rush of being afraid, that moment of being scared."

"Isn't life scary enough?"

"Sometimes. Maybe I watch so much horror to remind myself that things could be worse. I could be constantly running from someone who's going around killing my friends and going after me."

"Huh. I'd rather laugh." Just goes to show that people react to life experiences differently. We both shared the experience of childhood abuse.

"What's with the superheroes then?"

"The powerful savior. Someone out there looking out for those who can't protect themselves, fighting the evils of the world. Remember, heroes have a backstory too, a reason they became a superhero. Any one of them could have easily taken that pain and power and turned villain."

"I guess I can see that. The action movies?"

"Kind of the same thing. Usually good guys going after bad guys, right? Like the one we watched the other night, *Night Grooves*."

"Well, that one combined action with comedy."

"I guess it did," he said. I heard the smile in his voice. "What kind of cheerleader reads comic books?"

"A strange cheerleader, I guess," I said. "I don't really remember why I started reading comic books. I don't remember a lot about life before the lightning strike. What I sort of remember comes from what people have told me. When I visualize it as they're saying it, it's like I'm seeing it from outside my body. It's the weirdest thing."

"It must be hard to not remember so much of your life."

"I don't know. At least I don't remember all of the abuse. I know it happened before the strike, because it happened after. I sort of remember that."

I signaled as the next exit came up. We'd be able to get to the street we needed from there. It was earlier than I usually exited, but it would work. I pointed out my favorite seafood restaurant, Casper's, located in a building that looked like a ship as we passed. Mom and I used to eat there sometimes after flute lessons and doctor's appointments. I pointed out the music store where I used to take flute lessons before moving to the Poconos and taking lessons with Mrs. Bates. My former flute instructor had been a grad student at the nearby private college. She was great, but she'd graduated and moved to Colorado. I missed her sense of offbeat humor. Those lessons had been fun.

I turned down a familiar street, checked the street numbers and parked along a street side. I paid the meter. I didn't think we'd be walking far. The used bookstore was a block away, and Wilson's Leather should be on this block. We parked on the even side of the road, which meant that the store would be on the opposite side. We crossed the road and began to search the numbers. Wilson's Leather was on the second floor of a building with a cigar and tobacco shop on the first floor. It was an aromatic building.

We climbed the steps and entered through a door with bars on the window. A cowbell clanged as the door shut behind us. The store was the sort of place crusty old bikers would shop. The smell of leather was welcoming, but most of the leather I saw was decorated with American Flags, or motorcycle brands painted on them. I was looking for something more fetish wear. A burly bald man with a bear tattoo on his shoulder asked if there was something that he could help us find. I asked if he carried leather pants, skirts, or tops. He looked me over, nodded and sent us through a closed door to a back room.

I nodded in appreciation. Definitely more what I had in mind. I didn't want to run around on stage in the leather and chain bras, but they did have some nice bustiers and tanks. I found the leather mini skirts and pants on the far wall. I headed toward those as Ted checked out the fetish undergarments. I shook my head. The salesman pointed to a curtained booth where I could try on items, then returned to the front. Looked like the kind of place there might be hidden cameras. I looked around suspiciously before returning to the task of finding a stage costume.

Part of the problem was not knowing my size. I knew that the last size I bought was too big. I wasn't sure if I was the next size down, or if I'd lost more than one size. I pulled a mini skirt and a tank top in the next size down and headed to the booth. I was irritated to find they were too big. I returned to the racks and tried the next size down, found those were also too big. I sighed and tried two sizes down. They fit. I tried on a bustier that was more of a corset and had to have Ted come back to help with the laces. He really enjoyed the lift it gave my breasts. I told him I felt like I was going to spill out of it. He said he wouldn't mind. I bet.

By the time I'd finished trying on several pieces for Ted's opinion, I bought a pair of tight leather pants, a studded belt, a corset bustier, a side lace up cropped tank, and a mini skirt. At the counter, I added on an eye mask, biker hat, and cat o' nine tails for grins. I'd planned to spend a lot on the costumes, and I had. We still had to go to the mall for everyday clothes. At least I had an idea what size to look for.

I loaded the purchases into the trunk of the car and we headed for the used bookstore. I picked up a horror graphic novel and a book on music composition. I figured that learning some advanced music theory might improve our music. Ted waited at the register with his purchase already in a bag.

We left for the mall, getting there around noon. We walked one end to the other, stopping occasionally to check out something in a window display that Ted said would look good on me. When he told me that a 2-piece swimsuit would look great on me, I frowned.

"You do realize it's nearly winter. Swim weather is pretty much over. It's 50 degrees outside today."

"The hotel has a pool," he said with a wink.

I had major doubts about the swimsuit, but we went in and I tried it on. It actually looked fine. I bought it. I had a moment to wonder if the pool was indoor or outdoor as we walked out of the store, then mentally shrugged it off. I'd get to wear it eventually as long as I didn't regain the weight before summer.

He helped me find several outfits that fit incredibly well, but were more form fitting that I ever would have thought to try on. I didn't like to see my own body, let alone want to show it off to other people. The audience at our shows being the exception. On stage, I played a character, the Siren. She was different, sexy, and playful. She didn't care if people saw skin, the scars didn't matter, she wasn't ashamed. She didn't feel shame.

We left the mall several hours later and decided to stop for lunch at Frankie's Diner. The place had great shakes, burgers, and standard diner fare. I ordered a burger and a strawberry shake. Ted raised his eyebrows when I'd placed my order. I'd shrugged. He ordered the burger and a soda. I understood the look. The heaviness of the combined burger and shake might lead to bloating. The shake could make me phlegmy and mess with my voice. Neither would be great for tonight's show. I figured we still had hours for my body to process the meal before we showed up at the club. I'd be fine. I'd just be sure to drink plenty of water between now and then.

"Still got an hour and a half before we can check in. Anything else you want to do?" I asked.

"I don't know. What else is there to do around here?"

"We have time for the coal mine tour, then there's the railway museum, where they have the train exhibit. I doubt we'll be able to do the train ride today, but you could look at the pictures. We might be able to catch a movie if you wanted."

"Coal mine?"

"Yeah, there's an anthracite coal mine nearby that gives tours. You know, the hard kind of coal that they mine in the area? There's a museum and a tour that actually goes down into the mine. It's pretty cool if you don't get claustrophobic."

"That sounds kind of cool," he said.

The server brought our drinks, setting a water next to my milkshake. I thanked her before she walked off. I reached across the table to hold Ted's hand.

"Thanks for suggesting we skip," I said. "I'm having a good time."

"Me too," he said.

"I really appreciated your help with the corset," I said with a wink. His cheeks grew rosy.

"Any time," he said with an exaggerated wink and twist of the lips.

"I may need your help with the costume tonight."

"Happy to help."

Our food arrived and we ate. I didn't normally eat burgers at restaurants because they were too thick and didn't cook all the way through. I craved red meat today, and didn't care that the center was slightly pink. At least it wasn't bloody. The juice dribbled down my chin and I had to wipe it off. Gross. Still, it was delicious. Ted gave me an odd look as I ate.

"Hungry?" He asked, barely halfway through his burger when I finished the last bite of mine.

"I guess I was."

I didn't finish my shake. I drank the water and had it refilled twice. I wondered if I might be slightly dehydrated, then made myself use the restroom before we left. I didn't want to be stuck down in the mine needing to pee. Ted paid for lunch despite my offer to chip in.

"You paid for breakfast," he said. "Besides, it's a date."

The coal mine was a hit with Ted. He'd never visited the site before. I'd been there several times over the years and always loved it. My former school had taken us to the mine on field trips that I barely remembered and my parents had taken us there several times before and since the accident. The museum had improved a ton since I was little. The tour itself was very much the same, from the stuffed donkey to the narrative, but I loved the feeling of history as we walked through the dark mine shafts.

The hotel was across the bridge and several street lights from the coal mine exit. We made it there shortly after check in time. I expected it would be some time before the guys arrived. They'd planned to come up after school. School wouldn't let out for another hour. We picked up the keys for the double room at the desk, reserved under Zane's name, got our things from the car, and took our stuff up to the room. We claimed the bed by the window and tossed our duffle bags and shopping bags into the closet.

"I'm kind of tired," I said. "Mind if I take a nap?"

"No, I'll join you," he said. He sat down on the bed and removed his shoes. I kicked mine off and joined him.

I set the alarm for 5:00, assuming that would be the earliest that the guys would show up. We made out for a while, his lips warm and juicy against mine. Just in case, before falling asleep, I turned over, back against Ted. I figured it would be less upsetting if the guys walked in on spooning.

The click of the electronic lock and turning doorknob woke me at 4:30, according to the red digital numbers of the clock. I laid still with Ted's arm draped over my waist. I breathed in and turned my head. Barry.

"Hey, Barry," I said.

"Shell," he said, voice uncertain.

"It's been a long day," I said with a yawn. "Zane setting up in the other room?"

"Yeah, he'll be down in a moment."

I sat up, Ted moaned and turned over.

"Hey man," Ted mumbled.

"What's going on?" Barry asked quietly.

"We're together," Ted said.

"What?"

"Going out," Ted said. "Me and Shell are together." He rubbed his eyes.

"Is he talking in his sleep?" Barry asked me.

"No," I said. Well, I guess he wasn't going to wait until after the show.

"Zane's not going to like this," Barry said.

I shook my head.

"Maybe don't tell him about this before the show," Barry said. Wow, he could read my mind.

"I think he should know as soon as possible," Ted said.

"Know what?" Zane said, striding into the room. Barry and I turned to look at him in unison.

"Hey, where's Tara?" I asked, hoping to deflect attention from the situation at hand.

"In the other room. She's resting before dinner," Zane said. "What should I know?"

"Me and Shell," Ted said, "are together."

"Right, you drove in together."

"In a relationship," Ted said.

"Yes, you're friends."

"Dating."

"You're not allowed to date," Zane said.

"We are," I confirmed with a sigh. Might as well get it over with.

"You don't date," Zane gave me a look, challenging.

"I've dated. I'm dating again. Me and Ted." I said.

"No. Nope. Not happening," he said as his face drained of color.

"Not your decision," Ted said. Zane's face drained of color. At first, I expected him to turn beet red with elevated blood pressure at any moment. Now, I worried he might faint.

"He's right, Zane. It's not up to you," I agreed. "Moving on, what's the plan for tonight?" I knew it would take the guys time to adjust to the idea, Zane especially. Barry seemed pretty calm about the whole thing. I'd figured he'd be ok with it.

"How long?" Zane asked.

"Nope, moving on," I said. "Tonight. What's the plan for tonight?"

"We need to be at the club by 7:00 for sound check," Barry said. Zane wasn't used to being shut down by anybody. "We thought we might grab dinner around 5:00 or 5:30."

"Sounds good," I said.

I flopped back onto the bed, next to Ted. He laid down next to me. "You guys can watch TV or whatever, but we've had a long day and hoped to get a little nap in before the rest of the evening." I reset the alarm. Zane let out a huff, but I heard someone settle on the other bed. The television turned on, but the volume was low. Next to me, Ted's breathing slowed. I allowed myself to relax against him and drifted into a light sleep. When I woke, Ted spoke softly with Barry. Zane was no longer in the room. I checked the time, finding it was just after 5:00. I turned off the alarm and stretched, then sat up.

Ted walked over from the corner table as I stood. He pulled me into his arms and kissed me slowly. It was a great way to wake up. Barry cleared his throat. I guess we'd been lip locked long enough to make him uncomfortable. We came apart slowly, me dazed with a goofy grin. I turned.

"Hey, Barry," I said. I walked to the closet and pulled out my duffle. I grabbed my brush, tossed the bag back into the closet and headed for the bathroom. I heard the guys talking as I used the bathroom and got ready for dinner. When I came back out, Zane and Tara were waiting.

Ted wrapped his arm around my waist and Tara's eyebrow raised. "I thought Zane was joking."

"No joke," Barry said. "They've been making out like horny teens."

"Why would we joke about it?" I asked. "It's not funny."

"Definitely not funny," Ted agreed.

"Tried to call you last night," Zane said to Ted as we left the room.

"Stayed over at Shell's."

Oh boy.

"Sorry, I thought I heard you say that you stayed at Shell's place last night," Zane said.

"He did," I confirmed.

"Your mom is going to be so ticked," Zane said.

"Nah, she's ok with it," Ted said.

"Your mom knows about you and Shell, that you spent the night at her house, and she's ok with it?"

"Yep."

"Wasn't the first time," I said. I wasn't sure why I let that slip. Maybe I wanted to see how he'd react. He was acting like a jealous little jerk and I couldn't figure out why. I pulled my jacket on as we followed the others to the elevator. "Where did you want to go?"

"There's a restaurant a block down that the concierge said was good. Thought we'd give it a shot," Tara said. "American food."

Basically, what we'd eaten for lunch, but I was fine with that. I'd just try to avoid bloating foods. I felt fine and ready to eat again. Ted took my hand as we walked, lacing our fingers together. I welcomed the warmth as we stepped outside. A brisk wind rushed us, rifling through my braided hair and loosening strands. Looked like I'd be redoing my hair when we got to the club later. I'd planned to do my makeup there anyway. I was definitely changing there. I wasn't walking around in the outfits we bought.

Even though Zane was being a little weird about our dating, he was still taking it better than I'd expected. I think he'd already suspected that something was going on. We stopped at a door under a green awning that read Emma's Restaurant. Barry opened the door and Tara stepped through. The rest of us followed, Barry entering last. The hostess sat us quickly at a round top.

We placed orders with our server, Jennifer, and Tara started to ask me and Ted questions. We hadn't seen her in a while, so

I guess it wasn't surprising that she'd be curious what we'd been up to. She'd switched from Concert Band to Journalism and Yearbook, so we didn't see her much these days. She hadn't been the only one to be surprised by the dating news, although I think she was more surprised than the guys. They'd seen Ted growing more affectionate recently. She understood what an amazing feat it was for Ted to allow anyone into his personal space.

When the food arrived, the guys spoke around bites of food. Ted's hand rested on my knee, squeezing lightly when he sensed my growing discomfort. Zane, being Zane, had started with the underhanded comments about my stage presence and how tonight I really had to bring it. My eyes flashed as I glared at him and bit my tongue. Oh, I'd bring it alright. I breathed in deeply and slowly and let the air out in a rush.

"Ted," I said, turning to face him, "I can't wait to get the show started." I reached behind his neck and gently pulled him in for a kiss. I heard a strangled noise from Zane's direction and smiled. Ted didn't complain, just pulled me closer. I kind of wished that we had sprung for our own room tonight like he'd suggested.

"Guys, come on," Zane said.

"Oh, but it's so cute," Tara cooed. I very much doubted that what we were doing was cute. I drew back from Ted.

"Oh man, I'm going to be in a room with those two tonight," Barry groaned, then chuckled. "And tomorrow night." His face contorted into a mask of fake horror. We laughed.

10

We stopped at the hotel for gear and stage wear before heading to the club. When we entered the red brick building, a man wearing a shiny purple button up with black tie and black pants came out from behind the bar. He introduced himself as Lucio Mancini, General Manager of Club Del Sol, and told us to call him Lucio. Lucio was maybe 5 foot 2 with a paunch that hung over his belt. His dark hair, slicked back, and the stereotypical mustache made me stifle a laugh. What I saw looking at Lucio was Dini Bianchi, character from the Bianchi Brothers video game, running around jumping and smashing things with a hammer. We followed him through a doorway behind the bar and found ourselves in a dim hallway with worn wood floors. He opened a door labeled 2 and told us it was our dressing room. Other places we'd played didn't even have one green room. We'd just wait at a table in some dark corner until it was time to set up. We dropped off our gear and followed him further down the hall, passing the open door of room 1, the headliner's dressing room. It was much larger, better lit, and had a nicer couch.

Lucio took us through a door marked "Stage," and we were blasted by the sounds of some punk band that I'd never heard of. Their bass drum read, Pinhole Colada. The lead vocalist, if you could call him that, screamed out something in Spanish, then sort of sang a verse in English. It was total word salad, made no sense at all. Interesting. The guitarist sported a muddy blue spiked mohawk, and they all wore a mixture of metal studded cuffs, torn white tees and tight jeans. Weird. The drummer pounded out a few final beats and the lead mumbled into the mic before the band left the stage.

They walked past, nodding, but mostly ignoring us. On closer look, they appeared to be in their 30s, maybe early 40s. At least we could just do our merchandise sales, autographing and leave. Sure, we'd have to stay and listen a bit while we did that, but I couldn't imagine being stuck in the club until closing. We didn't have that large a following. Lucio told us to grab our gear and come back for sound check. The stage crew needed to rearrange some equipment for us. We were used to setting up on our own with minimal help from the club staff, and Ted and I looked at each other wide-eyed. Fancy.

When we returned, the stage was set up. We plugged in and jumped into our fast, classic punk Calabrias cover. Through the bright stage lights, I caught glimpses of the sound guy adjusting levels on the mixer. I sang while I strummed guitar. Lucio made a rolling gesture and we continued on to our next moderately paced song while the techs continued to adjust lights and sound. The exhilaration of standing on a professional raised stage nearly overwhelmed me. When Lucio applauded our second number and dismissed us to the dressing room, a wide grin spread across my face. I followed the guys back to the room.

I motioned for Ted to follow me behind the curtained changing area to help me into my trickier pieces. I pulled on fishnets and slipped into the leather mini skirt, which Ted helped fasten. I finished off the outfit with platform thigh high boots that Ted laced up. His fingers, warm, brushed my skin as he tightened the bustier. I had quite a mound of cleavage as I stepped out from behind the curtain.

I sat in front of a light framed mirror and applied makeup. The setup reminded me of my ballet recital days in the dressing rooms with all the mirrors surrounded by huge light bulbs, except that there was just one mirror instead of a long row of them with girls lined up giggling as they readied for the show. For a moment, I saw a younger version of me staring back with bright stage makeup and auburn hair pulled back in a bun, wearing a white sparkling headpiece that matched my glowing white leotard and fluffy tutu. I blinked and caught Ted's reflection eyeing my full-cleavaged, black leather wearing reflection and winked back. I ran deep red lipstick across my lips then tackled my hair. I kept the side plaits. No hiding behind the hair tonight. The Siren had arrived.

A knock on the door gave us our 3-minute warning and we piled into the hallway, tripping over each other in excitement. As opening act, it was up to us to warm the crowd. The rumble of voices increased as we neared the stage doors. Lucio gestured impatiently and rushed onto stage, wireless mic in hand. I gripped my guitar and prayed that I wouldn't puke.

"Here from the Poconos, we have an up and coming band, Toxic Siren! You may have heard them play at last year's Alternative Festival on the River, or recently on KNXT. Let's give it up for Toxic Siren!"

The band followed me up the steps and across the bright stage where we quickly plugged in, realizing too late that we should've just left our gear onstage. Barry tapped a quick 4-count and I belted out our retro punk cover. I threw in some old cheerleader moves as I hopped around stage in my minimal leather costume and hoped that my boobs didn't pop out. We transitioned into one of our originals, *Who Knew You'd Take It Away*, more of a moderately paced ballad, and I threw in some more sultry hip movements, not so easy behind the guitar. As the song finished, the crowd hooted and cheered.

Luckily, I wasn't able to see much due to the bright stage lights. I got stage fright sometimes, despite my past performance experience. It sounded like the place was full to bursting with people, but it could've just been that they were smooshed close to the stage. Greek letters and college tees spotted the crowd and I wondered if it was college night.

"It's great to be here tonight," I said. "Lovely town, Scranton. Great people, fun things to do, good food. We're having a wonderful time. How about you?"

There were a few 'yeah's hollered back.

"Awesome! I'm your Siren, we've got Bear on drums," I pointed to Barry, then gestured gameshow host style to Zane, "Zane on lead guitar," turned and motioned to Ted, "and on bass, our very own Ted. Hope you enjoy the show."

Barry counted off another quick 4-count and we ran through Ted's *Beatdown*. It was catchy in Ted's sexy growl, awful as the inspiration was. From there, we ran through our setlist with another classic punk cover, and completed the show with three more originals. As the strings rang out into silence, the crowd erupted into ground shaking applause and whistles. The stage quaked beneath us. I surveyed the guys, nodded, and we unplugged and left the stage.

Lucio waited to the side of the stage stairs, patting us as we passed. I got a slap on the butt and thought I heard Ted growl behind me. The stage crew took over, switching the setup for Pinhole Colada. To me, the band name sounded like two random words strung together. I'd never heard of them, and from their earlier equipment check, it was no wonder. We passed them on the way back to our dressing room.

I packed up my guitar, pulled my leather jacket on for some modesty and gestured to the door. We had merchandise to sell. We took over the table at the back of the club, where I had a better view of the ballroom floor and stage. The place was flooded with young folks. Lucio announced the headliners and they revved up as our table was flooded by fans wanting autographs. This part of the gig was difficult for me, plastering a smile on my face as people took pictures and asked for me to sign things, including body parts. One obviously drunk brunette sorority girl asked me to sign a breast. I shook my head, laughing, as I took a black permanent marker in hand and signed away.

"I love that *Beatdown* song," sorority girl said. "I just want to dance every time I hear it on the radio. Well, dance or hit something."

"You've heard it on the radio?" I asked. I knew Zane had sent the demo to all the nearby radio stations, but hadn't heard it playing yet.

"Yeah, the college station, KNXT. They play it on the night show. You guys are, like, number 5 this week."

I looked at Ted, who had been listening. He seemed as surprised as I was. I guess that explained why there were so many college logos tonight, and why less than half the people in the ballroom were paying attention to Pinhole Colada up on stage. Gosh, they were awful.

"Glad you like it," I said. "Thanks for listening!"

"You guys are great," said a familiar looking guy with dark auburn hair. I couldn't place him, but he looked like an older version of Joe, without the freckles, and wore a Bloomsburg University sweatshirt. He handed me a CD and I signed it.

"Thanks," I said. I wanted to ask if we'd met before, but there were still lots of people in line behind him. He smiled and left with a cute blonde. Something tugged at me from the murky marshes of lost memory, but I couldn't grasp it.

Ted ran his hand along my leg and I squeezed his hand and smiled before signing the next piece of merchandise. Our merchandise, CDs and posters, sold out before the line died down. We ended up signing napkins and taking photos with fans in front of the table. Way more physical contact than I ever wanted with strangers, but I made it through the end of the line. My face hurt from fake smiling, and my body hurt from being so tense around the strangers. I just wanted to go back to the room, shower, and go to bed.

Tara and Zane asked if we were sticking around for a while. I looked to Ted and shook my head. He shrugged and shook his head too. He wasn't huge on the social scene. I think he'd had enough crowding for the night too. Tara and Zane stayed at the club while Barry, Ted, and I returned to the hotel room like the introverts we were.

My foot slid with a whoosh as I stepped into the room. I bent down and picked up a manila envelope that lay on the floor. It had my name on it in block letters, but nothing else. I tossed it onto the bed, got my pajamas out of the duffle and requested Ted's help getting out of costume. Barry raised an eyebrow, but said nothing as Ted followed me into the bathroom.

"These clothes aren't comfortable," I noted. "Just for the record."

"You look good in them," he said, running his eyes down my body. "Really good."

"Thanks for helping me pick them out. Not sure I would've gotten a skirt this short. I was afraid to bend over on stage."

"Couldn't tell."

"I convinced myself that the guitar held it in place. I'm

wearing the pants tomorrow."

He nodded. I turned around and gestured to the ties and hooks at the back of the bustier. Ted slowly worked his way down from the top. The pressure eased with each loosened ribbon and released hook. I breathed more deeply than I had in hours as the bustier dropped to the floor. I bent down and picked it up, placing it on the counter.

"I see what you mean about the skirt," Ted said, smile evident in his voice.

"Told you."

"I saw lace," he said, low growl to his voice. My body heated.

I nodded, smile playing on my lips. At least Ted had chosen cute underwear. The color matched the dark leather. He undid the skirt and I stepped out of it as it hit the floor. The leather left me hot and sweaty where it had touched my skin. The air chilled my newly exposed skin, raising gooseflesh. Ted ran his hands over my breasts and hips before helping me out of the boots.

"I need a shower," I said.

"So do I," he agreed. "But you go first."

"You could join me," I suggested as I wiggled an eyebrow and grinned. He laughed and shook his head.

"Bear's in the next room." He stepped back. "I'll grab your pajamas for you. Go ahead and start your shower." He nodded toward the shower before closing the door behind him. I frowned as I stepped into water a bit too cool for comfort.

When I got out of the shower, I found the satin babydoll waiting for me. I slipped it over my head. As the fabric fell into place, I realized that it barely covered my butt. Great. Ah, I pulled on another set of lacy underwear that Ted had left for me and my lips twisted into a half-frown, half-smile. What was this? He wouldn't conserve water by showering with me, because Bear was in the next room, but it was fine for me to go out there like this? I quickly braided my damp hair, and opened the door. I shoved my dirty clothes into my duffle as Ted passed me, winking before he closed the door to take his turn in the shower.

Bear's look was priceless when I looked up from my duffle. A mix of disbelief, curiosity, and something I couldn't define, sprinted across his face. I tossed my duffle into a far corner and climbed under the covers. It wasn't surprising that Ted had chosen the more girly pajama gown over the standard tank and shorts, but now Barry kept looking my way. I focused on the television. I tried to figure out what he was watching on television. Late night MTV. Music videos played, flashing in the darkness of the room.

"Good shower?" He choked out.

"Yeah," I said with a sigh. "Leather's hot. I was pretty sticky and gross." I looked his way. "You showering tonight or in the morning?"

"Think I'll wait until morning," he said. I nodded and turned my eyes back to the television.

Ted came out of the bathroom, wrapped in nothing but a towel. I wasn't sure if that was his normal thing or if he'd just forgotten to bring his pajamas into the bathroom. He tossed the towel back into the bathroom before pulling on a pair of pajama bottoms. My first look at naked Ted and it was so brief. I half frowned, but his body was nice to look at. Lean, defined, impressive. Of course, he was the only guy I'd seen naked up close like that. That I remembered, anyway. He climbed in next to me and I slid closer to him after he'd settled.

"Night guys," I said.

"Good night," Barry said.

"Good night," Ted said as he touched his lips to my forehead and wrapped an arm around me.

11

My eyes opened to diffuse light. We hadn't closed the light blocking curtains the night before. I checked the clock and saw a red digital 9:05 AM. Too early for a Saturday morning, let alone the morning after performing. Performing again tonight, we needed sleep. The bed moved next to me. Barry snored lightly from the other bed. I rolled over to face Ted. His eyes glinted mischievously as he pulled me in for a kiss. The quick movement surprised me so much that I forgot to breathe and got lightheaded. I gasped as he drew back.

"Good morning," I said whispered.

Barry mumbled something and dragged blankets over his head. I ran my fingers through Ted's silky hair as I gazed into his eyes. A flash of blue eyes lit by lightning crossed my mind and I squeezed my eyes shut. Now wasn't the time to be thinking of a strange guy I'd met only once. I slowly blinked and smiled. Ted's pillow soft lips beckoned and I lost myself to the movements of lips and tongue.

"Guys," Barry said. He cleared his throat. "Guys, it's almost noon. Want to get some lunch?"

"Noon?" I mumbled against Ted's mouth. I drew back. "No way."

"Yeah, really," he said. Not only was it noon, but Barry was showered and dressed. He stood over us, hands on hips.

I untangled myself from Ted and pushed myself up to

sitting. Ted leaned back on his elbows and gave Barry a dirty look. I wanted to laugh. I'd never seen Ted look at anyone that way, annoyed. Ted was always so chill. I tumbled out of bed and started to get dressed. Barry's eyes widened.

"What?" I asked. I stepped into my jeans, pulled them up and fastened them. I realized Barry may have seen my scars when I'd turned my back. "Never seen the scars before?"

"Scars?" He asked.

Great. He was looking at me like I was a girl. I guess it made sense, since I'd been making out with Ted for hours. Not to mention that darned babydoll nightgown Ted had me wear last night. I sighed and decided to pretend he'd just noticed my scars. I turned my back to him and pointed at my exposed shoulder and upper back, where my Lichtenberg figures stood out in the daylight. I was surprised that he hadn't noticed them under the stage lighting last night.

"Scars, see? All over my back and down my left arm. From when I got struck by lightning."

Barry laughed.

"She's not kidding," Ted said.

In a masterful feat, I fastened my bra under the babydoll nighty and pulled a light tee over my head while removing the babydoll in almost one move. "I mean, it's not like I go around advertising the fact. I'll show you the articles sometime."

Ted stood up and started to dress while I got my shoes and socks on. Barry answered a knock on the door to let Tara and Zane in. I brushed my teeth and pulled my hair back into a loose braid.

"I don't think I can share a room with these two again," Barry said. "Too many pheromones."

"Pheromones, huh?" Zane looked at Ted, then sneered at me. He and I had a problem.

"Lucky you, Bear, it's just one more night," I said, turning to greet Tara. "Hi, Tara. How'd you sleep?"

The guys got into their own separate conversation as we left the room. Tara and I followed behind. Zane was excited about what he'd heard at the club after we left. As females, Tara and I became invisible.

"Sounds like you had fun at the club after we left," I said.

"Hmm? Not really. People kept coming up and telling Zane

what a great show you put on. We didn't get to dance much with all the interruptions."

"Sorry."

"Don't be. It was a great show. Where'd those moves come from?"

"What moves?" I feigned ignorance.

"All of them. You're usually so," her eyes looked skyward, "mechanical?"

"I've got my secrets." I said, facing forward with a half-smile.

"Yeah, you and Ted for one. Didn't see that one coming."

"Everyone saw that one coming," I said.

"No one saw that coming," Tara said with a laugh. I shrugged. It probably seemed surprising. It had surprised me. We left the hotel and followed the guys around the corner. A gust of wind lifted my hair and brought shivers. A cold front was pushing through. Good thing I'd be wearing pants later. "I think I got some good shots of you and the band last night."

"Really? I'd like to see them after they're processed."

"Sure thing."

A couple blocks later, we walked into a small cafe advertising the city's best Reuben. The staff took our order at the counter and we found a round table toward the back. Zane droned on about future concert dates while I barely listened.

"Wait, tour?" I asked, picking out something about a summer tour.

"Yeah, Shell. We've been talking about touring for ages. I think we can finally pull it together this summer. An east coast tour. Tonight's show is sold out. Lucio called this morning to book us in a couple months at his other club, Neon. Our songs are being played on the radio. I think we can do this."

I didn't want to get my hopes up. It only made the disappointment so much worse.

"When are we supposed to record our album?" I asked. "I thought we wanted to do that before we went on tour."

"I'm scheduling time at the studio starting in December during the break. We'll record what we've got down solid. You and Ted just need a couple more good ones."

"December? Do we have it in the budget?" I asked. I my eyes widened and my mouth went dry. I wasn't ready to record yet,

113

not with school and work going on.

"After this show, the band fund will have plenty to pay for enough studio time to record a short album," he said with a tap of pen on paper.

"A whole album? During the school year?"

"We'll split the studio time over non-show weekends, and winter break of course. I already worked it out with Bryce." Bryce owned the garage studio where we'd recorded our demo. We'd met him through Raif, of all people, one of his old college buddies.

"He was on the phone all morning," Tara groaned.

"It's going to be great!" Zane said.

I took a deep breath and exhaled. I knew we'd been doing more shows than usual, but hadn't realized we were so close to reaching our studio goal. Ted and I had worked on several songs recently, we just hadn't worked on them with the band. Maybe we could do the album. But a summer tour? That sounded outrageous. Once Zane got an idea in his head, the rest of us were along for the shaky roller coaster ride. Zane was a force, one not to mess with when he had his mind set on a career goal for the band.

A server brought our food to the table. We ate and talked about the upcoming shows, ten of them. Zane had been withholding, waiting for the perfect moment to unveil our show dates and locations. College towns, not just Pennsylvania, but neighboring states. It was almost an east coast tour already. Only problem was, it started well before summer, cutting into the school year.

"How do your parents feel about the schedule?" I asked.

"Haven't shown it to them yet," Zane admitted. For the youngest of us at 16, Zane had the best business sense, which was why he was the band manager. I certainly didn't want the job. He loved doing business with people. I just wanted to perform. The other two were too soft spoken and introverted.

"So, these shows are all on the weekend, right?" I asked. Pat wasn't going to like that.

"Mostly. Some are Wednesday nights," he said.

"What?" My eyes darted back.

"Wednesdays," he said with a nod.

"Uh, on a school night?" I felt like I'd wandered into an

alternate universe. I worked evenings and had homework to do. So did Ted.

"They're local, and should be over before 10. It's not like we don't all work that late or later on weeknights sometimes," Zane prodded. I just stewed over the fact that he'd scheduled weeknight shows without asking any of us first.

It was true, we all worked late on school nights sometimes. Barry nodded. Ted looked thoughtful. My heart raced. Ted's hand found mine and squeezed. I took a breath and nodded. I'd make it work. It was the dream. I wasn't sure it was my dream, but it was the band's dream.

We wandered the streets, checking out the neighborhood before returning to the hotel. Except for passing cars, there weren't many people on the streets. Housekeeping had visited while we were gone, and the unopened manila envelope sat in front of the television. I picked it up and slid a finger under the flap, curious.

I pulled out a glossy 8x10 black and white photo. The quality was poor, grainy, and taken through my old bedroom window. My eyes narrowed as I drew the photo closer to my face, as if doing so would zoom in and offer more details. Of course, it did nothing. In the photo, I sat at my desk, writing in my journal, wearing glasses I hadn't worn in over a year. My bedroom hadn't been in the basement for a year and a half.

"What's that?" Ted asked. I handed him the photo. "Whoa, I remember those granny glasses."

"Right?" I scrunched my face.

"I prefer your contacts," he said, chuckling.

"So do I," I agreed. "Picture sucks."

"Who's it from?" Ted turned the photo over. "Did you see this?"

"See what?"

He pointed to a single sentence, 'I see you.'

"Oh, that's nice," I said. A chill ran over my arms as it struck me, "you know, someone had to crawl under the deck to access that window and take the picture. That's creepy."

"Wonder what else they got pictures of," Barry wagged his eyebrows.

"Yeah, me too," I threw a pillow at him. I used to keep the

blinds closed. I guess that had been an unusual day. The blinds in the picture were obviously up. Of course, they were thin red plastic rolling blinds. I could almost see through them from the inside. It was probably the same from the outside. I glanced at the version of me in the photo. I wondered what the person was getting at. They saw a 40 pound heavier me when they looked at the Siren on stage? They saw a total band geek nerd? What was the message they were trying to convey? I slid the picture back into the envelope.

"They could've at least taken a better picture," I muttered.

"Aw, I thought you looked really cute and thoughtful," Ted said with a kiss to my forehead.

"I've seen worse," Bear said with a shrug.

I tossed the envelope on top of the dresser, next to the television. It slid until it came to rest against the wall. I flopped down on the bed and dramatically moaned, "I feel so violated." I really did. I didn't like my picture being taken, let alone by someone who dared sneak under the deck to snap secret pictures through the bedroom window. It was creepy.

Ted sat next to me and I glanced at him. I couldn't help smiling at the way he looked at me, interested. Nobody had looked at me like that in a long time. Wait, what? Not Joe, but someone else had. I heard springs creak as Barry sat on the other bed. I shook my head and returned to the moment.

"So, what are we doing for the next few hours?" I asked. I'd had enough contemplation of the photo. I wanted something mind numbing.

"TV?" Barry suggested, remote in hand.

"Sure," I said. "I may fall asleep. Just don't let me sleep through the show."

"Of course not," Ted said, laughing.

"Aw, come on, Ted you could totally rock the vocals without me. We all know it." It would just be a different sound. A good sound, actually. I loved when Ted took over lead vocals. It wasn't just my crush talking. He was more talented than he gave himself credit for.

"Nah, your range is so much wider than mine," he said.

"Yeah, yeah. You'd adjust, goofball." I nudged his arm.

"Shell's got a point," Bear said. I tossed another pillow at him. I hadn't gotten the first back. We weren't going to have any pillows left if I kept throwing them at Bear.

"I wouldn't have it any different," Ted said. I would've kissed him, but I had a feeling Bear would start beating us with pillows if we smooched any more. We'd pushed Bear's limits already.

I fluffed one of the remaining pillows and got comfortable as the guys picked something to watch. They found an action movie with lots of explosions and shooting. I watched for a while, then my eyes drifted shut. I startled awake with a knock at the door. Zane and Tara had come down to see what we wanted to do for dinner. They were an hour early. I guess they'd gotten bored. I took a moment to fix my hair and rinse the sleep from my eyes, then returned to the bed and sat. They'd come to no decisions on dinner, but it was early.

"What are we doing about merch tonight?" I asked. We sold out last night.

"Jay's bringing the last of our CDs and posters to the show," Tara offered. "Zane called him."

"Didn't know you and Jay were that close," I said. I couldn't remember seeing them hanging out or even talking in the school hallways.

"You mentioned he and some of your co-workers were coming tonight. Figured it was worth the call," Zane said. That didn't answer my implied question. I'd seen them talking, sure, but did I see them hang out? No. Did I go out much? No, so I guess I wouldn't know if they hung out, would I? Jay wasn't the best person for Zane to be hanging out with. Not a great example with the drinking and other things that I suspected he was up to.

"Lucky, I guess." I eyed him suspiciously. Wonderful, I'd have to be grateful to Jay. Sure, he'd been relatively human lately, but to feel like I owed him something? Yuck.

"Speaking of merchandise," Zane said, "we need new posters and have to start thinking about cover art for the album." Like the demo, we planned to self-produce our album. Sure, rookie move, but we needed more than demos and we had enough material for an album. We'd be recording in the same "studio" we'd recorded our demo in, a glorified garage studio, run by Bryce Armstrong, who graduated years before us. The studio did the job, but I always wondered what it'd be like to record in a real professional quality studio. "Time for another photo shoot," he said, slapping his knees.

"I've got some ideas," Tara said as she began to outline her plans.

I nodded. I really didn't like my picture taken. I wanted to zone out so badly, but made myself focus. This was why I wasn't the band manager. I couldn't stand the business side of things. I interrupted.

"Why can't we just use live concert photos?" I asked. I wouldn't even know they were being taken. Not with the show lighting and other flashing lights from the audience.

"We might be able to use some of them, maybe for the posters," Zane said. "We'll see." His eyes narrowed in irritation. "Go on, Tara. Tell us about those ideas."

"Well, I was thinking we could take pictures at the places you're playing, like the New York show."

"New York?" I asked. "Since when are we playing New York? As in City?"

"Was I not supposed to say anything?" Tara turned to Zane.

"It was a surprise, but now that it's out, yes, New York City. The Wolf's Den. We're scheduled for June."

"Sounds, um, lovely," I said, nose crinkling as I imagined some dank pit. Maybe a biker bar.

"Lots of great bands got their start there. It's just one night," Zane assured me.

"Right, well, I thought we might do some sightseeing while there, and get some pictures at landmarks and stuff," Tara said. Sounded like a school trip to me, but what did I know?

I shrugged. That would be fine. At least it wouldn't be in front of boring black or white curtains again. I couldn't believe how many photos she'd taken just to decide on one.

"I mean, it takes a while for the CDs to come back, so we'll have some time to put together the jackets," Zane reminded us. I'd been the only person voicing opinions. I shrugged and sat back.

"True," I admitted. The demo discs had taken forever, weeks.

Ted laced up the sides of my leather tank while I held my braids out of the way. The leather pants hugged my hips like a second skin. Ted finished tying the laces and let his hands drift back to my hips, where they stayed. I wrapped my arms around his neck and pulled him closer. Our lips met, gently, with the barest hint of tongue. His fingers squeezed and I let go. He motioned to the curtain with his head and I stifled a giggle. I hadn't forgotten the guys were all on the other side of the dressing curtain. I shook my head and stepped out from behind the curtain. Might as well get that stage makeup on.

Ted didn't immediately follow me. He needed to make some minor adjustments before leaving the dressing space. I sat in front of the mirror, not particularly comfortable in the new skin tight leather. It just didn't give. I applied my makeup carefully, applying extra eyeliner and lipstick, vampy when I turned away from the mirror. I stood on my platform Mary Jane's and stretched. As I exhaled, I eyed the guys suspiciously, they all stared at me.

"What, did I smear my makeup already?"

"No, you look great," Tara said. She snapped a couple photos. I shook my head. I hated being the center of attention. When could I go back to being invisible again?

"It's the cleavage, isn't it?" I asked. Great. The guys were seeing me like a girl again. Boobs. The push up bra under the leather tank worked extremely well, making the girls super perky, almost spilling out of the top.

"No, no, you look awesome," said Ted. His eyes roamed over my body, bringing warmth to my cheeks and lower places. Lucky for me, my arousal was less apparent than Ted's. My eyes rose as I pretended not to see.

"Thanks," I said, face reddening at the weight of eyes on me. The 3-minute warning knock saved me from further embarrassment. We hurried to the stage door, instrument free, already plugged in and set to go on stage. Tonight was sold out and sounded like it. The walls shook from all the noise. I wanted to give them a good show. I breathed in slow, feeling my belly rise first, chest last, then exhaled in the opposite way, chest falling, then abdomen. I let my mind go a little fuzzy and summoned the Siren from within. She walked confidently to the front stage in my mind. My body warmed as I let her take control and breathed deeply a couple more times before Lucio finished announcing us. It seemed that he dragged out our intro a little longer tonight, but that could've been my imagination on overdrive, making time slow.

We rushed onto stage, grabbed our instruments and jumped into *Medicated* with extra punk energy. I put more dance moves into our act, managing not to trip over any amp or mic cords, and had fun flirting with the invisible audience, or rather, the Siren did. There was no time for shyness on stage, it wasn't the place for it. The Siren rose above the former glory of Michelle, the old me. She didn't care about the scars, exposed under the hot lights. She wore them as natural skin, a part of her. The audience, captivated, erupted into thunderous applause and loud shouts after each number. It was intoxicating and I was afloat in the energy of it all.

I stalked around the stage, extra sway to the hips during our slower songs, eyes intent on the occasional visible guys in the front. Lighters came out on our last slow number, *Eyes For You*. When we left the stage, I thought I might fall from the trembling of the stage. I waved and smiled widely at the audience before stepping off the stage. The guys followed and we stumbled back to the dressing room.

I startled at a loud knock at the door. Lucio looked frantic.

"Do you have any more songs? They're calling for an encore."

"We're just the opening act," I stammered. Lucio gestured impatiently.

"Come on, let's go," Zane nudged.

I followed the guys back on stage. We played another punk cover and one of our newer originals, *Emergence*. Again, an echo of applause and shouts as we left the rumbling stage. It was scary, the response of the audience. When I thought about the upcoming meet and greet, my heart stopped. Could we handle it?

"Guys," I said once we were in the dressing room. "That was out of control."

"That was awesome!" Zane shouted. Bear nodded.

Ted lifted me up and twirled me around. "You've been holding back," he said.

"Maybe a little," I admitted. "Let's get out to the table before they start a riot."

Zane agreed with me for once. I checked my makeup in the

mirror, dabbed my face with a tissue and followed the guys out to the table. Jay had come through. Merchandise spread across the table ready to go. We took our seats and I grabbed a silver permanent marker, ready to sign the night away. Ted sat next to me with a black marker. I hoped to avoid signing body parts tonight. My hope was quickly dashed by a random dude with a black homemade "I Love the Siren" tee shirt came up and lifted his shirt for me to sign his belly. I shook my head and signed.

People flew by, one after another, buying up the remaining merchandise in record time. We got tons of names on our mailing list. Tara took hundreds of pictures, swapping out rolls of film like a pro. We continued signing napkins and taking pictures with fans long after Pinhole Colada finished playing their set. As the line finally dwindled down, Jay stepped in front of us along with a familiar face I hadn't seen in a while. Blond hair, blue eyes, gorgeous - Blondie! My heart stopped.

"Jay! Thanks for bringing the merchandise," I said. I wasn't sure what to say to Blondie.

"Daredevil! Great show," Blondie said. "Thought you said you weren't popular." He looked around, biting his lip. It was cute, he looked unsure of himself, less confident than at the beach.

"Thanks," I answered. "But, I'm not." Wow, he was more handsome than I remembered. Why was he talking to me? Oh, right. He just saw our show. Had I made a fool of myself on stage? The guys seemed to think we did ok. They weren't cracking up about my moves this time.

"Hi, I'm Ted," Ted held out a hand, face less friendly than the gesture.

"Dylan, Jay's friend," Dylan met Ted's hand with a firm shake and easy smile, composure returned.

"Haven't seen you before," Ted eyed him and put an arm over my shoulders.

"New to the area," Blondie said. "Starting school next week."

So, he hadn't been going to our school. I knew I hadn't seen him around.

"Cool, see you around," I said. Ted didn't share my

sentiments. I actually thought I saw a sneer stretch across Ted's lips.

12

Ted barely spoke on the way home. He'd hardly touched me after meeting Dylan at the club. Although he still shared the bed back in the hotel room, he'd turned away from me as soon as he got in bed. I'd missed his arms around me.

"Did I do something wrong?" I asked, gripping the steering wheel as music played quietly.

"Hmm? What? No," Ted adjusted in the seat and turned to look at me.

"You just seem really quiet."

"Just taking in everything. We had a couple of great shows. I can't believe the difference in you on stage. I mean last night, it was like you were a different person," he said. "I don't know you."

"I called on some old skills. I used to be a different person," I said. "I don't remember much about her." I didn't mention that on stage I also thought of myself as another person. I knew these were all aspects of myself, but they were so different from each other, separate.

"That's not really possible, you know," his voice, dubious as he shifted in the seat. "Turning into another person, I mean."

"No, seriously. After the lightning strike my personality changed. I lost years of memories. My family recognizes that I'm not the same person I used to be. Michelle was different."

"Michelle?"

"You don't think my full name is Shell, do you? My parents aren't exactly hippies." A half-smile played on my lips as I imagined my mother with long hair and a flower crown.

"Well, no. I'm pretty sure I've heard you called Michelle by teachers. It just didn't register."

"Michelle was really different. She shone like a star, had serious promise, tons of talent. I mean, dancing? Amazing talent. Piano? Crazy good, almost a prodigy."

"Wait, you play piano?"

"I don't. I guess I used to. You've seen the old black upright in the basement." My hand rose from the steering wheel in a shooing motion. I thought of the pictures and trophies in my closet. I couldn't remember winning any of them.

"Didn't think it worked."

"It doesn't. It's out of tune and some of the keys don't work anymore." Like my brain, I thought, broken.

"I really don't know you at all," he said. He crossed his arms. I risked a look at him before returning my attention to the road.

"I haven't played since the accident. I haven't danced since the accident. I haven't been a cheerleader since the accident. It's not me anymore. I lost those memories to brain damage when the lightning hit. Not to mention the loss of strength in my muscles. You don't know what it's like to have to recover from neuromuscular trauma. I couldn't dance now if I wanted to. You know the me that I am now." The doctors and specialists told me that it was common for personality to change after such an accident and the advanced level of changes within my brain. Some of those memories were just gone, and no attempt to reconnect would work. The tissue wasn't there anymore. What was left was fragmented, always would be. How could I explain that to Ted?

He went silent again. The radio played random songs, none of which I would've chosen to listen to. Ted watched the road. I pondered my losses, falling into a sadness I hadn't felt in ages. It wasn't just Joe and Christy I'd lost that day. I'd lost me too.

I'd offered to meet dad in Scranton to take Andy home with us, but dad said he'd meet me at mom's house later in the evening. Andy was hanging out with his old friend Shawn and wouldn't be ready to go home yet. I was happy that Andy maintained connections with his old friends. I hadn't managed it.

When I pulled into the empty driveway about an hour later, Ted unfastened his seatbelt, anxious to get away. He transferred his gear to the gold Toyota, not able to get away fast enough. My heart hurt. I'd thought we were getting close, really close.

"Guess I'll see you in school tomorrow?" I asked.

"Guess so." He got in his car and drove off. No goodbye kiss, no hug.

I checked my watch and unloaded the car. We'd made it back barely in time for me to get ready for work. When I entered through the kitchen door, I was greeted with the flashing message light. Mom working late again.

I rushed to get ready for work. We'd hit some traffic on the way back due to construction. I dumped my bags in the laundry room and guitar in the garage then changed into my uniform, swearing the entire time. I twisted my hair into a bun and rushed back out to the Olds. The drive to work was relatively quick. People must have been in church. The hordes would be unleashed soon enough. If I was lucky, work would be a great distraction from whatever gnawed on Ted.

I parked and rushed into the restaurant, catching a flash of blond hair in my peripheral vision as I passed the grill and sandwich area. Pat must've hired the replacement for Marcus. The assignment board had me back in my sanctuary, working salad bar. I clocked in, scrubbed my hands and headed back to the bar.

"Hey girl," Jules said, leaning against the back wall. The restaurant seemed fully staffed.

"Hi Jules. Busy yet?" I asked checking the space for work that needed to be done.

"Not yet."

"How's life treating you?" I asked as I gloved up to rotate out some vegetables.

She groaned. "Guys, you give it to them once and they want it all the time."

"Huh?"

"Sex," she said, rolling her eyes. She pushed away from the wall and stirred the marinara sauce. Her eyes drifted over the sneeze shield to the dining area, where Larry sat in a lonesome cloud of smoke.

"Ah." I wouldn't know. I frowned and picked up a cleaning towel from the sanitizer solution and wiped down the counter. "Rough time with Jay?"

"Pressuring me all the time. Sex, sex, sex," she shook her head in disgust.

"Sorry to hear that." Honestly, I was jealous. I sighed.

"What about you and Ted?" She asked, tossing the dirty spoon into the sink.

"Nope. Not yet," I said eyes roaming the area for something to do. It was good that Ted and I hadn't jumped into sex. Yes, we'd known each other for years, but whatever was eating at him and drawing him away was pissing me off. "He's mad at me about something, but he won't say what." I wrinkled my nose. What the heck was wrong with him?

"Already fighting?"

"Not fighting, he's just not talking much after last night's show."

"Heard it was a great show," she said, glancing back from her work.

"Thanks."

"Surprised you're here today. Didn't see you on the schedule." She looked down at her nails then brushed them on her apron.

"Weird, I was scheduled, but almost didn't make it. Hit a bunch of traffic on the way back from Scranton this morning."

Customers began to stream in, families large and small dressed up in their Sunday best. The salad bar was popular and I began to make trips to the walk in to get more refills for vegetables that were getting low. Jules kept the warm side stocked and I focused on the cold foods. Pat came out to check on us and asked if I could stay a couple more hours. I agreed. The light faded into darkness outside.

The stream of customers began to die down and Jules took her break. A blonde head popped under the sneeze shield, startling me. Kind of defeated the purpose of the shield.

"Hey, Daredevil," Dylan said with a grin. His blue eyes caught the light in a way that made them look almost teal. Beautiful.

"Hi. What are you doing here?" I asked, eyes wide. My heart did a little jig in my chest and I couldn't stop a smile from creeping to my face.

"Jay said you guys were short staffed and I needed a job." Oh my gosh, those blue eyes, so gorgeous. He walked around the bar and stood at the knee-high gate. "Permission to enter?"

"Granted," I said, withholding a giggle. He was tall, over 6 feet, and the gate looked like something he could easily step over.

"So, what do you do for fun around here?" He asked. Déjà vu.

"Seriously?" My eyebrow rose and my heartbeat quickened. "Thought you'd have it all figured out by now."

"Yeah, seriously," he frowned.

"Hike, read, do the band thing, there's really not a whole lot around here. It's a bit country." My mind blanked. Wait, did I do anything for fun?

"Hiking?" His lips spread in a big smile.

"There's a trail around the lake at the state park." The same park where we'd met.

"We should hang out sometime." He leaned close. I caught my breath. He smelled good.

"You wouldn't want to do that." I looked down and leaned back against the sink, nowhere to go.

"Why not?" He leaned back and sort of shrugged.

"I'm a loser." I met his eyes. It was true. Compared to my old self, in lots of ways, I was a loser.

"So am I. Come on, we could form a loser's club." Oh my, there it was again, a reference to one of my favorite books. What was his deal? He didn't look like the reading type.

"You don't look like a loser," I said. My eyes roamed his body as I crossed my arms and frowned. He looked like a popular football player. A golden athletic god to be worshipped from afar.

"Neither do you," he said quietly, leaning forward again. "Come on, give me your number."

"Sure," I said, drawing out the word. I grabbed the only paper I could find, a piece of brown paper towel and wrote down my number. He'd never call. Guys like him didn't call girls like me.

Pat called for him and he returned to the grill, stuffing the paper towel into his pocket. Weird guy. I appreciated the view as he walked away. Even in the uniform, he had a great body. Bulkier than Ted, but I knew it was muscle. He looked like someone who spent a lot of time in the sun and the gym. He had the body of an athlete, probably football. So not my type, not anymore.

I left work after 8:00, soon after Rob arrived. He let me know that he had tickets for an upcoming show and was really excited to be going. His hazel eyes glinted and danced as he pumped a fist in the air. During the shift, I'd heard Dylan and Jay talking about the Saturday show with coworkers. Of course, no one believed their tales of me being a sex goddess on stage, or whatever they were calling me. Most had seen me at small local shows, or Raif's private parties. Before this weekend, nobody had really seen the Siren. Me? I didn't feel the same raging sex appeal without the leather and stage makeup. I still felt like the same old shy Shell. How disappointing.

I pulled into the driveway to find dad's maroon AMC Eagle. Andy was home. I let myself in through the basement and walked up the dark stairs. Dad sat at the dining room table helping Andy with his math homework. I was grateful. Tired of my own math homework, I didn't have the patience to help Andy with his.

"How'd the shows go?" Dad asked.

"Pretty amazing. We've been invited to play at the manager's other club in a couple months. Pretty quick turnaround. We sold out."

"Sold out?"

"Yeah. Club was packed. They turned people away at the door. Pretty good for an opening band. The headliner sucked." Memories of the lead singer screaming and head banging to their odd punk rap mixture made me shake my head. Not to mention the green and orange outfit he'd been wearing. Yuck. "A couple of our songs are playing on KNXT, the college station."

"That's great!"

I nodded and joined them at the table.

"How's Shawn?" I asked Andy. He shrugged and continued working on his math problems, eyes never leaving the paper.

"How are things going with the boyfriend?" Dad asked. I raised an eyebrow, then squinted at Andy. He kept his eyes glued to his homework.

"He's upset about something. Not sure what. Didn't want to talk about it." Probably lots of things. It'd been a weird weekend.

"Try to work it out. Ted's a good guy. I want you to be happy." Dad's forehead furrowed, deep in thought.

"I'm not sure how to be happy," I admitted.

"Figure out what makes you happy and go for it."

"I'm trying." I hadn't found much that made me happy. I glommed on to what made others happy and gave it a try. I still hadn't found my key to happiness. Truth was, I wallowed in my misery. I'd gotten so used to being depressed that it was difficult to come out of it and see anything as positive.

"I need a shower, get some of this grease off me," I said as I turned toward the bathroom.

"Grease?" Dad laughed. "What grease?"

"Burger grease."

"That's not grease." Dad was a plumber. "Grease is what you get working on cars, motor parts, mechanical things that move, not food." He chuckled, shoulders shaking. He also worked on his classic '72 Mustang on weekends. He knew a thing or two about grease.

"I beg to differ. Anyway, I need to get this oily stuff off. It's gross." I stood up and headed back to my room to get a change of clothes. I wasn't sure dad would be there when I got out.

I hopped in the shower before it fully warmed and began scrubbing down. I washed my hair, scrubbing a delicious coconut smelling shampoo and conditioner through the strands. Having worked salad bar, the greasy burger smell was less pronounced than it had been working on the grill. I emerged from the shower, toweled off and dressed in pajamas. I wrapped myself in a pink terry robe, a gift from grandma, and combed out my hair and returned to the kitchen.

Dad sat at the table. He drank cola and motioned to a pizza box. My stomach growled.

"When did you order that?"

"Right before you got home," he said, gesturing for me to grab a slice.

"Wow, thanks," I said. I slid a piece onto a paper plate. I could have gotten take out from Norma's at 30% off with my employee's discount, but since I started working there, I couldn't bring myself to eat the food anymore. The smell of it turned my stomach. Pizza on the other hand may as well have been ambrosia. My mouth watered.

"I've got to hit the road. It's getting late. You should bring Ted up to visit. Your grandmother's excited to meet him."

"We'll see."

Dad stood and gave me an uncomfortable hug. He'd never been big on hugging. Andy chewed on pizza, legs swinging from the chair, toes scraping on the linoleum floor, his ADHD kicking in. I walked dad to the door and locked up behind him. We didn't expect mom home, so I was glad that Andy was there.

"No Ted?" Andy asked with a mouth full of pizza.

"Nope. Went right home. Besides, I had to go to work."

"Ugh, just like mom." He rolled his eyes.

"Not quite," I said with an unattractive snort. "Just a few hours." It wasn't like I had to work many unexpected shifts.

The phone rang. It was late for a phone call, almost 10:00. I picked up the receiver, expecting Ted.

"Hello?" I asked into the receiver.

"Can I talk to Shell?" Returned a male voice, not Ted's.

"This is Shell. Who's this?"

"Dylan."

I wanted to ask 'who?' But then I remembered Blondie. My heart sped up. He called? My hand grasped the receiver and I looked at my brother with apprehension.

"Didn't expect you to call." My heart in my throat, the words barely came out. I cleared my throat, holding the receiver away from my mouth.

"I said I would," he said. I could hear a smile in his voice.

"I didn't believe you." I twirled the long springy phone cord around my finger.

"So, you said. About hanging out, what are you doing tonight?"

"Homework." It was Sunday night, what else would I be

doing?

"We're going to a party. Want to go?" His smooth voice on the line was turning my knees to jelly. This was such bad timing. Why did he have to show up now?

"Um, no, that's ok." I looked at the clock and shook my head. "You know we have school tomorrow, don't you?"

"It'll be fine. Can I stop by on the way?"

"Am I on the way?" I asked, wondering where the party was.

"Sure."

He didn't know where I lived. I gave him the address and directions and we hung up. I figured whoever he was going with, probably Jay, would say no to stopping by on the way, and that would be that. He was odd. Just in case he wasn't pulling my leg, I changed from pajamas to regular clothes.

Andy went to bed, because it was a school night and he'd had a long day. He helped out at Shawn's farm with chores in the morning, then spent the afternoon playing video games. I was glad he'd showered before coming home. I used to hang out with Shawn's sister, Mary, and helping with chores usually meant time in the barn with the dairy cows.

After 11:00, as I watched music videos on MTV, there was a knock at the front door. I opened the door and found Dylan and Jay standing on the porch. I invited them in and showed them around. I brought them down to the basement so that we wouldn't disturb Andy. Jay went outside, leaving us alone. The next thing I knew, I heard the whiz of fireworks in the driveway. Not the best thing for a driveway filled with dry leaves, but whatever.

"My bedroom used to be down here," I said, pointing to the empty room across from the laundry room.

"I'm staying in the basement at Jay's house."

"Sounds cozy."

"It's got a bed."

I nodded. "Why are you here?"

"I want to get to know you. But," he said with a look out the basement door and nod of the head, "we need to get going."

I shrugged.

"See you in school," I said as I let him out the basement door and waved, watching them pile into a truck and drive away. I shook my head. Strange guy. I locked the basement door behind me before going back upstairs. They'd be so beat tomorrow morning. Probably hungover too. Who went to a party on Sunday night?

13

I made it to school early Monday morning and walked through the deserted hallway of red lockers to the Commons area. I sat in an abandoned corner and took out my new French novel, *l'Etranger*. I'd nearly finished it with only a couple of chapters left. Just as my mind started to understand the French effortlessly, the presence of someone standing next to me made me look up. Dylan grinned.

"What'cha reading?"

"Camus. In French." I showed him the cover.

"Sounds, um, interesting?"

"Reading it for French class. Independent study," I said. Frankly, it wasn't one I would have chosen on purpose. I would have preferred something by Victor Hugo or Guy de Maupassant. I mean, killing a person because the sun was shining like daggers into the eyes? Not a great excuse in my mind. There should be more motivation than that.

"Are you, like, smart or something?" he asked, eyes gleaming in the light as he grinned.

"Something." I smiled.

Bleached blonde hair jetted across the commons toward us as Stephanie grabbed Dylan from behind. I could almost hear her dry hair scratching the wind. "There you are!" She whined.

I raised a brow as he turned and hugged her back, picking her up and spinning her around. Interesting, but not so much.

She was a cheerleader after all. Born for each other. I stifled a snort with a fake cough but couldn't stop my eyes from rolling. Ted came toward us and I put my backpack on the floor to clear a spot. He sat next to me and leaned in, bumping me shoulder to shoulder.

"Ted, you remember Dylan?" Ted looked up at Dylan, assessing the tall athletic guy standing in front of us, football ho hanging from his arm. "He's new, a friend of Jay's."

"Nope." Accenting the p with a popping noise. Sax case between his legs, he leaned his knee against my leg. "Hi, I'm Ted," he said with a nod.

"Dylan." His eyes drifted to mine.

"Come on, Dylan. Let's go!" Stephanie simpered, dragging him toward the football team. He looked back at me, shrugging in a what can you do gesture. I wondered how they knew each other, then wondered if I really cared.

"Do you have time for extra practice this week so we can be ready for the next gig?" Ted asked. I frowned at the question.

"I'm only scheduled to work Wednesday night. I didn't take extra shifts this week so we could practice more."

"Awesome." He drew out in a low growl, hooking his arm around mine and leaning back. I reclined and look up at the recessed lighting. "Listened to our recording from the weekend."

"Yeah? Thoughts?"

"Focus on your dancing." He laughed.

"Hey, that wasn't on the recording." I play punched him and couldn't help laughing with him.

"Your voice is amazing." He looked at me. "Seriously you're getting better, just remember to stay loose and have more eye contact with the audience."

"Anything else?"

"Yeah, but more for the other guys than you." He raised a hand and I looked in the direction of his eyes to see Zane, Tara, and Barry walking our way. "Speaking of."

"Practicing tonight?" Zane asked.

"Yes! Tara, you going to come check us out?" I looked to Tara.

"Nah, I've got to take photos of cheerleading practice tonight for the paper. I'll catch the Saturday show." She flipped her curly gold-brown hair behind her shoulder with a flick of the wrist. She tilted her head to the right, looking at me and Ted, brow furrowing. "'Kay. See ya later." She pecked Zane's cheek and joined the gaggle of cheerleaders standing next to the gym.

I nervously rubbed at my scarred arm. "So, what's the plan this week? I'm working Wednesday night, but otherwise I'm free."

"We should get together whenever you're not working. Anyone have other plans?" Zane looked around. The guys shook their heads.

"Shell, is your mom cool with us using your garage this week?"

"May have to keep the amps down, but sure. She's been working crazy mixed shifts."

"That's fine. How early can we show up?"

"5:00?"

"You guys ok with that?" Zane asked. The guys nodded. "Great. It's a plan."

The first bell rang and we split up for class. I felt eyes on my back as I hugged Ted and kissed his cheek. I turned to see Dylan walking my way.

"Where's your next class?" He asked, walking at my side.

"Where's Stephanie?"

"She's got Gym."

"I've got Study Hall in the Cafeteria, lots of Precalculus to catch up on."

"Cool, my class is close, I'll walk with you."

"If you want." I hitched my backpack more securely onto my shoulder and continued walking.

"Precalculus, reading books in French. You really are smart." He nudged my arm.

"Total nerd," I said, nodding.

"Yet so much more." He faced me with a raised brow, "thought you didn't have a boyfriend."

"I do. I just don't call him my boyfriend," I said with a shrug. I still hadn't come up with a term to adequately define what I had with Ted. It was complicated and the new phase of our relationship was evolving.

"That guy? Tom, was it?"

"Ted. He's my bass player, best friend, boyfriend."

"You spend a lot of time with him?"

"Yes, all my free time." I held back a snicker.

"Does he know he's not your boyfriend?"

"He's a boy and my friend. We're dating. I'm just not big on the word "boyfriend." Why is everyone so concerned about labels?" I stopped outside of my classroom. "Here I am. You better hurry. You'll be late for class." There weren't any classrooms near the cafeteria besides the gym.

Labels, labels, why so concerned with labels?
Tease me, tease me, my desires freeze me.
Shattered, I'm stronger than most.
Can't let these walls down, unwilling host.

I know your type, conquer and leave.
All those tricks up your sleeve
Use those labels to amuse

Labels mean nothing, hold no promises
Lead to broken souls and dead kisses.
You promise a future with each gaze,
Then you with her, doesn't cease to amaze.

I knew your type, conquer and leave
No more tricks up your sleeve
Used those labels to abuse

Twisted and broken I knew from the start
You'd leave me alone with a black heart.
Labels, they change, why must we define
Heart's desires, you have yours, I had mine.

Labels!
No more labels!
No more labels!

Aaron sat next to me in study hall, tapping his pencil on the table. His leg bounced and I wondered how much caffeine he'd had today. He pulled out a notebook and leaned forward.

"Monica wanted me to pass along she's having a get together at her place Thursday. Want to come? She'd love to see you," he said as he doodled on lined paper.

"Depends on the time and how long practice takes."

"I think there'll be people at her place pretty late. I'm staying over. Her parents leave for Spain tomorrow and won't be back until next Sunday."

"That's cool that they trust her on her own for that long." Elbow on table, I leaned my head on my hand. My head too heavy to hold itself up, I was tired.

"Yours wouldn't?" His eyebrows rose in surprise.

"Heck no!" The study hall monitor looked over with disapproval, eyebrows furrowed and eyes narrowed. "My mom doesn't like leaving us alone for an evening," in a lower voice. "Although I have been gone a lot. Andy's been by himself a ton lately. Poor kid."

"I saw you and Ted this morning looking pretty close."

"Yeah, in a physical sense. Neat, huh? With his touching thing, I'd say progress."

"Are you interested in him or something?" Aaron leaned closer, voice low.

"I like him a lot. We're kind of going out. He's been my best friend for a while, you know. We have a lot of fun together. We work well together creatively and that's awesome."

"Be careful. Looked like he's getting attached, and not in a just friend's way."

"Yeah, that's the point of dating." I doodled in my notebook. "Used to seem like guy friends were easier than female ones. You're just complicated in different ways."

"You're just not paying attention," he said with a smirk.

"What should I pay attention to?" I leaned in, wanting all the advice I could get.

"You catch him looking at you when you're not talking about anything." He counted off on a finger. "Um, he moves closer when he talks to you." He ticked off another finger. "He physically touches you when talking. Leans close, pulls you in when there's another guy nearby, kind of protectively."

"Sounds like stuff a friend might do. Well, crap, I do those things to my friends." I looked at him. "What if more than one guy does this?" My stomach churned.

"I guess you'd have to make some decisions. May want to rethink the signals you're giving off." His brow furrowed, "are you interested in any of these other guys?"

"I may feel certain ways around certain guys, but it's confusing."

"You're interested in more than one," he said with a nod and a tap of his pen.

"Maybe." I groaned and dropped my head into my hands.

Mr. Seagram, in standard foul mood, stood at the podium adjusting musical scores into an order. I held my flute on my lap waiting for instructions and stared blankly at the music folder. He announced the afternoon's song order and opened the first score as we shuffled our sheet music into order. He held up the conductor wand for us to ready our instruments, counted to 3 and we began our 3/4 melody. As usual, he stopped early, although we made it almost halfway through the song this time. He wanted to hear the French horns and trombones. It always amazed me that he could tell which instruments were messing up. I was so wrapped up in playing my own part that I couldn't tell.

I slouched into the chair, focused on my part and played along silently with the French horn and trombone as they tried to correct whatever was going wrong. My eyes briefly shifted up and I saw Juan staring at me from the clarinet section. I averted my eyes as Aaron's words ran through my head and sank further into my chair so that I couldn't see over the stand. I craved a protective touch right about now.

I sat up straight and raised my flute as Mr. Seagram told us to resume at measure 24. We made it to the end this time and moved on to the next song. Felt like a half-hearted practice today. His emphatic gesturing was tight and confined today. He didn't yell or throw his wand at us. We made it through all songs but one before the bell rang. I grabbed my things and turned to Ted and Zane.

"I'll see you at my place in a bit ok?"

"See you there," Ted said with a nod and a side hug.

As I walked out the door into the parking lot, a warm hand

touched the small of my back and slid around my side casually. I jumped a little at the unfamiliar touch. Dylan glanced down at me. I raised an eyebrow in response to his overly familiar touch.

"Hey, let me walk you to your car." He swiveled his head around quickly surveying the people exiting the building.

"Sure, but what's up?"

"Trying to avoid Stephanie." He looked around acting nervous. I knew it was an act for my benefit, but I played along, laughing on the inside.

"Why?" I said with quirked lip and brow.

"She's really, uh, how can I describe it… perky."

"Not how I'd describe her, but ok," I said, continuing to smirk.

"Plans tonight?" His voice light and questioning.

"Practicing with the guys most of the week to get ready for the upcoming shows."

"Right, what about after?"

"Not sure how long we'll be working." Not to mention I might spend time with Ted after practice.

"Call me after?" Hope hid behind his stunning blue eyes.

"Don't have your number," I said with a shrug.

"Thought you might say that." He handed me a folded piece of paper. I shouldn't have said anything. I tucked it in my pocket, having no intention of using it. I mean, Stephanie. Stephanie?

"Thanks. Hopefully we won't be too late. We're kind of loud and it won't go over well with the neighbors."

"It's ok. I'm a night owl," he said with a wink.

"Talk to you later." I unlocked the car and got in. He walked away as I backed out of the spot and drove away.

Mom reclined in the living room watching television when I got home. I dropped my backpack on a dining room chair. Andy sat on the loveseat making his usual odd unconscious noises.

"Hi mom. The guys are coming over for practice in a bit."

"Ok, honey."

"We'll be practicing almost all week. Except Wednesday, because I'm working after school."

"Sounds fine. I may be home. My schedule's posted on the fridge, but you know how it can change." She sighed and took a sip of her beverage, ice clinking in the glass.

Ted knocked on the door and mom let him in with a glint in her eye. "Hi, Ted. Good to see you." She gave me a wink and dorky thumbs up behind his back.

"Talked to Zane and they're on the way," he said

"Excited about the upcoming shows?" Mom asked Ted.

"Yes, ma'am." He gave me a side hug and hung on to my shoulder. "They're going to be awesome. Shell is amazing. Have you heard her lately? She just keeps getting better."

"She's good, huh?"

"Aww, you're making me blush." I gave Ted a shove and he released my shoulder. "Let's go to the garage and get set up. Want some water?" He nodded and I grabbed a couple bottled waters before we headed downstairs.

"Gotta get the bass." He walked out the basement door and returned with his black Fender.

He plugged the bass into the amp, turned it on, slung the bass over his head and across his shoulder. Beginning slowly, he played some basic riffs and transitioned into arpeggios and scales. I picked up my candy apple red electric Luna and played some scales before launching into random chords. I found a progression I liked and switched to finger picking, my preferred method. I started humming as Ted joined in. I tried out some of my *Labels* lyrics as we faced each other, jamming, when Zane and Barry walked in. They stood at the door for a moment before coming in and sitting down with their instruments.

I put my guitar down, still messing with the lyrics and tune, having figured out a chorus that I liked, and headed over to the work bench to grab a pencil and write down some notes and chord progressions. I tapped my pencil as I hummed, and Bear started drumming along with my pencil before adding fancier beats. I took the pencil and paper back to my stool and placed them on a music stand before picking up my guitar again. I joined the guys with my guitar and started messing with the lyrics and melody. Zane quickly picked up the chord progression by ear and did some improv. Ted got the recorder running. After about 30 minutes, we'd worked out a rough version of the song and were able to play it from start to finish. I added in some growl for the ending chorus. Not perfect, but something new.

"We could work this into the weekend shows," Zane smiled widely. It's kind of angry Shell. I like the screaming."

"Yeah, who pissed you off?" Barry looked from me to Ted.

"Wasn't me. I don't think?" Ted's eyes widened. He had irritated me over the weekend, distancing himself as he had.

"No, not Ted." I winked at him. "So, Ted had some ideas based on our session last week."

"Were those suggestions about your dancing?" The guys laughed. Hard.

"Well," I turned red, "he did tell me to keep working on it."

"Please don't! They'll run from the building and stampede each other to death. We need more fans, not fewer." Zane held his stomach and bent over trying to breathe.

"Yeah, yeah. Ted, you want to share?" I turned to him, hands on hips as my guitar swung with my movements.

"Zane, you missed your solo cue on the first punk number and Bear slowed down when the rest of us were keeping up. The song is fast. It doesn't change tempo."

"Was that it?" Barry looked up tapping a stick on his fingers.

"No, but that needs more work than the other stuff." He looked at all of us. "Let's practice that next, then try *Storm*. Might be able to use that with some of our covers."

Zane counted off and we got through the punk cover twice, sounding all right. I'd been working on *Storm*, again practicing some screaming and high-pitched wailing. Ted called for time out after the second chorus and looked at me.

I feel it getting closer
Each day darker than the last
We're heading for skies overcast
As the storm gets closer

Can you hear the thunder?
On the distant shore
Come to rip my heart asunder
As I grow to love you more
My emotions you will plunder

141

Until I reach the distant shore

Will I breathe again
Once the storm has passed
Taken away my love at last
Heal this dreadful pain

Can you hear the thunder?
On the distant shore
Come to rip my heart asunder
As I grow to love you more
My emotions you will plunder
Until I reach the distant shore

It's a dark storm
Coming to wash it all away
Take it all away

"What if at the end of the first chorus, instead of going up in pitch, you keep it lower. In the second chorus, raise a couple pitches. I think it'll give it more punch," Ted suggested. I nodded. "Let's try it again." Barry counted off and we played. Ted was right, it did sound better to mix it up like that. We made it to the end, where I landed a high wail.

"Better." Ted looked pleased. "Zane, did you have a set list for us yet?"

"I'll bring one tomorrow. How do you feel about adding in our oldie *You Suck*? Too juvenile?" Zane assessed our reactions.

"I'm ok with that. It's probably good to play as much of our own stuff as possible. Start removing the covers. Might be one of our first creations, but we can start with it before people are really listening, you know?" I suggest.

"I agree, play it early and follow with a newer number and it'll be fine." Barry adds.

"Not our best, but wouldn't hurt playing it early." Ted nods. "The fans used to like it."

"Or it could be an encore number. Leave 'em with energy. We good for tonight?" I asked. The others nodded. They packed up and I put my guitar down on the stand.

I walked them out, gave hugs all around and watched Barry and Zane drive away. Ted stayed behind, arm around my shoulders. "Thanks for the suggestions. They were really helpful." I looked up at him, under the blinding glow of the flood light.

"Andy will be hanging around this week," I said. "He may check out a practice."

"Really? That's cool. He's a funny kid."

"Sometimes." I thought about the earlier near-incident with mom due to my brother's big mouth. "When he's not running his mouth about my boyfriends."

"You have boyfriends?" His brows rose comically. "Like, more than one? What is this, Utah?"

"That's backwards, it's the men that get multiple wives. The ladies don't get more than one man, and they have to share. Totally unfair."

Ted laughed and kissed my forehead. "I'll see you tomorrow."

"Uh… ok. See ya." Well, that was new. I scowled at the butterflies in my stomach. I stood in the basement doorway and watched him drive away. Things had been off since Scranton. He'd been distancing himself. Was he not interested anymore? I missed his kisses.

"Shell!" Mom called from the covered porch.

"Yeah?"

"Phone call."

"Be right there." I went back inside, locking the door behind me and turning off lights as I hurried back upstairs. I took the phone from the counter. "Hello?"

"Shell?"

"Yes?"

"It's Dylan."

"I'm starting to recognize your voice. I thought I was supposed to call you." I sighed as I leaned against the retro 70's kitchen island in all its brown and orange glory.

"I was worried you wouldn't."

"You may know me better than I think you do." I held back a yawn, suddenly tired.

"Done with practice?"

"Just finished." My fingers played with the phone cord, stretching and releasing the coils.

"Ted gone?"

"Yes, the guys are gone, why?" I stood up and inhaled a deep breath.

"I overheard your mom saying something to your brother about your boyfriend staying behind."

"Yes, Ted's my boyfriend." At least, I thought Ted was my boyfriend.

"Keep saying that, you might believe it one day." I heard irritation over the line.

"Huh - what?" My forehead scrunched and my eyebrows drew together.

"How many dates have you been on recently?"

"A couple." My tone rose slightly at the end, almost a question.

"I was hoping we could hang out sometime," he said. I could almost hear the smile in his voice.

"Not sure that's a good idea," I said. I knew it wasn't a good idea.

"I think it's a great idea."

"I hardly know you." My eyes sought out recognizable shapes in the random patterns on the countertop. I traced the brown veins with my fingertip.

"Don't you want to?"

"I think I might." I felt heat deep in my gut as my heart beat faster. I knew I did. I also knew I should steer clear.

"I want to know you," he said, voice low.

"You sure?" He didn't know what he was asking for.

"Yes, I'm sure. Give me a chance."

"I don't trust easily," I said, thinking there had already been plenty of clues not to trust him already.

"I sense that." He laughed. "So, you're closing at Norma's on Wednesday, right?"

"Yeah."

"Me too. Could we spend some time together after?"

"Hold on," I looked at mom's schedule on the fridge and saw an evening shift highlighted. "Uh, yeah, I should be able to do that." She should be home soon after my shift ended.

"Great. I'll see you at school tomorrow." His tone upbeat, I worried he'd soon be disappointed by me.

"See you. Bye." I hung up and sat down at the dining room table, pulling out my homework.

"Who was that, honey?" Mom asks, bringing a dirty dish to the sink.

"This guy, Dylan. He's new at school and work."

"Just be careful. Would hate for someone to come between you and Ted. He's such a nice and talented young man."

"Yeah, he's great. I hope we'll be friends for a long time." I realized I'd just called Ted a friend, not my boyfriend.

The more I thought about seeing Dylan at work on Wednesday, the more wired I got. I couldn't stop thinking and I couldn't get to sleep. I felt guilty. That meant I was doing something wrong. I hated being wrong. I sat at my desk, leaning my head on an arm, pencil hovering over a piece of paper. I let my hand write and doodle whatever came to mind. My eyes drifted to the glowing red numbers on the alarm clock. It read 3:35 AM. I decided that it would be better to at least try to lie down. I flipped the light switch and stumbled over to the bed and stared at the dark ceiling.

I practiced breathing in deeply and out slowly. I tried to let my muscles relax, visualizing them sinking into the bed, heavy and warm. My thoughts kept rushing between Ted and Dylan. I didn't know Dylan, but I had an intense physical reaction to him. I could feel him looking at me from far away, like an actual connection, a line that pulled me to him. When Dylan was near, I had to restrain myself because I just wanted to reach out and touch him. Anxiety rode me like a wave and I struggled, but I was caught in a line that just kept tangling around my internal organs, squeezing my heart and guts until I could barely breathe. Dylan was a dangerous unknown. I didn't know what to expect and it scared me.

Ted had been my friend since moving to the Poconos two years ago. He'd been a reliable and stable friend, kind. Took a while to get to where we were and chip away at that personal force field that he used to keep others away. I didn't want that barrier to shoot back into place. I'd hate his absence in my life even more. We were good together, creative partners, comfortable. I loved being close to him. There was something there. Definitely friendship and something more? I knew that I felt safe with him. Was I attracted to him? Yes. He was attractive in a unique artist kind of way. I always thought he was cute and goofy. I didn't want to lose him.

I also wanted to see if there was something with Dylan, if anything. Give it a chance. At the least, he'd expressed an interest, and God, he was so hot. I didn't think I could trust him and that really bothered me. And, he was friends with Jay. I wasn't liking Jay so much these days. Jay had always been questionable. Then there was that darned bleach blonde bitch Stephanie. Ugh. Handsy bitch.

14

When I got to school in the morning, Dylan greeted me with a hug and we sat on the steps in front of the auditorium, across from the principal's office. My heart beat faster when I saw Ted standing at the far end of the Commons. He walked over and sat on my other side.

"Hey, man, what's up?" Ted nodded a greeting to Dylan.

"We were just talking about hanging out after work tomorrow," Dylan said. I swallowed, hard.

"Hanging out?" Ted's voice cracked and he cleared his throat.

"Yeah, we're hanging out after work tomorrow." Dylan smiled at me. I wanted to punch him and cover his mouth. "So, coffee?"

"Don't drink it, but I could drink something else. Janelle's Cafe is near work. They're open 'til midnight."

"That works."

Bear joined us, eyes flitting between the three of us, sitting oddly close.

"Barry, you know Dylan?" Ted said flatly.

"No." Barry looked at Dylan then at Ted, sitting next to me, holding my hand, leg leaned against mine. "Um," holding a hand out, "Barry. I play drums for Toxic Siren."

"Saw you at the show," Dylan said with a grin.

"They're hanging out after work tomorrow," Ted said in monotone, looking at me.

"Hi, I'm Zane," he held out a hand. Dylan shook it, from the looks of it rather firmly.

"Dylan."

"How do you know Shell?" Zane's odd inquisition began. I gave him a dirty look, but he stood and waited for an answer.

"Met through a mutual friend and we work together," Dylan stated, referring to Jay.

"You don't look like the usual type she hangs out with. Interesting," Zane said, tapping a finger against his lip.

"What's her usual type?" Dylan asked with widened eyes.

"Dark and psychotic." Zane looked at me, a question in his eyes.

"You never know." I said quietly, thinking about Joe.

With a couple hours before the band was due at the house, I took a trip to the lake to clear my head. I sat on the sand and watched the water roll in and out along the shore. A few ducks swam nearby calling out in melancholy quacks. Alone on the beach, I leaned back letting my hair flow free in the cool breeze. The edges brushed the sand, stirring a small cloud into the air. My eyes closed. I took a deep breath of cool damp air. The fishy smell of the lake calmed my troubled mind. I opened my eyes to the gray clouds above, enjoying the subdued light. Rain threatened, but didn't come.

I leaned forward, picking up my notebook and pencil, and began to write, smirk pulling on my lips. Dark and psychotic, huh? I suppressed a laugh and a light snort escaped.

Standing in the smoke-filled room
Your eyes burn me, I'm in a tomb
I'm burning, feeling the ache
Desire, dark and deep

You're just my type
Dark and psychotic
Chains and leather

I fell back into the sand, laughing. I did like leather. Since the accident, my crushes had dark hair and darker eyes, not Joe. He'd been a redhead with green eyes and freckles. It was more accurate to say that since the accident, I'd gone for the broody type. Before Ted, it was Carlo. Black hair, nearly black eyes, and olive skin. Italian. Leather jacket, black tees, pants, and boots. Mr. Monochrome to my Ms. Monochrome. I own a lot of black. And plaid flannel. I might mix it up more now, but then, I wore a lot of black and dark lipstick against my vampire white skin. I was 16, He was 19. He was squeamish about the age difference at first, but I was tenacious. I pursued him, and I conquered. Despite his looks, he was timid, a poser, disappointing. I broke him. He was right, I chewed people up and spit them out. I wasn't a nice person.

Depression set in as my thoughts turned to my effect on people, I stood with notebook in hand, picked up my things and walked back to my car distracted by thoughts. An 80s band with a driving beat played when I started the car. I sang along as I drove home. Ted waited in the driveway as I pulled in.

I got out of the car, rubbing my scarred arm before closing the car door. A cold front was blowing in. My arm ached like this when the weather changed. He pulled his bass and an acoustic guitar out of his car.

"Thought I'd get here a little early so we could work on something."

"Sure. Come on in" I unlocked the basement door. Andy hadn't come home yet because of an afterschool sports practice. Mom was late because she'd taken him to practice and to watch. He usually just took the late activity bus. We walked through the dark laundry room and I flipped the switch to the garage lights. They flickered before lighting up.

Ted sat on a stool and started tuning his acoustic guitar.

"Sometimes I forget you play guitar too."

He looked at me. "I'm hurt." He pouted, beautiful full lips drawing down, and held a hand to his chest. "I'm, like, a serious musician. I play a lot of instruments. And mix tracks."

"Ah, yes, I remember now." He not only played a lot of instruments. He was good. I mean, really good. Almost prodigy good. "How do your parents feel about being away for the weekend?"

"They're supportive of the shows. Not really happy about the hotel stays."

"I hear you. My mom wasn't happy about that either. Are they upset you're missing work this weekend?"

"Nah, my uncle's covering for me."

"That's good. We sharing a room next time?"

"No. I think we should put the brakes on. Just for a while."

"Oh," I said, hurting, an ache building in my chest and gut. Did Ted just break up with me? Then again, I'd basically accepted a date with another guy.

Ted started playing something pretty. He began crooning a slow melody. I didn't get to hear him sing much. His voice was mellow, nice, a tenor. I sat down on the stool next to his. It was one of his original songs, a new one. A ballad, not really a love song, but slow.

I've been down this weary road
I've been empty so long
Never taking what's owed
Giving it away for a song
I've always got you on my mind
But wonder if you'll find
A way to rise above

Rise above the pain
Above the rage that turns
Those tears that rain
Will you rise above
The painful heart that burns
Rise above it all
Till you see me

It's been a long time feeling down
I'm waiting on your call
I'm getting tired of this frown
And always giving you my all
And I wonder if you'll find
A way to rise above

Rise above the pain
Above the rage that turns
Those tears that rain
Will you rise above
The painful heart that burns
Rise above it all
Till you see me

He ended the song and looked up at me.

"What do you think?"

"I like it. What do you call it?"

"*Rise Above*. Thought we might make it a duet." He handed me some notes with lyrics.

I grabbed the extra mic and set up the stand for him. "Let's give it a go." He interpreted his notes for me, pointing out our parts. He started playing and sang the first verse, nodding at me to cue the chorus, and I joined in. Our voices intertwined in a beautiful harmony. I sang the next verse as we gazed at each other. He smiled as we got into the second chorus together and continued through the final verse and chorus together.

"Beautiful," I breathed. He nodded, looking down at his guitar.

"Again?"

"Yeah."

We were on our third attempt when the guys walked in, stopping at the door to listen. They clapped loudly as we finished. Startled, I dropped my pick and looked at them.

"Nice!" Barry grasped his hands in front of his chest.

"Yeah! You guys are seriously prolific this week!" Zane smiled widely.

"The muses are kind." I grumbled, then smiled. "That was Ted's."

"We need that in the show. An acoustic, no-screaming number, just you two." Zane pulled out copies of the set list and handed them around.

"I'll work on memorizing the lyrics." I thought about the other two new songs we'd be doing and wondered when I'd have the time to memorize and practice three new songs before our next gig. I knew we had to use Ted's song. It was better than either of mine.

"Sure." Ted grinned.

"And you should do it just like that. Sitting on stools close together. You guys looked intense." Barry interjected.

"Yeah, way better than Shell's dancing." Zane snickered.

"I'm working on it." I whined.

Zane sang a line from an old disco number in falsetto. Yeah, I was dance royalty alright. I rolled my eyes and laughed.

We ran through our entire set list, placing R*ise Above* second to last and *Labels* last. Seemed a good idea to leave with energy. I glanced at the clock and saw that the set took 42 minutes. Not bad. Looked like I wouldn't have much audience interaction after all. I wondered if Zane might interact for me, since he was the people person.

"What're you guys up to tonight?" I asked.

"Homework." Zane and Barry said in unison and laughed.

"What's up with that Dylan guy?" Zane asked me, eyeing Ted.

"No idea." I said, exasperated. A faint smile drew at my lips as a mental image of him standing next to me at the lake flittered through my head.

"I thought I saw him with Stephanie and the football team the other day," Zane said.

"Uh huh," I nodded, thinking about her poofed up hair, grating voice, and acne.

"She's the football 'ho." Bear reminded me.

"I know," I said with a shrug and a snort.

"Like, more than half the team 'ho," Zane said. Not to mention the basketball team, I thought in an uncharitable way.

"Yeah. I think he played football at his old school. I guess she wants him to get to know the guys here," I said, guessing at her motivation.

"Seemed kind of clingy yesterday," Zane said, tone full of sarcasm.

"She di-i-id." I drew out.

"Jealous?" Zane raises an eyebrow.

I cleared my throat and looked away.

"And I thought he wasn't your type." Zane grabbed his drum sticks. "Anyway, me and Barry need to go."

"Don't joke about that," I said. "Ted's my boyfriend."

Ted cleared his throat and packed up his bass. Well, he had been.

Ted stayed behind to help me work on stage presence. We brought the boom box down to the basement, mumbling hellos to mom and Andy who had returned from team practice while we ran through our set. We returned to the garage and Ted set up the stereo, starting up our demo CD as he sat in front of me on a stool.

I stood in front of the mic, looking at him and glancing around the garage, pretending there was an audience. "We're Toxic Siren and we're super excited to be here tonight at Club Neon!" I left my guitar on the stand and started singing along to the demo and swayed to the music behind the mic. Ted stood and walked up behind me. I continued singing, holding the mic in my right hand, leaving it on the stand. He placed his hands on my shoulders and pressed down.

"Relax your shoulders. They're ear level." He whispered in my ear as he squeezed them in a light massage. I leaned back into him and started to relax. He took my left arm lightly in his hands and shook it. "Loosen up. Let your arm hang down and let it move with your body." He stepped back and returned to the imaginary audience area.

"Try to make eye contact with at least one person in each region." He sat, head bobbing with the music, foot tapping. The song ended and he clapped. "Better."

"At the beginning, when you introduce the band, say a bit more. Also, you started off talking really quiet. You're excited to be there - you need to act like it. Think cheerleader style and pump a fist or something." This brought to mind Stephanie and I frowned.

"Cheerleader, huh? You sure that fits with our image?" I asked, thinking about my Siren persona. She wasn't exactly cheerleader material, she oozed sexuality, not cheer.

"It'll have to do for now. Got to get their attention. Maybe end with a "woo" or something too." He flicked his hand in a dismissive gesture, as if that were no big deal.

"Woo?" What the heck was a "woo"?

"You know, that high pitched, 'wooooo!' that people call out when they're excited at football games and stuff." Now I was thinking about Dylan's abs. I shook my head.

"Ok, woo! Like that?" I asked after sort of screaming it out and jabbing a stiff fist in the air.

"Yeah, but louder. Let's practice stuff you can do with slower songs, especially ones where you don't play guitar. Remember, keep your shoulders and arms relaxed." With a serious look, "now add in some hip movement, sway with the beat. When you're about to sustain a note, grab the mic with both hands and turn your head to the left, well, pick a side." He started up the music again, a cover of one of the new grunge bands' songs about daddy issues.

I started to sway, looking down as I sang, feeling self-conscious. My hair fell forward and covered my face. I felt warm hands pulling my hair back behind my shoulders. "Head up." He instructed. "Watch your shoulders." He again placed his hands on my shoulders. "Now the mic, both hands and turn." I sustained, turning my head. His hands slid down to my hips and he whispered in my ear, "more hips, relax." He guided me, turning me around to face him. "Rise and fall a little with the hip movements and add in some steps." Ted demonstrated and lifted my arms around his neck. He placed his hands on my waist. We continued to move. "See, like you're dancing."

"Shell!" mom's voice called from upstairs and I caught my breath.

"Yeah, mom?"

"Dylan's on the phone."

"I'll call him back." I looked at Ted, realized we were still holding each other, I let my arms slip down his chest and back to my sides. "Thanks."

"Well, I gotta go. You're getting... better." He looked at me, picked up his bass and acoustic guitar and walked out the door.

"Dylan?" I spoke into the line. He made me nervous and I played with the phone cord, twisting the little rings around my pointer finger. It was an annoying habit that sometimes tangled up the cord. Drove mom nuts when she had to fix it.

"Hi, Shell." It sounded like he was smiling. I could see the image clearly in my mind.

"What's up?" A smile formed on my own lips, hearing him speak my name.

"Wanted to hear your voice."

"We'll see each other tomorrow." I chuckled, feeling it absurd that he couldn't wait a matter of hours to hear my voice.

"Just wanted to hear your voice." He confirmed. Well, alright.

"It's nice to hear your voice too." I admitted, heat burning my cheeks.

"So, I was thinking about what your friend said this morning…" He started and I immediately began to wonder which friend he was talking about and what had they said.

"What thing are you thinking about?" I asked, heart beating faster.

"Your type. Dark and psychotic." His tone lowered and I giggled. Wow, I actually giggled, like a girl. Crap.

"I wouldn't exactly agree with him." I had the phone cradled between ear and shoulder as I rubbed my scars. I'd been trying to push Dylan away, and now felt anxious that he might be drawing away.

"So, dark and psycho?" He asked again.

"There were only two and they may have looked dark, but only in looks. Psycho is relative." My voice drifted as thoughts of Carlo floated into my brain. He'd been a little possessive, had issues with breaking up, and some stalking behaviors. Did that qualify as psycho? Perhaps. Ted wasn't psycho, but at times was dark and broody.

"Relative?" He asked for clarity.

"I'm not a nice person. I'm more psycho than any of the guys ever were." I explained. My opinion of myself was pretty low, especially since the accident. I had traumatic brain injury, amnesia, and nerve damage. I'd been on lots of psych meds for a while. I thought that qualified as a little clinically psycho.

I heard nervous laughter on the other end, "You don't seem so bad."

"Looks can be deceiving," I said, voice flat.

"So, what's the story with the last guy?"

"Before Ted? Not that interested, and I was the villain." As in, I wasn't that interested after finding there was no chemistry, and he decided I was the villain when I tried to break up with him. I really didn't want to talk about Carlo, but now he was running through my mind.

"I'm definitely interested now," his voice strong and conspiratorial.

"Ok, but you have to tell me about your last girlfriend too. Quid pro quo."

"Squid what?"

"You know what I'm talking about," I said. He wasn't as stupid as he liked to play. "Basically, I give, you give. An exchange of information," I clarified. There was a certain cunning behind those eyes of his that I'd caught glimpses of in our short exchanges.

"Deal."

"Carlo lived a couple of blocks over. I knew he was a senior, I was a sophomore. He drove a motorcycle, had the leather jacket and boots, wore black. My vision of a cool guy. He didn't talk much, was a loner."

"Sounds like the typical bad boy," he interjected.

"That's what I thought. I started to really watch him. I'd go over to his house and talk to him as he worked on his bike. Made my intentions of going out with him clear. He was really concerned about my age, being sixteen while he was 19. I got kind of stalkerish until he agreed weeks later. I quickly realized he wasn't nearly as awesome as I expected. I had to make all the moves. He wouldn't even hold my hand for a month." I shivered remembering how I'd been the initiator of the whole ordeal.

"Wow, what a weirdo." That was putting it mildly.

"Finally got him to kiss me and it was so awful I decided he wasn't for me." I sighed." He had a totally different experience, and thought we were meant for each other."

"Then what happened?" He prodded.

"I broke it off. Told him we weren't going to work. Then stalker became the stalked. He wouldn't stop calling and watching my house. I'd find him in random places I'd be. The mall, outside a doctor's office, even at my brother's soccer game once."

"Creepy."

"Yeah." I paused. "I'd had enough. He came up to me in the hall at school one day and kissed me. Hard. Jay was there. I stomped his foot, kneed his groin, and punched him in the face. Broke his nose. Told him to leave me alone. We were over and I wasn't changing my mind. I got suspended."

"Harsh," Dylan said with a long laugh. The situation had been scary, not particularly funny.

"I told you I'm not a nice person. I couldn't shake the feeling he needed a strong message. Seemed like things were escalating and I was worried. Luckily, he graduated and went off to college in August."

"You think you're dark and psycho?" He asked. His voice had gone quiet again.

"I know I am," I said, thinking about a variety of things that made me both dark and psycho.

"I want to kiss you so bad," he said. How random.

"Huh?" I froze, phone cord hanging from my hand.

"What would you do if I came over tonight to kiss you?" He had to be joking.

"Wouldn't you like to know… Seems like a long drive for that." I said, doubtful. He may have a little crazy in him after all.

It was around 10:00 when I hung up with Dylan. I settled at the dining room table to do my homework. Mom walked in and sat down across from me. She looked at my arm, seeing the skin pink from rubbing.

"Everything ok, Shell?"

"Yeah, I'm fine."

"You sure?"

"Yeah, just stressed about the shows." I shrugged. "We just added a third new song to the set. Ted brought a really awesome ballad in. We're going to do it as an acoustic duet."

"That sounds like a change from your normal sound," mom said, touching my hand.

"I know, but it's a really good song." My eyes met hers as I smiled.

"What I could hear from up here sounded good tonight."

"Thanks."

"Dylan mentioned something about a date when he called.

Asked if it'd be ok to borrow you tomorrow night after work." Her brow furrowed. "I told him yes, but you know how I feel about you going out when I'm not home. On a school night too, and I thought you were seeing Ted. What's going on with that?"

I look at her, surprised, "You're ok with it? Hanging out after work on a school night?" My eyes widened and I took a deep breath. "I'm not sure what's up with Ted. He's been distancing himself since we got back from the shows. Said we need to slow it down for now."

"This time. I'm ok with it this time." She looked toward the living room. "Andy and I talked earlier and he's really growing up. He'll be fine until I get home."

I got up and hugged her. "Thanks mom!"

"I really appreciate all that you two do. I know I'm not home much these days." She got serious, "just make sure to keep the communication open. I want to know what you're doing."

"Yes, mother."

"Ok, I'll let you get back to your homework. I'm going to catch some z's. Tomorrow's a long day."

I opened my Chemistry book and got out the study guide to work on the practice questions. I briefly thought of Marcus' empty chair before I began balancing formulas. I quickly finished the sheet and moved on to my French novel. Tomorrow, I'd meet with Madame Bouvier to discuss the book during study hall. There was a knock at the door and I turned on the front light to peek out the window. Dylan stood outside with hands in his jeans pockets. I stuck my head outside and whispered.

"What are you doing here?" My eyebrows rose and my breath quickened.

"I told you I was coming over." He smiled and gestured for me to join him on the deck.

I stepped onto the deck and closed the door behind me. "Kind of thought you were kidding." I looked down at his truck, where a dome light illuminated a passenger. "Who's in your truck?"

"Scotty from school."

"Star athlete Scotty?." I had a class with Scotty, but there were 500 people or so per class, it's hard to know everyone. I followed Dylan into the shadows and we sat on the bench.

"We're on the way to a party."

"What is it with you and parties late on school nights?" I asked, eyebrows furrowing.

"What's wrong with that?" He asked, voice light.

"Don't you need sleep?"

"Who needs sleep?" He leaned in.

"I do."

He kissed me, soft and sweet, open mouthed, no tongue. Pulling away, he left me wanting more.

"I've been dreaming about that since I met you." He brushed my cheek with the back of a hand, then pushed a loose strand of hair behind my ear. He stood, leaving me glued to the bench. "See you tomorrow, Daredevil."

Speechless, I waved and watched him leave.

15

"Looking good - for a night of partying." I walked up to Dylan and he pulled me into a hug. We walked down the hall to the Commons. "It was nice to see you last night. Thanks for stopping by on the way to the party."

"No problem. Couldn't wait," he said. I raised an eyebrow, finding it hard to believe. We found a bench and sat down. "Looking forward to tonight," he said in a low voice that tickled my ear.

I laughed, "Work?"

Students pooled into the hall. I was surprised to not see the guys. I shivered as I felt someone's eyes fix on me. I turned my head to see Jay staring at me. He headed toward us. I didn't see Jules.

"You sure left early, Dylan," Jay sneered and swiveled his head between the two of us.

"Wanted to see my girl," Dylan wrapped an arm around my waist and kissed my cheek.

"Your girl?" I say with Jay. "Jinx." I punched Jay's shoulder hard. He flinched, backing up and rubbing his arm.

"Watch out for this one. She's rough," Jay said, giving me a suspicious look. He was probably remembering the crunch of Carlo's nose as I punched it.

I shrugged. Yeah. I hit harder than I needed to. To remind him that I could. Dylan pulled me back to his side.

"Easy slugger." He laughed. He pulled me against his side

and squeezed.

"O-o-kay." Jay sighed.

"I can't be possessed." I pouted. "Besides, I'm seeing Ted. I'm a person, not a possession. And, I hardly know you." Well, I wasn't sure I was still seeing Ted. We may have been on a break. He'd been unclear.

"You will." He smiled.

Other than French independent study, the day flew by. Although I had no problem reading the Camus' novel, discussing it in French was totally different. I was distracted by thoughts of dancing with warm hands on swaying hips, and light kisses beneath the night sky. Madame Bouvier grew tired of prompting responses from me and sent me back to study hall.

I joined Aaron at our normal table. I dropped my backpack on a chair and sat down across from Aaron, slumping into the chair. He looked up from the notebook he wrote in.

"Monica wants to know if you think you'll stop by tomorrow."

"I could use a party. Sure. Might be 10:00 or later."

"That's fine. We'll probably go until at least 1:00 AM. Bringing anyone?"

"Can I?"

"Sure."

"Maybe. Depends on who's available."

"Great. We'll see you then. So, any thoughts on the whole "guys are complicated business" thing?"

"Yeah. I'm paranoid now. Thanks a lot," I mumbled, opened my notebook and pretended to work on precalculus problems.

"How so?" He asked, tapping his pen.

"I've noticed a lot of guys look at me. Several of my guy friends sit close to me, hug me, put their arm around me, lean toward me when talking, etc...." Particularly Dylan, who I hardly knew. He'd become familiar really quick.

"Interesting." He looked me over. "Well, you are cute."

"Not." I looked at my pen and the doodles it had been drawing, mostly squiggly lines. So much for Precalculus problems.

"Like a pocket ninja," he said, words flying out of his mouth.

My eyes rose to meet his and an eyebrow crept up.

"What?" My pen hovered over the paper and my grip tightened. Had he just insulted me?

"Never mind. At the very least, you're different. You don't go throwing yourself at guys."

"Anymore," I said. I'd learned my lesson.

"Right, anymore… wait, what?" Now his pen hovered over the paper.

"You didn't really hang out with me outside of classes and recitals last year. I made some mistakes." The bell rang and I left a confused Aaron behind. Guess he didn't know about Carlo.

When I got to band class at the end of the day, I found that the period had been made into a combined band/chorus study hall. Mr. Seagram was out sick, so the Choir teacher, Ms. Moss stood to the side of the podium.

"I'm ok with you all talking as long as you keep it down. Otherwise, work on homework. If you want to practice, use the practice rooms." Ms. Moss walked away toward Mr. Seagram's office.

I took a seat in the front row and pulled out a random textbook, English. *To Kill a Mockingbird,* it was. The air moved as someone sat to my left. Expecting it to be Vicki, I glanced over. Dylan smiled and leaned in for a shoulder bump.

"Daredevil," Dylan whispered in my ear.

"Oh, hello." I smiled back and thought for a second. "Chorus, right?"

"Yep. Forgot already?" He leaned back. I did kind of remember him telling me something about chorus during a phone conversation.

"Sorry." I shrugged then noticed Stephanie glaring at us from behind the bells before she dropped down to the floor. She was two years younger than me. He looked in that direction questioningly.

"What's up?" He asked.

"Stephanie's over there, spying on us." I pointed toward the bells.

He laughed and leaned in, whispering in my ear, "nothing to worry about."

I put my book away. He reached over to hold my hand,

resting it on his leg. I pulled my hand back and looked at him, trying to get comfortable just sitting next to him. I wasn't used to guys like him paying attention to me. Couldn't see his fascination, but I tried to roll with it. I turned to the right as I felt a warm leg brush against mine and a long-fingered hand closed around mine. Ted smiled at me.

I looked at Ted, lifted my head and turned to look at Dylan, then back at Ted. "Hi, Ted," I said.

"Listened to your demo. It's really good," Dylan said, leaning over me to talk to Ted in a quiet voice. I guess he'd gotten hold of Jay's copy.

"Thanks, man." Ted looked at Dylan. "Glad you liked it."

"Would love to see you perform again sometime."

"Have you seen her dance yet?" Ted inquired.

My eyes widened and I bit my lips.

"No. Well, sort of last weekend, on stage," Dylan said thoughtfully, a playful glint in his eyes.

"You're in for something special," Ted said, bumping my shoulder with his.

My face burned, but I also fought an eruption of laughter. I tried to hide my face in Dylan's arm. I could only imagine what I might look like based on the reaction of the guys, and it wasn't good.

"Can't wait," Dylan said. He grinned and grabbed my free hand to give it a squeeze.

"Speaking of dancing, my friend Monica is having a get-together tomorrow night. Either of you free?" I asked. "I'm going after practice."

"I'm free," Dylan said.

"I'm free," Ted echoed.

I looked at both of them, surprised.

"Cool. Ride together from my place? It's in a development a few miles from my house."

I was happy for the short evening shift when I arrived at work after school. I was nervous about hanging out with Dylan, but excited to find what new things I'd learn about him. I clocked in and headed to the sandwich station to check supplies. Everything was ready to go. Sal, the day shift worker, left the station to me, all prepped and ready to go. Dylan walked in, tying his apron as he approached the grill.

"Hey! I didn't see your name on the grill!" I squeaked.

"Switched with Jay. He had other plans." He winked. "Makes our date easier anyway. We're both closing. We'll just go straight to the coffee shop from here."

"Makes sense." I smiled, happy to spend more time near him.

"So, about tomorrow, when should I show up?"

"We start practice early, around 5:00. My guess is we'll be done before 9:00. You can watch us play if you're early. I get performance anxiety, so practicing in front of people is good for me," I said, feeling a flutter in my stomach as I thought about him watching us practice.

"Cool, cool. I'll plan to show up around 9:00. If I'm earlier I'll watch." He grinned, "will I see some of this dancing?" He wagged an eyebrow.

"I'm trying to refrain from dancing while performing." I stifled a laugh. My hand traced circles on the counter.

The restaurant was devoid of customers, not a single one in the dining room. Vicki stood at the register, but wandered closer. She leaned in

"Did I hear the word date?" She looked at me, "as in you, Shell, have a date?" I nodded.

"Our first." Dylan said. His lips stretched in a sexy grin.

"But," Vicki looked at me, then focused on Dylan, "she's dating Ted." The words rushed out of her mouth.

"He put the brakes on. Whatever that means." I folded my arms. Her reaction seemed suspect. Why would she care?

"Some of the guys might not be happy about that," she grumbled in my ear as she pulled me into the back room.

"What are you talking about? They can't tell me what to do." I crossed my arms and leaned against the industrial sink. My feet slid on the soapy floor and I readjusted.

"No, you don't understand." She lowered her croaking voice to a near whisper. "A couple of the guys have been trying to ask you out." She looked over her shoulder at Dylan. "For a while now. Me and Jules have been holding them off, discouraging them."

"What? Why?" My eyebrows crept toward each other. The girls were crotch-blocking me?

"Well, you can be kind of scary sometimes. We didn't know how you'd react and we didn't want to be stuck working with a bunch of angry guys." Her hands were on her hips and I felt like a child getting scolded by a parent. She had no right to make decisions for me.

"Oh, come on." I eyed her. "Who?" My heel tapped involuntarily.

"Well, there was Rob, and Marcus for starters," she said, eyes to the ceiling, counting on her fingers.

"No way. Poor Marcus." I thought about Marcus laying in ICU covered in bandages. "Any news?" It felt like I hadn't thought about Marcus in a while. It was like he was disappearing from my memory. My heart beat an extra strong pump before returning to normal rhythm.

"Jules said that his heart is getting stronger and beating more regularly, but he's still in a coma. Doesn't respond." Her head lowered as she shook it side to side. Her brassy permed hair swayed despite its heavy coating of hair product.

Dylan stuck his head through the door. "Customers coming in."

"Thanks." Vicki returned to the register. I washed my hands and gloved up before heading back to the sandwich station. A steady flow of customers kept us busy for the next couple of hours. When there was a lull, Raif took over the grill and sandwich station while we headed to the back for supplies. Dylan followed me into the walk in. The light dim as we gathered lettuce, tomatoes and onions on a tray.

I turned to walk out and Dylan removed the tray from my hands, setting it next to a tray of patties on the shelf. He took me in his arms and pressed his warm lips to mine. It was a soft kiss with a smile building behind it.

"Can't wait to get out of here." He gazed down at me, holding me hip to hip. I was electric, a circuit overloading. Didn't know what I felt about him, but he was a bright fire that drew me in. I just couldn't help myself, like the bugs that flew into the electric blue light of a zapper, unable to stop before popping and burning.

"Me too. We need to get back." I pulled his head back to mine for another short kiss before we grabbed our trays. Wait, what the heck was I doing? Ted. Dylan carried the meat to the grill as I washed and prepped vegetables. Vicki came back to help, running the onions through the slicer.

"Raif was about to send me to look for you guys," she said, with her dry smoker's voice.

"He's just so, hot," I said with a quick exhale. It wasn't the kind of thing I'd normally say, but I couldn't help myself.

"Yeah, he's cute," she agreed. She assessed me with one eye squinted. "Doesn't seem your type."

"Um, well, I'm not sure I have a type. He's shown interest and made an effort. That's something." He called, he kissed me. That was showing interest, right?

"There's a bunch of guys interested in you," she reminded me.

"He asked." If she wasn't just jerking me around, about the other guys, they hadn't really been showing their feelings toward me. Not that I'd noticed. Besides, Rob? Rob? Come on, he treated me like a little sister. How were two guys suddenly a bunch of guys?

"There's more to it than just asking, Shell."

"I feel this… I don't know what when I'm with him. Drives me crazy. I've never felt this way."

"You hardly know him," she said with narrowed eyes. "Be careful."

"I know." I frowned. Be careful? She was always telling me I needed to get laid. What was her deal?

"I thought you and Ted had a thing," she said, voice sharp. What was with her tonight? She was being so catty.

"What? Well, yeah." Sort of. Seemed over to me.

"Denial ain't just a river in Egypt, girl." She rolled her eyes and carried the onions back to the line.

I frowned and finished prepping the tomatoes and lettuce. I took them out to the sandwich line.

"Why don't you go ahead and start closing the dining room?" Raif pointed. "It's mostly empty. Start in the atrium and stack the chairs."

"Will do." I went out to the dining room and nodded to Gwen behind the salad bar before I got to work scrubbing tables and stacking chairs. The last customers left and I finished up. Raif locked the doors and I dragged the vacuum out. Raif had already closed out the sandwich area and Dylan scraped the grill. Raif took the cash till to the office and told Vicki to help me.

"Vacuum or mop?" I asked.

"Mop," she said, as I'd expected. The area was much smaller. She rolled her eyes at me. What the heck was that for? I plugged in the vacuum and began vacuuming while Gwen carried wrapped salad bar containers back to the walk in. Floors mopped and vacuumed, Vicki and I helped Gwen finish closing down the salad station. Dylan had finished wiping down the back-room prep areas and washed the dishes. We double checked our close out duties and checked in with Raif. He wasn't done with the nightly paperwork quite yet, so everyone changed into regular clothes and returned to the dining area where we waited for him. Dylan leaned against the wall, wearing light jeans and a darker tee shirt, beckoning me to join him. Wow, he looked great in those jeans.

"Raif's almost ready to go." He dipped his head to look into my eyes. "I'm so ready to go."

"Me too."

"Wow, your eyes are seriously bright blue. Could've sworn they were a different color before," he observed.

"They change sometimes," I said with a shrug.

"They change?"

"Depends on the environment and what I'm wearing."

"No, they're really, really blue."

I reached into my purse for a compact and looked.

"Weird. Never seen them look that bright before. Cool."

"Cool?" He asked, as if I should be having a more intense reaction to my eyes being electric blue like a neon light.

"Don't need to pay extra for colored lenses, do I?"

"Guess not. Well, they're pretty," he said with a frown.

"Thanks." Raif came out of the office deposit bag tucked under an arm. We followed him out to his car and watched him drive away.

"Meet you at Janelle's?" He pointed down the road.

"Right behind you." I watched his butt as he walked away, thinking how muscular he must be under those clothes. Gosh, that butt! My mouth watered. What's gotten into me? I got in my car and followed him down the road, parallel parking a couple spots away from the cafe. I met him outside the door, which he held open for me. What a gentleman! I hadn't expected that from him.

We ordered our drinks and sat in facing overstuffed armchairs in the far corner. A small candle flickered on the table between us. I placed my drink on the table to let it cool. He sipped his coffee, black.

"So, you never told me about your last girlfriend." I prodded.

"Oh, that's right." He looked at me with a twinkle in his eye, but saying nothing more.

"You sure don't share much about yourself."

"I'd much rather hear about you," he said, deflecting the inquiry. He took another sip from his steaming mug.

"And I want to know as much as I can about you," I said as I leaned forward.

"I'm not that interesting." He waved a hand as if to shoo away some annoyance.

"You're interesting to me."

"Fine. My last girlfriend, Sara, was a cheerleader. We spent a lot of time together on buses to and from games because, as I told you, I was on the football team. Running back."

"Go on." I gestured with my hand for him to continue.

"She was a redhead, um, adventurous." His eyes glinted and a corner of his lips rose. He sipped his coffee, looking at me. "It didn't work out."

"Adventurous, huh?" I wondered in what way.

"Yeah, it didn't work out," he repeated as his eyes drifted away.

I leaned forward, ran a finger down his chest, and looked into his eyes. "You are so hot." My mouth snapped shut and looked at him, "I didn't just say that out loud, did I?" My hand rose to my lips, covering an embarrassed smile. Did I just touch him in public like that?

"You just said I was hot," he said in mock indignation, eyes wide. "What am I? A piece of meat?"

Blood rushed into my face and I started laughing.

"Why are you laughing?" He asked, eyebrows raised as he leaned toward me.

"I didn't mean to say that out loud. It just kind of escaped." I covered my mouth again.

"What's that?" He pulled my hand away from my mouth and looked at the visible scarring on my forearm. Wow, he noticed? I'd known Ted and the guys almost three years and I had to point out the scars last weekend.

"I was in an accident." My eyes lowered to my arm, where my hand rubbed the scarred area. I hadn't realized I'd been doing it.

"What kind of accident?" He prodded.

"Struck by lightning." It came out more like a question than a statement.

"Wow."

"Can we talk about that another time?" I looked down and leaned back in my chair. Did he have to be so observant?

"I'd really like to know," he said. His voice, low, as he lightly lifted my hand from my arm to take a better look at the scarring. I'd seen his scars the other night. It was only fair.

"My boyfriend, best friend, and I were at my grandfather's lake when a storm came out of nowhere. We all got struck, only I survived." I didn't want to go into what we were doing there. It was messy, and my memories detached.

"Recently?"

"No, a little over three years ago." I stared at the scar and traced it with a finger, holding it forward. "That day is pretty foggy in my memory. Lots of things are, but I still have nightmares."

I looked over at Dylan, finding concern, but understanding as well. "I woke up restrained in the hospital. They kept me in the psych ward for a month on heavy medication. I didn't talk for a couple weeks. I'd sit and stare at the therapist in our individual sessions and wouldn't participate in group sessions." I breathed deeply. "I was just angry, sad, and really confused. I couldn't remember what happened, let alone who I was, and so much memory was just gone." I had also undergone rehabilitation after the hospitalization, lots of physical therapy, and therapy in general.

"I know angry," he said. There was something there, but I wasn't ready to prod yet.

"I bet you do."

"Come here." He held out his arms and gestured for me to sit on his lap.

"I'll crush you. I'm really heavy."

"No. You're not, come here." I walked over and he pulled me down, giving me a big hug. I sank into him, vulnerable.

"Tell me about Ted." He murmured into my ear.

"What about him?"

"What's your relationship with him?"

"We're friends, more than that. Things changed recently, but I'm not sure what's happening. I'm confused."

"Confused?" He whispered in my ear.

"Yeah." I nodded, rubbing his arm with my free hand.

"How so?"

"You really want to know?" I raised an eyebrow, skeptical.

"I asked, didn't I?"

"I've known him since we moved here over two years ago. He's my best friend. We're good together. We just started dating and I thought things were going well. Fast, but well. He said we needed to slow things down."

Dylan nodded. "Ok."

"Ok?" My voice cracked and I cleared my throat. He nodded.

"How do I make you feel?" He said low. I felt his warm breath against my hair.

"Alive." I looked at him. "How do I make you feel?"

"Excited," he said, glint in his eyes and grin on his face. Charming.

"Hmmm…"

"In many ways," he said. My thoughts returned to his comment about the adventurous ex as he raised an eyebrow and gave me a roguish half smile.

I wrapped my arm behind his neck and kissed him.

"You wanna jump my bones." He grinned.

"Huh?" It took me a moment. "Oh." I looked at his eyes. "There's a difference between wanting and doing."

"You're kidding."

"Serious." I crossed my heart with a finger. "I have some self-control." I leaned away and placed a hand on his hard chest.

"One way to put it." His eyes searched mine. "You're just so…"

"Weird? Naive?"

171

"Different," he said, eyes darkening as his voice deepened.

"That's bad, right?" I stood. "Sorry to waste your time." I walked outside and left him sitting there. I took a deep breath of cool air. My arms wound tight around me as I walked to my car. The door opened behind me.

"It's not bad!" Dylan called after me. "You've got to stop thinking about yourself like that." He walked up and wrapped me in his strong arms. "I know we have our differences." He lifted my chin with a finger. "But we'll share some interests too. Experiences. Memories. Give us a chance." He leaned down and his lips were on mine, firm, confident. It left me breathless.

"I should get going. School in the morning," I mumbled against his lips. I stepped back.

"We good?" He held his arms out and I nodded.

"Good," I said with a nod. I did feel better.

"See you tomorrow." He winked before walking away. My heart jumped as I watched him walk away. What was this feeling? Hope?

"Tomorrow!" I got into my car. A band resembling Pinctada Falls, but not quite roared to life as I turned the ignition.

16

I discovered Ted and Dylan talking as I walked into the Commons. They were early this morning. They greeted me with stereo smiles and separated to offer a seat between them. I sat suspiciously between them as Ted nudged my shoulder. Dylan kissed my cheek.

"Enough PDA already, gross." The nasal voice of Stephanie, the cheerleader, intruded. Like she had any right to talk. I looked up to see her standing hands on hips, hair crunchy as ever, bangs teased high, but the rest pulled back in a tight pony tail that stretched her face. It was a great look. For a poodle.

"Dylan, you going to the team's party tonight?" She asked, eyes and smile bright and vacuous.

"No, I've got other plans," he said, arm squeezing my shoulder.

"Ugh. Fine. I'll tell George you won't be there." She huffed away, pony tail shifting stiffly with each step.

Dylan grinned at me. "So, where were we."

Ted cleared his throat. "Whose party are we going to tonight?"

"Monica's," I said.

"Haven't seen her in a long time," Ted emphasized "her."

"How long's it been?" I asked, wondering if he'd talked to her since I had.

"Since she dislocated her shoulder at the game." He shivered. "Saw her fall. She was screaming, her arm just hung there. It was terrible." Yes, it was. I'd been there too. I'd seen her since at one of the recitals Aaron and I performed at, maybe even more recently. She'd still been on crutches with a knee immobilizer.

"Well, she's obviously better now. I haven't seen her in a while either. Not for several weeks anyway." I tried to remember when I last saw her but came up blank. "Looking forward to it."

I turned to Dylan. "You still coming?"

"Wouldn't miss it," he said, nudging my arm with his elbow.

"I think you'll enjoy her friends. They're interesting. Well, not actually sure if you'll like them. They're not all football players." I gave him a weak punch. Some of them were. She had been one of the cheerleaders after all.

"I'm not just a dumb jock, Shell." He winked at me. I looked forward to finding out what else hid behind those gorgeous aqua eyes.

Jules made an appearance in gym class. Her make up darker than usual, especially around her right eye. Almost as if she wore foundation a shade or two too dark. I hadn't seen or talked with her in days, which was unusual. She sat on the bleachers instead of warming up with the rest of class. I ran over and sat next to her.

"Hey Jules, how's it going?" I asked, short of breath.

"Could be worse." She bit a nail. Her nails were bitten down to the quick. Some had bled recently.

"Where've you been?"

"Haven't been feeling well. Stayed home most of the week," she said, not looking at me.

"Feeling any better?" I asked. She gripped the bench as her knee bounced. Her eyes darted around the gym.

"Huh?" She looked at me like she'd forgotten I was there, eyes barely focused.

"Do you feel better?" I asked slowly, knowing from the way she looked that she didn't feel well.

"Oh, yeah, sure," she said with a dismissive gesture.

Normally, Jules would be talking my ear off about Jay and what they'd done over the weekend. This was like digging treasure from granite using a toothpick. She wore a long-sleeve turtleneck under a sweater and sweats. This wasn't normal for Jules either. Not even for gym class. She was going to get really uncomfortable when the teacher got our activity started. The school gym uniform was a white tee and red shorts. If the teacher made her participate, she'd get really hot.

"Aren't you going to change?"

"No." She looked up at with a jerk. "I just want to sit out today."

"Ok. I'll check with you later. I'm going to warm up."

I was happy to hear that we were being given the chance to choose between step aerobics or basketball today. I chose aerobics because I sucked as a teammate. I was a loner. I happily spent the class stepping up, down, and sideways until the teacher blew the whistle signaling the end of class. When I headed to the locker room, Jules was already gone.

On the way home, I made a quick stop in the family planning isle of the drug store. I grabbed some condoms, not wanting to spend too much time looking at the selection. I'd checked my stash and found they were expired. The way my body was going haywire, I figured it was better to be safe than sorry. I sure as heck didn't want a sexually transmitted infection, virus, or disease. They'd called them STDs in sex ed. Although I had the IUD, it didn't protect against disease transmission. I didn't think I was ready for sex yet, but after listening to my older friends over the years, unexpected things happened. I didn't want to be one of the statistics.

I stopped my musings as I paid for the condoms, blushing as Monica's older brother, Chris, checked me out and winked. I'd forgotten that he worked at the drug store. Stupid. I shouldn't feel embarrassed for being responsible. I shook my head. I walked out the door, putting the bag in my purse self-consciously. I drove home and hoped the guys weren't there yet so I had time to stow my purchase. It would be too embarrassing to have the condoms fall out of my purse in front of them or something. I was really clumsy and it could totally happen.

I was relieved when I pulled into the empty driveway. I hurried up the deck stairs and let myself in. I called out for Andy, then remembered he had team practice again. Was he in basketball now? Gee, I couldn't remember. I hurried back to my room and stashed my purchase in a desk drawer. I quickly changed and went to the garage to check the state of things. It looked fine. I took out an extra folding chair and put it in front of our practice area in case Dylan arrived early, then got nervous at the thought.

Tonight's plan was to go through the set a couple of times. At the sound of gravel crunching, I headed outside to meet my guests. Bear and Zane pulled up in the van followed closely by Ted. I held the door open for them as they carried in their instruments.

Ted gave me a big hug. I tried to pull him in for a kiss, but he pulled away. I frowned, then walked to the mic as the guys tuned and warmed up. I ran a couple vocal warm ups. Tonight, we planned a full rehearsal. When Zane signaled to begin, I took the mic in hand.

Bear counted off for the fast punk number and we were off. I jumped with the beat and occasionally added in some fist pumps, hops, and head banging. We transitioned into a song from our demo CD, to the cover of a grunge daddy issues song, to a couple more songs from our demo. As we neared the end of the set, I pulled a stool over to sit by Ted, who switched out his bass for his electric acoustic and we faced each other for our *Rise Above* acoustic duet. The other guys sat back as we sang and played. I was staring so intently at Ted as we rehearsed *Rise Above* that I didn't notice Dylan standing in the doorway. We finished and I heard an extra set of hands clapping. I looked up with a smile and gestured to the chair as I took the mic back to the front of our make-believe stage.

"Our final song for this evening is called *Labels*. Hope you enjoy it." Barry counted off and we finished our set with the most scream-y number we had.

"Those last two were new, weren't they?" Dylan asked. "I don't remember them from your CD.

"Yeah, just this week actually. *Rise Above* was all Ted," I answered.

"The band's really good."

"Thanks," I said as I returned my guitar to the stand and stretched.

Although we'd only run the set once, Zane suggested that it was such a great run through that we not jinx it and called it a night. We agreed not to mess with something that seemed to be working and packed up the gear. Ted and Dylan waved as the others left.

"I guess we won't be late to the party after all." I looked at them both. "Come upstairs and I'll finish getting ready." They followed me up the stairs and sat on opposite ends of the sofa. I hurried back to my room to grab my purse, then stopped to check my hair and makeup. Satisfied, I returned to the living room where the guys talked with my mom. Andy sat in the dining room drinking a large cup of water.

I returned to the living room after changing, let my hair down, and applied light makeup. "Ready to party?" I looked at my guys.

"Yeah!" Dylan yelled with a fist pump.

"Uh-huh." Ted stood up.

We walked out to my car. Dylan took front seat and Ted got in the back. As I drove the five minutes to Monica's house, the guys joked around. I was a little weirded out by how well they got along. I parked in front of Monica's house and we walked up to her door. I rang the doorbell and Aaron answered.

"Shell! Ted! Good to see you."

"This is Dylan," I said, putting an arm around his waist.

"Good to meet you Dylan." Aaron gestured for everyone to come in. "Welcome. Monica's out back. Grab a drink and head on out." He gestured toward the backyard. I'd been there a couple times before and knew the way.

I nodded and we went to the kitchen to grab a drink before exiting through the sliding glass doors onto a beautiful redwood deck. Monica talked to a guy I knew by sight, but wasn't acquainted with. She waved and came over to hug me.

"So glad you could make it, Shell. It's been too long!" She looked at Dylan and smiled, "I'm Monica."

"This is Dylan," I said.

"And Ted! Great to see you too. It's been ages." She hugged Ted. "You know Aaron and our friend Shane, right?"

"Not familiar with Shane." I waved at him and he smiled

back.

"Expecting a few more to show up in a bit." She gestured to several available chairs, "please have a seat. Enjoy yourselves." She looked at me. "Girl, we need to catch up." She took my arm, hooking hers through mine and led me away. "Wow, just look at those two."

"Yeah, Dylan seems to make friends easily. He and Ted are getting along."

"That's not what I meant."

"Hmm?" I stared at the guys, slight smile on my face.

"The way they look at you," she whispered conspiratorially in my ear.

"How do they look at me?"

"Like the world revolves around you." Aw, how sweet. Not true, but sweet.

"That's kind. I've only hung out with Dylan once. You know Ted's been my best friend for a while, right? We sort of started going out."

"Those looks aren't friendship or just hanging, girl. It's more like you're the air that they breathe."

"Well, that just sounds creepy."

"Or, lucky. Aaron said something about you being interested in a couple guys. My guess is those two?"

I nodded. My face relaxed into an adoring expression.

"It doesn't look one sided to me."

"Well, crap." I knew she was right, but was confused why Ted was putting on the brakes if he liked me so much. He hadn't kissed me since he'd "put on the breaks."

Music flowed from outdoor speakers. Tea lights and fairy lights provided an enchanting ambiance. It was almost warm outside, but my skin crawled, feeling as if unseen cold hands brushed down my arm. I looked around, seeing nothing out of the ordinary. Small tendrils of fog rose from the lawn.

"Well, I'll let you return to your other guests. I'm going to get back to my guys." I wanted to smack my forehead, remembering how irritated I'd been that Dylan had called me his girl just the other morning.

"Good luck," she winked and walked back to Shane.

Dylan asked Ted about the likelihood of our band touring someday.

"I'm hoping to tour as early as this summer. Small clubs and summer music festivals. Zane has been sending queries with our demo for months now." Ted looked up as I approached. As usual, they'd left a chair for me between them. I sat down.

"What about touring?" I asked.

"Dylan wanted to know if we were thinking about touring."

"Ah, the touring debate. Will we or won't we. Kind of depends on opportunity, doesn't it?"

"We're working on it." Ted grinned.

I was a lot less optimistic about the possibility of touring, especially this summer. It was only months away, and I couldn't see my mother being fine with me leaving for a couple months with the band. Of course, I'd be 18 well before then, so technically she couldn't stop me.

What we had going at our next gig was an unusual deal. Touring, we would be paying our own hotel costs, and that meant one room for all of us. I wasn't sure how I felt about being one of the guys for the summer, especially if things were still off with Ted. It was one thing to hang out with them every day, but to have to live with them 24/7 was a totally different creature.

Dylan looked at me, "are you excited about touring?"

"I'm not sure yet." I looked at him, then at Ted. It made me sad to bring down Ted's excitement. "I haven't traveled much, I'd be stuck sharing a room with these guys for weeks, and up on stage and around people all the time, which is really hard on me." My eyes skipped back and forth between the two. "Don't get me wrong, I'd work on it and get over it. It just wouldn't be easy for me."

"Ah, our lovely Siren, it's a good thing that you don't know your own power." Ted leaned over and put an arm around my shoulder, leaning his forehead against mine. "Can't imagine how different it could be if you'd let yourself be free once in a while."

"Isn't that the danger though. You just can't tell." I laughed uncomfortably.

Ted leaned back, eyes on me. He breathed deeply and nodded. He stood, holding out a hand. "Love this song, dance?"

I looked at Dylan, who shrugged. I shrugged, and took Ted's

hand. He led me to an empty space on the deck. The fog rose beneath our feet as we stepped, swayed and moved with the beat. As usual, Ted was loose and lovely to watch. At first, we danced a few feet apart, but he slowly approached me until his hands found their way to my hips. My arms snaked around his neck and we danced, inches apart. The warmth of his body caressed me, embers radiating heat after a bright fire. I wanted to sink into his warmth.

Ted released my hips and turned me so that my back was against him. Dylan danced toward us. We continued to dance and I reached out for him. Dylan danced at my front, Ted at my back. I danced between flames, one an out of control bonfire, the other a comforting hearth fire. We danced for several songs before I begged out to get something to drink. I felt like I'd never smiled so big before, happier than I could remember.

I returned to the kitchen and surveyed the snacks and drink options. Since I was driving, I opted for bottled water. I was gulping it down when a familiar voice startled me.

"Wasn't expecting to see you here," Jay said as he leaned against the frame of the kitchen doorway.

"Oh, hi. Didn't expect to see you either. Didn't know you knew Aaron or Monica. Wait, aren't you supposed to be at George's party?" The words flew out of my mouth.

"Friend of a friend," he said, smirking.

"That's nice," I said. I took a deep breath and looked down at my water.

"What were you doing out there?" He asked, continuing to smirk.

"Dancing," it came out like a question.

"You were dancing awfully close with your bassist," he commented, eyes narrowed as he leaned toward me.

"We're dating," I blurted before remembering we were kind of on a break.

"Dance that way with all your friends? You leading Dylan on?"

"Ted's my boyfriend. I've hung out once with Dylan. He's not my boyfriend or anything," I said defensively. I crossed my arms and leaned back against the counter.

"You might want to talk with him about that." Jay tapped

his chin.

"And?" I stepped forward. "This is your business why?"

"He's my friend. Just looking out for him." For a moment, it looked like he would say more.

I stepped closer. "So, where's Jules?"

"Julie? Uh, haven't seen her in a couple days." He looked down, eyes shifty as his fingers tapped against a cabinet.

"Really. She didn't look very happy today. I was just wondering if you had something to do with that." I took another step. He held his hands out defensively.

"No, I talked to her on the phone. She's just been sick. Stomach flu or something." His eyes widened and he held his hands out. If I didn't know better, I'd think he was remembering the time I broke Carlo's nose.

"Right." I drew out. I didn't believe him. "Gotta get back to my guys." Crap, I said it again. I walked outside and joined Ted and Dylan who were laughing.

"Jay's here," I said, breathing out in a huff.

"Didn't see him." Dylan said. He shrugged.

"Got here while we were dancing." I grinned in a half-smile and Dylan grinned back at me before leaning in for a kiss. "Mmm. Thanks for asking, Ted. I really enjoyed that."

"I could tell." Dylan looked me in the eyes. "Your eyes turned that bright blue color again."

"I've never seen them that color before, Shell. Beautiful." Ted sighed. He turned to Dylan, "Yeah, her eyes have always changed with her mood, but this color is new."

"So, what mood was this?" Dylan asked, while Ted looked at me intently.

"Happy?" I said meekly, thinking I might have been more horny than happy. "Maybe?"

"I don't know, Shell. I've seen you happy before." Ted looked at me.

"When?"

"When we're practicing as a band. Sometimes when we're hanging out."

"How can you tell I'm happy?"

"Uh, you smile. You rarely actually smile, that real smile. Your eyes turn a sky blue."

"Sometimes when we're alone, your eyes turn almost

indigo." He says quietly.

"When was that?" I asked, never having seen my eyes that dark.

"When we were working on stage presence for example." His voice deepened as he leaned in to speak into my ear, a secret for just the two of us.

"Oh," I said, beginning to understand. "It's hard to hide stuff when my eyes give it away."

"The indigo, it's your special message to me." He looked into my eyes. "I haven't seen it around anyone else." He looked toward Dylan. "I've only seen the bright blue around him." He breathed deeply.

"Weird, right?"

"You're my Daredevil and his Siren." Dylan shook his head.

"What's so serious?" Jay walked up to us and put an arm around Dylan's shoulder. Well, he tried to. His arm reached up and touched a shoulder. Jay was quite a bit shorter and rounder than Dylan.

"Yeah, guys, what's so serious? It's a party." Rob towered over us from behind, handing Jay a beer.

"Just thinking about our next gig," I redirected. "You know Dylan and Ted?" I looked up. Rob shook his head.

"I've heard about both of you. Ted, you're in the band, right?" Ted nodded and shook his hand. "And you, Dylan, is it? I heard you've been dating our Shell."

"Yeah, she's great, isn't she?" Dylan looked into my eyes, and whispered in my ear, "he's a little old, isn't he?" I smirked, but I didn't correct him. I guess he'd overheard Vicky last night.

"We've hung out once. It wasn't a date," I protested. "Rob, I didn't expect to see you. Do you know Monica?"

"Chris is a frat brother. We're all going to your show tomorrow night." Chris was Monica's older brother, the one I'd seen during my responsible purchase earlier in the afternoon.

"Very cool. Is he here? Haven't seen him in ages," I said, not wanting to admit I'd seen him earlier in the day.

"He's on an ice run." Rob returned his attention to Ted. "So, Ted, how long have you known Shell?"

"What, like almost three years now? We've been in school

band together and had the occasional class together. Started Toxic Siren a year and a half ago," Ted reached out to hold my hand. I squeezed his hand and let go. It was hardly the time to start showing interest again.

"Awkward, angry, depressed stages and all," I piped in uncomfortably, rubbing my scar. "Oh, hey, guys this is my jam! You mind? I gestured to Dylan and we headed to the area cleared for dancing again. He took me by the waist and kissed me quickly, then we danced, setting my body dancing with electricity. I heard thunder rumble in the distance and lightning burst in the sky. I laughed. Soon, Ted joined us and we all danced together, close with sensuality and heat. Lightning flashes became more frequent and the thunder got louder as the storm approached.

We left the party as the first raindrops began to fall.

When we got back to my house, the storm still raged. Ted and Dylan decided to wait it out. These storms didn't usually last long. Sudden, unexpected storms sometimes lasted twenty minutes, rarely more, before lightening up or stopping altogether. We rushed into the house through the basement and I turned on the lights.

"I'll be right back. Going to check in with mom and see if anyone's still up." I said, heading upstairs. "You want anything?"

"Nah, I'm good." Dylan smiled. Rain dripped from his hair onto his rain drenched shirt.

"No thanks," Ted said, droplets flying as he shook his head.

"You can put your shirts in the dryer if you're sticking around. There should be some towels on the shelves." I headed upstairs.

Mom had left the light over the stove on, but it was otherwise dark. Looked like mom and Andy were already in bed. I went back to my room and changed into some warm PJs, cute, but modest with a cloudy sky pattern. I also grabbed a couple of random tees and the afghans from the sofa before going down to the basement again. It was chilly downstairs, but I didn't want to hang out upstairs because we might wake mom or Andy. The boom box was still down in the garage.

"Hey guys." I walked into the laundry room where both

guys stood shirtless. Yum. "I brought down a couple tee shirts and some blankets if you're interested." I tossed the tee shirts over. Dylan caught them and handed one to Ted. Dylan took his time putting it on, while Ted slipped his on quickly. "Want to hang out in the basement or the garage?" I pointed to the next room and then the garage.

"Basement. Didn't I see a heater in there?" Dylan asks.

"Yeah there's a heater. No furniture though," I said, thinking about the futon in the back of the garage. The garage had a space heater, but was a larger area and there was a constant draft.

"I'm good with the floor," Dylan said as he took a blanket from the pile.

"Me too. A heater is good." Ted chimed in, teeth chattering.

"Ok." I handed Ted a blanket and gestured for them to head in while I went into the garage to grab the boom box. I joined them in the carpeted, but bare basement room and turned up the heater. I scanned my former bedroom, where the creepy photo had been taken and double checked the blinds. I sighed and plugged in the boom box. Our demo played at low volume.

"Your band really is good." Dylan looked at us.

I sat down and took one of the blankets, cuddling up between the two for body warmth. "Thanks," I said. "We practice a lot and the guys are talented."

We talked about upcoming shows and school-related activities for a while. The rain slowed. Ted looked at his watch and decided it was time to leave. I frowned as he stood, waved, and walked out. His car started with a rumble and gravel crackled as he drove away.

"Mind if I stay just a bit longer?" Dylan asked.

"If you want. I need to go to bed soon. School tomorrow. I need rest."

We sat against the wall and he leaned over to kiss me. The kiss went from soft and sweet to hard and intense before I knew what was happening. My arms swept around his neck, and suddenly I couldn't get close enough to him. My body buzzed with spreading warmth. I crawled on top of him and he pulled me closer, chest to chest. His hands slipped under my top, skin against skin. My fingers ran along his abs, pulling the tee up and he let me remove the shirt. I breathed hard as I leaned in to kiss him. It was the most amazing thing that I'd ever felt. Alive. Burning. I reached down, but Dylan took my hand.

"Whoa, slow down there."

"Hmmm?"

"You're going to get more than you bargained for tonight if you don't stop."

I got off of his lap, cooling off significantly, breath ragged and lips burning.

"You don't want me?" I asked, hurt.

"Oh, I do. Tonight's not the time or place." He pointed up, reminding me that my mom and brother were upstairs.

"Well, I guess I just confirmed it," I said dryly.

"What?"

"I wanna jump your bones," I said as a smile curved my lips. Dylan cracked up.

"Big time." My eyes grew wide as my mouth exaggerated the words. This got him laughing even more, sending him into a coughing fit. "Damn it." I looked down. I couldn't resist smiling.

"When's your birthday?" He looked at me.

"Next month. In a couple weeks, actually. Why?" I leaned back against the wall and shrugged before pulling my knees into my chest.

"That's not too far off." He evaded as he turned his body to face mine. "So that'll make you, what, 17?"

"No, 18. I should've been graduating this year." My eyes nearly rolled out of their sockets.

"Why aren't you? You're smart, aren't you?" He loosened one of my hands from its grip. I released my knees and let my legs slide forward.

"After the accident I was hospitalized for months. I missed so much school they held me back. It's not like I didn't catch up with the work, but it's school policy." Thinking about it still stung.

"That sucks," he said with a nod.

"It does. But it is what it is. So, I've still got a year left. Lost some credits in the transfer too." That irked me even more and I struggled to fend off the angry tears I'd held in for years, well mostly. My eyes burned and I blinked hard as my smile quivered.

"Really?" His eyes widened.

"Extra slap in the face, right? It's not like I got struck by lightning on purpose." What I failed to mention was that I'd hurt myself a month after I was released, leading to additional time in a mental hospital due to being a risk to myself. Knot in my throat, I changed the subject. "So, you're in chorus. Do you like to sing?"

"I need the credit to graduate," he said. "It was that or another science class and I wasn't going to do that."

"Must be good for picking up girls too," I said, thinking about the cute chorus girls, one in particular.

"That too," he said with a grin.

"Girls like Stephanie," I said with a grimace, thinking about Miss Poodle hanging all over him.

"What? She's nice." My left eyebrow shifted up and he shrugged. I wanted to punch him.

"Because you're a guy. She loves the football players," I rolled my eyes.

"You're not a fan?"

"You could say that," I said as I looked away at the wood paneled wall where a Calabrias poster used to hang.

"Nothing happened," he assured me. His voice called for my attention and I turned my head to look at him.

"Huh?"

"She and I kissed, that's all. Nothing else happened. I turned her down. She's hot and cold, plays games. I'm not into games." The words rushed out, as if he felt guilty, though he had nothing to feel guilty about. Not really. It's not like he and I were together.

"Ah." Gross. Like Stephanie, he'd turned me down too. Then again, he and I didn't really know each other. It's not like I was experienced. Unlike Stephanie. I didn't like the pressure in my chest. I tried to smile, but it was unnaturally pinched.

"You're with Ted," he reminded me.

"Maybe. It's hard to tell these days." Ted rejected me, and he knew me. Yet another person to desert me. My eyes drifted away again.

"What's the deal with Vicki?" He asked. My eyes darted

back to him, narrowed.

"From work? We're in band together. Why do you ask?"

"No, with her and her boyfriend." He stretched his legs out in front of him and leaned back.

"Um, they've been together a long time. She's leaving for college in May and she's worried about what'll happen to them after she moves. He's not going anywhere."

"She keeps talking about the size of his package and how it's so big."

"Does she?" I asked, eyes narrowing. I'd never heard her talking about Brent's junk. Maybe she talked about it while she was working front line with the guys. Who knew? She was always telling me I needed to get laid. It wasn't impossible she'd talk details with the guys. Was there a point to this?

"All the time," he said, rolling his eyes.

I shook my head. "Not that I remember. It's never come up in conversation. Then again, I haven't experienced much to compare it to. Didn't realize there was much variation. Kind of thought they were pretty much the same."

"Oh yeah, there's variation. More than just circumcision. There's length, girth, growers, showers, some are curved, lots of variations."

"I had no idea," my lips had turned up in one corner as I leaned forward. How had we gotten on the topic of penises? "What are you doing here? With me?" I asked.

"Trying to get to know you." He shrugged. Felt like he was playing with me.

"I'm not your type." Michelle might have been. Cheerleader, peppy, she put on a good show of being happy, unlike me. I didn't pretend.

"You don't know my type," he eyed me in speculation, doing that elevator thing.

"I think I get the picture. I'm no Stephanie." I shrugged and leaned into the wall. Examining him, his flirty smile and mischievous blue eyes, I almost wished there was a little bit of Michelle left in me.

"I told you I'm not interested in Stephanie," he said. "Like I said, hot and cold. I don't like games."

"What was that stuff about Vicki?" I was no Vicki either, thank goodness.

"Something that almost was, but didn't happen," he said, looking off to the side. He looked back at me with that sorry, not sorry look.

"Sorry, what?" I asked. What the heck did that mean?

"She'd broken up with Brent and the guys were pushing me to hook up with her. Since she was always talking about how big he was, I thought why not?"

"Oh." Yuck. What did the size of Brent's junk have to do with Dylan? Was this some competition thing that guys did?

"Well, I couldn't even get it in, so instead she blew me in the bathroom at Norma's."

"Oh my gosh. You didn't!" What the heck was wrong with this guy? Vicki? Vicki! Standards, what kind did this guy have? Was he working his way through the girls of Norma's in some twisted game?

"Yes."

"I mean, if Vicki's your type, I'm nothing like her," I said. I didn't hook up in fast food bathrooms. Gross.

"Well, you know, she has that big jaw, and I thought she'd open up like a snake or something."

I kind of thought Vicki looked more like a frog than a snake. She had a square face and no chin, but, whatever. My stomach churned. Yuck. He really was making the rounds. Such a man slut. Really hot. And, just like that, an image of Joe and Christy in bed popped into my head. Oh no. Flashback. What the hell? Joe and Christy? He was cheating on me? I doubled over, hugging my knees and closing my eyes.

"Are you ok?" Dylan asked.

"Sometimes something triggers a memory. You just triggered one," I said into my knees, causing the sound to come out muffled.

"Not a good one?"

"No, not a good one," I said, taking in a deep, but shaky, breath. This guy was the same. Claiming he was interested and all the while hooking up with every girl that caught his attention. Except me. I didn't believe for a second that he'd turned down Stephanie. No one turned down Stephanie. "The shock will wear off soon."

"What did you remember?"

"Don't want to talk about it right now," I said with a sigh. I sat up and leaned back against the wall. I took another deep breath. If Ted were there, I might have shared with him but, Ted wouldn't have triggered the memory to begin with. If there had been no accident, would I have gotten over the cheating?

17

Mom read the paper at the dining room table. I sat next to her with some toast and orange juice and browsed through the sections. When I saw myself staring back from the front page of the Entertainment section, I picked it up and pointed to it frantically, rattling the paper, trying to get mom's attention. I couldn't speak. I pulled down the paper that she held and thrust the Entertainment section in front of her.

"Oh my gosh! That's you!" She held a hand in front of her mouth and began reading out loud as Andy joined us, standing behind me.

"Shell Dean, of Toxic Siren, enchanted the audience in Scranton, PA Club Del Sol on Friday night, leading to an even more energetic sold out show on Saturday. If sirens exist, Shell is one of them. Her voice calls out to the listener, drawing them in whether singing a cover or one of the band's original numbers. The band mixes the sounds of punk, metal, and grunge into a wonderful fusion that excites and delights the audience. Toxic Siren produces an impressive driving sound with *Beatdown*, performed by bassist/songwriter Ted Levins. Band members were personable following the show, taking photos with fans and signing autographs well after the show ended..."

The story continued with praise for the band, and ended with the reporter stating that we had a new fan. I was excited, and anxious. I wondered if the band had seen the article yet. Andy punched my arm.

"Way to go, sis!"

"Mom, forgot to tell you, when we play at Club Neon, it's the same deal, hotel rooms are covered and the manager is doubling our compensation. Lucio, he's the manager, told us he'd try to get his producer friend out to see us. Cool, huh?" I grabbed my book bag and left for school. My mind raced as I drove to school. The odds of a summer tour had just increased.

Students lined the rows of lockers as I walked toward the Commons. They spoke quietly, eyeing me as I passed. I checked my watch wondering if I missed the first bell. No, I was early. I still had 15 minutes until first bell. Midway down the hallway, I heard someone shout, "let's hear it for our very own superstar! Shell Dean!"

The horde erupted into clapping as I froze, waiting for them to start taunting or throwing stuff. My schoolmates just kept clapping. The principal rushed out from the crowd holding a copy of the newspaper out. "Shell Dean!" Was this some weird dream about to turn sour? Like the one where I'm sitting in class and the teacher announces that it's a test day, but I didn't know we had a test?

The students continued clapping as the principal led me away to his office. "Well, Ms. Dean, this is certainly a surprise." He dropped the paper on his desk and gestured for me to sit. I took a seat in the bright orange plastic chair facing his desk.

"I had no idea we had such a celebrity at our school." He looked at me over his brown plastic frames. "I don't want this affecting classes or disrupting the school."

"I hope not," I said, squirming. How on earth would my being in a band disrupt the whole school? What a stupid idea. I gripped my hands in tight fists and refrained from rolling my eyes.

"If it becomes a problem, we'll have to look at alternative teaching options for you, maybe even homeschooling."

"Are you serious? But my friends are here!"

"And, you are nearly a straight A student in pre-AP classes. I'd hate to lose you," Mr. Dirk said leaning forward, "but, we can't allow the school to be impacted by this kind of publicity, or disrupted by crazy fan behavior."

"I don't have fans at this school. I just have friends." Fans at school? These people have known me for a couple years and generally avoided me like a diseased animal. Come on.

"Didn't you just see those kids out in the hall?"

"They must have been joking around is all." I crouched down. "Making fun of me or something." I was lucky they hadn't been tossing notebooks and pencils at me.

"That certainly wasn't the case, Ms. Dean." His eyelids lowered as he again looked at me over his frames.

"Will you be having this conversation with my bandmates?" I asked, wondering if any of the others had received a similar welcome this morning.

"Wait, bandmates? The people in your band go here too?" Mr. Dirk fanned a hand over his shiny balding head. "You were the only one in the paper." That wasn't true. Ted was mentioned too.

"I'm just the singer."

"At this time, you're the only one causing near riots."

"I'd hardly call that a riot." I couldn't stop my eyes from rolling and my hands flying into the air.

"Go home, Shell." Mr. Dirk sighed. "You can't be here today." Say what?

"Serious?" My hands again flew into the air as my voice rose.

"I'm serious," he said, voice stern. "Out. Now." He turned his attention to various folders skewed across his desk in a dismissive gesture.

I sighed and stalked out of the school. Mr. Dirk hadn't allowed me time to seek out my teachers to get my assignments. He also hadn't mentioned when I could return to school. I pulled my keys out of my pocket and unlocked the car door before I noticed a piece of white paper under my windshield wiper. I grabbed the paper and got into the car, unfolding it. It was a photocopy of a picture of me and Dylan kissing. On my deck. Eew, gross. I tossed it onto the passenger seat. I wondered what kind of creeper went around taking photos of private moments late at night. I shivered.

I drove through Tobyhanna, passing the army depot.

Thoughts of some random person taking photos of me in personal moments without my knowing wouldn't stop stampeding around my brain. An elephant stomped around in my stomach, bringing on nausea as I drove past the base. A boa constrictor tightened around my lungs, making it hard to breathe. When I pulled into the parking area at Tobyhanna State Park, my stomach began to calm and my breathing came a little easier. I knew my face was drained from lack of oxygen. I peeked in the rearview mirror. Yep, my eyes had darkened to storm cloud gray. Yikes.

I sat for a moment, facing the lake. I took a deep shuddering breath. Thank goodness it was just anxiety and not a full out panic attack. Those were far worse. I unfastened the seatbelt and got out of the car. I leaned against the car breathing in the damp air. Although the forecast called for clear and sunny skies, in the distance, dark cumulonimbus clouds built quickly and overshadowed the sun. Thunder crashed and lightning brightened the clouds. I stood watching the storm in the distance.

The lightning chased paths through the clouds in trails similar to my scars. The wind picked up, blowing my hair almost straight up before dropping and whipping it in my face. I took the trail to the beach and let myself fall into the sand. I sat there watching the distant light. Whitecaps churned the water as wind whipped the waves toward shore. I enjoyed the cold wind, although I wasn't dressed for it. The cold kept me present. The storm must have shifted because it didn't get any closer.

I contemplated the state of my life. I liked a stranger. When I was with Dylan, thoughts of Ted fled my mind. I liked Dylan a lot, despite his questionable behaviors. There was just something about him, something hiding under the jock appearance, something deeper. I couldn't pinpoint it, sadness, anger? There was something primal in my reaction to him. The band was taking off. I was kicked out of school, possibly for a while.

My thoughts turned to Marcus. It'd been ages since I'd heard anything about him. His empty chair continued to haunt the classrooms. It was getting harder to place an image of his face in my mind than it was to imagine the empty space that

Marcus used to occupy. I could've used his tutoring services. I was still nearly failing Precalculus, but I was acing Chemistry. I didn't want to ask Juan for help. He'd get the wrong idea. I wondered who had been driving the car that ran Marcus off the road and if they felt anything about the consequences.

On top of everything, someone was sending me photos of myself. Me, at my house doing private things. I didn't like that. I didn't like that the last photo was taken late at night, and that although grainy like the previous photo, probably required specialized photographic equipment. The only person I knew who was into photography was Tara, but I couldn't see her skulking around to take random photos of me. She didn't seem the type.

Dylan called after school to ask where I'd been. I explained that I'd been kicked out. So embarrassing to be tossed out of school when I'd done nothing. Rain fell outside, hitting the window in somber ticks and taps. Andy would be home soon.

"I've been kicked out before. Several times. Want to hang out?" Dylan asked. I thought I heard a hint of a chuckle under his words. I wondered what he'd been kicked out for.

"Sure. I could use some physical activity. I know it's raining, but would you mind going to the lake?"

"That's fine. Be over soon."

I knew it would take him at least twenty minutes. I changed into jeans and a tee, pulled my hair back, and got my school jacket out. Andy's rushed footsteps clambered up the deck stairs. I opened the door for him.

"Argh! It's wet outside," he complained. He sounded like a pirate and the image of him with an eyepatch popped into my head. He'd worn one for several months as a child, trying to fix a lazy eye. It hadn't worked.

"Yeah, it's raining," I said dryly.

"Where's mom? She's supposed to be here." He opened the fridge door and pulled out a can of soda. He popped the tab and took a sip. "She's never here anymore."

I shrugged. She hadn't called and wasn't home when I got back from the lake. "You sure she wasn't going to be late today? Wouldn't be surprised if it was just the weather."

I heard Dylan's truck in the driveway, an early 80's model

Chevy.

"I'm going to hang out with Dylan for a while. We're going to walk the trail at the lake. Want to come?"

"Nah. I've got homework," he said. I got the feeling he wasn't a fan of Dylan as he walked off to his room.

I let Dylan in. He brushed off the rain. Although it was chilly outside, he wore a light tee and gray cut off sweats. I shook my head. He'd freeze on the hike.

"Want me to drive?" I asked.

"I'll drive."

I followed him out to the truck. He opened the door for me. I hadn't been inside the truck before. Bucket seats. Interesting. All of the trucks I'd been in before had bench seats. A box sat between the seats, holding a collection of cassettes. He motioned to them and I picked through, choosing an 80s rock album.

"I've only been to the lake once. You'll have to navigate," he warned.

"Not a problem."

He backed out of the driveway and I pointed him toward Tobyhanna. The hoarse voice of one of my favorite 80s musicians filtered through the speakers and I smiled. I loved this song. I sang along gave the occasional instructions on where to turn.

He pulled into the gravel lot and parked. We sat there for a moment, bracing for the cold and wet day. I knew it wouldn't be that bad wetness-wise once we got under the cover of the trees. We got out of the truck and hustled toward the tree line. The gravel crunched beneath our feet and the scent of wet leaves still smelled of fall even though winter had officially begun.

When we got to the beach, Dylan took off, running across the sand. I stared as I carefully walked through the sand. He ran back.

"They say running in sand strengthens the ankles," he said.

"Oh, ok." I wondered who 'they' were.

"I didn't know how to tell you this before, but I enlisted in the Marines. I'm leaving for basic after graduation," he looked down at me, eyes searching for a reaction.

What? My stomach dropped. I had to like a guy that was

leaving in a few months? I wasn't sure why I liked him so much so quickly. It made no sense, but I couldn't control the way I felt. I really, really liked him. At least that's what I thought. My heart sped up when he was around, blood rushed through my body, I felt alive. It was the first time I'd felt alive in years. Even Ted hadn't woken me like this. Of course, there were things about him that hurt too. Stephanie, Vicki, and now, he was leaving in a few months. Big things. When I checked in with myself, it didn't change the way I felt. I wanted whatever time with him I could get.

"That sucks," was all I could say. It came out strangled and strange.

We continued walking the trail as it rained, running into a fisherman just off the path. Dylan greeted him. I was lost in my mind. How was this fair? Just as I started to feel like I was awake again, feeling this weird and unexpected *something* for another person for the first time, and he was being taken away from me. By choice. He'd chosen this. Thunder crashed overhead and we turned back.

Walking across the sandy beach, hot tears mixed with the cold rain. The best thing about crying in the rain was that no one knew. Unless you were sobbing, which I wasn't. We got back into the truck, soaked. We sat there for a while, running the heat. Maybe Dylan had been onto something wearing shorts. My jeans were going to hold onto the water until I put them through the dryer.

"Want to see something cool?" He asked.

"Sure. I don't need to be home any time soon." The band was taking a break tonight.

In the drizzling rain, he drove toward the Henryville Inn, a gorgeous old resort from the late 1800s that had long been abandoned, then turned onto 715 and soon after onto a side road. Along the rolling and curved road ran a rocky stream with small falls. It was gorgeous. The only thing to mar the location were the occasional signs for animal research facilities. As we rounded a corner, he slowed and pulled over. We got out of the truck.

The damp and musty smell of the woods was pleasant. The ground, carpeted with dead leaves, slightly damp from the falling rain. Mist hung in the air. We walked down the hill and stopped at the mouth of a waterfall. The crashing water created a calming white noise that drowned out the sounds of humanity. The spray of water added to the already misty and chilled air creating a late winter feel. Birds flew overhead, perching on branches before flying off.

"This is a special place for me." Dylan explained. "When we were kids, me and Jay used to come down here."

"Thanks for sharing with me. It's gorgeous." We stood there for a while as the water poured over the edge to land below. The day had a surreal feel to it, an almost dream quality with the misty atmosphere and Dylan by my side.

"I have a lot of good memories of this place." His voice faded to a whisper. My eyes wandered to him when I saw the sad look on his face. I put my arm around his waist and drew him close.

When I walked into the house, the answering machine flashed angrily. Several messages waited. The first was Mr. Dirk telling me not to come in for the rest of the week. There were two hang-ups, a message from a reporter at the Pocono Record, and another from a Scranton paper wanting to set up an interview. Andy sat in front of the TV. I laid down on the sofa and pulled a blanket over me. I felt sick, like there was a heavy rock bobbing around in some foul, oily acid in my stomach.

"How was school today?" I asked.

"It was ok. Lots of the kids were asking about Toxic Siren."

"Really? In your grade level?" My senses perked. I didn't think people in his grade would have any interest in the paper beyond the comics section on Sundays.

"Yeah, they saw your picture in the paper this morning." He leaned over, looking closely at my face. "Shell, you don't look good. Can I get you something?"

"Water?"

"Ok." Andy jumped up and got me a glass of water. I guzzled the water, swallowing a couple ibuprofen pills in a big gulp.

"Thanks, little bro I really appreciate it." Around 9:00, the phone rang. I told Andy to not answer it, but he did anyway. It was Dylan, thank goodness, and not a reporter.

"Hi Dylan. I'm glad it's you."

"What's the matter, you don't sound right."

"Not feeling great."

"Really?"

"Oh, it's not every day that the guy I like tells me he's enlisted. Oh, and Mr. Dirk told me not to go to school the rest of the week."

"You're kidding."

"No, I'm not."

"I'm sorry. I enlisted before I met you."

I sighed. "I just want more time." My words brought to mind the accident. I'd been given more time. Who knew how much time they had left? Christy's and Joe's time had ended that day.

"Have you told your mom that you were kicked out of school today?" He sounded concerned. Maybe I should be more concerned. I'd never been kicked out before. Not that I could remember, anyway. I'd forgotten to ask him what he'd been kicked out for.

"No, she's not home yet." I checked the schedule on the fridge. "She may be back around 11:00. I guess I'll either stay up or camp out on the couch until she gets home." I tapped my fingers on the counter. "You mentioned earlier you'd been kicked out of school before. What did you get kicked out of school for?"

"Fighting mostly. I was an angry kid," he said, but didn't elaborate.

When I hung up with Dylan, I decided to give Jules a call. We hadn't talked in a while. I dialed her number and listened to the phone ring. As I was about to hang up, Julie's little sister picked up.

"Hello?"

"Beth? It's Shell. Is Julie home?"

"Not yet. She should be any minute now. Should I tell her you called?"

"Yes, if you would please."

"Will do. Congratulations by the way."

"Hmm?" For what?

"On the shows this weekend. Saw you in the paper."

"Thanks, Beth. I appreciate it."

"I'll let Julie know you called."

"Awesome. Bye, Beth."

All I wanted to do was take a nap. I walked back to the living room where Andy played video games. Serious depression was coming back with a vengeance.

"Andy, I'm just going to lie down for a nap. Wake me up if you need me."

"Ok." He mumbled absently, continuing to jump around with the controller in hand. I curled up on the couch, pulling the blanket over me. I fell asleep.

I woke to the sound of the front door opening. I sat up, rubbing my eyes. Andy had left a dim side lamp on for me, but had since gone to bed.

"Hey, mom."

"Shell." She dropped her purse and keys on the table and joined me in the living room. She sat on the love seat. Dark half-moons under her eyes told me she was exhausted.

"The principal kicked me out of school this morning. Says I can't go back this week," I said in a rush.

"For what?" As in, what'd you do, Shell? She didn't sound surprised. I wondered why.

"For being in the paper and disrupting the school."

"That's ridiculous." It didn't sound like she believed me.

"I walked in and there were students in the hall cheering for me." I frowned.

"That doesn't sound so bad. Classes weren't going on, were they?"

"It was before first bell. Mr. Dirk acted like I was inciting a riot. I kind of thought the students were playing a mean joke on me."

"Things are changing, Shell," she said quietly.

"Tell me about it."

"It's not going to get any easier with growing popularity. What about the rest of the band?"

"I haven't heard anything about them. The principal didn't seem concerned about them. They weren't the ones with the big picture on the front page of the Entertainment section."

"Hardly seems fair." Placating. Maybe she was too tired to process that I'd been kicked out of school. But, yes, totally unfair.

"They should've been in the photo too." That was definitely uncool of the paper.

"Not what I meant, but yes, it would've been nice for the whole band to get more credit."

"Mr. Dirk also told me that he may have to kick me out indefinitely, make me do independent study or homeschool. Something about safety of the students, school disruptions, or whatever. Can he do that?"

"I think he can. I'm not sure." I could tell she didn't want to talk about it, but couldn't stop the self-pity from pouring out.

"I wonder if I even have a job anymore," I said sullenly.

"When is your next shift?" She leaned back into the loveseat and let her head rest.

"Tomorrow night."

"I guess you show up like normal and see what happens." Totally reasonable. She always had a reasonable response.

The phone rang and I got up to answer it. "Might be important. I've been waiting to hear from Jules. Something's off."

"Goodnight, Shell," she said, lifting herself from the loveseat with a groan.

"Goodnight, mom," I called over my shoulder as I reached for the phone.

I picked up on the third ring. "Hello?"

"Shell?" A tired voice responded.

"Jules? Thank goodness. I've been worried about you." I breathed a sigh of relief. She was alive.

"Went to work after school. Just got home." Another reasonable response. I don't know why I always assumed the worst.

"Feel like we haven't talked in ages. Do you have some time?" I asked, anxious.

"Sure, a few minutes before I go to bed."

"Great! I've missed you. How've you been?" I'd missed her gossip. Her life was so much more interesting than mine.

"Thinking about breaking it off with Jay. He's been acting kind of crazy lately." What?

"Crazy how?" I mean, sure, Jay was kind of a jerk.

"Like angry. He socked me in the eye last week for asking him about Marcus' accident, if he remembered anything more than what he told police."

"I thought your eye looked like you had a healing bruise. I'm so sorry Jules, you don't deserve that."

"I know. Just for asking a question. He was really apologetic about it, but then he got this look in his eyes, like I owed him. I didn't want to, but he forced me to have sex with him. It was bad, Shell. I was scared to push him away or say no." She sounded scared, voice quiet and meek, so unlike the vivacious Jules I knew. "I had bruises after, on my arms and legs."

"You've got to get away from him. That's not ok."

"I'm worried what he'll do if I break up with him. Friday, he insisted we go to your show. It's not that I didn't want to see you perform, Shell. But I didn't want to be in the car with him that long. Feels like I'm a hostage and I have to go along with whatever he says."

"Is there any way you can get away for a while? Visit out of town family?"

"I'm afraid he'll follow me. He came over Sunday morning so angry. For no reason. I thought for sure he was going to hit me again."

"Did you know he came to our Saturday show?"

"No. I thought he was working closing shift."

"He was there, in the club." I thought back to the look on his face as his attention swiveled between me and Dylan. It hadn't been a happy look.

18

Dylan showed up around 10:00 the next morning. I let him in and we sat on the sofa. I tucked my legs under me. He rested his cheek on top of my head. The house was a chilly, so I pulled down a blanket and offered it to him. He took it, draping the blanket over his lap.

"So, I got into the clinic early this morning," he said, leaning back to look me in the eye. "I've been swabbed and had blood drawn. Should have results back in 24 to 72 hours is what they said. Happy?"

"Mm-hmm." Sounded about right. I'd heard back after 3 days. When I'd gone in for the annual exam, they'd run an STD panel just in case. With the missing memories, who knew?

"I'm sure I'm healthy, Shell," he said.

"How can you be sure? You never did tell me about your former partners," I said, arms crossed. Well, except that Sara had been "adventurous."

"There were two. You'd be number three." He looked at me. I felt my brow tighten as it furrowed. "What?" He asked, raising his hands in the air.

"You sure?" I was skeptical. With his looks and, well, charm I suppose, I expected the number to be much higher.

"Yes, I'm sure." He laughed.

"Sara?"

"Yes."

"How long ago? You're counting Vicki?" The number definitely didn't sound high enough.

"Well, let me think. It's been... um... three months. Counting oral? No."

"Oh. That's not very long." My eyes narrowed. "Oral totally counts." I knew there was something off about his headcount. I felt slutty too, with my desire to just jump him. Maybe I was taking out my insecurities on him.

"It wasn't that serious, Shell."

"Not that serious, but you had sex with her. That's great. So, you haven't actually been tested since Sara."

"I guess not."

"Eew." I closed my eyes and breathed in deeply. "I'm guessing she wasn't a virgin."

"No. Why does that matter to you?"

"Haven't you ever heard the saying that when you have sex with someone, you're having sex with everyone that person slept with?" I felt hysteria coming on. "Depending on how promiscuous your partners were, it could be like sleeping with hundreds of people by having sex with you." I couldn't hold back my anxiety, wondering what other acts and partners he had omitted from the count. I let out the nervous giggles. Dylan looked at me like I might pick up a sharp object and stab him.

"So, was the person before Sara a virgin?" I looked at him, pulling away.

"No," he said cautiously. "She was older."

"Could be worse I guess." I stared at him. Lots of my friends had been sexually active early and had more than one partner. "Are you expecting to have more partners while you're with me?"

"No." He shook his head and held his hands up in surrender.

"Then I guess we're good." Gosh, I was acting crazy. Was I the Jay of the relationship? I didn't want to be. But I didn't want to get a nasty disease either. "Gee Dylan, this is so romantic, huh?"

"We should talk about it. It affects you too." He took my scarred arm in his hand and ran a finger down my raised scar, not the Lichtenberg one. "We should probably talk about this too."

"I suppose that might affect you as well." I didn't want to talk about the incident post-accident now. He deserved to know.

"What happened after the accident?"

"I spent time in the hospital, then another hospital for mental health issues." My head shook involuntarily, muscles stiff. Dylan continued to run his finger along the jagged line. "I was hospitalized after the accident when I lost my sense of hope. My friends were dead, I should have been too. I hurt myself, was found before I died, and was checked into the hospital after my wounds were treated. If mom wasn't a nurse, I wouldn't have made it." I took a breath. What I didn't mention was that it was Andy who had found me. I still felt guilty about that.

"Do you still feel that way?" He asked, eyes moving from my scar to meet my eyes.

"From time to time. Not as severely, but I do have my low times." I sighed. "Sometimes they last a while."

"What do you do when you feel that way?"

"Sleep a lot. Get irritable and anger easily. Other times I get insomnia and can't sleep."

"Do you still see a doctor about that?"

"I stopped going. Didn't seem to be helping." My brows drew together. "The ones in the hospital certainly didn't." My breath rushed out in a huff.

"What was that like?"

"They gave me medicine all day. I was so fuzzy headed I could barely function. I sat around staring at walls a lot. Didn't talk much. We had individual sessions and groups every day."

"How long were you in?"

"About a month."

I pulled into Norma's deserted parking lot five minutes before my evening shift. I parked and walked inside, hat and apron in hand. The tables were empty and there were no customers in line. No one manned the cash register. I wondered where everyone was and headed to the back to check my assignment and clock in. Raif sat in the manager's office speaking with Pat in hushed tones. Sal prepped vegetables for the next sandwich station worker on the metal table surface. I examined the board. My name was written over the salad bar and dining room hostess stations in Pat's unsteady hand. I clocked in.

Soon after checking in, I had the salad bar prepped for the evening. Raif asked me to join him in the office. I followed him back and took a seat. He closed the door behind him. I frowned.

"Shell, we've had some sad news today. Mrs. Jones called to let us know that Marcus died around 3:00 this afternoon." He said with a deep sigh.

"I thought his vitals were improving," I said, rushed.

"Well, he appeared to be doing better and even seemed to be responsive the past couple days. Then, this afternoon, his heart stopped again. They weren't able to revive him." His eyes creased in concern, in search of some reaction that I wasn't giving. I wondered why Raif was giving me the news instead of Pat.

"I'm really sad to hear that. He was a nice guy," I said with a break in my voice. We hadn't been close, but my stomach dropped. I guess there would be no future tutoring.

"He was. When I talked with his mom a little while ago, she said she found something of yours at their house. She wants to bring it by tonight." His green eyes held mine. My brow creased.

"I don't remember giving him anything." I looked at the ceiling as I tried to remember letting him borrow anything of mine. Nothing came to mind.

"Well, she's stopping by later. I wanted to give you a heads up. Also, we'll be sending around a sympathy card for people to sign. I know he was fond of you," Raif said. I didn't know that Marcus was particularly fond of me. We barely talked until he asked me if I wanted help with Calculus. I thought he was just being kind.

"He was nice, but we weren't close or anything. Just had some classes together," I said, voice hushed.

"Don't tell his mom that. Just tell her you're sorry for her loss or something, ok?" He suggested, touching my arm. I looked down at his long fingers resting on my skin and frowned.

"Sure, thanks for the heads up," I said, suddenly exhausted.

"Oh, and great show last weekend, really, it was awesome," he said with a voice that betrayed emotional exhaustion.

"Thanks." I left the office trying to remember Raif being at either of the shows before my thoughts returned to Marcus. It was nearly 5:00 and there still weren't any customers. Weird. I walked the dining room, wiped down clean tables, straightened chairs, checked trash bins, and stocked the condiment bar to near overflowing before moving on to the restrooms. I cringed while cleaning the restrooms. Visuals of Vicki and Dylan persisted like an incurable plague. I'd avoided checking on the restrooms earlier, knowing I had to, but not wanting to.

Dylan arrived around 5:15, called in to replace Jules, who called in sick. He worked the grill, but had less to busy his time than I did. He came back to check on me while I swept the tiled area around the salad bar.

"Hear about Marcus? I know you didn't know him, but it's sad," I said. I emptied the dustpan into the trash. Not much came out of it, just some dirt and a couple pieces of broccoli I must have dropped while setting up.

"You knew him though." He leaned against the counter, legs and arms crossed. Even in the uniform, he looked good. It was sweet of him to care.

"Sort of. We've had classes together and worked together for a couple of years. He was kind of shy. Offered to help tutor me with math a few times." My voice drifted off near the end.

"Apparently had a crush on you," he reminded me. "I overheard Vicki saying he was going to ask you out."

"Must've been a recent thing. I didn't know until Vicki said something the other day," I said, brushing it off. We walked behind the bar, where I put the small broom and dust pan away before washing my hands. His arms snaked around me as he kissed my forehead. Not wanting to think about it anymore, I changed the subject. "What are you doing after work?"

"No plans," he said.

"Follow me home? I'm not going to school tomorrow."

"Sure, if you want. Will your mom get mad?"

"Maybe, I don't know. She's been uncharacteristically calm about stuff recently. She works at the hospital. She probably knows about Marcus." I looked to the door as a woman with shoulder length black hair and a purple top came in carrying a bag. "Hey, there's his mom now."

"Shell!"

"Mrs. Jones," I said as I stepped out from behind the salad bar and gave her a hug. She grasped me like a drowning woman, heaving in a silent sob. Her eyes, pink and puffy, spoke of recent tears. With a shaky breath, she let go, collapsing against the bar.

"Last weekend I went through Marcus' bedroom to look for a couple things to bring to his hospital room, you know, bring him a piece of home? I found these." She pulled out a small photo album, some letters, and a couple of notebooks. "I put them to the side, just in case. I had a feeling he wasn't doing well." She sniffed, putting the items back in the bag. "He'd want you to have these. You meant a lot to him. It's a comfort to know he had someone like you in his life."

"Thank you, Mrs. Jones. I'm so sorry for your loss. I'll miss him." I hugged her again, confused by her choice of words, and she hurried off. I wouldn't consider myself as a part of Marcus' life, so how did she find comfort in that? I sighed and picked up the paper sack.

I carried the bag to the back room and placed it on the employee shelf to retrieve on the way home. I wasn't in the mood to look at the items now. Despite what she told Raif, none of those items were mine. They were all Marcus'. To look at them seemed an invasion of privacy.

I returned to the salad bar, where Dylan stirred marinara sauce. "What was he holding onto?"

"It wasn't my stuff. She just thought I should have it. Said I meant a lot to him, and she was happy that he had someone like me in his life." I shook my head. "I can't look at it right now. Feel like I'd be prying into his personal thoughts or something, you know?"

"Um, sure." His eyes shifted down and away. Seemed like he didn't get my moral quandary.

"I mean, he wasn't even what I'd consider a friend, more of an acquaintance, you know? We barely talked. Even here, we didn't talk much." I cringed, "Jay's more a friend than Marcus was." I shook my head.

"Jay isn't that bad," he insisted with a light nudge to my shoulder. "He took me in, right?"

I eyed him and nodded slowly, thinking about Jules, her black eye, and other injuries. I wasn't convinced.

Dylan pulled into the driveway behind me. I brought Marcus' stuff into the house and left it on top of the old piano in the basement. I didn't want to touch it. Felt like the stuff was haunted and I didn't want it near me right now.

Upstairs, mom sat at the dining room table reading a book. She looked up as we pushed through the door. She placed a bookmark between the pages and laid it on the table.

"Not a very comfortable place to read mom," I noted, shifting foot to foot. Her set expression made my heart race.

"Wanted to be here when you got home. You heard about Marcus?" She gestured for us to sit.

"Yeah," my voice tired. "Raif told me, and Mrs. Jones stopped by work to drop off a few of his things for me," my voice barely above a whisper. A hand rested on my shoulder. I shook and leaned into Dylan.

"She's a lovely woman," mom said. "She was there every day by his side. She kept a picture of you and him next to his bed." I raised an eyebrow. Where did she get a photo of the two of us together? There couldn't be many of those.

"What?" I couldn't process the reasoning behind the photo. Mrs. Jones must have had photos of Marcus with lots of his friends.

"You doing ok?" Mom asked "You're whiter than usual."

"Guess I'm kind of shocked. We weren't really friend friends. We had a lot of the same friends. I think what bothers me the most is that he's my age. People my age aren't supposed to die that easily." I sniffed. Dylan moved in and hugged me from behind. Of course, I knew people my age died. Joe and Christy had died even younger.

"I'm sorry honey. Young people die all the time." Mom looked at me. "You know that," she reminded me, eyes shifting down, reluctant to bring up Joe and Christy.

"What happened? I thought he was doing better. Were you there?" My heart raced and my throat tightened. I didn't want to cry, but my eyes held the telltale burn of tears.

"I was at the hospital, but not in the room at the time. He woke up. Talked with his mother. Seemed to be doing well. Then all of the sudden he wasn't. He was gone. Happens that way sometimes."

"He woke up?" My eyebrows flew up. I wondered what he'd said to his mother. Was it normal for a person to wake up from a coma and then die like that?

"Briefly."

"That must be so horrible for his mom, to have him back for a moment, then lose him like that. Oh my gosh…"

"Or, a blessing. Not everyone gets that chance." She patted my hand before drawing away. Her eyebrows pulled together. "Shell, did you say something to make Mr. Dirk angry?"

"No. Haven't talked to him since yesterday morning." I looked at Dylan and back at mom. "Why?"

"He left a message saying you're out for the next two weeks."

"Is that even legal?" I screeched. "I didn't do anything." She shook her head.

"Might be a good idea to start looking into the GED." She looked at me shaking her head. "I don't like it, but I have a feeling you're not getting back into that school." So much for all of my pre-AP classes. I lost the will to stand and collapsed into a wooden dining room chair. I slumped onto the table, drained.

"Can Dylan stay tonight? Since I don't have school and with all the other stuff going on, I could use the support. Please?"

"You know how I feel about that, Shell," mom narrowed her eyes and leaned back.

"Please mom? I'd feel safer. I need this. I'm sad, pissed off, anxious. I'm asking for help." I didn't ask for help. Dylan was not Ted.

"Well," she assessed me, conflicting thoughts obvious, "ok, but leave the door open." She shook her head, resting her head on her hand.

"Whatever you want, Mrs. Dean." He agreed with a squeeze of my leg.

"Call Jay and let him know you won't be back tonight," I said. I stood and stretched, taking in a deep, shaky breath.

"Yeah, I should. I'll make sure he knows about Marcus too.

They were friends, right?"

"Yeah, they were." I pointed to the phone and he called Jay while mom and I moved to the living room.

"Lots of changes all at once, Shell." She hugged me. Concerned, she searched me through tired eyes.

"I know, mom. But, Dylan's helping, a lot."

"He's a big part of those changes."

"Yes, but, I'm happy about that change." It was a change I'd chosen to make, not one of those unexpected ones that caught me tottering on the edge.

"Oh, call Zane. He called several times while you were at work." She pulled a piece of paper from the coffee table and handed it to me. It listed a few messages, Zane's name and number among them.

"It's late, but sure. Soon as Dylan's off the phone. I want to work on some songs, I'm not sleepy. May go down to the garage for a bit, or maybe the basement since there's a heater." I wouldn't keep anyone up downstairs. Besides, the slightly creepy atmosphere of the basement fit my mood.

"Don't stay up too late," she chided.

"Ok. Goodnight mom," I hugged her when she stood.

"Goodnight," she called over her shoulder as she walked back to her room.

Dylan returned soon after mom closed her bedroom door. He put an arm around me.

"All good?" I looked up.

"Yep, all good. I think Jay's annoyed that I'm not spending much time with him. It's like he's jealous or something."

"Sorry."

"I'm not," he said with a huge grin before taking me in his arms and kissing me until I was breathless. I caught my breath and got control over my goofy grin. I pointed to the kitchen.

"I need to call Zane. Apparently, he's been harassing mom all evening. Need to see what's up." I headed for the kitchen and dialed Zane's number. He picked up on the second ring.

"Shell?" The line clicked and crackled a bit.

"Yeah, it's me. Mom said you called?"

"Damn, I've been trying to reach you all night. Worried you wouldn't call. Your mom said she'd ask you to."

"She did. What's the emergency?"

"Where've you been? Things are nuts at school!" He said, either annoyed or excited, it was hard to tell with the raised voice.

"You're still in school? Principle Dirk didn't kick you out too?"

"You were kicked out?"

"Yeah, I've been told at least two weeks. I might not be able to go back at all," I said. My hand fisted and my nails dug into my palm.

"You're kidding!"

"No, I'm not," I said through gritted teeth. Talking about was bringing on the anger.

"Lucky."

"So? The emergency?"

"Oh, clubs all over the place want to book us. We need to schedule. Sounds like your schedule is clearer than expected?"

"Might be. I'll still have to clear it with mom."

"That's true for most of us. Have to clear it with the parents. We need to set up rehearsals."

"Right, what were you thinking? I'm still working."

"Shell, I don't think you need to worry about working right now. Our rate has increased. Clubs are bidding on us right now."

"What do you mean bidding?" My brows furrowed as my fist relaxed. Did clubs do that? Bid? I picked up a pencil and started chewing on it.

"For priority. You know, who gets us when. Those who want to book us now are offering to pay big bucks."

"You're kidding. How big?"

"The highest so far was $2000, not including a percentage of ticket sales."

"Not bad."

"Before long, we'll need an actual business manager, Shell. I'm serious. I can't handle these darn phone calls. Phone's been ringing non-stop. I have to unplug it at night."

"Whoa," my voice trailed off.

"Can we rehearse tomorrow night?" His voice got my attention.

"I guess so. What time are you coming over?"

"Five?"

"Great, see you then. Bye." I hung up and turned to find Dylan leaning against the wall, arms crossed, watching me.

"The band is still in school, huh?" Dylan asked.

"Sounds like it."

"Hardly seems fair," he said, lip turned up in a smirk. I tilted my head. I didn't think he had the same thoughts about school that I did.

"Exactly," I drew out. "Anyway, I want to grab my acoustic guitar and a couple blankets, then go downstairs."

"Sure." He followed me back to my room, where I picked up my acoustic guitar and gestured around the room.

"You want anything to read while I'm working?" He shook his head. "You sure? You might get bored. Magazine?"

"No, really, I'll be good."

"Ok." We grabbed a couple blankets from the love seat before going down to the basement. I leaned my acoustic against the wall of my old room, turned on the heater, and headed into the garage for a couple of stools, my notebook, and a pencil. I brought those back into my former bedroom, then returned to the garage for a music stand to hold my notebook.

Rather than sit on a stool, Dylan spread a blanket on the floor in front of the heater and laid down, watching me. I set up a stool nearby, bringing my guitar and stand closer and sat down with notebook and pencil in hand. I looked up at the ceiling trying to let my mind go blank, as the pencil drifted to my mouth, but I felt Dylan's eyes on me and it was distracting. I looked down at him. He smiled at me, the rogue.

"What?" I spoke around the pencil.

"It's just interesting to see your process," he grinned, finding something amusing. Probably that I was sitting there chewing on a pencil and staring at the wall instead of writing in the notebook or strumming on the guitar.

"I'm not making much progress right now," I whined, taking the pencil out of my mouth and tapping it on my knee.

"I'm sure you will."

"I'm going to keep trying. I need a topic." My eyes rolled skyward and I stared at the ceiling tiles for a bit as if inspiration might fall through one of the white textured squares.

"What about Marcus?" Dylan suggested.

"I didn't know him that well," I said, voice distant as I

continued to stare at the ceiling.

"Sure, but he died young, right?"

"Right," my throat tightened and the back of my eyes burned as images of charred red hair and fading green eyes filled my mind. Joe.

"You could write about that, dying young." He was right, I could. I might end up sobbing on the floor, but I could.

I nodded and tried to bring a picture of Marcus' face into my mind with as much detail as I remembered. Luckily, there were no actual memories of Marcus in ICU, only those I'd imagined. I visualized Marcus sitting in class, standing at the grill at work, getting books out of his locker. I revisited my last memories of Marcus, sitting with him on the beach, the wind blowing through our hair as he asked me if I needed tutoring, as we talked about general life stuff, as he walked me to my car in the rain. He'd been so sweet to offer tutoring. It was sad as heck that he wouldn't ever have the chance to have a serious relationship, go to college, maybe get married and have children. The mythical image of the Fates drifted across my mind. Life cut short by the cruel shears of Atropos.

Scarred wood marks the tree
Where a cruel turn did take
The cruel hand of fate

Will you remember
When you close your eyes
What no one denies
A heart from beat has severed
Loss hidden with lies

Do you slumber restfully
Now that you are free
Or wander aimlessly?

When we close our eyes
Will we remember
Your departure premature
From the earthly domain

Toxic Siren: Awakening

By the shears of Atropos, one dies.

I picked up my guitar, experimenting with minor chords, and found a progression of mixed chords that sounded vaguely eerie. The lyrics were iffy, but a start.

I went ahead and tried another, considering the symbolism of the willow tree and its association with death.

I will be your willow tree
Weeping long after you've gone
I'll wait until you return to me
A last vestige of light undone.

In the darkness I have danced
To the tune of your heartbeat
For a while, life enhanced
You, earth under my feet.

I'm crying out for you.
Wailing!
Can't you hear my pain?
Wailing for you
You gone, I'm insane

Do you hear me calling out for you?
Your lips of blue
Unflattering hue

My limbs dance in the breeze
Beneath a moon full
Of broken promises given with ease
My heartstrings did you pull.

I'm crying out for you.
Wailing!
Can't you hear my pain?

Wailing for you
Mind lost from pain

Your weeping willow
Dancing in the breeze.

Dylan left before the guys arrived, but promised he'd return after closing. I gathered the laundry and began sorting by color. As I reached a pair of my brothers tighty-whities, the sight of tracks made me quickly toss them into a pile. Gross. I sometimes wondered if it would help him to have a responsible male to look up to. I mean, basic hygiene kid! I certainly didn't want to take responsibility for hygiene talks. Next thing I knew, I'd have to give him the sex talk. I thought he was at or past the age of the initial sex ed in school, but couldn't be sure. I hadn't seen him bring home any permission slips like I'd had to bring home back in the day. I wondered if Andy and mom had had the talk. I took the laundry to the basement and started the first load, whites first, in hot water. I smiled when I found Dylan's tee mixed in with the laundry. I sniffed it before tossing it into the machine.

I heard a car in the driveway and looked out the window as mom got out of her car. I opened the basement door. She carried two plastic grocery bags from the A&P.

"Any more bags in the car?"

"No, this is it."

"Take one for you?" I asked, reaching for the heaviest one.

"Sure." She released it as my fingers closed around the handle. She nodded her head toward the laundry hamper. "Doing laundry?"

"Um, yeah." Seemed kind of obvious to me with the clothes arranged in a parfait of colors and the washing machine running.

"Thanks."

"No problem. The band is coming over tonight for rehearsal. We have that big gig in a couple weeks. Zane's freaking out. He's been getting calls asking for us to perform all over the place. Clubs are actually bidding for us."

"Bidding? I didn't know they did that," she said.

"Neither did I." I opened the kitchen door and placed the

bag on the counter, unloading items one by one. "He thinks we may need an actual manager or agent soon. It's kind of scary."

"Oh, I brought something home for you." Mom pulled a GED prep book from her shoulder bag. "Just something to think about. See how prepared you are right now and what might need more study."

"Thanks, mom. I appreciate it. It's actually really boring sitting around the house all day. I may want to ask for additional work days this week. I'm not sure yet."

"Where's Dylan? Thought he'd be here when I got home."

"He's working tonight. He'll be back after work. Hope you don't mind. I'm still feeling kind of freaked out about a lot of things. I feel better and more grounded when he's around."

"That's fine, dear." Mom observed me with an expression I wasn't familiar with. Eyes sad, smiling a little, arms crossed, she leaned back on the counter. "This isn't the life I'd planned for you."

"Plans change." I said with a shrug.

"I suppose they do."

"The band will be over a lot this week. After school."

"So, they really are still in school?" She asked.

"Somehow."

"You know, if you really want to go to school, you could always move in with your dad and go back to Blue Ridge. You still have friends there."

"Friends I've barely talked to or seen in over three years." I'd let them go when I moved, wanting a new beginning. Besides, a lot of them had taken issue with my brain damaged personality makeover.

"It'll be like hardly any time has passed," she urged. I'd just be living up the hill from my dead boyfriend and a couple houses down from my dead bestie. Nothing could go wrong in those circumstances. It was better to fall into the abyss of lost memory of my old friends than be the weird girl who used to be popular and smart.

"And Toxic Siren? Just the other day, you were concerned about the band. What happens to them if I move back to dad's?" I crossed my arms and gave her the side eye.

"I don't know." She sighed. "Do you really want the band, fame? Being in the spotlight, where everything you do becomes everyone else's business? You'll have no privacy." I hadn't even told her about the photographs.

"I don't know, mom. I want to make it work. It's all I can do for now." I picked up the GED practice book then let it drop to the table. "This isn't my dream either, but it's an option. I'll consider moving back with dad, but I doubt I'll do it. It'd be the end of Toxic Siren. We're just taking off."

"You have lots of family up there," she reminded me. "You'll have a lot of support."

"True. Lots of aunts, uncles, cousins, and the grandparents." I shrugged. The kitchen door opened and Andy rushed through, dropping his backpack loudly just inside the door.

"What's up, Andy?" I asked.

"There were, like, 20 photographers outside of school all day. The principal sent us to the gym and locked us in. It was so boring," he said. The words poured out in a rush. He stopped to pull in a breath.

"What do you mean, they locked you in?" I asked.

"To keep us away from the cameras."

"Why were the cameras there?" Mom asks, voice rising.

"They were looking for Shell's brother." Andy pointed at me. "But they didn't know what I looked like, so they were taking photos of all the boys," Andy said with a laugh. Mom groaned.

"School's out tomorrow while the principal tries to figure out how to keep the photographers out." Andy laughed. "Way to go, Shell! Soon, I'll be home all day too." He hopped up and down excitedly.

"Not as fun as you think buddy." I tossed a balled-up napkin at him. "I'm going to check on the laundry. Be right back." I went down to the basement, unloaded and loaded clothes, and leaned forward against the dryer to let out a silent scream, more of a prolonged throat whistle really. I looked up, startled to notice a shadow blocking part of the basement door's window. Air whooshed back into my lungs when I realized it was just Zane.

"Hey Zane, come on in." I motioned him forward and into the garage where we sat down on a couple of stools. "Right on time. Where's Barry? You guys normally ride over together."

"Barry has a big Physics test coming up Wednesday and

said he had to study. He won't be here tonight. Ted begged out too. Something about practicing for district band tryouts." He shrugged, eyes cast to the floor, hiding something.

"You're not trying out too?"

"Me? Heck, no. Got enough to do. Figured we should talk anyway, even though the guys couldn't be here."

"About what?"

"Why you haven't been in school."

"Principal Dirk kicked me out," I said, voice flat.

"Right, but why?"

"He said I was disturbing school, or inciting riots, or something."

"You weren't though."

"No," I said, drawing it out. It's not like I'd done anything on purpose to get kicked out of school. Dirk had barreled out mad. I hadn't provoked.

"Well, school operations, as he put it, are definitely disturbed. Photographers keep infiltrating the school and snapping photos. Reporters wait outside, trying to find you or interview other students about you. They could care less about the rest of us."

"Why is the rest of the band not kicked out too? How are you guys still going to class?"

"Nobody seems to realize that we're in the band. Apparently, Shell, you are Toxic Siren." Zane shook his head with a smirk. "The guys are kind of ticked."

"I am too. I don't like how this is affecting my life. I can barely leave my house, and the number of messages every day is ridiculous. I'm afraid to answer the phone without screening first. I can't believe you're all still able to go to school."

"No need to tell me about the phone calls, we've got more offers out there for club shows than we could fill a summer tour with. They're starting to spread beyond Pennsylvania. Even got another call from New York City today."

"No way."

"We're on the edge." He leaned forward. "Do you understand, Shell? We could really make something of ourselves, get out of here."

"What's wrong with the Poconos? I like it here." Not that I'd planned to stay here. My plan was to go to Penn State, Main

Campus, hours away. "I'm tossing around the idea of taking the GED. It doesn't look like I can go back to school any time soon. Mom even suggested I move back in with dad and go back to my old school."

"Where's your dad live? Not far from here? Don't think going back to your old school's the answer. Same media frenzy would happen there," he said. He didn't realize my dad's house was hours away. It would make practices difficult.

"I guess so." I looked around the garage. It felt so bare without the other guys. "I miss seeing you guys every day." It had only been a couple of days, but I even missed Zane. There was an emptiness in my stomach and a tightness in my throat. "Don't suppose you'd all like to take the GED with me and tour early?"

"Hmmm…" Zane seemed almost speechless as he absorbed the idea. "Barry and Ted are 18, you and I have to get parental permission, right?" He asked. I'd be 18 next week. There was a little more to it, but I didn't want to go into it. "Ted is having a rough time. Have you talked to him?"

"No, what's going on?"

"I'm assuming it has something to do with you and Dylan being so close so fast," he said, voice accusing. My heart dropped.

"He encouraged it," I said, defensive.

"He wants you to be happy, even if it means that he isn't."

"Crap. It's hard to tell what he wants."

"You know nothing about his childhood, Shell. Before he was taken in and adopted by the Levins, things were a lot different." Zane looked down. "Ever wonder why no one gets anywhere near him? Why he doesn't let people touch him? You were breaking down his walls. He hugs you for goodness' sake!" Zane shook his head. "Doesn't even flinch when you touch."

"He never talks about his childhood, and it's taken years for him to feel comfortable enough to let me touch him and vice versa."

"He's different with you."

"I know. He's my best friend."

"He's more than that. At least to him, it's more than that."

"It's hard to define." I looked up, then my eyes fell back to the concrete. "Then Dylan showed up, and Ted just kind of pushed us together, and stepped back? I don't know how to explain it."

"He's trying to make you happy."

"I miss him."

"Well, you two need to figure it out. It's messing with our vibe."

"I'll try."

"You've been working on some new material?" He asked, changing the subject. Zane rubbed his hands on his jeans and looked ready to get down to business.

I nodded.

"Care to share it?"

"Sure. Let me get set up." I plugged in the acoustic electric guitar, turned up the amp, then the mic. "I've been thinking about Marcus the past couple of days." I started playing, then changing, the chord progressions and rough lyrics of Marcus' song, *Atropos* followed by *Willow*.

"Obviously, rough, but that's what I have so far." My eyes darted to the garage door, "Wait a sec, I've got an idea." I opened the door, switched out the laundry again and sat down on the piano bench, where I used the same chord progressions, but on the piano instead of the guitar. Gosh, the piano was in bad shape. So out of tune. It gave the song a different sound. Not that great because of the tuning, but I could play with my electric piano if I pulled it out of my closet later. I liked the idea. Made me wish Ted were around. He was great at smoothing out rough lyrics and offering constructive criticism.

"Let me get the tape recorder." Zane hurried into the garage, grabbed a fresh tape, hit record and I started again at the piano with *Willow*. It began slow in a minor key with me singing a mixture of high and low notes, but more in the upper register. It didn't have any of the growling scream that I enjoyed, but the melody was pretty, even if the words weren't perfect yet. I liked it better with the piano than the guitar. I decided to try Marcus' song with the piano as well. It was rougher than *Willow*, but still worked well substituting piano for guitar. A mixture of guitar and piano might work.

I felt like I was creating a new sound for myself as I worked with the piano and I enjoyed it. It was different than working with Ted and the band, but also freeing in a way. It was a far less finished sound than I got with the band, but it could work in a pinch. Amateur nights maybe, for the ones I liked, but didn't fit with the band. I needed to improve my piano and guitar playing skills, whether for self-improvement, or for the band's overall sound. Lucky me, it looked like I had the hours that could be dedicated to such practice in the near future.

"Shell? Hello?" Fingers snapped in front of my eyes.

"Hmmm?" Dazed, I looked up from the piano, my fingers pressing firmly down on a final set of chords.

"Where'd you go?"

"Sorry. Brain's on planning overload." I shook my head, trying to fling outside thoughts away. I breathed in. Stay in the moment, Shell. "Just thinking I need to put more time and cash into piano lessons and practice."

"Wouldn't hurt. Sounded good. Places you could improve; work in the weeping willow line a few more times and that will help, end of the chorus I think."

"Thanks, Zane." I began again, allowing words to change when they fit better and added in repetitions of the weeping willow line to the choruses. From the corner of my eye, I noticed the bobbing of Zane's head as I played and sang.

"I like it." He nodded. "Just fancy up the piano and tighten the lyrics and you've got a good one." A notebook fell onto the piano keys with a cacophonous ring. Zane picked it up. "New lyrics notebook?"

I shook my head, looking at the cover. "No, that's a notebook that Mrs. Jones brought me after Marcus died. Said she found it in his room and that I should have it." Zane thumbed through the pages.

"Have you looked at this?" He asked, eyes wider than usual, and growing wider as he turned the pages. Something wasn't right.

"No, just put it all on top of the piano when I came home," I said with a shrug as chills ran down my spine.

Zane held the notebook out to me, opened to a page with "Mrs. Michelle Jones" and "Shell Jones" and other variations of our combined names written all over the pages surrounded by hearts. "Ni-i-ce." Zane drawled, grin creeping into his voice. "Dylan see these?"

"I don't think he's been down here going through my stuff." I pulled the notebook from Zane's hands and begin paging through it myself. Zane took the photo album from the top of the piano and started going through it.

"Oh boy." Zane stifled a laugh. "Shell, this is really weird." He held up the album to show me a collage from a magazine with my yearbook photo face pasted to a swimsuit model. The yearbook photo was so unflattering!

"Oh my gosh! His mom gave me his stalker spank bank?" I went back to the journal, seeing page after page of doodles and variations of my name merged with his last name. Marcus had seemed so normal. "I thought only girls did this kind of thing." I sighed, putting the journal back on top of the piano. "Didn't his mom look this stuff over before deciding to give it to me? What was she thinking? Did she think it was sweet? Cute?"

"Shell, maybe she thought you two were dating, or that those were your notebooks." Zane raised an eyebrow and smirked. "Shell, these aren't your notebooks, are they?" I tossed a pencil at him, hitting his chest.

"Of course not. Idiot." I took a deep breath. "She told Raif that she'd found some of my things in his room. Then she showed up with this stuff and gave it to me. She said that she thought I should have them."

"Wow, check this out." Zane held out a photo of me talking on the phone. I was in my old basement bedroom and it looked like the photo was taken from the window under the deck. At night. I took the album from Zane and checked the photos. Some of them were group photos with our shared friends. Others were photos taken of me when I wasn't aware that I was being watched. Some of them, like the one with me talking on the phone were of more private moments. I felt violated.

"Crap, stalker. Like, for real." I continued paging through the photos, unable to stop. There were a few more pictures where Marcus apparently cut my head out of photos and pasted them onto other people's bodies, sometimes in pictures of him with other friends. In one, he'd glued both of our heads onto some magazine advertisement where the couple was dressed in fancy clothing. I showed this gem to Zane. "I had no idea he was doing this."

"Creepy, huh?"

"He barely said a few words to me at a time. Vicki said he'd been planning to ask me out before the accident, but this is ridiculous!" I placed the photo album on the piano bench like a dirty tissue and picked up the last journal with my fingertips like it might be contagious. "I don't even know if I want to look at this."

"Go for it. How much worse can it be?"

"Who knows." As I opened the journal, a folded copy of one of Toxic Siren's performance flyers fell out. Zane leaned down to pick it up. It was from one of last year's local shows, one of Raif's backyard bashes, actually. Zane opened it up and I watched his mouth drops open.

"What?" I asked.

"Uhhhh..." He looked from the paper, to me, and back to the paper again.

"What is it?" I made a grab for it before Zane could fold it back up or hide it away. I looked at the flyer, finding lots of scribbles over my bandmates, while my photocopied self had a doodle of a flower bouquet where my mic would have been. A crude drawing of a dress, I guess, drawn over my flannel top and jeans, and something that could be a veil drawn on top of my hair. It looked absolutely grotesque.

"Oh - my - gosh!" I dropped the flyer like it was on fire. Mom must have heard my scream because the door at the top of the basement door suddenly flew open and mom rushed down.

"What's wrong, Shell?" She yelled, out of breath. I pointed at the flyer on the ground and started laughing hysterically.

"I didn't do it, I swear!" He said, stepping back with hands raised in the air.

"Seriously, mom, we need to talk." I picked up the photo album and journals and we all walked upstairs. I laid the evidence on the dining room table. I told her how Mrs. Jones brought me the items and how she'd told Raif that Marcus had some of my things in his room that she wanted to return to me. When she gave them to me, she knew they weren't mine, but told me she thought he'd want me to have them. Looking at the journals and album now, I had to wonder what the heck she'd been thinking.

"Maybe she thought you'd be flattered that her son thought

so… highly… of you," mom said, searching for the right words, trying not to offend.

"But, mom, it's obvious that he's been taking pictures of me without my knowledge. Pictures from outside my old bedroom window. Gross!" A thought smacked me in the face and I nearly recoiled. "Oh my gosh, someone left a copy of a photo of me and Dylan on the deck the other night on my windshield. Marcus was in the hospital. How many people are sneaking pictures of me? Someone's still taking pictures of me!" My breathing quickened and my vision began to blacken at the edges, narrowing as the darkness tried to overtake me.

"Shell! Shell!" Mom's voice muffled as pressure and buzzing filled my ears. She leaned over me and shook me by the shoulders. "Head between your knees and breathe!"

"Why?" I pointed to the journals and photo album. "Why?" I whined louder, angry tears dripping from my eyes.

"Why not?" Zane looked at me.

"Huh?" I tilted my head and sniffed.

"If not you, it would have just been someone else." His eyes turned toward the ceiling and a finger tapped his chin. "Although, you do attract these obsessive types, don't you?"

"Honey, maybe you need to stay with your dad for a while." She looked at me, forehead creasing with deep lines as her brows crawled together, "you said Dylan was in that photo that was left on your car? Maybe he should go up there with you. I could talk to his father. We'll talk when Dylan gets back tonight." I nodded.

"Dylan's staying here?" Zane's eyes widened and he looked from me to my mom and back.

"Sort of." I felt a corner of my lips lift and tried to return to a neutral expression. "He's helping me through a difficult time." I fingered my scar. "One that keeps getting more and more complicated."

19

Mom and I sat at the dining room table with the journals and photo albums on the table when Dylan walked through the kitchen door. I'd lent him the spare key before he left. He eyed us as he placed his apron and hat on the counter.

"This doesn't look good. What's going on?"

"Have a seat, Dylan. Let's talk." I invited him to sit between me and mom. "Remember that photo that I found on my windshield Monday morning?"

"Yeah, a little weird."

"Well, those things that Mrs. Jones gave me are even more creepy weird." I pointed to the photo album and journals and invited him to take a look. He picked up the photo album and began looking through the photos and collages. His mouth dropped open and his forehead wrinkled as he continued paging through the photos.

"What the…" he trailed off and looked at me, eyes narrowed, "what are these?"

"They were with Marcus' things." He started to see some of the more personal photos, like those taken from outside the window of my former basement bedroom.

"Oh my gosh, Shell," he said, voice hushed. Dropping the album, he pulled me into a hug. "How long had he been doing this?"

"I don't know. Remind you of that photo left on my car?"

"Similar in theme, photo taken during a private moment. But we weren't inside the house."

"Yeah, but taken in night vision or something? Come on." My head shook so violently that some of my braided hair came loose. "Take a look at the journals."

He picked up the Mrs. Marcus Jones journal. Nothing but variations of Mr. And Mrs. Marcus Jones, Mrs. Michelle Jones, etc.… Disturbing as heck.

"Didn't know guys did this." He mumbled. I snorted.

"That's what I said!" My hands gestured wildly. "Anyway, you get the idea. He was creepy obsessed. I didn't even know. I don't know why his mom would think I wanted this stuff." Maybe she wanted me to know that he liked me. "What bothers me more is that the new photo was taken after he was in the coma, and it was definitely left on my car while he was in the hospital. That's someone else harassing me, well, us."

"Sure, it's upsetting when you put it that way."

"See if Zane put the band flyer back. It was in the other journal on folded orange paper. I didn't actually look at the other journal, just the flyer." Dylan pulled the flyer out of the journal.

"Those are some serious elementary school art skills," he said with a laugh.

"All my bandmates are scribbled out of the picture and I appear to be in a dress and veil. I'm kind of freaked out."

"I can see that," he said, trying to look serious, but failing.

"Mom suggested that I stay with dad for a while, maybe go back to my old school if I don't want to do the GED. She also suggested that you might want to come with me. Dad would probably allow it if I asked. It might be good to get away for a few days, or a week or so. Even if we don't transfer to my old school."

"I haven't spoken with John yet, but I'm sure he wouldn't mind," mom said. I could tell she was judging dad's difference in morals by the sour look on her face.

"Let me think about it." He shook his head. "I've been to a bunch of schools, Shell. I wanted to make this one work. It's only a matter of months to graduation."

"If you change your mind, let me know," mom said,

standing. "I could talk to your father." Mom left us to talk.

"I don't think that's really necessary," he said. "Moving, that is."

I shrugged. "I don't like being watched." Chills rushed down my spine.

"What about that Carlo guy, could it be him?"

"Carlo? No. He's at NYU. Working on film." Oh. He'd have fancy cameras. The grainy photos could be stills from film. I cleared my throat. "No. He's gone." I tried to assure myself. "Haven't seen him since graduation last year." I shooed the thought away with my hands, brushing the table with my fingertips.

"Any chance he was a friend of Marcus?" Dylan asked.

I shook my head. "They ran in different circles. Carlo knew Jay. Never saw him with Marcus."

I picked up one of the journals and flipped through it, finding lists of my daily activities. Days I'd been in school, or hung out with Ted. He'd been watching me for a while. If he hadn't been in the accident, I never would've known. Some of the entries were pure fantasy. Very detailed fantasies. I cringed and closed the journal. I tossed it onto the table and wiped my hands on my pants.

"Carlo?" Mom asked from the other room. "From the neighborhood?"

"Yeah mom. Remember, we went out briefly."

"Black hair, rode a motorcycle? I ran into him at the grocery store last weekend," she said.

"What?"

"We didn't talk, but I'm sure I saw him." She stood in the doorway, finger to her chin, eyes to the ceiling. "He was stocking produce."

My skin prickled. He was home? Working? Maybe it was just a weekend visit, home to see the parents. People didn't usually work on weekend parent visits. The thought unnerved me. Things hadn't ended well with us. It was a while ago. I was sure he'd moved on. My hands fisted. I was torn between running over to his house and demanding to see him so I could kick the crap out of him and locking myself in my room. I was angry, scared too. There was a chance it wasn't even Carlo taking these pictures.

Dylan left the spare key with me and returned to Jay's for the night. I wanted him to stay, but he had homework. For once, he wanted to focus on school. Besides, mom was home and Andy would be home tomorrow, school being shut down. Before I went to bed, I worked on music. I pulled my electric piano out of the bedroom closet and set it up with headphones plugged in. It sounded better than the out of tune upright in the basement. My fingers yearned to run across the keys, an itch I hadn't had for years. Until Zane stopped by, it'd been years since I touched piano keys. Not since the accident. Now, I wanted to see if I had any skill left. Michelle, I, used to be good. Award winning good. Probably not concert pianist good, but maybe recording artist good.

My fingers hovered over the keys. I let them drop and began running old warm up drills. Although my fingers moved slowly at first, I picked up speed. I didn't make it to my former speed, but did pretty well considering how long it had been since I'd played. I flexed my fingers and began playing *Moonlight Sonata*. Not a particularly difficult piece, but I liked it. It had been one of my early performance pieces.

I took out my lyric notebook and made some notations on short chord progressions before trying out rhythm patterns on the keys. Ideally, I needed to pick up some music composition paper. In the meantime, I made do with my clumsy tinkering and notebook paper.

Sometimes I wonder what it's all about
Drowning myself in pools of doubt
Running through my failures and deadly sins
There's no salvation for this girl
No way in hell as the world on its axis spins
There's no redemption for this girl

I've been so low without you
Hoping things will turn around
That someday happiness will ensue
But there's no joy that I've found
Outside of your arms

And bitter charms

Since you left, it's been so gray
No spark to the light the day
Not a thing to break the pain
There's no redemption for this girl
No way to break these heavy steel chains
There's no redemption for this girl

So low, so low, without your smile
So low, so low, without you

I've been so low without you
Hoping things will turn around
Someday happiness ensue
But there's no joy that I've found
Outside of your arms
And bitter charms

I turned off the electric piano and went to bed. I dreamt of piano lessons with Mrs. O'Brien, Joe, Christy, smoke, and dead green eyes. I woke screaming.

20

When it was a reasonable hour, I called Ted. We hadn't talked since the show and I missed his voice. He'd be leaving for school in an hour. His voice, sleepy, didn't sound happy to hear mine. I wasn't surprised, but sad.

"What do you want, Shell?" He grumbled.

"I miss you. I hoped we could spend some time together."

"What about Dylan?"

"What about him? I thought you liked him," I said.

"I'm working tonight."

"When do you think we could practice?"

"I'm not sure. I'll have to ask the guys. Why aren't you in school?"

"Didn't Zane tell you? Principal Dirk kicked me out. I don't have a choice."

"When are you coming back?"

"I'm out at least two weeks. Mom wants me to move back with dad and go back to my old school." I waited for a response.

"Might be for the best," he said. It wasn't the response I'd expected from my friend. He said it so casually. He knew how far away my father lived. He understood that meant I'd be out of the band.

"Might be," I agreed, rock in my throat, eyes burning. I doubted my former classmates would still give me the looks of horror that I'd confronted after the accident. It was like they thought I was a zombie, or cursed. Sole survivor of three teens struck by lightning. They probably wouldn't recognize me anymore. "What would that do to the band?"

"Does it matter?" So angry.

"It matters. Ted, we're doing so well. We've got all those show dates to consider. The producer to impress."

"We could practice on weekends. Just reverse the typical visitation schedule," he said.

"I guess that might work. I'm also considering the GED."

"Seriously?"

"Yes, seriously. Should've been graduating this year anyway. I really miss you, Ted."

"Gotta go."

He hung up on me. He'd basically told me to go away. I'd screwed up the band for a hot football player. The urge to punch something strained the muscles in my arm. I breathed in and out several times before my arm relaxed. Ted didn't even want to see me before I left, if I did go. If I stayed, missing so much school from my suspension could hold me back another year. I didn't want that.

Mom emerged from her room, awake and ready to go to work. I'd made breakfast and had a plate ready for her. She sat. I poured some tea.

"Maybe it is a good idea for me to transfer back to Blue Ridge," I said.

"What brings about the change of heart?"

"I don't want to be held back again," I said, staring at the steam rising from my mug.

"I doubt you'll be held back."

I gave her a dubious look. It'd happened before, despite passing all my classes.

"I want to talk to Dylan first. Ted thinks it's a good idea."

"Ted? Are you sure?"

"I talked to him this morning. He thinks I should go. Practice here on weekends."

"Don't you have gigs on weekends?" Mom asked, sipping her tea and wincing at the heat.

"Yep." Not sure that Ted really thought that one through. Don't know what we'd do about the Wednesday night local shows either. They wouldn't be local for me anymore. We had one of those coming up next week. I sighed. School, or the band. I eyed the GED prep book that sat on the table. Its bright red and white cover invited me to open it and take the practice tests. I didn't want to take the GED. I wanted to graduate with my peers this year, but that wasn't possible. In a long shot, I might still graduate next year. I wasn't stupid, just a victim of stupid policy.

Mom shook her head and took a last bite of toast before carrying her plate to the sink. "Keep thinking about it. You don't have to go back. You do have other options."

I wished her a good day at work as she walked out the door. I opened the GED book and grabbed a pencil. Although my options might be more limited than mom wanted to admit, Andy would most likely be transferring back to our old school. I'd miss my little brother.

I checked the clock after finishing a math practice test and nearly swore. I'd worked out extra daytime shifts with Pat to keep me occupied. I'd need extra money if I moved back to Jackson. It wasn't like there were jobs near that little town. I rushed to my room and changed into my uniform. I braided my hair and checked in on Andy, curled up in his room with a stack of comic books, happily reading away.

"You good for the day?" I asked.

"Yep," he said without taking his eyes off the book. Looked like one of the vigilante comics, artwork dark in theme.

"Leftovers, cold cuts, and stuff to make sandwiches in the fridge," I reminded him.

"Got it," he said, waving me off. "Be careful, sis." I wondered how much he knew about what was going on in my life. I didn't want him scared, but he needed to know enough to be alert.

I pulled on my jacket and left the house, lungs seizing mid inhale as I hit a wall of cold air. With effort, I breathed out, air escaping in a fog of tiny ice crystals. I rushed to the car and slammed the door behind me. My breath continued to fog until the heat started working several miles down the road.

I parked next to Raif's car and hesitated before I opened the car door. I took a deep breath before I stepped back into the cold, slammed the car door, and rushed to the rear of the building, where I pressed the call button. I didn't understand how Raif did so many opening shifts with the nightlife he had. He let me in, no one else there to do it. I hadn't worked a day shift when school was in session before and wondered if anything would be different.

"Why aren't you in school?" He asked. Despite dark half-moons under his eyes, he still looked good. I shifted foot to foot as my eyes dropped to the floor.

"I got kicked out for a couple of weeks for disturbing school operations. Something like that," I mumbled.

"Awesome. Wouldn't take you for the type. How did you do that?" His voice held a tinge of amusement. I looked up to find him smiling.

"My face was featured in the paper."

"Oh, that story about your band. I saw that. It was a good review."

"I thought so. I just wish it'd used a picture of the entire band rather than a headshot of me. Maybe then the whole band would be suspended, not just me."

"Throw yourself a pity party why don't you? Do you know what I would've given for a two-week suspension when I was in high school? I wouldn't have been working. That's for sure."

"I'm bored. Besides, it's more like an expulsion. I can't set foot on school grounds."

"Bored," he scoffed. "Hot Lips, you don't know what bored is."

I checked the board. Cashier? I'd never worked cashier before, although it was the position listed on my hiring paperwork. Could be interesting. Trusting me to smile at customers? Not a safe bet. Cashier made me think of Vicki, ugh. Vicki usually got assigned cashier duty, but it was a school day. Damn frog face. I'd never found her particularly attractive, and now I wanted to puke every time I thought of her. Nauseous, I stood in front of the cash register memorizing the placement of keys.

I turned around and set up the drink dispenser. I pulled out the metal shake cups and set them on the counter next to the machine. Easy tasks I'd done before. I wondered what took the cashiers so long to set up mornings. I went back to Raif's office and asked what I needed to do, as it was a new station for me. He pointed to the cash drawer and told me to count it out.

I sat next to him and counted the till, finding $200 in small bills.

"When you cash out at the end of your shift, the amount above the $200 is the sales for the shift," he said. "At the end of the day, everything over that $200 should equal the total on the sales report generated by the register at the end of the day."

"Doesn't sound bad."

"It's not," he said with a smile. He walked me out to the register, dumped the tray in and shut it. "We'll go over the register when customers start to arrive."

"Should I set up the salad bar?" Like I'd said, I was bored.

"Sure," Raif said before returning to the office.

I hadn't checked to see who was supposed to be covering it, if anyone, but nothing was happening back there. I headed toward the walk in. I let Sal in when the buzzer sounded. His eyes widened when he saw me.

"What are you doing here?"

I ran through the explanation and continued the setup routine. We crossed paths several times between walk in and prep area as he got the sandwich and grill stations set up. I knew daytimes were generally slower, but wondered if they actually operated with only three employees during the day. Salad bar set up, I returned to the front. I glanced toward the grill, for a moment mistaking Sal's tall frame and dark hair for Marcus. My breath caught.

I quickly turned my attention back to the register keys and did my best to memorize where food items were located. As long as I kept busy, I didn't think about Vicki and Dylan in the restroom. But, staring at the register wasn't enough.

"Sal, need any help?" I asked.

"All set up," he said.

Darn it. There was the image again. Then, an image of Christy and Joe. In his room. Wow, vivid. I'd walked right in, the door ajar. The smell of sex in the air, fresh, but I hadn't known what it was. I'd been shocked. Naked, tangled limbs, and Christy's moans of delight. Light skin moving against white freckled skin.

I'd spun on my heel and walked out, but not before they'd

noticed me. The look Christy gave me, the pity look. Not apology. Then I realized it wasn't pity, it was more like claiming a victory.

Joe? He'd had his usual look of confusion, eyes wide, hair wild and damp. He wasn't the brightest. Too many blows to the head maybe. He must've gotten tired of waiting for me to give in. Christy had obviously been willing.

I'd driven out to the lake. I didn't have a driver's license yet, but dad had been letting me practice at the family farm. I'd taken the old family station wagon. I smelled the musty scent of the car despite the window I'd cracked open as I drove toward Thompson. I hadn't even fastened the seatbelt.

"Shell?" Raif touched my shoulder. I startled.

"Sorry, what?" I turned to face him, releasing the firm grip I held on the cool countertop.

"I've been trying to get your attention. You ok?"

"My mind was somewhere else."

"It sure was. I'm unlocking the doors now."

I nodded and took a deep breath. Well, now I knew why I'd been at the lake that day. I remembered. Raif returned and began to walk me through orders as customers came in. Larry came in, cigarette dangling from his lip, cologne sweet and strong. He mumbled something about fries and a black coffee. I keyed it in. I took his cash and poured the coffee while Sal got the fries.

"Hit the deck!" Larry bellowed. I dropped to the floor and crouched behind the counter. I wasn't sure what was going on, but Raif and Sal looked at me wide-eyed like I was the crazy one. I slowly straightened and brushed at my apron. Larry stared into the void. Today he was dressed in a sailor's uniform. Navy top with white piping. Reminded me of black and white photos of Grandpa O'Carroll and I shivered. Larry placed a pack of cigarettes on the tray, slid it from the counter, and wandered back to his normal 8-seater bench, because a person with so much personality needed that much space.

"He does that all the time," Raif said, eyebrow raised.

"I thought there might be a reason," I said shakily.

"Not that we can figure," Sal said.

It was a while before more customers streamed in. Good thing, too. Larry had plenty of time to add a smoky haze to the dining room ambiance while chatting away with himself. Walking past as I bussed tables, I heard separate voices. Had I not known he was the only one sitting there, I would've thought there were multiple people at the table.

The shift was uneventful after that. Working the day shift was slow, but I got to work multiple stations, so it wasn't bad. We took turns taking breaks. I left as Jay and Vicki came in. I may have vomited a little in my mouth before I swallowed and forced a fake smile on my face. I was good at it; I just didn't like to be fake. Old cheerleader tricks.

Dylan was on schedule to work and I wondered if he'd keep it in his pants or end up back in the restroom with his pants down. Not that anyone would tell me. Vicki hadn't said a word about the hook up. She hadn't told me about the trouble with Brent either. I probably meant as much to Dylan as she had, but I still wanted him. There was a lingering curiosity, and an undeniable desire for him. It wasn't like he'd be around much longer.

I drove away, wishing I could talk to Ted about what was going on. He didn't know about the journals or the second photo. I hadn't told him. He wasn't the only one hurting. I hurt too. He'd pulled away first.

I pulled into the driveway as images of Joe and Christy crashed through my mind. Joe bursting out of his red truck followed by Christy. Once a flashback started, it was unstoppable. I parked and leaned back into the head rest. I let myself fall into the swampy reservoir of memory.

I sat on the lake shore, turning around at the sound of the truck doors. It was a beautiful day. The sun was out and a breeze blew my reddish hair into my face, where it stuck to angry tears. Christy yelled at me and I turned back to face the water. I wasn't in the mood to deal with the two of them.

"You can't ignore us forever," she said.

I didn't answer, just breathed in the grassy scent of early spring. My heart hammered and my face went numb.

"Michelle, it didn't mean anything," Joe said.

"What? You know it did!" Christy screamed at him. "Don't lie." She turned to me. "Boyfriend's been screwing me for months."

"Months?" That drew me out of my stupor. "Months?" I asked louder. My hair stood on end. They both moved closer.

"Well," Joe looked down, "I have needs."

"You're 16," I scoffed. "Needs? I have needs, too. I need you to go." I shooed them away, but they came closer.

"You're such a prude," Christy said, crossing her arms.

Thunder rumbled in the distance and heat rode the air. A sharp prickling stabbed my back, then darkness. I opened my eyes and fought to draw in a breath of burning air. The air, heavy with smoke and other foul smells, fought against my lungs and I rolled over coughing. Green eyes. Orange-red hair. Joe. His eyes, dull, stared at me through smoky air that carried the scent of burning flesh, hair, and vegetation. Part of that smell, I realized, was me. To his side, Christy's darker green eyes stared sightlessly to the sky, mouth open, blonde hair charred, and body smoking. An old elm tree I used to climb burned from the center like a fireplace, smoke pouring through the top, a chimney from hell. What'd happened?

I sucked in air, finding myself back in the Olds and blinked a few times. I knew what'd happened. We'd been struck by lightning.

Like happened so often after a heinous flashback, aches wracked my body. I dragged myself up the deck stairs. I bent down to pick up a manila envelope and groaned when I found my name in large block letters on it. I let myself into the house, dropped the envelope on the table and headed straight for the shower.

I wondered if the nightmares would stop now that I'd remembered. The last thing Christy had done was call me a prude. If she'd seen me a couple of nights ago, she'd have a different descriptor. A half smile crept to my lips.

A shower, brief, but refreshing, woke me up enough to get changed and take another go at the GED workbook. I tried a science test while Andy continued his comic book binge. I was surprised he hadn't switched over to video games.

The manila envelope distracted me while I took the practice test. Halfway through the test I grabbed the envelope and tore it open. I dumped the contents out, finding another glossy 8x10. In it, I was in the school parking lot facing the camera, paper in hand, as I unlocked my car door. On the back of the photo was another note. 'You can't hide.'

Really? I can't hide? The heck I can't.

"Andy?" I called out.

"Huh?"

I rushed back to his room, stopping in the doorway. "Has mom talked to you about transferring back to Blue Ridge?"

"No. I think I'm going back to school tomorrow."

"Would you go back to Blue Ridge if you had the chance?"

"I don't know. Maybe. Mom's got custody."

In reality, mom had only offered for me to go back to our old school. I was the only one who had the choice in whose custody I lived. I'd chosen mom. Andy didn't get a choice. I didn't want to leave him alone.

Wait. Why was I scared? These were just stupid photos. Not even good ones. The notes were pretty vague too. They weren't overtly threatening, just violations of my privacy.

I stomped back to the kitchen and picked up the phone, dialing a number I hadn't called in over a year. After three rings, a male answered. I asked to speak with Carlo.

"He's not here. He's off at college."

"Is he?"

"Of course, he is. He won't be back for a couple more weeks," his dad said. I recognized the voice. "Want me to pass along a message?"

"No, that's fine."

I hung up, embarrassed. I hoped his dad hadn't recognized my voice. Carlo nearly had a breakdown after I broke things off with him. Who'd have known he was so sensitive? He played a tough guy so well, all black clothes and biker boots.

If not Carlo, who? Not Tara. Her photos were of such high quality that I couldn't imagine her taking crappy stalker photos. If it was her, I'd have looked good. I picked up the photo and eyed it again. Nope, I did not look good. It wasn't Marcus. He was dead.

Marcus had some similar photos in the album his mom had given me. He was in some of those photos. Who had taken them? Jay had told Jules that Marcus had been racing someone right before the accident. Didn't seem the kind of thing Marcus did. Who was in the other car? Had the police looked into that lead? Was there a connection between the photos and the accident?

21

I hadn't heard from Dylan in a couple of days, and the band hadn't gotten back to me about practice. I'd been keeping myself occupied working the day shift while everyone else was in school. Evenings, I hung out with Andy. He'd gone back to school, like he expected. Even when he was home, I felt alone.

The GED prep book was completely marked up and scored. That morning, I'd gone to the bookstore to pick up another, larger book of practice tests. The thing looked like a monstrous encyclopedia of knowledge. I was certain that I'd pass the GED tests based on the first book of practice tests, but needed something to fill my time. I chewed on a wooden pencil as I reviewed a math problem that I'd gotten wrong. It certainly wasn't Calculus, just simple Algebra. My eyes drifted to the window as my mind wandered. Marcus, smiling at me across the Chemistry classroom as one of our classmates was made to do ten jumping jacks, counting them off loudly. All for a simple yawn in class. I smiled. Then I dropped the pencil with a frown, stood and marched over to the fridge to brainstorm dinner ideas.

Andy and Mike played a fighting game on the video game system while I prepared dinner, rosemary chicken with roasted potatoes and green beans. The volume of the video game music invaded the air and a headache threatened behind my left eye. I drizzled olive oil over the chicken then covered it with foil and put the tray in the oven, setting the timer for 30 minutes. I washed my hands and sipped some water. My head throbbed.

I sat at the kitchen table, rested my head on my arms, and waited for the timer to go off. Occasionally, I sipped water and hoped that a migraine wasn't coming on. My gut, warm and bloated, had ached all day. I mentally calculated the last day of my period. I was a little late. I groaned and got up to check.

I wasn't disappointed. I changed from my jeans into some gray sweats and geared up with the feminine products. The IUD pamphlets had been right about increased cramping and flow. Gross. Well, one period started, one more to go before I had to go back for a checkup. I washed up, pretreated my stained clothes, and took the hamper down to the laundry room.

Laundry started, I returned to the kitchen as the timer went off. I checked on the chicken, not quite ready, and set the timer for another 15 minutes. Electric ovens were tricky. I'd grown up using a gas oven and preferred gas over electric, they just seemed to work more efficiently. The food just tasted better when cooked over fire, more organic and less electrical fire. The current house came with an electric stove, and that's what I was stuck with.

"You guys doing ok?" I asked the boys. They were both jumping around in their seats with the controllers as their characters fought on the screen.

"Yeah," Andy mumbled. His arms jerked him to the right, nearly hitting Mike in the face with his controller.

"Dinner'll be ready in about fifteen." I sighed and returned to the kitchen. I picked up a viral pandemic novel I'd been reading and finished a chapter before the timer buzzed again.

The boys joined me at the table and we ate. We talked about what they'd worked on in school and jealousy roiled in my gut. I missed my friends. I missed Dylan. Hadn't even run into him at work. We hadn't talked on the phone either, which was odd, but I hadn't been answering the phone either. Jay hadn't said anything about him at work and I hadn't asked. I still fumed on the inside every time I saw Vicki. Good thing I was working days and avoiding her. Patterns. Sometimes I fell into them.

"This is good," Mike offered after I hadn't said anything in a while. My eyes met his and I forced a small smile.

"Thanks. Tried a new recipe." It was healthier than what we usually ate. "How's your grandmother?" Besides making conversation, I was curious. Mike lived with his grandmother. His mother wasn't fit to take care of him and had remarried a man who wanted nothing to do with Mike. He was better off living with his grandmother, a sweet lady named Lily. I'd spoken with her on the phone last week, but hadn't seen her in person in a while.

"She's good. We're going to visit my aunt this weekend," he said after he swallowed. Ah, manners. Kid had that going for him.

"Really? Are you close?" I asked.

"To my aunt? Not really." Mike said. "She's in Philadelphia for work."

"Oh? What's she do?"

"Not sure," he said with a shrug. He forked more chicken into his mouth. When he swallowed again, he said, "I think grandma said something about money. Working with money."

"Like an accountant maybe?" I asked. Mike shook his head and opened his mouth to say something.

"I thought Lily said she was an estate-something," Andy interrupted, mouth full of half-chewed chicken.

"I don't remember," Mike said, shoulders slumping. He leaned over his plate and shoveled more food into his mouth. The way he was devouring food, it looked like he hadn't eaten all day. Either that, or he actually liked it.

"Is there a time you need to be home tonight?" I asked. Being Friday, there wasn't any school tomorrow.

"Grandma said I could stay over if it's ok with you," Mike said.

"It's fine with me," I said. Apparently, I was granting overnight privileges now. Mike and Andy high-fived and hooted. "Do you have what you need?"

"Yeah, in my backpack."

"Just remember I've got work in the morning." I stood and cleared the dishes. "Done, or do you want more?" I asked Mike.

"Do you have more chicken? It's really good. Grandma's

picking me up at 8:00 to go see Aunt Tunia." Tunia? Lily named her daughter Tunia? It was probably Petunia, which was, well, less common than some names.

After dinner and dishes were done, I put away the leftovers and headed back to my room to continue reading the book. I'd decided that my brain deserved some play time after all the GED practice tests that I'd been running it through. As I lay in bed consumed by tales of strangers meeting after a deadly epidemic, the phone rang. Andy called out that he'd get it. It was after 10:00 and I assumed it was mom checking in. The phone calls had died down and it was the first call of the day.

"It's for you!" He called down the hallway.

I groaned as I placed the book face down on the bed and walked to the kitchen to pick up the phone. A familiar voice greeted me.

"Dylan?" A smile rose, then the anger started burning in my gut.

"Of course. Who'd you expect?" I could hear the smile in his voice. The smile that melted my heart.

"You kind of disappeared. I wasn't sure I'd hear from you again." Great, the pissiness was coming out in my voice. Not that I couldn't have dialed him myself.

"It's only been a couple days. I've been busy. Got a second job."

"With school going on?" What high schooler takes on a second job? That was crazy. When did he do his schoolwork?

"Could use the money. Pays more than Norma's. Construction." I wondered why he needed the extra money, but didn't ask.

When I thought construction, what came to mind were the road construction crews, standing on hot asphalt in their bright orange vests directing traffic or working heavy machinery. "Construction?"

"Houses, pools."

"Ah." Unseasonable time for pools.

"I'm working tomorrow but wanted to know if you had plans on Sunday," he said.

"No plans on Sunday," I said, smile returning.

"Can we hang out?"

"Sure." Us and my period. What a group. "Looking forward

to seeing you again. I miss you."

"Miss you too."

We hung up and I returned to my room. Mom would be home soon. The boys had moved back to Andy's room, and were squealing about something. Reminded me of childhood sleepovers with Christy. My heart dropped. I closed the bedroom door behind me and crawled into bed, picking up the book. I couldn't get back into the story now that Christy was flitting through my memories.

Christy was my hero growing up, my best friend, my soul sister. Our moms were best friends and we spent most of our days together until she started school. I'd always looked up to her and was so jealous when she'd started school the year before me.

I'd taken dance and piano lessons, she was more into climbing trees, playing soccer and basketball. She exuded confidence and fearlessness. As Michelle, I often sought approval for my actions, for being me. I wasn't sure I could even define who I was. I was whoever the other person wanted me to be. Christy never questioned who she was. She never cared what other people thought of her.

Christy had an older brother, Roy. She adored him. He worked on cars and played on the school's basketball team. His best friend, Conor, was always hanging around. When we got older, we'd all play 2 on 2 together. Conor was Joe's older brother. It was a small town. Everyone was related. Hadn't thought of Conor in forever. Handsome, 3 years older, green eyes, dark auburn hair and so similar to Joe, taller and no freckles. We'd… we'd…

Mom walked into my room and sat at the foot of the bed. Face numb and breathing shallow, I had no doubt my face was whiter than usual. Her brow furrowed and she touched my hand.

"What's wrong?"

"Just memories mom."

I was not about to go into what I'd just remembered. I didn't think that she'd react well. I wasn't reacting well. Christy wouldn't have called me a prude if she'd known what I'd done. I wondered if I'd even been upset when I caught Christy and Joe. I'd strayed first. I wasn't as inexperienced as I'd thought.

22

Dryness plagued my eyes from staring at the ceiling all night. Flashbacks had followed me through the night. Once Conor's face had penetrated my thoughts, there was no escape from the flood. I couldn't begin to judge Dylan based on the things I'd done. I blushed as a memory of the older O'Brien above me in all his pale glory crashed over me. No wonder the women's exam hadn't been as painful as I'd imagined it would be. Michelle had secrets.

I rubbed my eyes and turned off the alarm clock as the sun's rays began to brighten the room. It was hours before I was expected at work, but I wasn't getting any sleep. My feet carried me to the shower and I massaged my scalp with shampoo, thinking again that it was time to get a haircut. I conditioned, lathered up with shower gel, and rinsed off the floral and coconut scented products. I dressed and stumbled out to the kitchen.

"You look pale," mom said.

"Period," I said. "I probably look puffy too."

"Maybe a little." Thanks, mom. I nodded. "When's the band coming over?" She asked.

"I don't know. They never called me back." She eyed the schedule on the fridge. I nodded. "We have a show Wednesday night. I should call them."

"Working today?" She asked.

"Yeah, until 7."

"That's a full shift."

"I know. It's been almost full-time this week. Raking in the big bucks. I don't know how you do it week after week. It's so boring."

"And you can have this life too, if you get that GED," she said with a smile.

"Well, not as a nurse, mom."

"Of course not. You'd have to go to college for that. Have you started looking at any colleges?"

"I'm not sure I want to go."

"What do you mean?" Her voice rose. I worried she'd wake the boys.

"I'm not sure I want to go right away. I was supposed to have another year to explore colleges, remember?"

"Well, if you're not in college, you'll be working a full-time job." A minimum wage job, implied by her set jaw.

"Of course," I agreed. I'd been sleepwalking through the week. I could sleepwalk through my life. Wouldn't be fun, but I could do it. I'd been sleepwalking through it for years.

"Haven't seen Dylan lately."

"He's been busy."

"You sure you're ok? You seem kind of down."

"Yeah, I'm down. My band's not talking to me, Dylan's been MIA, and I can't go to school. Another photo showed up," I said, pulling the envelope from the kitchen counter and handing it over.

"Another one? We need to call the police."

"What are they going to do? Take prints off the thing? I've already touched it, and now you have too."

Mom shrugged. "Still, they need to be aware of the situation. What if it escalates?"

I sighed. My eyes burned and I rubbed my fists against them. "Fine. If that's what you think is best."

Mom picked up the phone.

After an hour of inquisition and handing over evidence, I dressed for work. Cramps had nearly doubled me over as I'd dressed, but I'd taken some pills and hoped for the best. The

IUD pamphlets weren't kidding about severe cramps. I'd never experienced anything like it.

I drove to work in pouring rain. The medication left me lightheaded and I struggled to walk straight as I was let into Norma's by Jules. She didn't look happy to see me, a normal reaction these days.

"Where have you been?" She demanded. I looked at my watch.

"What do you mean? I'm early." I didn't want to go into the morning police business.

"School, you idiot. Why haven't you been at school?"

"Principal Dirk kicked me out. I can't go back for at least another week. It's, like, a two-week suspension. It's not like I want to be home bored all day."

"It's been a circus. Reporters and people taking pictures. Strangers asking about you."

"Ah yeah, the whole disrupting operations thing…" I mumbled. "Still happening?"

"It's calmed down, but it was really bad for the first few days."

I checked the board. Ugh. Vicki. Then again, could I really judge? Dylan really made my body sing. I sighed.

"What's up with you?" She asked, eyes wide.

"I'm just glad I don't go around blowing random guys in the restroom."

"What?" She asked, eyes wide.

"Sorry, thought just ran right out of my mouth," I murmured. "So, Vicki's working today?

"Yeah."

"Thought her and Brent were pretty tight," I rambled.

"What are you going on about?"

I walked back to the walk in to gather supplies for the salad bar. Nothing was getting done standing around yakking with Jules. She followed me and picked up container of cauliflower and another of sliced tomatoes. We walked out to the bar and dropped the vegetables in their proper places then returned to the walk in for more.

"Did they take a break recently?" I asked.

"Yeah, but they're back together."

"Huh."

"And?"

I shrugged. "How big do you think his Johnson really is? I mean big, like long or big, like thick?"

"What?"

She was very monosyllabic today.

"I hear she talks about it all the time, but I wondered what exactly she says about it. I've never heard her brag about the size of her boyfriend's weiner before."

"I guess she has a couple times. No specifics. Why are you asking?" Her eyes widened. "Oh my gosh! You know."

"Yeah, I know," I said with a sigh. "I'm just hoping it was a one-time thing."

"Well, I mean, are you and Dylan even a thing? I thought you were with Ted"

"Who knows. Me and Ted are done," I said. "Does Dylan screw anything with boobs, or what?"

"Oh, you didn't," she said, eyes popping.

"Oh, not yet." My shoulders drooped and I leaned back against the wall. I wanted to cry. At least Conor had cared for me. Dylan? Who could tell? All I knew was that my body wanted him desperately every time I saw him. He made me laugh. I hadn't laughed in a long time. He also made my insides ache. He was leaving in a few months.

"And?"

"We're hanging out tomorrow." Me and my period. A small smile crept to my lips. How awful.

23

Sunday morning rolled around and started with a phone call from Zane. The band would be over Monday after school. I guess the boycott was on hold. I dressed in fitted jeans, tight black tee, and left my hair down. My leg bobbed anxiously as I waited for Dylan to show up. He arrived, sunburnt, but hot as ever. I let him in, afraid to touch him.

"Wow, that looks painful," I said, hand hovering over his hot skin.

"We were outside all day working on a pool."

"It rained most of the day."

"You can still get sunburned when it's cloudy outside."

I nodded. It'd happened to me before.

"Did you have anything in mind today?" I asked. We hadn't discussed what we'd be doing. It was cold outside, but the rain had stopped. The ground was crunchy and white with frost.

"Just spend time with you. Where's your brother?"

"With Mike. Mom's at work," I said. I reached my arms around his neck and pressed my lips to his. I was so horny. I released his neck, remembering the sunburn. "Sorry."

"Don't apologize."

"I'm on my period," I blurted. He chuckled. "It's not funny." I pouted.

He shook his head and held up his hands. "Let's get out of here."

I nodded and grabbed my jacket. He led me out to his truck and helped me up. He drove us out to the lake. When he parked, he turned to me, leaned over and drew my face to his. His lips opened and tongue dove inside my mouth. We made out for a while before getting out. I couldn't help it. It was hard to keep my hands off him when I wanted more. The windows, completely fogged over by the time we got out gave away what we'd been up to.

He helped me out of the truck, my legs weak from the little we'd done. We took the lakeside trail. The wind stirred the branches of the skeletal trees. Gravel crunched under our feet with each step. We held hands as we walked.

"Wish we had more time together," I said.

"Me too," he stopped and turned to me. I looked up. "We should elope," he said. "We could run off to Vegas."

I cocked my head. "Would if I could. I'm not 18 yet." I meant it. I would. I could be crazy spontaneous sometimes. I didn't think he took me seriously. He grinned and swept me into his arms. My fingers touched his hair, soft, the softest I'd ever touched, except for a couple bits of something that felt crunchy. Paint maybe? "What's in your hair?"

"Concrete mix. Couldn't get it all out."

I shook my head and laughed. "Sounds uncomfortable."

He shrugged.

We continued along the path, stopping to stare across the lake when we came to the beach. He wrapped an arm around me as the wind brushed past. I turned and kissed him, nearly knocking him to the sand. We continued through the path, stopping when we reached the drains that led to the swamp. I liked swamps. To look at. They're beautiful and eerie, but I didn't want to swim in them.

When I turned around, Dylan was gone. I spun around, searching, but found no trace of him. I leaned over the guardrail and there he was, peeking out from one of the large drains. I shook my head.

"If you're not careful, you'll get stuck down there," I called out.

"Nah." He shook his head. "You should come down and check it out."

"Uh, no thanks," I said with a laugh and shake of the head.

Thoughts of snakes and large frogs filled my head, followed by an image of Vicky's froggy face. My face scrunched.

He climbed up from the ditch, wiping his hands on his pants. "It's pretty cool down there. You sure you don't want to check it out?"

"I'm sure."

He shrugged. "Your loss."

We continued on looking for the next branch of the trail, but ended up in the campground. We walked the circuit of abandoned camping spaces with no success and ended up lakeside at the boat launch. Ducks quacked and waddled toward the water. Seemed unseasonably cold for the adorable creatures. They should've migrated long before now. Dylan ran toward the ducks, chasing them into the water.

"What are you doing?" I called, laughing.

"What?" He looked over his shoulder, arms outspread to keep his balance.

"Your feet are going to freeze."

He stood ankle deep in the water, having skidded just enough into the lake to get his shoes submerged in cold water. He walked back to dry land, shaking his feet. I smothered my laugh with a hand.

"Guess it's time to go back," he said.

"Guess so," I agreed. I wanted to spend more time with him at the lake, but with the chill and his now wet feet, it just wasn't a great idea.

We walked back the way we'd come, his arm around my shoulders. His body was warm, but wouldn't stay that way with cold, wet feet. His shoes squished with each step.

He dropped me off at the house, with another deep kiss that left me crazy with wanting. I think I'd scared him off with the period disclosure. Who wanted to mess with that? I didn't. A manila envelope waited for me at the basement door. I picked it up, looked around and let myself into the house. I got the laundry out of the dryer and brought it upstairs. I left the basket on the sofa and opened the manila envelope.

I pulled out another 8x10 black and white photo. This one was clearer, taken in brighter light, and showed me and Dylan kissing in the school hallway with a pissed off Stephanie in the background. I giggled. I didn't remember her being around at any point when we'd kissed. He made me forget everything when he was around. I turned the photo over to see what the person had written this time. 'YOU'RE MINE.' All caps. Well, that was difficult to respond to when I didn't know who was sending the photos.

I placed the photo back in the envelope with a snort. The sender was a little late to be claiming me. I tossed the envelope onto the kitchen island and decided to leave it for mom to deal with. I wasn't calling the police on my own.

I checked the messages and found one from Ted. I called him back. His mother told me he wasn't at home so I hung up. I wondered where he'd gone. The hardware store was closed on Sundays.

Shoulders slumped, I grabbed a bottled water from the fridge and returned to my room to try to get back to the viral pandemic novel. I hoped it would take my brain away from the drama it was generating for me. I wondered how many other things I'd done as Michelle that would shock me. From the pictures in the albums, I'd figured I spent all my time dancing and playing piano. How would I have had time for Conor on top of Joe? It'd all started with those blasted piano lessons. Always had more in common with Conor, the music, the reading, the arts.

I laid back and opened the book. I reread the same paragraph three times and gave up. I wondered if Dylan would have stayed longer if I'd told him what was going on with the new pictures and memories. He might get a kick out of some of Michelle's exploits. He still hadn't seen the albums.

I moved over to the piano and began messing around with chords.

Just a memory or a dream
I can't hold on to it for long
Soon you'll be lost to the fog
Nothing left but this song

I'd give you anything you desire
If it would make you stay
You burn me like fire

Toxic Siren: Awakening

> With eyes so cold
> Don't say a word
> I'm already sold
>
> Before you drift away
> I ask this one last thing
> Could I just hear you say
> You feel the same way
>
> I'd give you anything you desire
> If it would make you stay
> You burn me like fire
> With eyes so cold
> Don't say a word
> I'm growing cold
>
> We're two of a kind
> Flawed, damaged, alive
> Another like me you'll never find
> Together we could try

The phone rang and I rose to answer it. I didn't make it to the phone before the machine picked up. It was Ted. I smiled, hand reaching for the receiver, when I heard the familiar piercing squeal in the background. Stephanie. No thank you. I returned to my room and closed the door. Whatever Ted wanted could wait.

Dark thoughts whirled through my head. It wasn't my business if Ted wanted to spend time with Stephanie. He could date whoever he wanted to. He could screw whoever he wanted to. I returned to the keyboard.

I understood on some level that I chose to isolate myself. There were other people I could call if I really wanted to be around others. It was a symptom that the depression was coming back. Either depression or severe PMS. The thought brought a small smile, making me think it was more likely a case of menstrual mental issues.

I continued to work on my song until the room got too dark

to see my notebook clearly. I moved over to the bed, switched on the bedside lamp and fell into the tales of rebuilding society after a plague. When the phone rang again, I ignored it and continued reading.

The sound of the front door closing brought my attention to the fact that it was after 10:00 PM. Andy's voice carried through my closed door. I sat up and crawled out of bed. I followed the voices into the kitchen and found mom checking messages while Andy put away groceries. I held a hand to my mouth to cover a yawn.

"Did you know Ted called?" Mom asked.

"Yeah? Must have missed his call."

"He called twice."

I shrugged. "I'll see him tomorrow. The band's coming over for practice."

"You ok?"

"Still don't feel great. Cramps."

"That's normal with the IUD. How's the bleeding?"

"Heavy. Not as bad as yesterday. It'll stop eventually, right?" I'd never bled like this before. Horrendous.

"It should," she said with a smirk. Smart ass. "What's this?" She asked, eying the envelope on the island.

"Another photo. Didn't want to call the police on my own."

"Police?" Andy asked.

"Yes, give Detective Daniels a call. Now. I've got his card on the fridge," mom said. "Andy, if you see anything strange, let one of us know. You know, people around that shouldn't be. Someone's been taking pictures of your sister."

"Everyone's taking her picture," Andy said.

"This is different," I said. "Like someone hiding and taking pictures of me. Someone creeping around who shouldn't be."

"You have a stalker?" Andy asked. He knew what a stalker was?

"I think I might."

"Why would anyone want to stalk you?"

"No idea." Why would a football player be interested in me? No idea. Must be some kind of freak factor thing. Let's follow around the depressed girl in layers of black and see how long it is before she hurts herself again. The stalking had obviously been going on longer than Toxic Siren had been performing publicly. It wasn't related to the band.

"You're kind of boring, Shell," Andy said. I laughed and nodded. I agreed. I was far more interesting before the lightning strike. Well, except for the band.

A knock at the door surprised all of us. We all turned to the door. I didn't want to check. It was late. Nobody should be outside the front door at this hour. Mom looked at me and I shook my head. I didn't want anyone going toward the door.

"Who is it?" Mom called.

"Ted."

I let out the breath I'd been holding and opened the door a crack. "What are you doing here?"

"Can I come in?"

I looked back at mom. She looked back expectantly, as if asking what the heck I was doing. I opened the door.

"Can we talk in private?" He asked, voice pinched. As if he had a reason to be irritated. I shrugged and led him to my room. I closed the door behind us. Against the rules, but whatever. We weren't going to be doing anything.

"What's up?" I asked as I hopped onto the bed.

"Just like that? Why didn't you answer my calls?"

"How's Stephanie?"

"Huh?"

"Stephanie. How's Stephanie?"

"Fine, I guess. What are you going on about?"

"I heard her on one of the messages."

"She came over with Zane."

"Did he and Tara break up?"

"Wow, you're really out of the loop."

"No duh."

"Yeah, they broke up, and all of a sudden, he's dating Stephanie."

I sighed. I'd caught them making out a couple months ago behind the school where the kids smoked. I'd hoped it was a one-time thing, that she'd trapped him in one of her little games or something.

"You don't look surprised," he said.

I shook my head. "So, what's up? What brings you to my front door so late on a Sunday night?"

"You haven't been in school."

"I told you, I got kicked out."

"I was worried. You haven't called."

"It was weird when we talked. You hung up on me. I didn't want to make it worse."

"Well, I can't pretend that I'm not hurting," he said, looking at the brown shag carpeting.

"Why did you pull away from me?" I asked.

"That's not why I'm here," he said, shaking his head.

"Why are you here?"

"We need to talk about the band."

"Are you kicking me out?" My voice raised and broke.

"No! Not at all." His eyes widened. "It's Zane and Barry. With you gone, it's like they can't stand each other. They've been close since we were kids. Now there's this mess with Tara and Barry's on the warpath."

"I'm not gone, I'm right here."

"You know what I mean. We haven't seen you."

"You guys bailed on practice and I haven't been able to work out a practice schedule with you. It's not like I wasn't trying." I looked down at my hands.

"Did you know we had a rule in the band?" He asked. When I shook my head, he continued. "No one dates Shell. I broke the rule."

"I didn't know there was a rule. I just figured it was a bad idea," I said. "I chose to cross the line, and so did you. I thought things started off well."

"Barry was pissed. Super pissed."

I'd never seen Barry get mad about anything. He was like a big cuddly teddy bear. If he'd been pissed, he'd hidden it well from me. Jay had hinted about something with Barry. I couldn't quite place it. My forehead crinkled as I tried to remember.

"That's why? Barry? You pushed me to Dylan because of Barry?"

"I wouldn't say pushed," he scoffed. "You kind of ran to him."

"He's leaving in a few months," I said, voice hitching.

"What do you mean?"

"Dylan's leaving for basic. He joined the Marines."

"I'm sorry, Shell. I didn't know."

"Well, I guess we all get hurt, don't we?"

Ted pulled me into a hug. I sniffed. I didn't want to cry in front of Ted, but it happened anyway. His arms, stronger than I remembered, comforted me. I let him hold me and I hugged him back. I breathed in his scent. I still cared for him, more than just cared for him. I let go and scooted back onto the bed, leaving a safe distance between us.

"How's Tara doing?" I asked.

"Better than expected. Of course, she's probably not going to be doing our photos anymore."

"Of course not. It's a pity. I loved her photos."

"Yeah, she's good." His eyes met mine, the same deep brown I loved to fall into. "We still on for practice tomorrow night?"

I nodded.

"Good. I need to get back. See you tomorrow. Just wanted to make sure you were ok."

"Wouldn't exactly say ok, but I'm working on it."

He squeezed my hand and stood up.

"What's with the keyboard?" He asked.

"Been working on some stuff. I'll play for you sometime."

I walked him out, watching from the deck until he'd driven away.

24

"Still suspended?" Sal asked as he let me in Monday morning.

"Yep, one more week," I said as I tied my apron. "It's ok. I can use the money from the extra work. How do you do it? Work every day." I shook my head.

"It's not so bad." He shrugged and continued to wash tomatoes while I checked the assignment board. Cashier again. In reality, floater. I counted the till, got the front counter ready to go then got to work on setting up the salad bar.

"I'm bored out of my mind. I miss school," I whined.

"You learn to have hobbies outside of work. Keeps you sane."

"What?" Raif said. "You don't need hobbies when you have friends." He walked out from the back. "You're bored after one week?"

"Well, yeah."

He shook his head. "You should be having fun. Can't believe you volunteered to work while you're out of school."

"What else is there to do?" I asked.

"Anything else."

"Anything else doesn't earn a paycheck," I pointed out.

"She's got you there," Sal said.

"So, even working all day, you're bored?" Raif asked.

I nodded, picked up a cleaning cloth and wiped down the counter.

"Come over to my place. We're getting together after closing tonight."

"Like 10:30?"

"People will probably start showing up around 11:00, but yeah, you can come over at 10:30 if you've got nothing better to do."

"How do you get here for opening shift when you're up so late?" I asked, curiosity overcoming my irrational fear of authority. He'd always made me nervous, being my manager. Especially as good looking and flirtatious as he was with all the other girls. I wondered if Vicki had hooked up with him too. The ho.

"Coffee."

"Coffee?"

"Lots of coffee and cigarettes."

I frowned. I knew he smoked. Being allergic to smoke, it wasn't a habit I liked to be around. It made breathing difficult. Not a great allergy to have when playing in clubs. Always had my inhaler with me and hoped for the best.

"Sure. I'll come over." Hadn't been to his place since we'd played there over the summer.

"Really?" He asked, eyebrow raised.

"Yeah, really."

"You're going to leave your house on a weeknight?"

"Why not?"

"You never hang out with us."

"Like I said, I'm bored," I said with a shrug.

"Cool, looking forward to it."

That was how I ended up at Raif's after an uncomfortable practice with Ted and the band. We made it through the songs without side conversations and made plans to meet up the next night to prepare for Wednesday's show. I let mom know my plans. Luckily, she hadn't been called out for a night shift.

I left the house around 10:30 and made the right onto Sterling Road. I wondered who would show up, if anyone. In the back of my mind, I wondered if Raif was setting me up. I checked in with security and made a series of turns through the maze-like development until I found myself in front of his house. I took a deep breath and got out of the car.

Raif let me in, looking slightly disheveled and roguish. He

really was good looking, film actor good looking. I followed him into the house and took the beer he handed me. I didn't generally drink, but whatever. It was just beer. It wasn't like he was plying me with hard liquor.

"Happy birthday," he said, raising his beer to mine.

I stared at him blankly.

"You didn't tell me that today was your birthday," he said with a wry grin.

Was it? Had I forgotten my own birthday? I looked down at the date on my watch. Yep. My eyes widened. I was 18.

"You can't tell me you forgot your own birthday," he said, laughing. I couldn't help it. It was contagious. I started laughing too.

"So, you seeing anyone these days?" He asked. I raised an eyebrow.

Was Raif trying to ask me out?

"Sort of."

"You and Ted still seeing each other?"

"No. Ted's complicated." I hadn't been seeing much of him lately. Hadn't been talking much either. I would've preferred to be seeing much more of him and repairing our friendship.

A knock at the door and Raif motioned for me to hold that thought. He let Jay, Dylan, and Jules in. Dylan took a seat next to me.

"Happy birthday gorgeous!" He said, leaning in for a soft kiss.

"What are you doing here?" It was nice that he'd rather hang out with the gang than talk to me.

"Raif invited us over. Told us it was your birthday. How was practice?"

"It went ok," I said with a shrug. So, these were the parties he'd been going to. I knew some of them had been at Jay's and other kid's houses, but really? Raif's actual parties were known for drugs, booze, and hook ups. Tonight wasn't going to be one of Raif's big parties, just hanging out with the friends, if he could be believed. "Didn't take as long as I'd expected. They were in a rush to get back to their lives."

"Didn't hang out with Ted afterwards?"

"Nope. He left with the others. Why?"

"Nothing."

"Yeah, he dropped by unexpectedly yesterday. He was worried about me. It's what friends do."

"Why was he worried?"

I shrugged. Neither of the guys knew about the night of flashbacks. Ted would've been a lot more worried if he had.

"I didn't answer his phone calls yesterday. He's not happy, but I think we'll be ok."

Raif sat across from us, listening in. Jay returned from the kitchen with more beers and Vicki. Ugh. I rolled my eyes. I chugged the beer. Jay stared at me wide-eyed.

"Whoa, slow down," Dylan said, touching my arm.

I tossed back the rest of it. Jay offered another and I took it. "You're not the boss of me," I said and took a swig of the new beer.

"What's got into you?" Jules asked, sitting on Jay's lap. Why was she on his lap after what he'd done?

"Reality," I glared at Vicki. She gave me a dead froggy stare.

"It meant nothing," Dylan whispered in my ear. "It was before you."

"Still bites," I said. He chuckled. I guess she didn't, bite. A half smile crept to my lips. He leaned in and kissed me. I kissed him back. Like I could judge. Still stung. I mean, look at her. Then again, look at me. I was no supermodel.

"I like you," I said, drawn to the blue in his eyes.

"I like you too."

"Well, it's just that you left so quickly."

"I was tired and had school stuff I needed to work on. Some of us are still going to class. I do want to graduate this year."

"That wasn't my choice." Why was everyone so irritated with me not going to school? It wasn't like I didn't want to go. I wasn't partying the days away. I took another long pull from the beer bottle. Gross. How did these guys drink all the time?

The others were engrossed in conversations around us and someone had turned on some low-key music. The lights were dim and Jules and Jay had disappeared. I had a feeling they were hooking up in another room. Rob had joined Raif and Vicki on the sofa. I wondered if Brent ever came to these things. Not that it mattered.

"Ever tell you about the effects of getting struck by lightning?" I asked Dylan.

"Struck by lightning?" Wow, talk about short term memory loss.

"Never wondered about my scars?" I looked at him. Rob's attention turned to me.

"What scars?" Rob asked. Wow. He was so observant. We'd only worked together for over a year.

"Remind me to show them to you sometime," I said. Some of them anyway.

"You don't have any scars. I've seen you," Rob insisted.

"Not all of me. They're not as dark as they used to be. They used to be red, they're more pink now. Hard to see if you're not looking for them, but they're still there. Followed the path the lightning took through my body. They're on my back, left shoulder, and arm."

"You were struck by lightning? Are you putting me on?" Dylan eyes widened. I knew I'd told him about the accident before. Selective amnesia.

"I really need to show you those photo albums," I said. "You can see me as a cheerleader and all kinds of things you wouldn't expect."

"You'd mentioned you used to be a cheerleader. I'd like to see that," he said with a goofy smile.

"It's something else." I gazed into his beautiful blue eyes. "I told you I have nightmares sometimes, and flashbacks, right?"

"You mentioned something about that. Your boyfriend and best friend died in an accident, right?"

"We all got struck by lightning," I said, nodding. "I lost a lot of memories, a type of trauma induced amnesia. Sometimes, something will trigger them. Well, our conversation the other day," I glanced over at frog face, "brought back a whole slew of memories."

"A whole slew, huh?" His forehead furrowed. "What kind of memories?"

"Well, I wasn't as innocent as I thought."

"What do you mean."

I shrugged. "I guess I got a little experimental. It was years ago."

"You and your old boyfriend. How old were you?"

"Wasn't Joe. It was his older brother. I was younger, but I understood what we were doing. We'd been together a while before Joe died." I didn't want to address the age issue.

"His older brother?"

I nodded. "I haven't seen him since the accident. The morning of the accident, I found Joe and Christy in bed together. I didn't know they'd been hooking up for months. It was a bit shocking." So was the lightning.

"I don't mind that you aren't completely inexperienced," he said. "It makes me feel better, actually."

"I wish I'd remembered. I feel like I lied. A total hypocrite." I'd been lying to myself for years. While Joe had been a dreadful kisser, Conor had been different. He'd been gentle, patient, and generous.

He leaned in. "It's ok. There are things I wish I could forget. Maybe you're lucky."

I hoped Vicki was one of those things. Ugh, she was looking at us. I closed the distance and kissed him. He had the worst taste in girls. I didn't want to know what his other former girlfriends were like. Yes, I guess that made me nasty too, but I already knew that.

"I want you so bad right now," I whispered into his ear.

"Thought you were on your period," he said.

"It'll be over soon." I hoped.

He laughed. "What are you doing tomorrow night?"

"Band practice. We'll probably be done around 7:00 or so if it's anything like tonight."

"I'm working, but want to hang out after?"

"Yes."

"Good." He drew on my palm with his finger. I looked down. "I want you too."

"Good," I said with a nod. I smiled.

25

"Happy belated birthday, Shell," Jules said, handing me a card as I walked toward the commons. It was my first day back at school part-time and other than a couple more stalker photos, things seemed almost back to normal. I still wasn't talking to Vicki, but we were to the point of ignoring each other.

I opened the card, a silly anime rabbit with a carrot on the cover. I hugged Jules. It was sweet. "Thanks for the card."

"Feel any different now that you're 18?" She asked.

I shook my head. "Not a bit. I thought I might, but I don't."

"Do anything fun to celebrate?"

I shook my head. "No, just practiced for the upcoming show," I said. "A producer's supposed to be in the audience to check us out. It's really important."

"Babe!" Dylan said, spinning me around into a hug and giving me a warm kiss that made me melt inside.

"Good morning," I said. I knew our relationship would end soon, but wanted to enjoy every moment we had. The thought made me sad. "Coming with us to the show this weekend?" I asked.

"Wouldn't miss it. It's a big one." He took my hand.

"Later!" Jules said, walking off toward the counselor's office.

Ted slouched low, his body nearly melting into the bench,

boneless.

"You ok, Ted?" I asked.

He looked up. "Yeah, fine. Why?"

"You looked kind of sad."

"No, I'm good," he said, pasting a small smile on his face. He wasn't fine. "Still on for tonight after school?"

"Yeah, 5:00 right?"

He nodded. Stephanie patted me on the shoulder. I rolled my eyes. Now that she was dating Zane, she thought we were best friends.

"What are your plans?" She asked. I sighed.

"Tonight? Just practicing with the band."

"You can't be serious," she said, rolling her eyes. "George is having another kicking party tonight at the lake house."

"Don't remind me," I said. I didn't need any more weeknight parties. I'd woken up the morning after my birthday on Raif's sofa, head splitting and burping up beer. The thought churned my stomach.

"It's like you're a real adult now," she went on. One of my eyebrows shot up and my lips pursed. "You can do what you want, stay out as late as you want. You don't even have to ask permission."

"Yeah, it's like, 'you're 18 now, you can vote and buy lotto tickets,'" I said. "Exciting." It wasn't true that I didn't have to ask permission. Not exactly. I still needed to check in with mom. Similar arrangement as Ted.

"You just don't realize how lucky you are," she huffed. "No curfew. You can get into R-rated movies without a problem. You can even get into some clubs now."

"I was already getting into clubs, because we were playing them. It wasn't that great," I said. The guys looked at me like I'd said something horrible. I eyed them. "The crowded floors, the smoke-filled air, the music's too loud, you can't hear yourself think, and everyone's drunk. It's not that great."

"And the crowd loves you," Zane said.

"I'm talking about it in terms of being a customer." I still didn't like dealing with the crowds after the show. It didn't matter that they loved me. They invaded my personal bubble. "You know I have issues being around lots of people. I do the best I can, but it freaks me out."

Zane shook his head and hugged Stephanie to his side. "It's just the way she is."

The bell rang and we separated. Dylan walked me to study hall and left with a hug.

Zane brought Stephanie to band rehearsal, which irritated me. Tara had come a couple of times, but I hadn't minded. She'd never tried to screw my boyfriend. Stephanie sat on the futon, coiling her crispy hair around a finger and snapping gum while we ran through the set. My personal goal was to finish as quickly as possible to get her out of my house. I didn't like that she now knew where I lived.

"Enjoying yourself?" I asked when I found Stephanie flipping through my photo album, which I'd left on the workbench.

"You were a cheerleader?" I was surprised she could recognize me in the old pictures.

Zane and Barry laughed, then Barry glared at Zane. It was as if the act of laughing together offended him in some way.

"Yes, I was," I said.

"Shell, you're joking, right?" Barry said. Zane continued laughing, thinking we were having some kind of funny moment. I shook my head. Stephanie turned the album around and pointed at pictures of me and Joe and Christy. I'd never gotten around to talking to the other two about my past. We weren't that close.

"Well, it does explain the sudden improvement in dance moves," Zane said.

"Why didn't you try out for the squad?" She scrunched up her face in confusion.

"Keep flipping," I said. She did, sometimes pointing out pictures to the guys, particularly pictures of me doing things they hadn't seen me do before, like ballet, gymnastics, and piano recitals. I doubt the piano playing was all that surprising, although except for Zane, none of them had heard me play. She finally got to the articles and gasped. She looked from the article to me, and back again. I folded my arms in front of my chest.

"Teens die in weather related accident," she read aloud. "Three teens struck by lightning, one survived... Memorial

271

services for Christine Smith and Joseph O'Brien will be held..."

"My boyfriend and best friend died in that lightning strike." Technically, we hadn't broken up. Joe had still been my boyfriend.

"You were the one that survived?" She looked up at me, gray eyes wide.

I nodded. "Things were different after getting struck by lightning. There was damage. It's not like the human body is equipped to handle a billion volts of electricity."

The guys, except for Ted, looked horrified. I knew I was a freak. It didn't hurt any less to have my friends look at me that way. It was why I didn't share the information with everybody. Stephanie just looked overly intrigued. Great.

"Yeah, things used to be a lot different," I admitted. "I danced, I cheered, I was on my way to becoming a concert pianist. Then, wham! Struck by lightning. Totally sucked. Lost a lot of my memory, woke up to my dead boyfriend and best friend. I was in pain for a long time, and I still have issues. My personality's different, and I sing and play guitar instead of doing things I used to do." I shrugged. "That's my life in a minute."

"But, how could you give up cheerleading?" Stephanie asked, missing the point.

"I joined the squad because Christy wanted to join the squad and my dance school had just shut down. It gave me a chance to keep dancing and doing gymnastics. After the accident, it reminded me of her." Duh, bimbo. I shook my head. Stephanie was dense. Most of the cheerleaders at my former school had been honors society students. Stephanie was not of that caliber. "I look at the album and think, 'that girl was something.'"

"You're still amazing," Ted said.

"Just different, I know." It's what my parents told me all the time. They lost their daughter on the day of the accident and got an awful substitute in her place. I was sure they felt it. I could see it on their faces, the loss. Michelle wasn't perfect, but she had promise. Of course, she was probably well on the way to becoming a teen mom too. Happened a lot in that region. Not much to do in the country.

The guys had questions. Lots of questions. So many

questions that they were still there when Dylan walked into the garage.

"Thought you said you'd be done by 7:00?" Dylan asked.

I looked at my watch. It was after 10:00. Mom would have come down to let us know it was getting late, if she was home. Andy was staying at Mike's for the night. Dylan hugged me and drew me into a soft kiss. It may have been for Stephanie's benefit, but I enjoyed it.

"We've just been talking about the accident," I said. I picked up the album and flipped to the articles before handing it over. He scanned the articles and flipped to the front of the album, checking out the pictures.

"You really were a cheerleader! What's up with the blonde hair?" Dylan asked.

"I bleached my hair when Christy went a lighter shade of blonde. Frosted my hair actually. Didn't work really well with my skin tone," I said with a chuckle. The hair made me look like a washed-out ghost, or would have if I hadn't worn so much bright makeup.

"We should head home," Ted said, gesturing to the others.

"Thanks for hanging out. See you at the show tomorrow night," I said. I stood and walked them to the door. "Thanks for coming, Stephanie."

"It was fun," she said. She didn't seem to catch the sarcasm in my voice.

I locked the door after them and turned to face Dylan. "So glad you're here." I pressed my lips to his, warm and firm. He smelled of mint, earth, and rain. My fingers pulled the shirt from his jeans and ran along the small of his back, enjoying the heat of his taught skin. I wanted skin on skin contact, craved it.

Kissing, tongues dancing seductively, we stumbled into my old bedroom. That was as far as we made it before we started losing items of clothing. As his tongue dove into my mouth, heat flowed through my skin. Dropping to the carpet, our hands and mouths explored each other as passion took control of my body and everything but sensations fell away. My reaction was primal, instinct. I couldn't get close enough.

As our bodies merged for the first time, not exactly effortlessly, I winced, trying to relax as we kissed and moved together slowly, trying to make the pieces fit. There was an almost painful stretching fullness in the act that lessened and turned to intense pleasure as my body adjusted to Dylan and our movements became more frantic and less cautious. My hands grasped his back as we lost ourselves in mounting pleasure until release came in waves. My body shook with each contraction and he shuddered, sweating above me, eyes intently staring into mine.

We continued to kiss until he became aroused again. He urged me to stand, picked me up and pressed me against the wall.

Dylan stayed over. It had been a long day for both of us, and he was exhausted after our vigorous and passionate activities. I couldn't blame him for being exhausted. He'd performed a pretty incredible feat of strength, nailing me against the wall like that. I giggled at the euphemism.

"What's so funny?" Dylan asked.

"You nailed me against the wall," I said.

"I did," he said, gazing into my eyes and kissing me with lots of tongue. It excited me all over again.

When we finally made it upstairs, we took turns in the shower. He was in the shower when mom came home.

"How was practice?" She asked.

"Not bad. Hope you don't mind if Dylan stays over. It's been a long day and it's late. I'd rather he not drive back to Jay's tired."

"Keep the door open," she said with a smirk. I nodded. My guess was that she'd seen at least one of the many love bites. Too late.

"Don't suppose you'd let me have the basement room back?"

"Maybe. Let me think about it."

Dylan joined us in the kitchen. We talked about school and work for a bit, mom turning in before we did. I followed him back to my room, enjoying the view. He looked over his shoulder at me from my doorway, a silhouette against the dim light.

"Are you checking out my butt?" He asked

"Maybe," I said with a giggle. It was a nice view, what I

could see in the dim light.

He slept hot, so we only covered up with a sheet. I would've been cold if he hadn't been there to hold me. Without the blankets, he didn't feel as warm as he claimed he was. His body wasn't as furnace-like as Ted's. I couldn't remember ever actually sleeping with Conor, so I couldn't compare.

26

A rare mid-week in-service day, we had the day off from school. Dylan went to his construction job before the sun rose and Andy was at Mike's house for the day. With the house to myself for a few hours before I had to leave for work, I sat in front of the keyboard and played a couple old performance pieces before jumping into a song I was working on. I jotted down some notes and returned to composing.

Your skin smooth under my fingertips
Your breath warm and sweet on my lips
Just want you by my side tonight
Staring into your eyes so bright
I just want you to stay tonight

You offered me forever
How could I say no
I look at you and never,
I don't want to let you go

A knock at the front door surprised me. I slowly crept from my room, not wanting to alert the person that I was home. I wasn't expecting anyone. Being home alone, there was no way I was opening the door to a stranger. The person knocked again, louder, announcing that it was Detective Daniels. I released the breath I was holding and sucked in air as I opened the door.

"Officer, you scared me," I said.

"Sorry. Is Madelyn here?" He asked.

"Mom already left for work. Can I help you with something?"

"She left a message that you'd received another photo. I came to pick it up."

I nodded, grabbed it from the kitchen counter and handed it over in the envelope. "It was outside the basement door when I came home."

"Did you notice anything odd, besides the envelope? See anyone?"

"No."

He made a couple notes and left. I watched him walk down the deck stairs and climb into his car. He sat in the driveway for some time before actually driving away. He'd made no mention of any progress, which left me to assume that none had been made. I locked up and returned to my room.

Larry puffed away industriously, murmuring and staring while I wiped down the counter. Pat assigned me to cashier and salad bar again. Sal shimmied around to the canned music and I couldn't help but smile. As far as I could estimate, he was in his early 30s, but I'd never asked. He was married and had a young child at home. He'd shown me a picture of his son just the other day.

I straightened as another customer walked in, greeting them with the almost automatic cashier smile. It wasn't that hard, it was becoming second nature, like the cheerleader smile I used to do. I'd come to realize that although Michelle smiled a lot in the pictures, she wasn't that much happier in her life than I was. I relayed the order over the microphone and keyed in the items. The customer handed me cash and I returned change. Easy. I was beginning to think that I was better at the whole cashier thing than Vicki. I was definitely a better multitasker.

Pat came out and snapped a Polaroid of me. I blinked. Um, what?

"Employee of the month," she explained. "Congrats."

"Thanks?" I'd never gotten employee of the month before. I guess that was cool. I could kick butt at work. I stifled a snort. It wasn't like the job was hard. Dealing with the ungrateful people all day was tiring.

At a lull in business, I strolled out to the dining room and wiped down tables. I replaced Larry's ashtray with a fresh one. His overflowed with crushed butts and ash. My nose wrinkled as I carried the dirty tray away. Today, he wore a Hawaiian shirt, 1970s shades, and a bandanna. He'd been in a conversation about 'Nam when I'd passed by. It seemed most of his themes were military by nature. I wondered if he was an actual vet and if his behavior might fall under what used to be called shell shock, but was now known as PTSD.

I checked the salad bar and found a note on the prep counter behind the bar. The block letters rang of familiarity as I read, 'it's not over.' Well, could've been left for anyone. It wasn't addressed to me. I hadn't noticed the note earlier, but whatever. I left it on the counter, wiped the salad bar down, and returned to the register.

"Everything good?" Sal asked.

"It's all good," I said with a nod. Yep, all good.

The rest of the shift went well, but slow. Vicki sauntered in around 4:30. She was an hour early for her shift. I sighed.

"Good evening, Vicki." I'd nearly called her frog face. It'd come out 'Fricki.' I bit my lips to keep from smiling.

"Hot Lips," she said, voice husky, with a nod as she passed by. Well, fine then, if we're back to that. I shook my head. I wondered where she'd heard that from, and if she was thinking Hot Lips like on the TV show, or like, "the guys voted and…" I shrugged and eyed Sal with a raised eyebrow. He shrugged.

"Pat says you can move out to salad bar now," Vicki told me on her return.

"Sure thing. How's Brent?"

"Fine. Why do you ask?"

"Just wondering about that big dick of his." Her eyes widened, then narrowed. "I wonder what he's going to do with it while you're away." Not my finest moment. She took a swing at me and I ducked. Wow, I was such a beast. I held my hands up and backed away. "Just sayin'."

I walked through the tables and wiped down those that needed to be cleaned. I was surprised to find Larry still sitting at his bench table. I walked by carrying a couple of dirty trays.

"Hit the deck, sailor!" He yelled.

I ducked down and dropped the trays. He'd done it again. My eyes searched the room before standing back up. Jumpy? Me? I sighed and stood up. I only had about 15 minutes to go before I left. Then, the mid-week show. It'd be a rush home to shower, then speeding to get to the resort. I hated rushing. I should've asked to leave early.

I drove, freshly showered toward a resort I was unfamiliar with using the directions that Zane had given me. I'd memorized the instructions as well as I could before I left, knowing it'd be dark before I got there. The sun set so early in the winter. I'd decided on leather pants, white top with flowing sleeves and black leather vest for the evening show. It reminded me a little of my favorite glam rocker, king of elves, on *Maze*, a movie I'd loved as a child.

I managed to find Briar Hills Resort after I drove past the entrance. I turned down the first road I found, drove around the block and got back on track. I hauled the guitar from the trunk. I was happy that I'd avoided Vicki's punch earlier. A fresh black eye would've been a gnarly thing to try and cover up before the show. I hurried in through the lobby and the concierge directed me to the ballroom. I speed walked down the carpeted hallway and pushed through the ballroom door.

Ted and the guys were setting up at the far end of the room. I joined them, plugged in and helped finish setup. The stage was low and I wondered if we were playing a private party or something.

"No, we're the resort's entertainment for the evening," Zane said. I frowned. Who was going to be at the resort looking for entertainment mid-week in early winter before the slopes were snow-covered? There was a makeshift bar setup along a side wall, but it wasn't a permanent fixture. To go from sold out club shows to this kind of venue was a shock to the system. The good news was, they were paying us regardless how many people did or didn't show this evening.

We ran through a couple songs to warm up and test sound levels. Like our old shows, there was no sound tech, and the lights were being handled by staff, but nothing complex. The sound echoed through the empty space. Hopefully, we would sound better with people in the room.

The doors opened right at 8:00 PM and we started. No one showed to announce us. People filed in and the room slowly filled. Drinks poured and there was applause. It was a pretty sedate audience, but they seemed to enjoy the show. We played a few encore numbers for grins and left at the end of the set.

Driving home, fog obscured the mountain roads. I'd never minded driving in the fog. It was just a matter of taking it a bit slower and being cautious of potential deer and other drivers. As I pulled into the driveway, Conor's face popped into my head. I parked. He'd been handsome. Some evenings we'd sit next to the pond near his house as the fog rolled in and the fireflies began their glowing dance. It'd been magical.

I unloaded my guitar and dropped it off in the garage before heading upstairs.

27

"How was the show?" Dylan asked, voice tinny through the receiver.

"It was fine. Not as fun as the club shows," I admitted. "How was work?"

"Heard you and Vicki got into a catfight," he said with a chuckle.

"Not exactly, but she did take a swing at me."

"Why'd she do that?"

"I kind of deserved it."

"What do you mean, you deserved it? What did you do?"

"I may have inferred some things about the use of Brent's dick while she's gone next year."

The line went silent.

"It really bothers you, doesn't it?" He asked.

"It really does," I said.

"You were with Ted, as in, not available," he said. Next thing, he'd be talking about his needs.

"Sort of." It sure didn't last long. "If I'd known you were interested and going to be around a while, I could've changed that. Instead, you were hooking up with everything that had boobs."

"Two girls. I only sort of hooked up with one. I told you that."

I looked at the clock. "I know. We've got to get to school."

"Why does it bother you so much when we weren't even together?"

"It bothers me because instead of coming for me, you just went for the easy ones." It made me wonder about myself.

"I asked for your number."

"Before or after the other two?"

"Before. The night we met. You didn't give it to me."

"You could've gotten it from Jules if you really wanted it."

"You kidding? Jay doesn't like me talking to Jules."

"I'm not surprised." I checked the clock again. "Seriously, we're going to be late."

"Are we ok?"

"Of course, we're ok."

We hung up.

"You can't go around fighting with your co-workers, Shell," Raif scolded as we sat in the manager's office. I nodded, wishing I hadn't agreed to work partial day shifts while I was on probation at school. I hated getting in trouble, especially when I'd done something wrong, and I had. Still, I couldn't believe Vicki had tried to hit me. I thought she was a bit classier than that. Then again, she was blowing guys in the restaurant's restroom. How classy could she be?

"It won't happen again," I said. What I meant was that it wouldn't happen again at work. I totally meant to let her have it every chance I got. I wasn't happy that Dylan's member had been in her mouth and had nearly made it into other places. Ugh. Gross. I didn't want to share a sex partner with a former friend.

"Shell?" Raif asked. "You're going to let it go, right?"

I huffed.

"It might be better for us to not work the same shifts for a while," I said.

"I'll see what we can do. I wouldn't have expected this from you. I thought you and Vicky were friends."

Neither would I. I knew I was crazy, but purposely pissing off Vicky like that? I shrugged. Having Raif discipline me was the oddest thing, but he'd been left with the responsibility since Pat wouldn't be back on duty until the next shift I worked and Vicky had filed a complaint against me. Maybe I should've filed a complaint against her since she'd physically made a move against me, but that would've just been evil.

"Am I suspended from work?" I asked. Might be for the best. I was under a lot of stress with the upcoming shows and the strange photos.

"No, but we're revoking your employee of the month award," he said. I laughed.

"Of course." Duh. Totally behavior unbecoming of an employee of the month.

"You should also leave by 4:00 today to avoid Vicki," he said. "Just to be on the safe side."

I nodded as he shooed me out of the office, to get back to work. I finished setting up the salad bar and front of house and waited for him to unlock the doors. Sal gave me the side-eye but said nothing as he finished prepping his area. He refused my help when I offered.

Larry waited outside, almost hopping foot to foot as Raif unlocked the doors. Larry's agitation continued as he ordered, fumbling with his cigarettes and blinking an unusual amount. He wore a khaki top, similar to his Hitler outfit, although he was missing the mustache today. His thinning hair, slicked back, had an extremely oily sheen under the track lighting. I keyed in his order, took his money, gave his change back, and filled his drink while Sal completed the rest of the order. I braced for the usual 'hit the deck,' but it didn't come. He walked off with his order, tray shaking.

Well, that's two of us off our game, I thought. Larry stared from his bench toward the counter, but his focus was somewhere far away. He puffed away at a cigarette and occasionally took bites of his food. There were days that Larry's behaviors scared me. Today, he was just sad.

More customers straggled in throughout the day, keeping me busy. The salad bar was particularly popular, so I ran back and forth to check on levels and refill veggies. By the time 4:00 came around, I was excited to leave. I let Raif know I was leaving so that he could replace me at the register until frog face came in.

"How was your day?" I asked Ted as he carried his bass in

through the basement door.

"You sound like my mom. The guys should be here soon," he said. "Zane said they were swinging by his place to pick up his guitar and they'd be right over."

"I've been working on a few things," I said. I pointed to the electric piano I'd set up on the workbench. It wasn't the right height, but the standup piano in the basement wasn't in playable condition. Ted gestured for me to play.

Just a memory or a dream
Can't hold on to it for long
Soon you'll be lost to the fog
Nothing left but this song

Give you anything you desire
If it would make you stay
You burn me like fire
With eyes so cold
Don't say a word
I'm already sold

Ted made some notations on my notepad and I altered the lyrics and chords. He always seemed to know exactly what to do to help make the song better. I nodded and smiled.

I'd give you anything you desire
If it would make you stay
You burn me like fire
With your eyes so cold
No need for word or whisper
My heart I can't withhold

The guys wandered through the garage door as I played, Ted standing to my side making more notes. Zane had seen me play piano before, but it was a new thing for Barry. Full of surprises, that was me. Seeing something in a photo and witnessing the act in person were two different things.

"Wow, that was different," said Barry. Zane made a sound

of agreement. It certainly wasn't something our band would normally do. It was much more indie than punk, metal, or grunge. I nodded.

"It's not something we have to do as a band," I said.

"Planning on going solo?" Bear asked.

"No. Just something I'm playing with." I'd been playing with several things on the piano lately. It was a time of rediscovery. Hadn't been much to do in my time off. Everyone else had been in school. "Some of them might convert to band numbers eventually."

"Like what?" Bear asked, pointing to the keyboard.

I will be your willow tree
Weeping long after you've gone
I'll wait until you return to me
Last vestige of light undone.

In the darkness I have danced
To the tune of your heartbeat
For a while, my life enhanced
You, the earth under my feet.

I'm crying out for you.
Wailing like a banshee
Can't you hear my pain?
Wailing for you
You gone, I'll go insane.

Do you hear me calling out for you?
Your lips an unflattering hue.

My limbs dance in the breeze
Beneath a moon full
Broken promises given with ease
My heartstrings you did pull.

I'm crying out for you
Wailing like a banshee

Can't you hear my pain?
Wailing for you
Losing my mind from all the pain

I'll be your weeping willow
Your weeping willow

Barry's eyebrows drew together. I guess it wasn't his idea of a chart topper. Couldn't blame him. It wasn't traditional Toxic Siren fare.

"You don't have anything more upbeat?" Zane asked.

"Is anything upbeat?" I pointed out. I wouldn't say that any of our material was particularly cheerful.

"You know what I mean. Driving, passionate, fast."

"I can do angry," I offered.

"Let's hear angry then," Zane said with a smirk.

I pounded the keys and began a furious fast paced bunch of chord progression with runs. A little cacophonous maybe, but it let out some of the pent-up irritation and anger I'd been feeling. The jealousy, the disturbance. I let out a breath, then breathed in.

Heinous little witch
With a frog-like face
Had to scratch that itch
Up your sleeve an ace
Like you didn't know
Put on such a show

Now I know who you are
I know what you did
Might as well go hook at a bar
Who do you think you kid?

"Whoa, whoa, whoa," Zane held a hand over mine, making a dreadful sound as my fingers smashed the keys. "Definitely not. We don't want any lawsuits. Who the heck pissed you off?"

"Vicki," I said.

"Vicki? You're kidding. She's your friend," Ted said.

"She does kind of look like a frog," Bear said with a snort.

"She's no friend of mine," I said with a shake of the head.

"If you say so. But what are you going to do when you're back in band and have to sit next to her again?" Ted asked. I hadn't been going to Concert Band since I'd returned to school. Principal Dirk had let me return on probation, but made me leave at lunch. Meant I was falling further behind in Precalculus. I was keeping up with French no problem.

"I won't," I said. I shrugged and stepped away from the keyboard. I pulled the red Luna over my shoulder and plugged in. "I just won't." I'd rather submit myself to the awful playing of last chair third flute than sit next to the beast. "Speaking of band, Ted, how is your district piece coming along?"

"It's good." He looked down. Apparently, something wasn't good.

"What's wrong with it?"

"Having a little trouble in this one section that has a bunch of accidentals."

"I could take a look at it with you if you want," I offered. I didn't have anything better to do. He nodded and the barest hint of a smile broke through.

The guys plugged in and we practiced our standard set. At the end, they decided to hang around and hear what else I'd been working on. I guess they wanted more laughs. I stuck with my guitar. I'd gotten to the point that I could switch fairly easily between guitar and piano on my songs.

Somedays I wish I could remember
The when I thought I was happy
A love the sort of May-December
Romance way too sappy

What happened to that simpler time
Some consider it a crime
Innocence isn't always lost
Learning love there's a cost

But don't let me go
You let me go

Life's full of firsts, you were mine
In more ways than one it was divine
As things begin so they must end
In a flash to fate's will we bend

What happened to that simpler time
It was never a crime
Innocence isn't always lost
Learning love there's a cost
But don't let me go
You let me go

"How depressed are you?" Zane asked flippantly.

I looked to the ceiling and thought about it longer than I probably should have. I shrugged. Yeah, I was definitely depressed. I did some of my better work that way. I was more prolific when I was slightly depressed.

Ted stayed behind after the others left. He decided to take me up on the offer to look at his district tryout piece. At least one of us should make a strong showing this year. He brought in his sax and set up in the garage. I sat on a bench next to him and started the metronome. I counted beat as he played and found sections where he slowed down that weren't marked as places to do so. We marked them as places to practice.

When he came to the section of accidentals, I saw what he meant. The key signature change was nuts to begin with, and the accidentals then double sharped some of the notes. It was really confusing. I penciled in some notes. He gave it another try with the notations and it played more smoothly. He'd been misinterpreting some of the notes, forgetting the original key signature. It happened. I'd done it before.

He packed up and left about an hour after the other guys. He hugged me and kissed my forehead. It was more than he'd done since we'd broken up. I appreciated the gesture.

I stayed in the garage for a while after he left to work on my songs.

I can't escape myself
I'm everywhere I look
Memories put on a shelf
Things the accident took
I can't escape

I'll just cry in the rain
Cry away the pain
Of losing me
'Cause no one can tell
My own personal hell
When I cry in the rain
Can't stop the pain
Of losing me

No matter what I try
When I look in the mirror
With that skeptical eye
I can only see clearer
That she's passed me by

I'll just cry in the rain
Cry away the pain
Of losing me
'Cause no one can tell
My own personal hell
When I cry in the rain
Can't stop the pain
Of losing me

She's not what I thought
It's not what I ought
To want to do
I think of her when I'm with you
I'm in that personal hell

I'm losing me
I'm losing me

I noticed a theme. Despite having people in my life, I felt alone. Really alone. I hadn't felt like this since after the accident. I'd been isolated because of the school suspension. All of my friends were separated from me because they had to go to school. I'd chosen to work days to keep me busy, when I could've just as easily continued to work nights with my friends, although that would've put me around Vicki more. At this point, I didn't want to be around her. I'd distanced myself from Ted by hooking up with Dylan. I wouldn't have cared about the whole Vicki thing if I didn't like Dylan the way that I did.

I didn't understand the way I felt about Dylan. It was an almost instant attraction, magnetic, animalistic, and intense. Maybe it was some form of crazy infatuation. Whatever it was, I'd never felt anything like it before. I didn't trust him, but my body lit up like a firework whenever he was near. I felt alive again.

It was different with Ted. Our relationship had bloomed and warmed up over time. At least it had until he'd turned on the cold water. I couldn't deny that my eyes had wandered, but I hadn't planned to do anything.

28

Mr. Fritz returned our tests. I'd managed an 80% and was happy with it. I'd bit back my pride and asked Juan for tutoring. We'd been staying after school twenty minutes two days a week and studied in the band room while Ted sat in the room with us. I felt more comfortable that way. Fritz went over the answers and reviewed a couple of the solutions on the board. Turned out I actually had an 82%. One of the questions marked incorrect was right. Things were looking up in Precalculus. It was nice to see less red ink on white paper. When Juan turned around to see how I'd done, I gave him a thumbs up.

Juan smiled widely and returned the thumbs up. Mr. Fritz nodded toward us and asked me to stay after class. The bell rang and I packed up, but stayed behind.

"Great improvement," he said.

"Juan's really helping. Thanks for the suggestion."

"Really didn't think you'd take it."

I shrugged. "Glad I did."

"Will I be seeing you in AP Calculus next year?"

"Not planning on it. I want to take AP Biology."

"Sad to see you go. I think you'd do ok in Calculus."

"Thanks."

"That was all," he said with a gesture to leave. I nodded and left.

A smile played on my lips as I hurried to the band hall. That was high praise from Mr. Fritz. He was tough.

Dylan caught me outside the choir room and gave me a gentle kiss before releasing me and reminding me he'd be by after work. I nodded and continued on to band. It had been a good day. I walked through the band hall doors and pulled my folder down. A loose folded piece of photocopied paper fell out. I picked it up.

Another bad surveillance photo with cryptic note. This was a photo zoomed in on me playing with the school band at a Veteran's Day event at Tobyhanna Army Depot, possibly last year. Great. The person had snuck past security at an army base and gotten a photo of me. Under the photo in permanent marker was written, 'I've always seen you.' Well, that wasn't creepy. I wondered why this one was photocopied instead of a blown-up glossy like most of the others. I took my seat at the end of the flute section and set up. Since my probation was removed, I no longer sat in the first seat. I sat at the end of the flutes, in the middle of the semi-circle. I reached back and handed the photo to Ted.

"Who's doing this?" He asked.

I shrugged. "No idea. Someone with access to the school. Looks like I'll be talking to Officer Daniels this evening." I sighed. Not something I wanted to do.

"Make sure you do," Zane said. "It would be best if they caught the guy. Could be dangerous."

The band was taking the photos more seriously than I was. I'd begun to think it was a really bad prolonged joke. I was more irritated that the photos were so awful and made me look ugly than the fact that I had a stalker. I wondered how someone could take such consistently bad photos.

Mr. Seagram tapped the conductor's stand with his wand a few times and directed us through the typical warmup. He waved his wand excruciatingly slow. The idea was to listen carefully to our neighbors and adjust pitch until we were in tune, but I just wanted to get into the songs.

Vicki glanced my way and I did my best to ignore her. We'd been doing a pretty good job of it lately. I focused more intently on Mr. Seagram. He signaled the end of our final note and called out the name of one of our marches. I shuffled through my folder and pulled out the piece of sheet music.

I looked straight ahead at Mr. Seagram, but could tell that Vicki was trying to get my attention. I continued to ignore her. I never would have thought there would be a day that I'd find Stephanie less irritating than Vicki, but here it was. Stephanie twirled her crispy hair around a drum stick and waited for Mr. Seagram to motion for us to start. I waited for her to get the stick caught in her hair. Today, she stood behind one of the snare drums next to one of the football players.

I rolled my eyes when Vicki whispered my name, then faced her. "What? Got something on my face?"

"We need to talk," she said, voice low.

"I don't think we do."

"It's important."

I shrugged. I doubted it. She probably wanted to jump me.

"Can we begin now?" Mr. Seagram asked with a sneer. I nodded. I'd just been waiting for his cue. He raised his wand, ticked off the beat and we began at a fast clip. As usual, we stopped shortly after we'd begun for a minor correction in the brass section. I looked down to avoid rolling my eyes. I didn't want to invoke the wrath of Mr. Seagram. His mood worsened as the class wore on.

When I raised my eyes, Vicki's attention was on me again. 'After class,' she mouthed. I nodded and sighed. Might as well get it over with.

Vicki walked up next to me in the parking lot. "Where did you want to talk?" I asked.

"Doesn't matter. Somewhere private would be better."

"My car's right over there. Private enough?"

"That'll work," she said and followed without a word until we were seated in my car. "Listen, me and Dylan, it was stupid and didn't mean anything. Serious."

"What the hell were you thinking?"

"I wasn't. Me and Brent had an argument and I was pissed."

"It doesn't excuse it."

"No, it doesn't, but it doesn't change the fact that he chose to be part of it too. I wasn't alone in there."

"I know."

"If you're going to be upset with one of us, you should be

mad at both of us."

"I know." I was.

"I miss you. I miss our talks."

I nodded. I didn't want to admit that I kind of did too. Girls were such backstabbing beasts.

"Truce?" I offered. It was the best I was able to offer at the time.

"Truce," she agreed. "You weren't serious about Brent…"

"No. I've got enough problems of my own. Dylan's leaving in a few months. It's going to break me."

"He's not good for you."

"Probably not, but I really like him." I kind of thought I might love him. Maybe just a bit. If not love, I didn't know what it was.

She shook her head. "Later, girl." She got out and closed the door.

I drove home in the post-school rush hour traffic. I slowed as I came to a red light. I stopped behind a school bus. Talking to Vicki delayed me enough to be on the road with the buses. I sighed. Ted would probably beat me home.

I reviewed a checklist for the evening. Dylan was working at one of the construction sites and would be over whenever he got out. There was no telling with that job. Whenever the work got done or they were released for the day. Ted and the guys would be over after school for practice. Mom was working late. Andy would be at Mike's overnight. Another lonely night.

I was surprised to beat Ted back to my house. I set up the garage and grabbed a couple bottled waters. He showed up shortly after I started fiddling with the electric piano. I let him in and he set up his bass. He was curious what I'd been working on. I wasn't sure he really wanted to know. I sat down and played for him.

It's a short road of passion and pain
This strange connection between us
Through troublesome nights we've lain
After times we've been so amorous
It's a short road to passion

But it's leading to pain

As much as I want you
As much as I need you
I know I can't keep you
It's been fun, it'll be over soon
If only you felt like I do
Maybe my heart wouldn't be
Breaking in two

It's a short road from pleasure to hell
Living without you I want to die
Can't you hear that tolling death knell
It's the one last death rattle sigh
It's a short road from pleasure
To the end of love's spell

As much as I want you
As much as I need you
I know I can't keep you
It's been fun, it'll be over soon
If only you felt like I do
Maybe my heart wouldn't be
Breaking in two

I'm falling to pieces without you
Wishing you'd return to me
But some things aren't meant to be

If only you felt like I do
Maybe my heart wouldn't be
Breaking in two

"Shell, you know it's not over yet," he said. "Dylan's still here."

"I know. But he's leaving soon and it kills me," I said. I met his brown eyes. "He says we'll keep in touch and he'll come back and see me when he's on leave after basic." I hoped that he would.

"Good. Luckily, we'll be busy with all the shows this summer. You won't have much time to think beyond the tour."

"I just worry. I mean, what if he gets hurt? What if he finds someone else?"

"If he finds someone else, he's an idiot," Ted said. "You're worth waiting for."

"Uh, thanks, I think." I still hadn't told Ted about not being a virgin. He had to suspect that Dylan and I had done the deed. I hadn't wanted Ted to know about that part of my character. I had mixed feelings about what I'd done prior to the accident. I wasn't sorry that I'd hooked up with Conor. I regretted not breaking up with Joe first, as I should have. I couldn't figure out why I hadn't.

The guys arrived with Stephanie in tow. I'd almost gotten used to her. It was kind of cute to have a band groupie. She seemed genuinely interested in getting to know us, and not in the hitting on all the guys way that I'd expected. She'd been helpful at the shows, selling merchandise while we played and autographed things afterwards. I hated to admit she wasn't the heinous beast I thought she was. Today, she sat on the futon in rapt attention while we practiced.

Dylan waved from the doorway as we were wrapping up. I nodded. He mouthed and gestured that he was going to take a shower. I gave him another nod. I looked forward to our alone time. It'd been about a week since we'd had any time to ourselves. He'd been working after school and I'd been practicing with the band or working at Norma's.

We completed our set and the band left. Ted hugged me before leaving. It was sweet. I hurried upstairs. Dylan was still in the shower, so I checked the voicemail. Mom called to remind me that she'd be home after 11:00 and that Andy wouldn't be home at all. It was nice to know that she still planned to come home.

Dylan walked into the kitchen naked and I inhaled his clean scent as he swooped in for a passionate kiss. His tongue dove into my mouth and explored suggestively. My body nearly went limp in his arms as we kissed. He tugged on my hair and gazed into my eyes.

"You're mine," he said.

I nodded. I agreed, I was his. We continued kissing and made it back to the bedroom before I lost all of my clothes. Although mom wasn't due home for a couple of hours, we easily lost track of time together. I explored his body with my lips, tongue, and mouth before we moved on to other activities and positions. His eye contact throughout was intense, almost spiritual. I loved looking into his eyes as we moved together. His eyes took in everything, and he smiled as he watched the dance of our union.

My breathing quickened and became shallow as my skin began to flush with pre-orgasmic tingling. Our bodies moved faster as the sensation of delightful champagne bubbles built through my body. We released in cries of pleasure.

We laid silent, catching our breath. I nestled my head against his chest and listened to his heartbeat return to a slower normal beat. This was what I wanted

29

I woke in Dylan's embrace, warm and firm. He'd spent the night so that we could leave early for Scranton and run some errands before the show. I heard movement coming from the kitchen, so either mom, Andy, or both were up. Dylan's breath, slow and even, tickled my ear. I twined my fingers with his and closed my eyes. The alarm wouldn't go off for another couple of hours. We had big plans to sleep in.

When the alarm did go off, we lazily made out for far too long. It was a wonderful start to the day. I didn't know what Jules was complaining about. Sex was amazing. I couldn't get enough.

I dressed in tight black jeans and black tee. Dylan chose a medium blue tee and light blue jeans. He looked good. Really good. The shirt brought out the blue of his eyes. We grabbed our jackets, bags, and my guitar, then headed for the car.

We stowed our stuff in the trunk and were on our way. Dylan took control of the music, choosing more of an 80s vibe than Ted would have. It was fun. Cruising down the highway, we sang along with the music, the parts that we knew anyway. Some of the songs I hadn't listened to in a while. I'd forgotten nearly all the lyrics except for the chorus on several.

"So, when are you leaving?" I asked, hating to bring it up.

"Sometime in June, after graduation."

Wow, that was vague. I nodded. The wheels hummed along the pavement.

"I don't want you seeing anyone while I'm gone," he said. This surprised me. I glanced at him.

"No?"

"I'll call you after basic and see you when I can."

"Ok, I won't." I really didn't want to. I only wanted him. I knew we were young, and it was probably stupid to make this kind of commitment, but I was totally willing to do whatever it took to have him in my life.

"We can write to each other," he offered.

"Definitely."

I exited at the mall. I needed a few more items of clothing. I'd shrunk a couple more sizes. Even my skinny jeans were loose. We'd be making a trip to the leather store too. Dylan was super excited by that prospect and hoped I'd pick up some kinky undergarments. When I'd last been there with Ted, I'd seen a couple interesting bra-like tops he'd probably like that combined chains and leather.

We went to Hot Topic first, where I picked up some new band tees. I picked up more conventional clothing at one of the department stores. Then we left for the leather store.

"You'll love the leather," I replied.

"Can't wait." I caught the smile from the corner of my eye. He rubbed my leg, making me warm inside. I longed for the hotel room. We had a couple hours to kill before check in. A smile crept to my lips.

I parked a block away from the store. It was the closest I could find without circling. We got out of the car and walked hand in hand to the shop. The stairs creaked under our feet as we ascended to the second floor.

A woman with teased blonde hair stood behind the counter.

"Can I help you find something?"

"Need to try on some pants and tops," I said, pointing to the back room. She nodded and gestured for us to go on back. I guided Dylan by the hand until we stood in front of several stands of black leather women's clothing.

He immediately reached out for the shortest skirt. I shook my head.

"For the stage, remember?"

"Oh, right," he said, eyes alight with mischief. He hadn't been particularly happy with my last mini skirt purchase, and that one had been slightly longer. I'd still flashed the band and audience during a couple local shows before I retired the skirt.

I pulled a couple pairs of pants, a leather and chain bra top, a leather halter top, and another bustier then took the items back to the dressing room to try them on. I required assistance on the bustier and called for Dylan. He happily waltzed into the dressing room and let his fingers dance along the fasteners and ribbons as he tightened them.

I took my purchases to the counter and paid, not surprised by the cost of leather, but frustrated at having to buy more so soon. I wondered if I might have a medical condition. I'd been eating fairly normally, yet the weight continued to drop.

Dylan helped carry my bags to the car and we stowed them in the trunk. We stopped for a late lunch at the seafood restaurant shaped like an old sailboat, Casper's. It wasn't a place I'd normally have suggested for minimum wage workers, but they had reasonable lunch specials. It wasn't like we ate there regularly. Lunch was leisurely and we talked about school, which brought up graduation again.

"You were supposed to be graduating this year too, right?" He asked.

"That's right," I said with a nod.

"Kind of sucks."

"Tell me about it. Would've been worse if I hadn't moved away. If I'd been watching my childhood friends graduate this year it would've torn me apart." Of course, they were still graduating without me this year. I just didn't have to watch it. He cocked his head.

"Think you'll go to college next year?"

"Probably. Mom wants me to. I've been thinking I might like to be a doctor someday. That requires college, then med school."

"Thoughts on where you might go?"

"Penn State maybe. Not really sure. Haven't thought much about it." If I'd been graduating as expected, I was sure there would've been more thought put into it. "I mean, pre-med can be studied just about anywhere. It matters more where you go to med school."

"Lead singer of Toxic Siren wants to be a doctor, huh?" He smiled.

"I kind of do. Maybe just a psychologist. I'm not sure yet. That wouldn't require med school. Still lots of school, but not med school."

"Zane's been talking about this upcoming summer tour a lot," he prompted.

"Yeah. Keeps assuring me that I'll be too tired to think about anything else while we're traveling from gig to gig all summer," I said with a sigh. "I'm really going to miss you."

"I'll miss you too."

After lunch, we drove to the hotel and checked in. I spent a few minutes removing tags from the purchases while Dylan checked out what was on TV. He found a snowboarding event and stopped surfing channels. A smile tugged at my lips. At least it wasn't football season. Although I'd played with the band at games, cheered, and dated football players, I'd never really gotten the game. I snipped another tag off and tossed it into the trash bin.

I hung up my new show costumes and left the luggage in the closet. I joined Dylan on the couch and nestled my head against his shoulder. He wrapped an arm around me and my remaining tension drained away. I watched as snowboarders took to the air and did amazing gravity defying tricks, and occasionally wiped out.

I startled awake when someone knocked at the door. Dylan released me and stood to answer it. A moment later, Ted was in the room with us. He'd ridden up with Bear and Zane. The two had argued half the trip about Tara, who still wanted to do the band's photography. Everyone but Zane agreed that Tara should do our photos. Zane continued to be a jerk about it. I was surprised Tara wanted anything to do with us after Zane had behaved so poorly, but she was an amazing person, and she was our friend, not just Zane's ex.

"When did Tara bring up the photos?" I asked. She'd mentioned it to me before school the week before last, but I hadn't thought the band would go for it.

"She called Bear last night then he called me. We both tried to convince Zane on the way here," Ted explained.

"Bad timing," I said. "Maybe you should've waited until Sunday." As in, after the shows.

"Probably," he agreed.

"You don't think he's going to be a problem this weekend, do you?"

"I think Stephanie's going to keep him occupied. She's coming up later tonight," Ted said. I nodded. She did seem to have a calming effect on him. I wasn't sure how she'd react to the possibility of Tara having continuing business with the band. The thought of a catfight between the two almost made me laugh, but then I remembered that I liked Tara and I was tolerating Stephanie.

I checked the time. Nearly 5:00, meaning I'd maybe been asleep for an hour. Poor Dylan. I stretched with a yawn, tucked my legs under and leaned against him.

"Looks like you're utterly stimulated," Ted commented. I covered another yawn with the back of my hand.

"Sorry. Just tired. So, what are you guys doing until the show?"

"Bear's watching some cop show and Zane stormed off to his room as soon as we got here."

I nodded. Figured. Zane was a real hothead. We'd learned that the only way to get him to listen to ideas he wouldn't like was to trap him somewhere, like in a car, or being his ride somewhere. He'd still storm off if you were his ride, but he couldn't get far. I bit my lower lip. I hoped that Zane chilled out before the show. It's not like he had any right to be mad at Tara. He was the one that cheated and broke up with her. She deserved way better, and yet she was still willing and wanted to work with us.

"You want to hang out with us for a while?" I offered.

"You mind?" Ted asked Dylan. Dylan shook his head. It wasn't like we'd been doing anything exciting. I'd been sleeping.

"Cool. Let's get some drinks," I said. I gestured to the door. Ted followed me out. "Be right back," I called over my shoulder. "Think Zane will be a problem tonight?"

"I really hope not."

We fed money into the vending machine and got a few cans of soda. "How's Bear taking the latest meltdown?"

"He's kind of moody. Moping around the room."

Typical. "So, you thought you'd see what we were up to instead?" I asked with a hint of a smile.

"I know what you're like before a show," he said. "Figured you'd be out like a light and Dylan would be bored out of his skull."

"You know me so well," I said. I couldn't help it, I laughed. We walked back into the room; Dylan looked expectantly at us.

"Just talking about Shell's love for a nap before a show," Ted said. Dylan nodded.

I handed Dylan a Coke and opened my own diet soda after sitting down. I took a sip and set the can down on the coffee table. Ted sat on my other side and I got comfortable between the two. I sank into the sofa and comfort of Dylan's arm. Ted's body heat radiated like a furnace. The guys cheered on the snowboarders. Dylan became more animated with Ted in the room. I grinned at the macho bonding.

Ted was a snowboarder when the weather permitted. I'd never seen him do it, but I'd heard he was good. Downhill skiing and snowboarding weren't activities that I did. Flying down a mountain on sticks sounded like a great opportunity for me to break a limb. Ted loved it. He'd spent some time on the slopes this year on artificial snow. It'd been cold, but hadn't snowed much.

Dylan, on the other hand, liked being outside, but wasn't one for mountain sports. Apparently, he enjoyed watching extreme tricks, but who didn't? Even I was enthralled by the high jumps and aerials. Rather than skiing or snowboarding, we'd spent time on the less frigid days hiking on mountain trails. I was fond of one that led to the swamp. The trails weren't as flat as those at Tobyhanna State Park and offered different kinds of wildlife sightings and were more secluded. I loved sitting by the swamp in the early mornings before the fog totally burned off.

When 6:30 rolled around, I dressed in the new leather pants and halter top and packed my small bag with makeup and hair gear. I'd finish getting ready there, because it was too windy outside to mess with the hair. The three of us stopped to get Barry, but there was no answer. Zane didn't answer his door either, so we left without them.

We arrived at Club Neon at 7:00 to the familiar sight of fans lined up outside. We walked around the side where a bouncer let us in. Lucio led us back to the dressing room. I had been surprised and delighted to see that we were playing with Bosley, one of my childhood favorite metal bands. They hadn't released anything in years, but still played the occasional gigs. Tonight, was one of those nights. I'd seen them play once before, and tonight they were our opening act? They'd been headliners since before I was born, in my parents' era. I wondered how many people would leave after Bosley's final chords.

"Sold out show," Lucio called in from the doorway. "Let's do the sound check so we can start letting people in. They're restless out there and it's cold."

We nodded and headed for the stage. My breath caught in starstruck awe as Evan and the guys of Bosley passed us in the hallway. We were playing on the same stage! Evan nodded at us as he passed. He acknowledged our existence!

The band was named after a character on an old TV show, not the hair club. I'd loved watching the show's reruns with my grandma as I grew up. Bosley had been comic relief. The guys still rocked the long hair and tight black pants and tops of their younger performing days. For older gentlemen, they still looked good.

We took the stage and played a couple songs. I heard adjustments as we made our practice run. Dylan stood in front of the stage and gave us a thumbs up. I winked at him and continued to sing and play guitar. When sound check finished, I rushed off stage.

Evan stood outside the stage door. "Great sound," he said.

"Thanks!" I said as the rest of the band continued past to the dressing room. Ted looked back from the door as Dylan came up behind me and placed a hand on my back. "I love your music. Listened to it all the time. Any plans for a new album?" I asked.

"Actually, yes. We're recording in a few weeks," he said with a smile. "Just wanted to say, break a leg." With that, he returned to his dressing room. I glowed with excitement.

Dylan followed me back to the dressing room. I fixed my hair and applied stage makeup, the room eerily quiet while I worked. I spun in the chair to face the guys.

"Come on, we're playing on the same stage as Bosley! Aren't you excited?" I asked.

"Well, yeah," Barry said. "Just wish Zane wasn't being a dick."

"Zane? Are you being a dick?" I asked, half my mouth losing the fight against a smile.

"I just don't like that you guys went behind my back with Tara," he said.

"She's still our friend, and she has serious talent," I said. "We'd be fools not to take her up on the offer."

He crossed his arms. "You too, Shell?"

"I told her it wasn't a good idea because I didn't want the conflict. But I really want her to do the photos, Zane. She makes us look good. I trust her."

He huffed.

"And, like the show, the price is right," Ted said. "We'll never find anyone who will work as cheap as she does. She only charges us the cost of film and processing. We should pay her more."

I really didn't want to discuss this before a show, but having him act out on stage wouldn't be good. Especially since we didn't know which night the producer would be in the audience. I sighed.

"Zane, we need her," I said.

"Fine," he said. His shoulders slumped and his arms relaxed. "If that's what you all want, she can continue to do our photos. I just hope Stephanie doesn't throw a fit."

I hoped Stephanie didn't throw a fit too. She had a mean streak. Tara didn't deserve to be on the receiving end of that fury.

"Three minutes!" Came our call from the door. We rose and grabbed our guitars then proceeded to the stage door. Bosley finished with *Fallen Angel*, one of my favorites, and left the stage. Lucio took the mic and introduced us as the Poconos sensation Toxic Siren, and we rushed onto stage, plugged in, and took off.

The blinding stage lights prevented me from seeing anyone in the audience, but I practiced pseudo eye contact by quadrants. I slinked and stalked around the stage. I danced, as well as I could behind a guitar, and sang my heart out. The audience reacted with enthusiasm and even sang along with a few of the covers and songs from our demo.

Blood hummed through my body with the energy of the crowd. The stage shook with applause at the end of each song, lighters came out with our slower songs, and silhouettes jumped around with the faster ones. From the quaking stage, I understood what the expression, bringing down the house, meant.

Ted and I finished with *Rise Above*.

Rise above the pain
Above the rage that turns
Those tears that rain
Will you rise above
The painful heart that burns
Rise above it all
Till you see me.

As the chorus faded out, we left the stage. The audience, stunned at first, broke into wild applause and called for an encore. We ran through *Labels*, *Willow*, and *You Suck*. We rushed off stage to even more thunderous applause, hoots, and hollers. Evan winked at us as we passed in the hallway. A sheen of sweat glistened over my skin as we returned to the dressing room to drop off our gear.

I opened a bottle of water and guzzled the entire thing. I crumpled the bottle and tossed it into the trash bin. We walked down the hallway to find a massive line waiting to greet us. It was going to be a long night. Dylan hugged me and whispered into my ear, "great show."

I smiled and took a seat behind the table. Dylan stood behind me and rubbed my exposed shoulders. The first people began to drift in front of me with items to sign. Halfway through the line, my wrist and hand were cramping. I circled my hand and opened and closed it repeatedly, trying to loosen the cramping muscles. I picked up the marker and continued to sign, smile pasted to my face.

A familiar guy with auburn hair walked up with a poster in hand. I cocked my head and squinted. "Conor?" I hadn't recognized him before with the college sweatshirt and facial hair.

"Yeah, that's my name," he said. "How do you know my name? Is someone punking me?" He looked around. I stepped out from behind the table and gave him a big hug. His eyebrows rose.

"I'm Shell, it's Michelle."

He looked at me, really looked at me. "No way." His face paled. "No way." He didn't look happy to see me. I stepped back and put my hands on my hips.

"This is how you greet an old friend?"

People in line stared. I guess he blamed me for his brother's death. I'd been blaming myself for years. Why make the situation worse? I sighed and stepped back behind the table. He stood frozen in place. I reached for the next item. Dylan put an arm around me.

"The Conor?" He said quietly in my ear. I nodded. We'd discussed him.

As I autographed with the band and took photos with fans, Conor disappeared into the crowd. Another piece of my old life gone. Hadn't meant to lose a fan. At least he'd have a story to tell. He'd once messed around with the lead singer of a band, after all. Before she was famous, but still. My heart rested heavily on my gut and I could feel it leaking through my eyes. No amount of smiling would fix that. I dabbed at the corner of my eye as I reached for another poster.

30

Zane wanted to practice early in the afternoon to prepare for the producer, and Lucio agreed to give us early access to the club. Ted, as usual, had notes for us. I'd thought the performance had been 99% flawless. Dylan chuckled when I'd told him that.

"Well, the show was amazing," he said. "But I get where Ted's coming from. The guys just want your chances of getting picked up to be as good as possible."

I nodded and bit my lower lip. We'd been intimate when we woke and I still blushed at the memories. I wanted to wake up every morning with him. The thought brought on a wave of sadness.

"What's wrong?" He asked.

"The usual," I said. "Already missing you and you're right here."

He gathered me in his arms. I slipped my arms around his back and squeezed, cheek resting against his chest. I listened to the beat of his heart. We separated and I checked the time.

"I need to get to the club," I said. "No need for you to go." I tossed him my keys. "Go explore. I'll see you tonight."

"You sure?"

"Yeah. It'll be boring. You've heard all the songs, and you've seen Ted's critiques before."

"I'll miss out on hearing how bad your dancing was."

"I've gotten better," I said with a pout.

"Yes, you have. You were super sexy last night," he said with a wag of the eyebrow.

"Thanks. Really, go explore the city. See what you can find. Ask the concierge for suggestions."

"Thanks, I will," he grinned with mischief. I grinned back. There were things in Scranton that couldn't be found in the Poconos. I made sure I had my room key and left.

Walking down the street, my skin crawled with the familiar sensation of being watched. I turned around, but saw no one. I rounded the block and walked faster until I got to the club door. I knocked and waited, hair at the back of my neck standing on end.

"Shell!" I turned. Jules walked up. "Didn't you hear me calling for you?"

I let out a breath I'd been holding, heart beating out of control. "Gosh, you scared the crap out of me," I admitted. I hadn't told her about the stalker and the photos. I knocked on the door again. "What are you doing here?"

"We're here for the show," she said with a smile. I didn't see anyone else.

"You're early. Doesn't start for another five hours," I said glancing at my watch and frowning.

"Speaking of, why are you at the club so early?" She asked.

"Pre-show practice. Tonight's an important show and the guys want it to go perfectly."

The door creaked open and a red-eyed yawning Lucio let us in. Jules followed me back to the dressing room. I was the first of the band to arrive. I hoped the guys hadn't forgotten. Jules walked around the room, dragging her hand across the makeup table. She stopped in front of the table and stared at me through the mirror.

"What is it about you?" She asked my reflection.

"Huh?"

"I mean, why do all the guys want you?" She leaned into the table, tapping her finger against the black surface. "What do they see?" She asked staring down at the table.

"I'm not sure what you mean. It's only Ted and Dylan."

"And all the guys at Norma's, including Jay," she said. "And Marcus..." she sniffed. She spun around, pulling a revolver from her purse. "He wouldn't shut up about you."

"Jules? What's with the gun?" Was this some kind of weird joke? Where did Jules get a gun?

"Shell, Shell, Shell…" she said with a nasal voice. "Always about Shell." Jules gazed at the gun in her hand.

"The guys always liked you," I said. "I mean, you're the gorgeous blonde. You're so easygoing, funny." Please be a joke.

"Funny?" Her eyebrows rose. She held the gun up, pointing it at me. "You think this is funny?"

"Is it supposed to be?"

"I'm pointing a gun at you, and you wonder if it's supposed to be funny?" She laughed, but not in a good way. She stepped closer. I stepped back and fell onto the leather sofa, sticky. So gross.

"Seriously, what's with the gun?"

"I'm so tired of you. You're the reason Marcus is gone," she said with another sniff.

"How so?" I asked, eyes darting around the room, but finding nothing useful.

"That morning," she choked. "We met at the lake, me and Marcus. He wouldn't shut up about how he was going to ask you out. He was actually going to do it. I told him not to. Why him? Why'd he have to like you?"

"I don't know. He only ever asked if I needed help with Precalculus," I said, keeping still.

"You're so clueless," she snarled. "Do you know how long I've loved him?"

"You've been with Jay for over a year," I started, but her eyes went distant.

"I followed him to stop him. But he was driving so fast. I pulled up next to him and a car came straight at me. I swerved…" and he drove into the tree. Jules had killed Marcus. Kind of by accident, like I'd killed my boyfriend and best friend.

"He's gone," she said, head dropping with a deep sob, gun still pointed at me, hand shaking.

"Yes, he's gone," I agreed, eyes searching the room. Nothing.

"He liked you," she said, gun trembling in her hand as she

began to squeeze the trigger.

"I know," I said. I dropped to the concrete floor in a spin and kicked Jules in the knee with as much force as my leg could muster.

The gun went off before it clattered to the floor and skittered across the concrete as Jules collapsed, knee at a sick angle. Her piercing screams followed me into the hallway as I half crawled out of the room. A man in dark uniform ran past me, gun raised, as another shouted at me to put my hands in the air and face the wall.

Facing the dark wall, with my fingers linked behind my head, I squirmed on the inside. My heart raced and I struggled to breathe in, my body finally catching on to the fact that I'd had a gun pointed at me. My vision began to tunnel from the edges and I shut my eyes, leaning my forehead against the wall. My legs shook, numbness spread fast and I barely registered hitting the floor.

From the darkness, and down a tunnel, someone called my name and I heard the police yelling at Jules to put her hands up, as another shouted that he'd found a gun. I opened my eyes and blinked, vision dark and hazy, but slowly shapes became recognizable. Ted bent over me, holding my hand and calling my name. I sat up too quickly and everything went black again. Hands pushed me back to the floor.

My eyes opened again, finding not only Ted, but a man in uniform wearing gloves and checking my vitals. I looked around, moving just my eyes this time and found I was still on the black concrete floor. Sound returned to my fuzzy and ringing ears. Jules whimpered nearby. Jules. My body jerked again, wanting to get up and out of the building. Ted and the gloved man held me down.

"It's ok, Shell. Stay down. You hit your head when you fell," Ted said, voice soft.

My hand reached up, pulling the other arm with it. Cuffed? I was cuffed? I touched the side of my head, where a radiating pain was giving me a headache. My fingers came away bloody. Just what we needed the night of our big show. Tears slipped from my eyes, falling to the concrete.

"Is it safe?" I asked. "Jules," my breath hitched, "gun." It was difficult putting full sentences together.

"An ambulance is on the way. You did a real number on her," Ted winced. "They have the gun." I could see he had questions. I wasn't sure I had answers.

31

Ted left a message at the hotel for Dylan to let him know that we were at the hospital to check out my head after I'd fallen at the club. He left it for me or one of the others to explain later. Ted asked him to bring my gear to the club around 7:00. We hoped to be back at the club by then. While waiting between tests, in an Emergency Room curtained bed, Ted shared his side of what had happened at the club.

Ted had arrived shortly after us and was outside the dressing room door when he heard Jules. He peeked through the open door before coming in. That's when he saw the gun, rushed back to the bar to tell Lucio, and called the police. When they arrived, I'd already subdued and disarmed Jules with the knee injury. Who knew where I'd learned that move. The police weren't sure who was who, so they'd cuffed both of us while they sorted things out, even though I was unconscious on the floor and Jules was broken on the ground.

I sipped water while I spoke to the police, who had followed me to the hospital and interrogated me after the doctor saw me and before the results of my CT scan and other tests were ready. Jules was looking at potential manslaughter charges for Marcus' death, and aggravated assault with deadly weapon for me. She'd been in love with her best friend for ages, but it hadn't worked out. I understood that feeling, twice over.

Wouldn't be difficult for those feelings to turn into obsession. I asked if they had spoken to Detective Daniels about the open stalking case. Daniels had followed up with them, and with further questioning, Jules denied being the sender or taker of the stalker photos. If not her, who would do such a thing?

I was released with my head bandaged, but no stitches, and instructions to watch for more severe symptoms, like my headache getting worse, memory issues, or if I lost consciousness again. They gave me some acetaminophen and sent me on my way. I was instructed to rest and drink fluids, but rest would have to wait. We picked up some bottled water and more acetaminophen on the way back to the club.

Dylan showed up within minutes of our arrival, bearing my costume and makeup. He looked confused as Ted explained what happened. I was too drained physically and emotionally to explain.

"You ok, Shell?" He'd asked. "Sorry, stupid question. I should have come with you." He looked afraid to touch me. I reached for his hand, finding comfort in its warmth and strength.

"I'll be fine. Still a little shaky. It hasn't caught up with me yet." From experience, I knew that with trauma, it could be days or weeks before I experienced, or rather re-experienced, any serious issues. I requested his help in the dressing area because I couldn't work the fasteners and ribbons of the bustier on my own. He helped fasten the leather pants when my shaking fingers refused to stay steady enough to zip up the side. He happily assisted me behind the curtain, holding me for a moment as I breathed deeply. Emotionally, numbness had set in.

"Wow," Ted said in a whoosh of air as I stepped out from behind the curtain. "You look great."

I hadn't even applied the stage makeup, not to mention the large white bandages wrapped around my head. Must've been the cleavage. "Thanks," I said with a half-smile.

I sat in front of the lighted mirror and applied makeup, then removed the bandages from my head and winced. The bandages weren't supposed to come off before tomorrow, but there was no way I was keeping them on for the show. There wasn't much I could do about the dried blood caked in my hair with the time that was left before the show. Bosley had already started. Their heavy metal sound pounded through the walls. I carefully brushed my hair, watching dried flaking blood fall to the floor and winced at the sting as I held the base of my hair against my scalp and pulled the brush through. Then I gingerly wound my hair into a loose braid. The guys talked quietly behind me. I heard Jules' name mentioned several times. It was a name I could do without hearing for a while.

Stephanie joined us ten minutes before showtime to hang all over Zane and let him know what a big badass guitarist he was. I'd hidden a smile behind my hand. Ted and Bear rolled their eyes. Zane didn't need a bursting ego. He was ok, but not legendary. Most of Ted's corrections had been directed at him. I'd been so caught up in my own performance the previous night that I hadn't been paying as much attention to the others as I could've been. I'd just done my best to give the audience a great show. I'd assumed that's what the others were doing too.

Ted was a multitasker. He could not only play bass and sing, but also paid attention to what everyone else was doing at the same time. Incredible. Suggestions for me? Continue to work on audience eye contact and shake my butt more. Seriously? Shake my butt more? Like anyone could tell behind my guitar. I'd laughed.

We hurried to the stage door when called. Dylan and Stephanie headed out to stand by security at the front of the crowd. We'd gotten to the stage faster than the previous night and Evan was introducing their final song. He winked at us and gestured in our direction.

"We'd be honored if the Siren would join us onstage for our last number, *Fallen Angel*. Shell, what do you say?"

I hopped and did a little squeal, making my head throb, before nodding and rushing onto the stage, leaving the guys stunned. Lucio handed me the wireless mic and I joined Bosley onstage. The intro played and I moved with the music and waited for a cue to begin. Evan sang the first verse and gestured to me on the chorus.

You're my fallen angel
Fallen from the sky

My own private angel
Don't ask me why
You rock me to my core
Alive like never before
Don't ever leave me
Fallen angel see me

The crowd went wild as we finished the song together in harmony. It was a dream come true, performing with a band I loved under the bright stage lights of a crowded ballroom. I waved as we left the stage. I handed the mic to Lucio and waited side stage with the band. Ted clapped me on the back.

"That was awesome!" He said.

"Totally awesome," I agreed. Not in terms of performance, but just in the enormity of the situation. My insides burned with excitement.

Lucio gave us a glowing intro and we skipped onto the stage. Reminded me of the old cheerleading days. We slammed into our punk intro, where I released some caged anger. Anger at Jules for threatening me. Anger at Conor for looking so horrified to see me. Anger at Christy and Joe. Anger that Dylan was leaving me. The audience thundered as we transitioned into our next song, *Thundering Heart*.

I reach for you through clouds in my dreams,
You're never there
I call for you over the thunder of my heart
Answer me, I'm dying in here

I reach for you through the thunder of my heart
Can't reach you with my shaking arms
I sing for you and give you all of my art
Wish you'd fall for me and all my charms

Can you hear me over my thundering heart?
Through the darkened night
And the dimming of sight
When you close your eyes

Do you dream of me
With your endless sighs of desire
Like I long for you
With my thundering heart

I oozed sadness and longing as the crowd listened rapt, drawing from that constant sadness that dwelled inside and the losses I'd survived and would survive again. Beyond the bright stage lighting, the firefly glow of lighters fluttered and flashed around the room. Beautiful. I thought about Ted and Dylan while I sang.

The rest of the set ran smoothly, drawing stronger reactions from the crowd than usual. The audience interacted and sang along with zeal. I was sweating like crazy from the leather, lights, and movement by the time we left the stage. They called us back for an encore and we didn't disappoint. We played another punk cover, *Willow*, and *You Suck*.

"That was crazy!" Stephanie squealed as we walked into the dressing room. I pulled some paper towels from a dispenser and blotted. My stage makeup was wrecked, old blood ran down one side of my face and neck, and my hair had frizzed from dampness. "You should've been in the crowd. It's like, they knew your songs, like actually knew them!" She clasped her hands in front of her and hopped up and down.

"I could hear them," I said, half a smile playing on my lips. That said something, hearing the audience sing over the amps.

Lucio came through the door, a rotund man in a suit behind him. "This is Al Goldman," he introduced. Al handed us business cards. The music producer wore a gold tie over a dark shirt, matching dark jacket and pants. I wondered if he always wore something gold, like a gimmick. We introduced ourselves.

"Haven't heard a sound like yours before, but the audience loved it," Al said. Did he not love it? "We should talk about the future of Toxic Siren with AG Records."

I looked around the room at the guys. We were still in high school. Should we be committing to a record label? The guys smiled broadly. I must've been stunned. I didn't feel a smile on my face.

"Not right now, of course. Call the office on Monday and

we'll set up an appointment," Al said. I nodded, mirroring the guys. "I know you've got tons of people waiting to see you. Talk to you next week." And with that, Al was gone.

Dylan rubbed my back. I got chilled as we stood around. I picked up my leather jacket and pulled it on.

"You heard the man," I said. "Let's get out there. Fans to greet."

32

After we'd finished up at the club, I followed Dylan into the hotel room. He pulled me in for a deep and passionate kiss, turning my legs to jelly. I held on to the back of his neck to keep from falling down. He lifted me up and carried me to the bed where he let my feet fall to the floor.

"Quite a night," he said as he helped me out of the bustier. As he undid the ribbons, I breathed more deeply, enjoying freedom. The top fell to the floor. His hands ran over my bare skin, leaving behind gooseflesh. He kissed my neck. His fingers drew down the zipper of my pants and he slowly peeled the leather from my legs, getting stuck at my shoes. I sat at the edge of the bed, enjoying the cool and smooth texture of the comforter while he removed my platform Mary Janes then finished removing my pants. I leaned back on the bed as he stepped back, eyes on mine.

I watched as he undressed, eyes glued to mine the entire time he stripped, losing contact only as his shirt brushed over his head. My eyes dropped as his hands reached his pants and my lips spread into a wide grin as they slid to the floor. He crawled on top of me.

"You're mine," he said, blue eyes intent on mine.

"I'm yours."